Praise for

The
FARWALKER'S
QUEST

"Joni Sensel writes like a dream—her language, her
settings, and her humor make a great read. Ariel's
world—part dystopia and part Eden—could be the future or
it could be the past, but it is still all unique and compelling."
—Karen Cushman, Newbery Award winner

"Absorbing fantasy. . . . Crisp dialogue, an exciting plot
and strong secondary characters." —*Kirkus Reviews*

"This is a solid and well-paced fantasy in which the journey is
more important than the conclusion. . . . The theme of finding
and accepting one's true calling resonates." —*SLJ*

"At once elegant and lyrical, while also offering an
intensely paced and action-driven plot." —*BCCB*

"Absorbing, moving and ultimately satisfying, [*The
Farwalker's Quest*] encourages readers to move beyond
ready labels and discover what role the world really
wants—or needs—them to play." —*Kidsreads.com*

"This stand-alone fantasy has a unique setting with an
intriguing history and a suspenseful plot. Ariel, as headstrong as
she is thoughtful, is an appealing character, and her strong bond
with her companions—Zeke and Scarl, her taciturn but caring
protector—makes their journey one to follow." —*Booklist*

Books by Joni Sensel

The Farwalker's Quest

The Timekeeper's Moon

The
FARWALKER'S
QUEST

JONI SENSEL

BLOOMSBURY

NEW YORK BERLIN LONDON

Published by Bloomsbury Books for Young Readers
175 Fifth Avenue, New York, New York 10010

The Library of Congress has cataloged the hardcover edition as follows:
Sensel, Joni
The farwalker's quest / by Joni Sensel.—1st U.S. ed.
p.   cm.
Summary: When twelve-year-old Ariel and her friend Zeke find a mysterious artifact
the like of which has not been seen for a long time, it proves to be the beginning of
a long and arduous journey that will ultimately reveal to them their true identities.
ISBN-13: 978-1-59990-272-2 • ISBN-10: 1-59990-272-9 (hardcover)
[1. Fantasy. 2. Adventure and adventurers—Fiction. 3. Identity—Fiction.] I. Title.
PZ7.S4784Far 2009   [Fic]—dc22   2008030523

ISBN-13: 978-1-59990-450-4 • ISBN-10: 1-59990-450-0 (paperback)

Typeset by Westchester Book Composition
Printed in the U.S.A. by Worldcolor Fairfield, Pennsylvania
2 4 6 8 10 9 7 5 3 1

All papers used by Bloomsbury U.S.A. are natural, recyclable products
made from wood grown in well-managed forests. The manufacturing processes
conform to the environmental regulations of the country of origin.

For all who wander

PART ONE

FINDER

CHAPTER
1

Zeke's tree wouldn't speak to him.

"Are you sure you've got the right tree?" Ariel asked when he told her. "Maybe you've been hearing another nearby that got tired of the confusion and gave up."

Zeke shook his head as the two twelve-year-olds hurried back across the meadow toward afternoon classes. At lunchtime, they'd dashed off to chase pollywogs in the creek. Their catch wiggled in the wood bucket that now dangled between them, and water splashed their legs with each step. Their free hands crammed their mouths with last-minute lunches.

"I think I know my own favorite tree," grumbled Zeke. "She's just stopped paying attention."

Ariel calculated. Today was March 29. "But Namingfest is only three days away!"

"Gee, really?" Zeke rolled his eyes. "I might . . ." He couldn't say he might fail. "I might have to wait until next year."

"What's your father say about it?"

Zeke watched his goat-leather boots squelch in the mud. "Haven't told him."

Ariel shot a sidelong glance at her friend. A Tree-Singer could be the most important person in a village. Hearing the voices of trees and coaxing them to share their great wisdom took special talent, however, and both of Zeke's older brothers had settled for more ordinary trades. Since then, Zeke had vowed that he would claim the Tree-Singer name of his father. But today his narrow face drooped in defeat.

If Ariel had chomped into her meat pie right then, or maybe just bitten her tongue, the next few hours—indeed, her whole life—might have turned out quite different. Instead, she wiped her mouth with her sleeve and said, "Maybe you're not a Tree-Singer after all, huh?"

Zeke's sausage roll dropped from his fingers. Seeing it fall, Ariel could practically hear her mother scolding her for her thoughtless talk. "Even a cart donkey can bray, love," Luna would say. "Take care you aren't mistaken for one."

"Or maybe your tree's sick," Ariel added quickly. "Maybe that's why she's quiet."

"Oh, and I suppose you're going to heal her?"

Ariel stopped. "Sure. Why not?" She was the daughter of Luna Healtouch, after all.

"What do you know about healing a tree?" Zeke demanded. "There's nothing wrong with her, anyway."

"Maybe I'll just go and find out." Ariel released the handle of the bucket, spun, and ran back in the direction they'd come.

"Ariel, wait!" Zeke struggled with the bucket alone.

"Come on," she shouted over her shoulder. "Leave the pollywogs there. We'll come back."

"What about class? I don't want to be punished for showing up late again!"

Not known for the effort she applied to her studies, Ariel

ignored the squirm of her conscience. Excitement propelled her down the path. Zeke's idea that she heal the tree was so good, she wished she'd thought of it first.

Everyone in Canberra Docks assumed she would become Ariel Healtouch in time. The bouncy girl with the apple-round face hadn't shown a talent for anything else. She would turn thirteen later that summer, so at Namingfest in a few days she could apprentice herself to a Fisher or Reaper. But the easiest course would simply be to learn from her mother. Unlike tree-singing and the more mystical trades, most of the healing skills could be taught.

Yet a nagging worry chased at her heels as she sped toward the woods. She didn't feel much like a healer. Ariel liked gathering herbs, but she found illness messy and unpleasant until the ailing person felt better—and paid off the debt with some interesting trade.

Healing a tree, though, would be almost like helping an angel. Some people said trees spoke directly with the Lord of All Things. Maybe Zeke's tree, grateful, would share an old secret, like where to find gemstones or the legendary treasures locked away in the Vault. If so, Ariel was confident that Zeke would understand the tree's message. Of course he would share it with her. He often acted grown-up and thoughtful because he was trying so hard to be a Tree-Singer, but Ariel knew his adventurous side. Together they'd trapped classmates in the outhouse, lowered each other into the village well, and set his family's laundry ablaze trying to send fire through a string as people were said to have done in the old days. They'd both been punished for that, but it hadn't stunted their curiosity or their mutual attraction to mischief.

Sure enough, Zeke's big feet soon pounded behind her. His

long legs easily caught up with Ariel's short ones, and they dashed together along the path, leaping root knuckles and dodging branches. Ahead, a grove of cottonwoods reached toward the sky. Smaller alder, cedar, and other trees shaded the creek below.

Ariel spotted Zeke's tree. They'd often sat in the moss beneath its curved branches, eating lunches of cheese curds and bread. Her legs slowed.

"That one, right?" she asked, pointing. Although much older than Ariel and Zeke, the maple was still young for a tree. Its trunk forked near the height of Ariel's chest. Below, roots humped from the ground, clenched to hold the tree firm against winter winds.

"Yes, that's her." Zeke peered wistfully through his sandy bangs to the flickering leaves overhead.

"I don't see any brown leaves," Ariel said.

"She's not sick, I told you." He crossed his arms and waited for her to concede. Sometimes he acted too much like a brother.

Turning away with a flounce, Ariel slipped closer to the craggy trunk. "Hello, tree," she said. "I'm Ariel. Remember me? I've been here before with Zeke. You know Zeke."

Zeke snorted. "That is *not* how you talk to a tree."

"*Your* way hasn't been working, remember?"

His disdain crumpled and he fixed his eyes on the dirt near his feet. Ariel sighed. It was for his own good, she reminded herself. She couldn't even try to help if he kept making comments like that.

She reached one palm to the rough trunk and circled it. Around back, where less sunlight dripped through the trees, moss draped the bark. Ariel paused in the shadows.

For someone named Ariel, she didn't look very airy. She was sturdy and short-limbed, and her black hair was chopped blunt near her chin. She did have light feet, though, and frequently skipped when she walked. Her eyes, a dark gray indoors, reflected blue from the sky whenever she went outside, which was often. Her mother had given up insisting on skirts, which ripped too easily on branches and stones. Instead, Ariel wore mostly wool trousers and sweaters.

She tipped her head skyward now and tried to remember the questions her mother asked neighbors who weren't feeling well. None of them seemed to apply to a tree. Ariel could see no wounds bleeding sap, no gnawing bugs, no breaks in the sturdy tree bones. The tree's breath smelled of honey, the balsam scent of nearby cottonwood buds. On high, sunshine glowed through the leaves, which flickered in the breeze. To Ariel, it looked as if the tree winked.

With a sudden insight that both her mother and Zeke's father would have recognized from their work, Ariel knew there was nothing wrong with this tree. She wanted to spank it for tormenting Zeke. Instead, she wrapped both arms around the trunk and rested her cheek against it, trying to think what to say or do for him.

"Why are you ignoring my friend?" She peeked around the trunk. Zeke sat on a knuckle of root, his pointy chin slumped in his hands. The dejection on his face rubbed a blister on her heart.

Zeke's tree felt that pain, too. But the kindly maple had known, in the way that trees do, that the boy Zeke by himself would never have done what was needed. So the tree quaked, shouting as loud as she could to this nearly deaf human girl.

And in a corner of Ariel's mind, an idea bloomed. Oblivious

to the rush of sap over her head, she turned the idea in her mind, wondering how to lure Zeke into a sport they both knew was forbidden.

The first time he had ever brought Ariel to his tree for a visit, she had asked, "How can you tell your special tree from the rest?" She'd envied his talent, since she seemed to have none of her own.

"The same way you know your best friends," Zeke had replied. "You recognize one another."

"But you must recognize dozens of trees. We've seen the same ones our whole lives."

"That's not what I mean. It's not what it looks like, branches and bark. It's . . ." He'd frowned, searching for words. "It's more like hearing it whisper in the back of your head. Some trees don't like to be bothered—"

"That big oak by the graveyard."

"Yeah. Anyone can figure that out. He'd get up and move farther away if he could. But some trees like people—one person, at least. They make you feel welcome. Sometimes a leaf will fall right into your hands. You want to curl up at their feet and be cozy."

"So you're basically a pet." Ariel had giggled.

"Probably." Unperturbed, Zeke had stroked the bark of his maple. "They live longer than us. They understand more." At Ariel's snort, he'd added, "Just because they can't walk around doesn't mean they're not wise."

Chastened, Ariel had inspected the woods around them. She could see how one tree differed from the next, but none looked particularly smart. If they were, why did they let their branches and some of their friends end up as tables and boats? Yet Ariel knew that certain trees had given Zeke's father all kinds of important information, including the locations of lost children and the truth behind quarrels. Some said wise trees knew the future as well as the past.

"I don't get it," she'd sighed.

Zeke had shrugged. "I guess you'd be a Tree-Singer if you did."

"Can I listen while you sing?"

Zeke had always shyly refused. Ariel had even tried to sneak up on him, but he always fell silent as she drew within earshot. Perhaps his tree warned him.

Today, though, either Zeke forgot Ariel's presence or desperation numbed his self-consciousness. As she watched from behind the mossy trunk, he gazed toward the maple's crown, leaf shadows dappling his face. A few lines of song, almost a whisper, slipped from Zeke's lips:

Hail to leaf and twig and bough,
Towering above me now.
I will listen, graceful tree,
Humbly—won't you speak to me?

Zeke's eyes closed. Riveted, Ariel strained with him to hear a response. Only the rustle of leaves and the creak of branches reached her ears. Zeke's face fell. He turned his gaze back toward the dirt.

Feeling angry for her friend, Ariel stomped to his side. Still, she smiled inwardly. Zeke had opened a door for the brash idea tickling inside her.

"Maybe she just can't hear you," she said. Drawing a deep breath, Ariel stepped onto a hump of root, braced her hand on the trunk, and boosted herself into the fork.

"What are you doing? Get down!" He jumped to his feet.

With all her weight on her belly, Ariel didn't have breath to answer. Her hands scrabbled across the bark. Gaining a hold, she wiggled higher until she could draw one knee into the fork and push herself up.

"Come on up," she said, climbing more easily now. "It's not as hard as it looks."

"It's disrespectful to climb trees!"

"It's disrespectful of her to ignore you, too. Let's get closer to her head. See if that helps."

"You don't—Ariel! Stop!" Zeke came after her. She could hear his grunting as he strained past the fork.

"Come on," she taunted. "Try singing up here, in her ears."

"Trees don't have ears, you goof."

"When trees talk to each other," she said, "it seems to me like they do it up high."

"Maybe they do," Zeke allowed, breathless. He was gaining on her. "But that's different from a tree talking to us. They hear us the same up here as down there."

"Then it can't hurt to try."

"It'll hurt a lot if you fall!"

Ariel looked down. Already she was higher than she'd intended to go. All she had really hoped to do was distract Zeke and perhaps make him laugh. Now she felt the urge to climb higher. In fact, Ariel had the strangest sense that the tree wanted to be climbed. Gazing past Zeke at the earth below, she knew she ought to be scared. The fear wouldn't come. There was too much to hold on to, and the route beckoned.

Reassured, she clambered up past the tops of nearby saplings, past a snarl of dry leaves that had sheltered some squirrel. Zeke's protests grew.

As the branches became slender and frail, he grabbed one of her ankles.

"Ack, don't!" she cried. The space between her and the ground seemed to throb.

"What if a branch breaks? The wind's starting to blow. Come down."

Ariel tightened her grip. While she was here, why not look around? Swiveling west, she could see the meadow and the creek running through it. Beyond that were thatched and tiled roofs, the docks, and the sea.

Zeke exclaimed. Ariel peeked down at her friend. One of his hands flattened against the trunk. His mouth dropped open.

"I hear her!" He turned a huge grin toward Ariel. "It worked! It really— I don't know why, but—" His grin faded. Head cocked, he listened again, brow furrowed. "She wanted us to come up . . . ?"

A hand might almost have tugged on Ariel's ear, twisting her head to the east. Braced for a squirrel or bug to leap into her face, she leaned to peer around the trunk in that direction. Her eyes widened.

"What is it?" Zeke called, climbing once more. "There's something up here, huh?"

Ariel tipped her head from side to side, afraid the bright brass surprise might vanish.

"Come see for yourself!" Heart tripping, she shimmied a few inches farther around. She wanted to reach it before he did.

Ariel had never seen a telling dart, but she had heard plenty of stories. The brass shaft was no larger around than the handle of a carved wooden spoon. Its tail bore three slender blades like the feathered fletches of an arrow. The dart had embedded itself in the underside of an upswept branch. Where the tip pierced the tree, golden sap bled. A fly struggled in the sticky drip. Although the dart itself must have been old, it could not have been stuck in the tree for very long.

Excitement bubbled into Ariel's throat. She reached up from her perch with one hand. The metal shaft felt cold, but its scored surface faintly buzzed under her fingers. Engraved marks circled the dart. The barrel would be hollow, or so she'd been told. Whoever had sent it might have slipped in nuggets of silver or gold, a ruby or two, or something even more priceless—a secret message.

She tugged. The dart didn't budge.

"It's stuck," she told Zeke as he climbed up beside her.

"Let me try."

Ariel gave way. She hated to admit it, but his hands were stronger than hers. The two shuffled awkwardly, trading places.

It took a few tries, but Zeke yanked the shaft free. Clinging against a sudden strong gust, they inspected it together. Ariel fought an urge to snatch the dart from Zeke's fingers. She marveled at the tiny bright scratches in the metal. Several she recognized as the signs of a trade: the Windmaster's ℗, the Tree-Singer's ↑, and of course the ω that marked the home of a Healtouch. Others were strange. But she knew they could speak, the way different flags on a mast could alert other boaters to schooling fish or trouble back home.

"I didn't think you could still find stuff like this anymore," she said. Darts that could talk were only one of the marvels lost after the Blind War and now known only in legend.

"Me either," said Zeke. "I wonder how it got up here. This isn't like finding it in a pile of old garbage. But I didn't think anyone still knew how to send them." They both gazed northeast, from whence the dart seemed to have come. Nothing interrupted the sea of trees but a passing bird and the distant faces of mountains.

"I thought telling darts were supposed to find the people they were sent to, anyway, not just stick in any old tree," Ariel said. "And why—"

"Shhh." Zeke cocked his head.

Ariel started to protest before she realized what he was doing. Sure enough, he took a breath and softly sang a few words she didn't recognize.

In a moment, he said, "It's been here since just before Thawfest—that night we had the bad storm, remember? It must have gone astray in the wind, or because of the lightning."

"That was only seven or eight weeks ago. How do you know?"

Zeke gestured to the tree.

Jealousy hummed along Ariel's arms. She told herself they were just getting tired of gripping branches. Yet she hesitated to climb down. Once they were back on the ground, some magic spell might wear off and their discovery prove to be only a twig.

"Let me see it a minute."

To her surprise, Zeke handed her the dart without argument. "Let's go down, though," he said. "We can look at it better out of the wind."

Agreeing, she considered her pockets. None seemed deep or trustworthy enough, so she slid the dart, tail first, into her boot. It rested snug against her anklebone.

Ariel led their descent, which proved harder than the trip up. The handholds and footholds seemed farther apart. Gusts shook the branches.

Halfway to the ground, she heard a scrape overhead—the sound of a boot missing its mark. Instinctively she hugged the trunk. Zeke's arms and legs, in a tangle, fell past. Ariel screeched as his flailing limbs struck one branch and slid off another.

Before her eyes, the tree reached to catch him—or tried to. Ariel never would have believed it if she hadn't seen it herself. Not even Tree-Singers claimed that trees could move, except with the wind. Yet as Zeke hurtled toward the earth, a long branch near the ground swept around toward him.

It was wood, though, not an arm. It couldn't bend far enough. The branch tangled with one of Zeke's legs without catching before springing back straight. An instant later, Zeke hit the earth.

His cry of shock and pain felt like a spike through Ariel's skin. As loud as it was, his yelp didn't cover the crack that accompanied it.

"Zeke!" Throwing caution aside, she scrambled down, calling his name and praying his head had not broken like an egg on a rock.

Her feet hit the ground. He was breathing, at least: sobbing gasps rose and fell. Nothing oozed from his head.

"Are you okay?" She jumped the last distance. Pain stabbed in both of her knees. She ignored them and rushed to her friend. He hadn't tried to sit up. "Say something!"

"She tried to catch me. Did you see that?" Zeke's face was screwed tight against pain. Tears leaked from his eyes despite his sturdiest blinking, but Ariel recognized what was meant as a smile.

"Yes! But the branch didn't reach. Does anything hurt?" Her eyes scoured his body. No blood soaked his clothes.

"It slowed me down." He wheezed. "I still hurt my arm,

though. Kinda landed on it." He clutched his right forearm tight to his ribs. A root humped nearby from the dirt. Ariel guessed he'd landed atop it, his bone snapping over the root like kindling across a bent knee.

"I bet you broke it." She resisted the itch to touch his hurt arm. "Can you move it?"

He puffed. "Don't want to find out."

"Okay. Just catch your breath." She thought rapidly. Ariel knew how to help broken bones, but most of the things Zeke needed weren't here in the woods. Unable to keep her helpless hands off him, she carefully petted his shoulder. His ragged breathing relaxed.

"I can run and get help while you wait," she said, "or I can help you walk back."

Though every motion made him wince, he insisted on walking. Ariel tucked herself under his good shoulder. Together they stood, Zeke sucking air between gritted teeth. That evidence of his pain made Ariel's stomach lurch.

"Are you sure about this?" she asked. "It might be better if—"

"I'm okay."

They made their slow way down the path toward the village. To Ariel's relief, the tension she could feel in Zeke's shoulder and ribs eased soon after they'd started.

"It's kinda gone numb," he explained.

As they entered the meadow, he halted. "Wait. You didn't drop it, did you?"

"Oh!" Her fingers poked into her boot, where the forgotten metal dart had grown warm until she could hardly feel it. "I've got it." She eyed her friend hunched in pain. A generous impulse moved her mouth. "You want it? It was in *your* tree."

No fair! insisted a more selfish voice in her head.

"No," Zeke said. "You found it. And I got what I wanted."

"A broken arm?"

He rolled his eyes. "Come on." He shuffled on without her aid.

Ashamed of her relief, Ariel caught up. "Was it hurting your tree? Is that why she stopped talking to you?"

Zeke shook his head. "I think she . . . Well, I don't understand everything she tells me. But the dart is for you. You'll take better care of it, or something like that. And, Ariel . . ." He gave her an odd sideways look. Maybe it was just shock and pain, but she had never seen him so somber.

He said, "My tree thinks whatever that dart has to say is important."

CHAPTER

2

Zeke insisted he could walk by himself, so Ariel retrieved the pollywogs on their way back to the village. When she lifted the bucket, the creatures' frantic swirling seemed to echo both her stomach and the increasing wind.

Even before they reached the first stone cottage, the storm bell began clanging. Gusts swept dirt into the air and sent chickens fluttering into roosts. Fishing boats crowded the mouth of the harbor, flocking home early. Under the darkening sky, villagers bustled to gather damp laundry and fasten shutters over a few precious glass windows. Advance scouts from an army of rain splattered on the cobbled lanes.

Ariel spotted some of their classmates rounding up siblings and pets to bring them safely inside. Apparently class had been released early so the students could help prepare for the storm. Any punishment she and Zeke might face for shirking their lessons would wait.

Ariel burst ahead of her friend into her mother's cottage. Luna was filling the peat bin for what looked to be a blustery night.

"Zeke broke his arm!" Ariel announced, dropping the bucket of pollywogs.

"I wondered where you were," said Luna. "Finding trouble, as usual." She took one look at Zeke's posture and turned back to her daughter.

"I'll save my questions for later. Run to Zeke's mother and let her know I'll be along with him shortly. On your way back, stop by the Flame-Mage and get another coal. It was so fair this morning, I let ours burn out."

"Can't I stay and watch?" Ariel had hoped to help splint her friend's bone.

"Go, before Zeke's mother gets worried." With one arm, Luna drew him into her workroom. With the other, she pushed Ariel back out the door.

With a frustrated huff, Ariel hurried off down the lane. The brass rod in her boot knocked against her ankle. If she ran, perhaps when she got back there'd be time for them to examine it more closely.

She swiftly dispatched her errand at Zeke's house and raced on to the Flame-Mage's workshop. After collecting a tender of hot coals there, she returned to the bluster.

She noticed the Windmaster, Leed, on the wharf, his gray hair tangling in the wind. He held his windpipe in his hand but not raised to his lips. Perhaps the weather was howling too loud to hear the notes, much less obey them.

"Will it last long, Leed?" Ariel shouted. She had once dreamed of becoming his apprentice, charmed by the way a fresh wind washed the thoughts from her head, mussing her hair and caressing the grass with the same invisible touch. The wind and rain never listened to her, though. Last summer she had tried to learn the windpipe under Leed's amused eye. He had finally pointed out, gently, what they both already knew: she did not have the gift.

Her question now seemed to startle him.

"Ariel," he said gruffly, without his usual toothless grin. He tucked his pipe into his coat. "It's a bad wind, child. I can't tell how long it will blow. I can tell this, though: something ill drives it, or arrives on it. It will bear away things we all value. Get inside."

Ariel nearly dropped her coal tender. She'd never heard Leed talk so ominously. Too stunned to disobey or delay, she lifted her feet to run. The wind hissed and snarled in her ears as she went.

By the time she reached home, Zeke's fingers poked out from the end of a two-piece wooden splint. With his other hand, he wiped away tears. Ariel pretended not to see them, shamed by the knowledge that she sometimes cried over banged shins and splinters.

"It's not so bad," Luna told her, knotting the bandage that held the splint halves in place. "He'll heal. Do you want to get him his sling?"

Ariel jumped at the chance. Her mother took the coals to restart their fire.

While Ariel folded Zeke's sling and tied it gently in place, the two whispered.

"Want to look at it before you go home?" Ariel asked.

Zeke's eyes shifted to the workroom doorway, looking for Luna. "Later. Let's keep it a secret."

"Why?"

"I don't know. Just because."

Ariel studied the furrow in his brow. She didn't understand it, but there were plenty of things, both in class and in village life, that he grasped better than she did, so she trusted Zeke's judgment.

Luna walked Zeke home. With the wind lifting and banging the loose slates on the roof, she had insisted that Ariel stay in. Once her mother was gone, Ariel pulled her stool near the fire, drew out the dart, and took a close look.

The firelight glinted from the shaft. Where it had entered the tree, the once-sharp tip had snapped off. Nearest that end were four rows of symbols, spaced equally around the barrel:

Ariel recognized those—one mark representing each of the twelve trades. A scored line separated those marks from the rest. More lines near the dart's tail fenced a symbol alone like a zigzag of lightning:

Ariel puzzled over this crooked mark, which looked to her like the arrow of a Tree-Singer mixed with the triangular mark of a Flame-Mage. Perhaps it stood for a person who was both Flame-Mage and Tree-Singer—a tree-burner, even. Ariel snickered, despite the horror of that idea. Everyone gathered kindling from wood that had already fallen, but the idea of a whole, living tree engulfed in flames gave her a shiver.

The squiggles and dashes carved at the dart's middle were stranger. They must have been some kind of writing, but Ariel knew nothing of that. Only the village Storian, to whom the children recited their lessons, might recognize those marks. Remembering things was his job, after all, even things nobody used anymore.

The brass shaft should open, but Ariel couldn't tell how. She twisted and pulled. Nothing moved. She shook it. Nothing rattled inside. Part of the message ought to be in there, she was sure. That helped keep the whole message private. Perhaps it opened only for the person to whom it had been sent. Ariel wondered who that might be. It had to be someone she knew, because the next coastal village was more than a whole day away. The dart couldn't possibly have gone that far astray.

She jumped at the click of the door latch. Stuffing the dart in a pocket, Ariel pretended to stir up her pollywogs.

Her mother had returned just in time to stay dry; rain and thunder joined the wind beating their house. Her lips tight, Luna heated their supper in silence. Ariel's father, a Fisher, had been drowned in a terrible storm. It had happened so long ago that she barely remembered him, but her mother still grew tense when the weather turned rough.

To fill the silence, Ariel chattered about pollywogs and Zeke's arm. Her mother scolded her for climbing a tree. Ariel nodded humbly, but her secret wouldn't stay behind her lips.

"Guess what Zeke and I found, though." She presented the dart with a flourish. Firelight glanced off it.

"My goodness." Luna set aside her chowder spoon. "Where'd you find that?"

"It was stuck in Zeke's tree." Ariel grinned and they ogled the brass shaft together.

"Did you know that your great-great-great-grandmother Mim got so many darts, she had to put up a dartboard to keep them from splintering the door?" Luna asked. Ariel clicked her tongue in awe, and her mother smiled. "She was a Healtouch, too. People for miles around would dart her when someone fell sick. Then she'd borrow a bike and go visit."

"A bike?" Ariel cried. She pictured a wheelbarrow, but with two wheels instead of one. Somehow, she knew, the person riding could make it go without someone else having to push. Such a thing was even more magical than a telling dart.

"Yes indeed. Some of the old things were still working back then." Luna winked. "Boys sent darts to girls with love tokens inside. Girls sent back locks of hair."

Ariel giggled. "Did you ever get one?"

"Oh no, they were gone by the time I cared about boys. That's just something my grandmother told me."

"Do you know what these marks mean?" Ariel asked. "The ones that aren't trade marks?"

Her mother studied the symbols. She sighed. "We've forgotten so much. The only one I know is this." She pointed: ☦. "It used to be painted on that old metal tree near the wharf."

Ariel and her friends sometimes dared each other to swing on the contraption her mother described. Serving no purpose anyone could remember except to provide scrap metal for boat keels and garden tools, the tower of linked metal strips would soon collapse in a jumble.

"What's it mean?" Ariel asked. "Metal tree?"

"No. It also was used to mark poisonous plants. It's a sign that means danger."

Ariel's bones tingled.

"Storian might be able to figure it out," Luna added. "Will you take your dart to class tomorrow?"

Ariel shrugged. "I don't know. Zeke wants to keep it a secret."

"Perhaps he's afraid you won't get to keep it. By rights, it belongs to the Storian."

"Storian? Is that who it was sent to?"

"I'm sure I don't know, but that's not the point," Luna replied. "It's his job to keep old things."

"Stories," Ariel argued. "Not old junk."

"Both."

Ariel's face slumped.

"Don't feel bad," Luna continued. "I have an idea for you." Rummaging in her sewing basket, she found two large knitting needles. One had been snapped off short.

"Your father made me this pair from whalebone before you were born." Luna ran her fingers along the smooth rods, smiling sadly. "The one has been broken for years, but I couldn't bear to throw them away."

She handed both needles to Ariel. Each was much lighter than brass, too long but nearly the same thickness as the dart.

"If you used a sharp pin, you might be able to copy the symbols from the dart to each needle," Luna said. "One for you, one for Zeke. A nice memory of your adventure."

Ariel wrinkled her nose at the age-yellowed ivory. Her mother's suggestion sounded like hard work.

"It's the best treasure I ever found," she complained. "You really think Storian will take it?"

"Probably." Luna nodded. "I know for certain, however, that you will offer it to him. I'll give you a few days to copy it first."

Feeling new kinship with the tumult outside, Ariel blew her own windstorm into her bangs and hunted for a sharp sewing pin.

She stayed awake late, scratching symbols into the broken knitting needle long after her mother fell asleep. The bone was not as hard as she feared, and she quickly discovered that her scratches didn't have to be deep. When a slip of the pin pricked her thumb, a dot of blood smeared on the bone, lining a groove so one crimson symbol stood out from the rest. Ariel licked her finger and wiped the spot clean. But the idea took hold, and soot from the hearth rubbed into the scratches as well. Soon even shallow marks stood out sharply against the white bone.

She'd nearly completed the copy when sleepiness overtook her. Unable to hold her hands steady enough for the finishing touches, she tucked everything into a clean sock and stashed it at the foot of her bed. Then she crawled under the covers herself.

Despite her drowsiness, Ariel slept restlessly, troubled by nightmares of strange symbols dripping with blood.

CHAPTER
3

Dawn arrived in a sickly green gray. The rain and bluster had eased, but the heavens looked more like a waterlogged blanket than a friendly spring sky.

"Go ahead to your classes," Luna told Ariel. "Don't be surprised if the Storian sends you home again, though. The tail of the storm is still coming."

Once in the classroom, Ariel struggled to keep her eyes open. Today's lesson should have been exciting, too: Bellam Storian was finally letting his class talk about Namingfest. Every month had its festival, but for a person of Ariel's age, April Namingfest was the best.

"So who will we lose from class this year?" the Storian began. He surveyed the two dozen students sitting cross-legged on the floor of the story-room. Gray hair kinked from his eyebrows, his jaw, and even his ears. It seemed to have gotten lost on the way to his nearly bald scalp. He stroked the hair at his chin. "Who do we have turning thirteen?"

Zeke raised his splinted arm proudly. Excitement clearing

some of the fog in her head, Ariel shot her hand up, too.
Another girl, Madeleine, wiggled her fingers shyly near one ear.

"Good," Storian said. "What happens day after tomorrow at
Namingfest, then? Ariel?"

She sat up stiff. It sounded like a trick question. "We get our
last names," she replied. "Like Healtouch."

"Or Fool," someone teased from the back of the class. "You're
lazy enough, and a goof, too, but I bet you can't dance." Ariel
whirled to fire a scowl.

"That's enough." Storian shifted his gaze to Madeleine.
"Yes, the naming, of course, but before that?"

"There's a test." Madeleine gulped.

"Yes. The trade test." Storian looked pointedly at Ariel. She
rolled her eyes to show him she knew *that*, for heaven's sake.
Frowning, he added, "What sort of—"

Thud. All eyes zipped toward the door. The knock repeated
twice, sounding sturdy enough to cave the door in.

"Excuse me, class," the Storian growled. He stalked to the
door. It had better be good, Ariel thought. He didn't like inter-
ruptions. She didn't suppose Storian would make an adult
stand and recite the entire calendar, as she'd done a few times,
but his scolding could be punishment enough.

He yanked the door open.

"Bellam Storian?" The voice did not match the pounding.
It was male, but almost a whisper.

"Yes, and you've interrupted my class."

Unabashed, the interrupter strode through the doorway,
looking to Ariel like a tall, storm-tattered crow. A stranger, he
wore an oilcloth coat with layers and flaps that fluttered about
his long legs. His trousers looked like oilcloth, too, rustling
stiffly when he walked. Both his coat and his knit cap were wet,

as though the storm still raged wherever he'd come from. Chestnut curls escaped his cap at his nape like ruffled feathers, and his dark, widely spaced eyes and sharp nose completed his avian appearance.

"A word with you, Storian. It's important." Those glittering eyes swept the young faces turned toward him. Seeming to change his mind, the stranger took half a step backward. He breathed, "Perhaps better outside."

"I'm afraid," Bellam began coolly, sounding anything but afraid, "that whatever it is must wait until—" He faltered. The stranger had raised one palm to show a bit of glass there. The Storian exhaled into his beard.

"Very well." Without a word to his class, he stepped out.

The stranger's eyes roved the students. Riveted, Ariel throbbed in fear of that keen gaze stopping on her. Her breath caught as their eyes met. With a soft thump of his heel, the man spun. His coat flapped. The door shut behind him.

The clunk of the door broke the icy spell on the class. Students surged to the two windows, the largest boys jostling for the best view. Zeke held back to avoid his arm getting banged. He and Ariel exchanged scowls of mutual frustration; then both looked at the door.

"They'll see," Zeke worried as they ran to it.

"So?" Ariel replied. "He didn't tell us to stay seated."

It was not their stubby old Storian, however, but the crow man who concerned her the most. She didn't want to attract his attention. Gripping the door handle, she put her face close so a slight gap would be enough. Zeke leaned on her shoulder to peek over her head. A younger girl scrambled to tuck herself beneath Ariel's chin. Ariel depressed the latch.

"Wait." Zeke slapped his palm over the door, keeping it closed. "Where is it?"

"It's home." She knew better than to name it aloud. Yesterday's surprise might be connected to this one.

Zeke moved his palm. Ariel eased the door open.

There were three people outside, not two.

Canberra Docks welcomed few strangers, but now and again an unknown Fisher sailed in to trade catches or seek shelter from storms. The men standing with their Storian looked more like they'd blown in with a swirl of dead leaves. Next to the crow fellow stood another man in oilcloth, not so tall and built more like a bear. He had ruddy skin, short yellow hair, and a patchy blond beard. A stiff leather hat dangled in one hand while he talked. Ariel did not quite believe the smile fixed on his lips.

When the blond man finished speaking, Bellam shook his head, adding a few words and a shrug.

A gust of wind flapped both strangers' coats. Abruptly, Ariel recalled yesterday's encounter with Leed Windmaster and his warning about the troubling wind.

She pressed the door shut.

"Hey," complained the girl crouched below her. But other students scattered as well.

By the time the door opened again, everyone was seated once more. The Storian entered slowly, his hands clasped and his brow wrinkled.

"Is something wrong?" Madeleine asked.

"Good question," Bellam said, mostly to himself. He fingered one hairy ear. "Perhaps. But where were we? Oh yes." He clapped his hands. "Namingfest."

For the next hour, students recited lessons that Ariel had heard every year: What the word "apprentice" meant. How the trades had emerged at the end of the Blind War, and why there were more Reapers and Fishers than anything else. What happened if you failed your test and had to spend a miserable year as a Fool. While her classmates described the symbol for each trade, Ariel thought about all the other marks on her dart. She could hardly wait for lunchtime, when she and Zeke could run to her house and inspect it together at last.

When the morning could stretch out no longer, Storian checked the weather at the door. The wind whooshed in past him.

"Come back after your lunches," he decided, dismissing the class. "We'll get a few more lessons today."

Zeke, who had jittered anxiously the whole hour, jumped up. Ariel got stuck behind somebody slower.

"Ariel." The Storian's voice held a silent command.

Her heart shivered. "Yes, sir?"

The other kids stepped wide around her. Whatever her crime, it might be contagious.

Storian did not go on until they had all filed out. Tortured, Ariel craned her neck, trying to see through the doorway whether Zeke awaited her outside.

"Did you think I didn't notice?"

Ariel's mind spun. Did the Storian somehow know what they'd found?

He continued. "You and Zeke did not return after lunch yesterday."

She tried not to slump in relief. "No, sir. We were catching pollywogs, and I guess we were late." It was true, partly.

"And how did that result in a broken arm?"

"Well, we climbed a tree, too."

"I see." Storian tapped his fingertips on his leg. "Don't be late today. The two of you will start our afternoon lesson by reciting the multiplication of numbers from one to fifteen."

A groan escaped her. "Yes, sir."

By the time Ariel fled outside, Zeke was racing up the hill toward the meadow, his splint hugged to his belly.

"Zeke!" she hollered. He had already run too far to hear her. She could guess where he was going, however, and he wouldn't want her there while he talked to his tree. She stamped one foot in annoyance. She wasn't sure how some silly tree—or even a smart one—could answer questions about strangers or anything else that didn't concern it. Meanwhile, he was wasting a good chance to look at the telling dart.

She scuffed through the mud toward home. At least she could finish her copy during lunch. Maybe Zeke would return with time to spare and come find her. She shot a last glance toward the tree line. He'd already disappeared into its shadow.

Ariel turned the corner of her cottage an instant before hearing the voices. Horrified, she stumbled back out of sight, praying she hadn't been spotted. The bearish stranger stood at her open front door. Since he didn't look sick, Ariel couldn't imagine why he had come—unless it had something to do with her dart.

Gripping the stone wall of her house, she peeked toward the blond man. He flashed his fake smile at her mother and lumbered away. Luckily for Ariel, he turned his back, not his face, toward her staring eyes at the corner. As soon as he vanished behind the next wall, she dashed for the door and burst in.

Her mother glanced up from tying herbs by the fire.

"What did he want?" Ariel asked, breathless.

"He's looking for something. He thinks it might be near here." Luna hesitated. "I told him I hadn't seen one since I was a child."

Ariel collapsed on her stool. Her mother had saved her.

But her mother wasn't done talking. "And you have something to deliver to Storian right after lunch."

Ariel gasped and leaped back to her feet. "You told him that?"

"No. I'm telling you that."

Ariel's heart started beating again. "But why? You said—"

"I know, love, but it isn't a toy. I just felt our own Storian should have a chance to see it before it went to a stranger."

Ariel pushed tears back down her throat and slouched toward the foot of her bed. What might have happened, she wondered, if she had kept her mouth shut last night? Could she and Zeke have held on to their secret once they'd learned the strangers were hunting for it?

"Why is some old metal stick so important?" she grumbled.

"I can't imagine." Luna sounded puzzled. "But giving it up is the right thing to do." She patted Ariel's shoulder. "Want something to eat?"

"No." She pulled the shining dart and her ivory copy from their hiding place. Inspecting her night's work, she raised the brass shaft to the light to compare. Her fingers, slowly twisting it, halted.

One of the symbols had vanished.

She turned the brass barrel the whole way around. All twelve trades had been marked on the telling dart last night, she was certain. Now one of the rows came up short. Bright, unmarked brass filled the space where one symbol had been. Ariel glanced at her copy to confirm which was missing: ✗ , the mark for a Judge.

Her mouth fell open. How could engraved marks disappear? That one may have been fainter than others, but she was sure they'd all been there yesterday in neat, aligned rows. She'd been careful to copy each in order, or she might have believed she had—

"Wait," her confused mind muttered. A shape had changed, too. Her mother had pointed out a crosshatched sign that meant danger: ╪. Now a second appeared on the dart in a place where it hadn't before. The sign that used to be in that spot—the mark she had copied onto her whalebone—had a little swoop instead of one crossbeam: ┣. Surely that swoop made it mean something different, something less threatening than an echo of danger.

Ariel dropped both hands in her lap, her mind racing. She had no idea how telling darts worked. Maybe changes were normal. She examined both shafts again. Her eyes were not misbehaving. Ariel heartily wished she and Zeke had studied it more closely while still in the tree. She believed her own eyes, but nobody else would, not even Zeke.

Ariel peeked up. Her mother had gone back to work. With a long, steadying breath, Ariel bent to finish her copy. Fortunately, all that remained was to smooth curves, deepen the shallower scratches, and add a few details to trade marks she knew. She didn't bother fixing her version to match the brass dart now. She wouldn't ever forget what had changed.

Ariel hurried back to class through a sprinkle of rain, chewing one of last fall's mushy apples on the way. She also bore a small linen bandage with the telling dart folded snugly inside. Her mother had made Ariel promise to turn it over right away. The bone knitting needle was hidden once more at home, and Ariel had made her own vow about that. Her copy would remain secret, no matter what the Storian or anyone else said.

CHAPTER
4

Ariel slipped into the classroom just before Zeke. He was breathless and looked a bit queasy, but the bell had been rung and there was no time for them to speak.

"Don't bother sitting," Bellam Storian said, as the two hurried in. Zeke halted, confused. "Perhaps your friend didn't tell you," the old man went on. "Stand in front here and multiply the numbers for us. Ariel, you start. I'll let you know, Zeke, when you can take over."

Zeke cast Ariel a frown. She ignored it. Her fist closed on the wrapped dart. She didn't want to relinquish it, but doing so now might at least get them out of their punishment.

"May I approach you with, um, something private?" Ariel asked the Storian. She could feel Zeke's eyes boring into the side of her head.

The Storian raised his bushy brows. Many students had tried to bribe him over the years. None had ever phrased it quite like this. Frowning but curious, he gave Ariel a curt nod.

Zeke grabbed her elbow. She shook off his grip to place her prize on the Storian's table. Moving her body to block as many curious eyes as she could, she unfolded the linen until the telling dart lay bare.

The mix of irritation and amusement on the Storian's face drained away. Pulling the cloth back over the dart, he addressed the rest of the class.

"The weather is growing nasty again more rapidly than I expected," he announced. "Your parents will want you home. Class dismissed."

The students remained frozen in their seats for much longer than usual. Nobody had gotten a good look at the thing on the table. Many wouldn't have known what it was if they had. All they knew was that a bribe had finally worked. Amazed, they shuffled toward the door, whispering, "What is it?" "What's in there?" "Is it gold?"

Storian waited until everyone but Ariel and Zeke had departed. Zeke shut the door against the weather and returned, his face dark. The Storian looked Zeke up and down. When Zeke just stared back, Bellam shrugged.

"Where did you get this?" he asked Ariel.

She glanced toward Zeke for help, but got only a baleful look in reply. She said, "We found it in the woods yesterday."

"Do you know what it is?"

"Yes, sir. A telling dart. Right?"

"And how did you know the visitors were looking for one?"

Ariel opened her mouth, but Zeke was faster. "We peeked out the door this morning," he said. "We heard them asking."

Ariel kept her gaze straight ahead, but she couldn't breathe. He was taking an awful chance, lying like that, and she couldn't imagine why.

Storian raised a disapproving eyebrow at Zeke. "I see. We'll discuss whether that was appropriate later. Why have you brought it to me, then?"

Zeke faltered. Ariel borrowed words from her mother. "You're our Storian," she said. "If it's important, you'd know and could decide what to do."

The Storian's eyes narrowed. He drew the dart out of its wrap. Zeke leaned forward, transfixed.

"Do you know how to use it?" the Storian asked. His voice was suddenly light, as if this were just one more lesson, and the rest of the class were simply out sick today.

Ariel shook her head. "I know some of the symbols, but—"

"Do *you* know how to use it?" asked Zeke.

The Storian probably should have taken offense, but he didn't. "Yes. But you see where it's broken?" He tapped the dart's point. "That's too bad. The inside message is lost."

"It fell out in the woods?" Ariel asked.

"No, no," Storian said. "The dart just won't unfurl to reveal it. Here's the idea." He placed his fingers along the three brass feathers. Ariel had done something similar while fiddling with it the previous night. "If you press these and twist, a seam appears and the dart springs open flat. The rest of the message is engraved on the inside. The barrel could hold something small, too, I suppose. But only the person who was meant to receive it could make it work."

"How could a metal stick know the difference?" Ariel asked.

The Storian smiled sadly. "How I wish I could tell you in detail. Particularly since you show less than avid interest in most of our lessons. But you've seen the luminescence in the sea at night, yes?"

Ariel nodded. She loved to stir the dark water and watch the sparks dance. Some nights the entire sea glowed.

"Imagine those sparkles not just in the sea or fixed in the night sky, but in and surrounding us all. Those before the Blind War learned to harness this Essence, which shimmers in every-thing, living and earthen. Your Essence tells who you are, and the darts use it—or they did, before the old things began run-ning down. I would never have guessed a dart might still be working. But it would be blank if it weren't."

Ariel mashed her lips between her teeth. Should they tell him it had been in Zeke's tree only a few fortnights?

Before she could decide, Storian shook his head. "Since it's been broken, however, it likely won't open at all. They made them that way to stop people from forcing darts that weren't sent to them."

"Was this sent to you?" Ariel asked. Who else but a Storian would know how to use it?

Zeke didn't wait for an answer. "What's the outside message say?"

Storian studied them, debate plain on his face. "Well, let's see," he said. "Even I may not remember some of the symbols."

Ariel didn't believe him. Not much of a liar, the Storian clearly did not want to tell them.

He tapped the smooth part of the shaft nearest the blunt end, above all the scored lines. "The mark of whoever sent it usually goes here."

"It's blank." Zeke sounded angry.

"I'm afraid so."

"Did everyone have their own symbol?" Ariel asked. "How could you know them all?"

"Oh, you couldn't," Storian said. "But each would be a trade mark, with a few changes to make it unique. You'd recognize the marks of your neighbors and friends, and even if you didn't, you'd know the dart came from some Storian or Healtouch, for instance. The sender's mark on this one probably wore off. Because it's so old."

"That lie was easy to spot," Ariel thought. The dart itself may have been old, but it had flown into Zeke's tree quite recently, so it must have been sent recently, too.

Storian's finger slid down through the most mysterious scratches in the middle. "This," he said slowly, "is a sort of invitation. To . . . it might be a party."

Zeke grunted. Wanting to elbow him to be quiet, Ariel pushed a cheerful grin to her lips. Did the Storian really think she and Zeke were that thick? That was the part of the message where the ‡ mark spoke of danger, not just once now, but twice.

"Fun," she said, hoping the rest of Storian's fibs would be equally obvious.

He hastily showed the trade marks near the broken tip. "Those tell who else was invited. You know those."

Ariel craned her neck for a final glimpse as he rewrapped the dart with the cloth. If his last words were true, the person who sent it had a friend in every one of the trades—until this morning, at least. It was possible, she supposed. But while Canberra Docks had more than its share of Fishers, she'd never met a Finder or Judge. And despite her friendship with Zeke, she knew Tree-Singers were rare.

"What about that first mark, below the blank part?" she asked, thinking of the lightning bolt.

"Oh, that shows who it was sent to." The Storian tucked the bundle into his vest. "Since we have two visitors here to collect it, I suppose that mark is for them. I'm not certain."

"Sure," Ariel thought, "if they were identical twins. Or the lightning bolt stands for the storm they arrived in." She stuffed back the sarcastic thoughts, along with questions she knew wouldn't be answered. Clearly the dart or the strangers made the Storian nervous.

He ushered his two students toward the door.

"I wish I could keep it," Ariel sighed.

Storian looked at her kindly. "I understand," he said. "Old relics are charming. A discovery like—" He rapped his knuckles on the doorframe, interrupting himself. "You might make a good Storian, eh?"

Before yesterday, Ariel couldn't have imagined anything more boring. Now she wasn't so sure. Storians seemed to have secrets.

"Well, hold on," he added. "I might have something for you." He retreated into his private half of the cottage.

Zeke stuck his head back inside. Rain dripped from his hair.

"What are you waiting for?" he hissed. "I have things to tell you."

"Me too!" she replied. "But—"

The Storian reappeared, his story abacus in one hand. Each bead in the eye-catching loop helped him remember a story. He untied the cord and slipped beads off one end, dropping them in his pocket. He removed beads of wood and silver and shell, a stone with a hole, a red knot of yarn, and other lumps Ariel couldn't identify.

"Here's the one I want." Storian's fingers reached a clear, greenish blob. One side was pinched narrow where the hole had been pierced. It reminded Ariel of a water droplet or a pollywog made of glass. When he passed it to her, it weighed heavy in her palm, smooth and cold. Flecks of gold sparkled deep in its belly.

"The Storian before me owned that bead," Bellam told her. "He never shared its story with me, and I've never found one that fit. So it's yours."

"For me?" Ariel squeaked.

"I wouldn't want you to learn that wondrous finds should be hidden, or that sharing them goes unrewarded." He began restringing the beads in his pocket.

"Thank you, sir," she breathed. Gazing at the green and gold bead, she stepped toward the door.

"One more thing," he called. "You still have multiplication to recite. But tomorrow will be soon enough."

She blinked, having trouble believing he still cared about that. When he neither smiled nor winked, she nodded reluctantly, closed her fingers over the bead, and ran out.

"My mother made me," Ariel blurted before Zeke could start. They huddled under the eaves of the classroom, although without much success. The wind blew the rain sideways.

"How come she knew? You were supposed to keep it a secret." He didn't sound mad anymore, though. Just sad. "Too late now. Maybe it doesn't matter."

"What do you mean? Why did you run off at lunchtime?"

"I'm freezing," he said. "Let's get somewhere inside."

As they ran toward her house, Ariel gripped her new treasure tightly. It might not be as intriguing as the telling dart, but it was pretty. Perhaps she could string it into a necklace.

Just before they arrived, they spotted a strange horse tied under a tree. He held his nose low, his ears flat, and his hindquarters pointed into the wind.

"It's probably theirs," Zeke muttered, although Ariel couldn't give up the idea that the strangers had blown into Canberra Docks on the wind.

"Where do you think they went?"

Zeke scowled. "Not far enough."

Even once they were inside, with cups of hot milk to warm them and Luna away out of earshot, Zeke wouldn't explain what he meant. He would admit only that his maple had hinted of trouble.

"Three bad things are going to happen, but I can't understand what," he moaned. He told her two would be soon, before the strangers left town. The last would come right as they left.

"Can't you just ask your tree what she means?"

"I tried." Frustration pinched the skin near his eyes. "I couldn't find the right questions, I guess. She kept answering, but not with anything that made sense."

A twinge of sympathy seized Ariel's belly. She imagined how overwhelmed she would feel if someone terribly sick arrived needing help when her mother was out.

"Maybe you should tell your father," she said.

Zeke's face cramped in reluctance. "Not this close to Namingfest. Not until after I pass."

In a moment, he mused, "It might not be me. My dad told me that when the trees sound mixed up, several very different things could happen."

"I thought trees knew the future beforehand," she said.

Zeke wobbled his head, not quite disagreeing. "They can feel the earth's forces, and the Essence Storian talked about, too. So they pretty much know what will happen. Usually. But my dad says that if some action will change things a lot, the trees can be confusing. They're actually telling us all of the futures that could sprout from that seed, but we're not smart enough to understand all at once."

"You think the telling dart is the seed," Ariel guessed.

Zeke stared into his milk. "Don't get scared," he said softly, "but if I understand the maple at all, I think the seed might be you."

She giggled, certain he must be teasing. He did not join her laughter.

"I know one thing for sure, though," he added. "You're going to get that dart back."

Afraid to get her hopes up and desperate to lift his creepy mood, Ariel showed him her copy, swearing him to secrecy with her. His face brightened for the first time since the crow man had entered their classroom. He even seemed to believe her when she whispered about the symbols that had vanished and changed. But when she promised to make a second copy for him, he shook his head hard.

"No. Don't make another."

She asked why. He repeated the rough shake of his head. "I don't know. Just don't."

Ariel studied him. He'd always been dreamy and unpredictable; that's why she liked him. This gloomy outlook was odd, though.

"Does your arm hurt?" she asked.

He looked at his splint as if he'd forgotten about it. "It does, actually."

"I'll walk you home, if you want."

"That's okay." He managed a smile. "You're a poke. I can run faster through the rain by myself."

In a burst of generosity, Ariel extended her bone dart to Zeke. "I've got Storian's bead. Do you want this?"

He regarded the white stem. "Not to have," he said slowly, "but I'll keep it for you for a while." He slid the bone along his palm and forearm into his splint, where it vanished completely.

"You are acting so weird," she said. "Are you sure you're all right?"

He nodded and finished his milk before heading back into the rattling storm.

Ariel had barely closed the door and moved near the fire when her mother raised her head from her sewing. She was finishing a new yellow skirt for Ariel to wear to Namingfest.

"Do you hear that?" Luna asked. "Is that the bell or just a ghost in the wind?"

Ariel's ears picked a clanging out of the roar. "It's the fire bell!"

Luna pushed aside her sewing and reached for her cloak. "Run across and make sure the neighbors have heard," she ordered. "Then come straight back here. Tend the fire. I'll be back right away if I'm not needed."

Wondering if Zeke might have rung the alarm, Ariel longed to dash to the square and find out. But the job her mother had given her might be important. She beat Luna through the door. Though the downpour had stopped, the wind battered Ariel sideways.

She banged on the door across the lane. It opened, but not by the hand of either Fisher who lived there. Ariel faced the crow man instead. She gasped. Out of his black flapping coat, he looked thinner and not quite so frightening—until he tilted his head like a bird watching an insect it would shortly snap up in its beak.

Jumping back, Ariel struggled to snatch a lungful of air from the wind.

"Yes?" he asked mildly.

Her breath returned. She remembered her errand. "The Fishers. Did they hear the bell?"

Burlingam Fisher stepped up behind the crow fellow, grabbing a storm coat and hat. "We have now. Rouse them next door, too, Ariel. It's hard to hear in this wind."

Ariel threw a last look at the stranger and fled. The clanging bell followed. Her heart couldn't quite separate the alarm from the stranger.

After banging doors at the two nearest houses, Ariel ducked back home out of the gale. Antsy, she busied herself with finding a ribbon to hold her new bead. Her mother returned not long after she'd strung it.

"It's a good thing the Storian dismissed you," said Ariel's mother, running her fingers through her wind-tangled hair. "His roof caught a spark."

"Storian's house is afire?" Ariel cried. Most of the building was stone, of course. But Storian's house was larger than usual to make room for his students. Smaller homes like her own were lidded with slate, but Storian's roof had been thatched.

"He's not hurt," Luna assured her. "The men will have the burning out soon. But someone could have been injured if students had been there and panicked."

Staring at the fire in the hearth, Ariel imagined it over her head. The back of her neck crawled, and she couldn't resist the urge to look up. Their dark beams sat silent and firm.

"Wait. How'd it catch after all that rain?" she wondered.

"This wind, that's always the danger," her mother replied. "Only bad thatch soaks through. A chimney spark must have blown up underneath."

Silently Ariel knotted her ribbon around her neck. The glass bead fell at her throat. Fingering it, Ariel wondered what the Storian had been doing when flames began eating his roof.

Quite possibly he'd been bent over the telling dart. That idea led too quickly to the stranger across the lane. Were the newcomers helping to put out the fire?

Despite Luna's explanation, a darker question rumbled in Ariel's mind: had one of them started it?

CHAPTER
5

Two things were on tongues in the morning: the fire and the Finders. The grim weather had blown away during the night, luring everyone outdoors to admire the blue sky and catch up on gossip. Once their trade became known, the strangers were offered more beds and meals than they could possibly use. Canberra Docks had gone a long time without a Finder to trade with, and the two men were kept busy. They located lost tools and fishing nets, wandering sheep, and the gold nugget that somebody's grandpa had hidden too deftly. The village needed a second well, too. Men dug where the Finders suggested and hit water before lunchtime. That prompted talk of a hunt for sea pearls. Their success was frightening for someone like Ariel, who had never seen a Finder at work—or who didn't want something found. Secretly, she feared that last night's fire might have been meant to scare Bellam Storian into turning over the telling dart.

His classes had been canceled until his roof could be fixed, so a troop of kids soon trailed the Finders, trying to spy the magic by which they worked. Ariel overheard someone using their names. The bear man was Elbert. The other was Scarl. That name sounded enough like the cry of a crow, she decided, to suit him. None too eager to know more, she spent the afternoon in her mother's workroom, fidgeting over tomorrow's Namingfest and wondering how she'd be tested.

Every test, like every person, was different. Aptitude mattered most. Skills could come later, once apprenticeship started, but some trades took talent or strengths. Someone who got terribly seasick wouldn't be wise to sign on as a Fisher, for instance. Ariel knew the traits expected in a healer: caring, calm, a steady hand, a strong stomach, a good eye for useful plants. The most important was also the trickiest: a healer's intuition. Wishing she could have used Zeke's broken arm as her test, she sniffed her mother's herbal concoctions and tried to feel a response deep inside. She noticed only her stomach craving a snack. If she had the Healtouch intuition, however, the test should bring it out soon enough.

Her thoughts strayed back to the Finders. If the telling dart had been meant for either of them, the receiver's mark would have been some modified ⊙ of the Finder trade instead of a lightning bolt. The event the dart invited old Lightning Bolt to attend must be something quite special, too, since almost no one ventured much beyond his or her own village. Storian had told his students that people once traveled for fun, but the Blind War ended that.

The Blind War nearly ended people, in fact. Uncountable hordes had crawled the Earth beforehand, although Ariel found that hard to imagine. Perhaps a struggle for land caused the conflict; nobody now remembered or cared. Entire cities had been flattened. Corpses piled up without a clear victor. And then someone had created an even more terrible weapon. A hideous twist on the past's wondrous knowledge of healing, this new weapon was meant not to kill, but to blind. If enemy forces couldn't see, they couldn't fight, no matter how great their numbers or reach.

The invention worked too well. Escaping control, the blindness ran rampant. Within a few days, or perhaps as long as a week, no eyes in the towns, in the wild, or beneath the wide ocean could see. With no warning and too little food or water easy at hand, nearly everyone died. Animals fared better than people. Yet the hardy—and those with hidden talents—survived. They began to adapt. Generations later, when the blinding disease had run its course and people began to see again, they'd lost the desire and the means to travel.

Ariel wondered what might lure travelers now. Maybe the dart announced some vast market or a dangerous contest with lavish prizes. More frightening, perhaps some mutual threat loomed, and every trade must send someone to meet and decide what to do. Unless the Storian had twisted the truth more than she thought, though, the time and place had been lost with the message inside. Even if they gained what they'd come for, the Finders would be disappointed.

With a twist of spiteful pleasure at that thought, Ariel decided to join her classmates as they snooped on the strangers. She had just risen to leave when her mother, who'd been out hanging laundry, stepped in through the doorway.

"Ariel." A troubled look darkened Luna's face. "Come outside. You've been found."

Ariel's first thought was that she'd never been lost. Then other meanings of her mother's words gripped her. She gulped and walked out to the Finders.

Both strangers waited outside the door. To Ariel's surprise,

Storian and Zeke stood there with them. A knot of gawkers hovered just down the lane.

"Ariel," said Elbert, the big one. He put out his hand. "It's a pleasure to meet you."

Ariel shot a glance at Zeke. His mouth remained a thin line.

Her mother tapped her shoulder, so Ariel shook Elbert's hand. It was meaty and warm, matching his face.

"I've given your telling dart to the Finders," Storian told her, his gaze on the cobblestones. He added, "They were looking for it," as if she hadn't known.

"Not exactly," said Scarl. "We were looking for you."

A chill ran down Ariel's back toward the stones under her boots.

"Zeke tried to take all the credit, but we were kids, too, long ago," Elbert said.

Eyeing him, Ariel could imagine a towheaded bully. It was harder to see a child hidden in Scarl.

"I know you found it together," Elbert continued, "but we figured that whoever turned it in was probably the one who had spotted it first."

She nodded, her thoughts racing. Zeke never would have taken credit that wasn't properly his, so he must have been trying to protect her. But from what?

"You see, Ariel, here's what happened—" Elbert stopped, glancing around the lane. "Might we step in?" he asked Luna.

"Oh, of course." She reached to open the door. "We just don't have much room."

Indeed, the main room nearly overflowed when they'd all filed in. Elbert encouraged Luna and Ariel to take the stools by the hearth. The men remained standing, with Zeke and Bellam hovering near the door.

"See, a Storian quite far away stumbled on a bunch of old telling darts," Elbert began when they'd settled. "He decided to try an experiment. He sent them all out, directing them to the nearest person in each trade who could still understand them. He didn't send much of a message, though. He wanted only to see if the Essence that once drove them still worked, if they could still find their targets—and if anyone but Storians could indeed understand. The darts went out a few weeks ago; then he sent us to find the results."

Ariel kept her eyes fixed on Elbert, though she wanted badly to check her Storian's face. What Elbert said matched rather poorly with what she'd heard yesterday. She knew Bellam had not told the whole truth, but she was certain he'd told more than this Finder.

Elbert pulled the dart from his pocket. She couldn't help but lean toward it, wishing to hold it again. He smiled.

"Unfortunately, the experiment has been a fat failure. The other darts all found someone—one stuck itself in the mast of an old Fisher's boat. But so far, no receiver has understood theirs or known what to do with it. Even other Storians like yours don't remember."

Alarms rang in Ariel's head. Her whirling mind suggested that if there had been a trade simply called Liar, Elbert would be in it. And if there were another called Fib-Spotter, she could apprentice today. But if it was important enough to make him lie in front of other adults, she had to be careful. Too much silence would reveal her disbelief.

"Gee, that's too bad," she said.

"Yes." Elbert bent his head and scratched his scrubby blond

whiskers. Speaking to the flagstones, he added, "You can't understand what's marked on it, can you?"

She shook her head.

"Are you sure?" He held it out toward her. "Take another look. What does it tell you?"

Her fingers trembling, Ariel took it. She focused hard on the brass. Even a stray glance toward Storian or Zeke would tell Elbert that they had discussed it. She had to guess correctly what the Finders already knew.

While she worked up enough spit in her dry mouth to speak, she noticed the telling dart's point. Its broken tip had been beaten or filed. Someone had tried to repair it.

"Well," she said, fidgeting to hide her surprise, "I know some of these trade marks. Like this one is Healtouch and that one is Tree-Singer and that one is Fool."

He stepped close enough to breathe on her neck. Ariel closed her eyes, quailing. He smelled like fish oil and mud.

"This is the only dart, so far, that delivered itself to a child." Scarl spoke in his shadowy voice from behind Elbert. "That seems a bit odd."

Thankfully, Elbert stepped back.

"Well, it really delivered itself to a tree," she said. "That's where I—we—found it." She hadn't planned to bring Zeke back into the danger, if there was any. She couldn't help it. She needed to spread out the fear.

Scarl merely gazed at her with those wide-set eyes, dark and unblinking. She felt as if they could see past her skin to find the secrets held by her soul.

"Anything else we can help you gentlemen with, then?" Luna asked. Her voice was pleasant, but Ariel knew the visit had ended.

Elbert tapped the dart on his thumb before he slipped it back into his pocket. "Just one thing," he said. "For their help with the experiment, we've been giving most folks a reward. Finding is what we do best. Can we do a bit of that for you now?"

"Goodness, a reward." Luna stood, giving Ariel silent permission to jump up as well. "None is needed, I'm sure. Besides, we've nothing lost or lacking that I can think of. Have we, Ariel?"

Ariel's eyes darted, her mind suddenly blank. Now that it was almost over, the strain wrung her out empty. She could only shrug.

"Well, we'll be here a few more days, I expect," Elbert said, as Luna ushered him out. "That may give you time to think of something you need."

Before the door closed behind them, Ariel decided what reward she wanted most. If she hadn't known her mother would scold her for rudeness, she would have begged the Finders to leave right away. The knowledge that the crow man slept just across the lane had given her nightmares last night. Ariel needed to sleep better this evening: her Naming test was only hours away.

CHAPTER
6

The whole village turned out for Namingfest. The chance to take time off from chores, play games with neighbors, and celebrate the first day of April in sunshine had everyone smiling.

Everyone, that is, except Ariel, Madeleine, and Zeke. Though the day was held in their honor, first they faced tests. Students hardly ever failed, but it did happen. Nobody wanted to spend a humiliating year as a Fool. Besides merciless taunting whenever adults weren't around, it meant sitting through another year of classes before the test could be taken again. The second time, most people settled for Fisher or Reaper, regardless of what they had wanted before, simply because those two were hard to mess up.

A few people remained Fools, of course. Some wanted to be Fools all along. They didn't often admit it beforehand because parents never approved. Sure, class clowns basked in attention, but once they'd grown up, Fools had to be awfully amusing to earn food from others every day of the year. Singing and juggling weren't really enough. Most Fools ate bugs for some of their meals.

The grown Fools of Canberra Docks lived for festival days like today, though. Everyone brought treats to the village square for a shared picnic around the sycamore tree. Ariel clung near her mother and watched her give away fresh bread and butter. Zeke's mother, a Kincaller, tended two cows, so Zeke's broken arm meant that Luna would have plenty of milk and cream for a while.

Ariel couldn't possibly eat. The tests would begin soon, and her stomach felt like a rock. Plus, she'd spotted Elbert and Scarl laughing with a handful of Fishers. She couldn't imagine why they didn't go home.

Restless, she paced the square. She spied Zeke with his family near the sycamore, a favorite of Zeke's father's. Since Canberra Docks had no Judge, Jeshua Tree-Singer and his old sycamore were clearly in charge of the village. Today would determine if someday that role would fall to Zeke.

When he saw her, she waved. He waved back, looking nervous. She remembered what he'd said about two bad things happening before the Finders left town, with a third coming as they departed. The fire must have been one of the two. She hoped the loss of the dart was the other.

Finally Zeke's father and the Storian stood up together in the shade of the sycamore. Luna and Madeleine's parents joined Zeke's mother at its base. The chattering stopped. The youngest kids drew close to watch. Ariel pressed her hands to her chest. She had to work for each breath.

Zeke, the eldest by a few months, went first. He stood straight before his father and the Storian.

"I buried something last night among the roots of our tree," Jeshua announced. He pointed out a mound of freshly tamped dirt. "Your test, Ezekiel, is simple—but not easy. Find out from this tree or any other what I've buried. No one else knows. Come back and declare it. We'll dig it up to see if you pass. You've got until nightfall."

"Yes, sir." Zeke no longer looked nervous. He gave the sycamore a long stare before heading slowly toward his maple. The villagers, cheering him on, parted so he could pass. His gaze never left the distant grove.

Ariel squirmed. She didn't know how he could keep from breaking into a run. When he passed the edge of the square, she dragged her attention back to his father.

Madeleine went next. Before Zeke's father had even begun, she declared, "I want the Kincaller test." Ariel had never heard the shy girl speak so surely.

The crowd hummed. Madeleine was the daughter of two Reapers, and nobody had guessed she might want to do something else. Even her mother looked startled. Many Reapers handled animals, but generally in slaughter. Kincallers befriended creatures that did not provide meat, including some that weren't useful at all.

Taken aback, the grown-ups in charge whispered together. Bellam Storian bent to consult with the mothers of both Madeleine and Zeke.

"We're not really prepared," Jeshua told Madeleine. "You should have said something sooner."

"I'm sorry. I wasn't sure sooner." Her voice had dropped back to its usual shy whisper. If Ariel hadn't been up front, she wouldn't have heard.

Storian straightened. "I'm told, Madeleine," he said, "that you've made pets of some pigeons. Are they caged?"

"Sort of," she said. "I made a coop from an old blanket."

"Your test, then, is this: Go put them in something smaller, a fish basket perhaps. Bring them here. Someone—" He scanned the crowd. "Someone will carry them a goodly way into the forest."

"I'll do it," said a voice in the back. Ariel turned. All eyes fell on Scarl, who added, "I've got a horse."

"Very good," Storian agreed. Ariel nearly fainted. She couldn't believe the Storian would let a stranger take part in a Naming test. He might do something mean to make Madeleine fail.

Another voice laughed. "The Finder will become a Loser for the day!"

Storian nodded. "Indeed. He'll take them away and release them. We'll limit how far he should go." He looked gravely at Madeleine. "Find them or coax them back here by nightfall to pass."

Madeleine blanched. "All five of them?"

When the Storian hesitated, Jeshua answered. "At least three. You've not made it easy on yourself, Madeleine. But that's not a bad thing. We'll all be hoping for you." Jeshua raised his eyes to the villagers. "Not helping, though." Heads nodded.

Ariel thought she would choke on her heart. Poor Madeleine! Not only would she likely fail the test, she'd lose her pets, too. This year's tests seemed many times harder than usual. Of course, she'd never stood with those tested before. Ariel watched Madeleine cross the square to gather her birds, not blaming her for dragging her feet.

"Ariel."

She jumped at Jeshua's voice.

"Healtouch?" he asked.

She nodded and clasped both hands around the glass bead at her throat.

"Your test has three parts," he said, glancing at Luna. Ariel wanted to stamp her foot at the injustice, but her mother nodded, approving.

"Unless someone has taken ill suddenly!" he added. The crowd laughed. Ariel held her breath, certain Elbert would claim to be sick and she'd have to heal him.

"All right, then," Zeke's father went on at last. "There are three things you'll need to bring us, Ariel. The first is a sample of your needlework. Healers must have clever hands to stitch wounds."

Ariel exhaled. She could stitch something that afternoon if she had to.

"The second," Jeshua said, "is a bucket of fish guts. Healers must not mind ugly sights or unpleasant things to touch." He surveyed the crowd. "I'm sure we have a Fisher who can supply what she'll need?"

A chorus of agreement ran through the crowd.

"Finally," Zeke's father continued, "you must bring us a certain few plants. Your mother says you know plenty already. It wouldn't be fair to expect you to say what they're good for, but you should be able to remember a list and recognize them. Are you ready to hear them?"

Grinding her teeth, Ariel nodded. This might not be so bad.

"They are foolsbane, marshyellow, fiddlefern, chamomile, goat ivy, and swarth. Your mother assures me they all appear this time of year. Do you see why we've chosen these six?"

With a gulp, Ariel nodded. Everything on the list had a twin that was either useless or poison.

"A healer's intuition should guide you in choosing which are wholesome, even if your eyes can't do it for you. Shall I repeat them?"

Hoping she'd simply remember the telltale signs, Ariel nodded stiffly. She ticked a finger for each as he went.

He finished, "You, too, have until nightfall."

Unlike her two friends before her, Ariel didn't care what anyone thought. She set off at a run.

The fish guts would take the least time, so that's where she started. She tapped the arm of a sturdy woman who lived on her boat at the docks.

Felia Fisher winked. "Oh, have I got fish guts for you." She led Ariel to the pier and what looked like a pile of seabirds. As they reached it, the birds lifted off, their wings beating a stench into the air. Ariel had certainly smelled it before, but it still turned her stomach.

"Borrow a bucket from my boat if you like, child," Felia said. "Your mother might not want hers smelling so fresh."

"It's got pollywogs in it, anyway," Ariel told her.

Felia laughed. "Remind me not to drink water at your house!"

With a shout of thanks, Ariel ran to the boat for the bucket, glad she hadn't worn her new yellow skirt. If all went well, she could don it later, along with her new last name.

When she returned, the birds had gone back to their feasting. She shooed them away, held her breath, and dipped the bucket. It scooped up loops of fish intestine, loose scales like stinky snowflakes, and putrid, unidentifiable ooze.

The villagers in the square smelled Ariel coming. Heads turned. Palms waved at the air before noses. Ariel walked up the aisle they formed, wishing she hadn't filled the bucket so full. Her arm ached.

"That's close enough," laughed the Storian as she

approached. Ariel set the bucket at his feet. "No, no," he continued. "Please take it away now!"

"That's not what Jeshua told her!" someone shouted. "There was nothing in the test about taking it back!"

The crowd erupted in hoots and pleas for Ariel to take it away. Giggling, she hefted the bucket again. Cheers followed. She was filled with a prickly love, not just for her mother and friends but for all of Canberra Docks—even the guts pile.

No longer nervous, she went next to her house for a needlework sample. The most artful work she'd ever done with a needle or pin was her bone dart, but she didn't want to show that. Zeke still had it, anyway. She dug through the sewing kit her mother had given her long ago. There wasn't much in it; Ariel considered stitching only slightly more fun than chores. But she found a half-complete handkerchief she'd embroidered with a sun and a cloud. She stuffed it into her pocket. If she had time after collecting her plants, she would add a nice flower.

Running across the meadow, she chanted in time with her footsteps the names of the plants that she needed. Foolsbane, marshyellow, fiddlefern, chamomile, goat ivy, and— She halted. What was the sixth? She repeated the first five, tapping each finger. Her second thumb remained silent.

A tornado spun in her belly. She'd forgotten one! She walked on, shaky, trying to keep the whirlwind in her guts from rising into her head. She told herself she had all afternoon. She would carefully collect the first five. Then she'd sit and name every plant in Luna's workroom, every plant she'd ever heard of. When she said the right name, she'd remember.

Despite this plan, she still felt like throwing up.

Marshyellow was easy. It grew near the hole in the creek where the pollywogs lived, and it didn't look that much like its twin. Wishing she'd thought to bring a basket, Ariel yanked a handful from the water.

True chamomile flowers dotted the meadow. She resolved to get those on her return.

As she entered the woods, she yearned to stop by Zeke's tree, but she decided she'd better not waste any time. With marshyellow slapping wetly against her calf, she found fiddlefern and, after a long hunt, a goat ivy vine. To her relief, she remembered the notched leaf shape that identified the ivy. The fern's sharp scent confirmed that find.

She had just started her search for foolsbane when she felt something odd—not a healer's intuition, but the tickle that suggests somebody watching. The skin between her shoulder blades crawled.

"Zeke? Is that you?" She swiveled, searching. "Madeleine?" Maybe the other girl had come this way after her birds. "Madeleine, it's me. You can come out. There's no rule against talking. Just helping."

The wind sighed. The birds had stopped chirping. Someone was definitely here with her.

Ariel bent back to her hunt for the foolsbane. Although her eyes roamed the ground, her attention remained tuned for the crack of a twig or a movement.

At last she heard the footfall. She jerked her head up. He stood in full view before her, no longer trying to hide. It would have been difficult anyway, so close and with a horse at his side.

CHAPTER
7

Frozen, Ariel stared at Scarl. He'd ridden out in the fair weather without his coat, so nothing hid the long knife he wore at one hip.

The plants in her hand slipped to the ground. Just before she whirled to escape—as though he'd been timing her courage, in fact—he spoke.

"Well met."

She didn't believe for a moment that their meeting was any accident. Nobody could sneak up so well in the woods without trying. Her limbs shook in anger as well as in fear.

"What are you finding today, Ariel?" he asked. She could barely make out the soft words over the rustle of the forest.

"Only what I'm supposed to," she said.

He ducked his head as if amused. "Of course. That would be plants for your test, yes?"

When she refused to even nod, he added, "Watch out for the swarth. Its poisonous brother is plentiful here. I passed some just there." He jerked one thumb back the way he had come.

Ariel's breath caught. The sixth plant! Her test, though, felt distant. She narrowed her eyes and tried to guess what this stranger wanted.

When she still didn't respond, he shifted and patted the neck of his horse. A cold twist of pleasure unfurled in her chest. She'd discomfited him—not much, but a bit. Her pinching fear eased slightly. Ariel noticed then that his horse was lathered with sweat. He'd ridden hard, either before releasing Madeleine's birds or on the way back. Ariel could only hope the horse was tired and that she could dodge through the trees better, if she had to run.

"Healtouch." Scarl turned his penetrating eyes back upon her. "Are you sure that's the right trade for you?"

"I would *never* want to be a Finder, if that's what you mean." The hot words slipped out and then hung in the air like a mistake. Precisely because of that dread, she pushed herself a step closer to him.

"I'm not afraid of you," she added. Her voice remained steady—almost.

Scarl raised one eyebrow. "I can see that." Inside, he was laughing, she was certain.

"Go away." It sounded more like a plea than she wanted. To make it stronger, she added, "You're not supposed to bother people who are taking their tests."

He did smile now, a thin stretch of the lips. He tipped his head at her politely and swung onto his horse. In a breath, the pair had passed into the green flicker and vanished.

Ariel collapsed to the ground.

After a moment of inhaling the familiar, safe smells of leaf mold and dirt, she sat up. The words she'd exchanged with Scarl were burned into her brain. As her thoughts found their way back to her test, though, a grin spread on her face. He'd mentioned the one plant she couldn't remember. He'd meant to scare her, she thought, and he certainly had. But he'd helped, too. As birds began warbling again, Ariel jumped to her feet and collected the plants she'd let fall.

Another thought dashed away her victory grin. Helping was against Namingfest rules, and he'd been in the crowd when Zeke's father said so. Maybe the Finder had done it on purpose.

Ariel couldn't cheat. The idea churned in her stomach. She probably would have remembered the swarth on her own, but now she'd never know. And what if Scarl told someone that he'd met her and brought up the name of a plant? One of his comments rang horribly in her ears. "Healtouch—are you sure that's the right trade for you?" He had found her in the woods specifically to make her fail.

Tears rose in her throat. She was stuck. If she went back and confessed she'd had help, they would thank her for being honest, but she would fail nonetheless. If she stayed mum, but he talked, people would believe him because cheaters had something to hide. She would fail either way.

Her only hope was that she was wrong. She could say nothing and pray that he did the same. But even if no one ever found out, her Healtouch name would always feel like a cheat.

In a daze, Ariel got herself moving again. Her heart felt as though it hung near her knees. Dragging her feet, which were heavier from the weight of her heart, she plucked a few strands of foolsbane. She kicked at a swarth fungus where it sprouted low on the side of a tree. Snatching it, she would have rather stomped it to pulp. She'd never wanted so badly to run away.

Ariel haunted the forest until the spring air grew chill. As she returned across the meadow, she remembered the chamomile. She picked a single flower before continuing on to the square.

Zeke had returned, probably long ago. His face glowed. That was all Ariel needed to know he'd passed his test. Madeleine was nowhere to be seen, but she still had an hour or two. More time couldn't help Ariel now.

The crowd welcomed her back. Unable to match their smiles, she trudged to the sycamore. Zeke's father, the Storian, and Luna came together from conversations they'd been holding with friends. Seeing her daughter's downcast look, Luna tipped her head inquiringly. Ariel pressed a stiff smile to her face and laid her pickings at Jeshua's feet.

"Needlework?" he asked.

"Oh!" She drew the balled handkerchief from her pocket. She could still add better stitching, but it no longer seemed to matter. She handed it over.

Inspecting it, the adults looked disappointed. "It's a start," Storian said. "And for the last part of your test . . . ?"

Jeshua called out the names one by one. For each, Ariel held up the plant. Luna raised her eyebrows at the lone chamomile flower.

As "swarth" fell from Jeshua's lips, Ariel's ears buzzed. She saw his lips move but couldn't hear it. She was too busy waiting for a cry of "Cheat!" from the crowd.

Jeshua twitched his hand and repeated the word. Hardly believing the silence, Ariel grabbed her last plant. Her heart soared. She raised the fungus to Jeshua—and froze.

"Ariel!" Her mother gasped.

Ariel saw it plainly at last. Somehow she'd done exactly what Scarl had warned her against: picked a fungus that looked much like swarth. But this one was deadly.

Jeshua's face collapsed into wrinkles. A small groan rippled among those near enough to see. The fungus tumbled from Ariel's hand.

"It's not swarth," she said, too late. The idea Scarl had planted had sprouted in the fear he'd sown with it. She'd simply been too distracted to notice its bloom until now.

Her heart thudded and ached as if she had actually poisoned someone. The adults in charge whispered together. Luna bowed her head and shook it slowly once: no.

Jeshua looked at Ariel gravely, his eyes sad.

"I'm sorry, Ariel." He said more words, like "taking more time" and "next year" and "partial." None of them mattered but "sorry."

"Something scared me. I got confused," she whispered into the fog around "sorry." She didn't expect her explanation to change things. It didn't.

Tears flooding her eyes, Ariel let Luna lead her home through the whispers. A few young voices taunted, "April Fool!" Those were hastily hushed by parents. She didn't look up from her feet until she thought she'd passed every face in the crowd. When she finally raised her eyes, she discovered she still had a few more faces to pass. One belonged to Scarl. She gazed back at him dully, not caring if his eyes glinted in pleasure or triumph.

Neither appeared on his face. If anything, he looked ill. One hand kneaded his temple as if his head hurt.

The other gripped the hilt of his knife.

CHAPTER
8

"It was a hard test," Luna said. She sat by the hearth and scooped her daughter into her lap. Like a toddler, Ariel hid her face against her mother's collar. "But I thought you'd do fine. I know you've learned your plants better than that."

She awaited some explanation. Ariel's tongue felt too wooden to give it. Words couldn't turn back Jeshua's "sorry."

"I know it feels awful now," Luna added, accepting the silence. She patted Ariel's back. "But you won't die of it."

In the hours that followed, three people told Ariel they were partly to blame. The quickest to say so was Zeke. The first time he knocked on the door, Luna took one look at Ariel's face, bent to whisper to him, and sent him away. When he came back just before bedtime, she let him come in.

By then Ariel's stomach, unaware she considered her life over, had rumbled angrily awake. Zeke sat beside her while she nibbled cheese and leftover bread.

"I'm so sorry," he told her.

"Don't say that. I hate that word." She would never hear "sorry" again without reliving this day.

Zeke studied his hands before trying again. "It's kinda my fault. My dad didn't want anyone saying he'd been easy on me because I was his last son. And then I think he felt he had to make all the other tests hard, too."

Ariel looked up from her bread crust. "Did Madeleine fail, too?"

Not sure what she wanted to hear, Zeke gnawed his lip. "No. She came back just before dark. She spent all day looking and calling. I even saw her trying to talk to the horse to figure out where he'd gone. She captured only two birds, but another flew by itself to her coop."

Ariel gazed at him sadly, trying to imagine Madeleine's day. It was tempting to want company in failure, but she would never wish her own roiling shame on somebody else, least of all gentle Madeleine. Ariel managed a shallow smile.

"She's lucky," she said. "I think her test was the hardest. It's not your fault, though, Zeke. I just—" She shuddered. She couldn't bear to revisit it yet again. "I goofed up something awful," she said instead. "I guess this is the second bad thing that was going to happen."

Zeke sighed. "I'm not too sure about that."

Unable to imagine anything worse, Ariel just blinked at him and let blankness fill her head. It was so much easier than thinking about what he'd just said.

"What was buried under the tree, anyway?" she asked, changing the subject.

Zeke shared the high points of his test. He hadn't bothered trying to catch the sycamore's attention. Instead he'd walked to his maple, sung her a few songs he thought she would like, and asked if she could help him. Although even trees have enemies and allegiances, they rarely hold secrets from one another.

After an hour or so, the maple gave him an answer. He returned to tell his father that the thing in the ground was a spoon with a bootlace tied around it. Jeshua dug it up. That was that.

He made it sound easy. Ariel knew that it wasn't. Having already done well enough to be a Tree-Singer himself, Zeke would now start as his father's apprentice. She hugged him and cried. In the part of her that still could feel at all, she was honestly pleased. Yet his success also lit up her failure.

The second person to shoulder some of Ariel's pain, the next morning, was Bellam Storian. He didn't use the word "sorry." He just came by to ask how she was.

"I feel somewhat responsible for what happened yesterday," he added. "All that fuss about the telling dart was quite a distraction. I should never have mentioned that two of my students had found it."

"Why did you, then?" Ariel grumbled.

"Ariel, what manners!" Her mother clicked her tongue.

Ariel shrugged one shoulder. She thought she had nothing left to lose. Why be polite?

"That's all right." Storian whisked his hands together slowly. He gave Ariel a lopsided look—part amusement, part chagrin. "You haven't had much experience with Finders, have you? No one but them understands how they work. But those who eat regularly have to be very good at their trade." He paused, letting Ariel decide that a Finder as big as Elbert must be skilled indeed.

He cleared his throat, stared out the window, and continued. "You heard them say what they sought—not the dart, but its receiver. They would have found out sooner or later.

I thought sooner was better. I thought then they'd just leave. It never occurred to me—" He faltered. "Well, I guess I was wrong."

"Nonsense," said Luna. "You told the truth and should make no apology for that. I can't see how it changed yesterday. Some things just don't turn out as we'd like."

Ariel choked on a protest. When she'd first opened her eyes that morning, her waking brain had forgotten, just for an instant, that she was a Fool. Memory had crashed down upon her like a wave crushing a seashell.

She and Storian now swapped a look of regret. "I'll try to make the next year of classes as interesting for you as I can," he said. His eyes dodged away, and he added, "Once we start again, of course."

It wasn't until after Storian had departed that Ariel decided he might deserve just a teaspoon of blame—not for giving her away to the Finders, but for letting Scarl release Madeleine's birds. If he'd stayed in the square, she might be Ariel Healtouch now.

That wistful notion made Ariel's third apologetic visitor doubly surprising. She and her mother had just eaten lunch when a tap came at the door. By then, as much as she hurt, Ariel was starting to imagine that life could go on. She might even comb the tide pools that afternoon.

"Why don't you answer that, love?" Luna didn't add that it was probably another well-wisher anyway.

But when Ariel opened the door, Elbert stood on the threshold. A cluster of pink heartthrob flowers trembled in his fist.

"Supposed to help a broken heart," he said, extending them

toward her. "Although a Healtouch probably knows better than I do."

If Ariel's teeth hadn't been well attached, they would have dropped from her mouth. He grinned at her expression. It was the first honest smile she'd seen on his face.

"These are for you," he said. "But I also would speak with your mother, if I may."

Ariel stumbled backward. Luna came to the door. After a blink of surprise, she swept her hand back.

"Would you like to come in?"

Elbert rested his bouquet on the table. "I don't blame you for being suspicious of these," he told Ariel. "I know we have frightened you, being strangers and all. Too intense in our interest, perhaps. We were only excited by the end of our quest, and surprised where it led us."

Feeling defenseless after yesterday's havoc, Ariel tucked herself behind her mother's left hip.

"No harm done," Luna said. "What can I do for you, Elbert?"

He clasped his hands over his belly. "We're preparing to leave, Scarl and I."

Trumpets rejoiced in an unbroken corner of Ariel's heart.

"I wonder," he continued, "if you've thought of that reward we discussed."

Luna smiled down at her folded hands. "If you could turn back the days, I'm sure Ariel would choose that. Since I doubt even you can find a way to do that, then no. There's really no need."

He chuckled and scratched at his whiskers. "I've hunted for 'do overs' myself more than once. I haven't found any. Yet. But since you haven't thought of a suitable reward, I'm happy to say that I have. If you'll hear me."

"Go on," Luna said doubtfully.

He reached one hand into a pocket. When his chunky fingers emerged, the telling dart rested between them. Ariel edged out a bit from her mother.

"We're going to Libros to take this back to the man that I told you about." His eyes flicked between Luna and Ariel. "We have a few more to find, but our orders are to return with each singly. We'll be back for another, not far from here, soon. That being the case . . ." He pressed his lips together, choosing words. He focused on Luna, but the hand holding the dart drifted toward Ariel. "Ariel could deliver this dart herself."

Ariel wasn't certain her ears had worked right. Elbert hurried to explain before he heard "no."

"It would be worth a great deal for him to meet her personally, be able to talk to her, get some idea, perhaps, why the dart came to her. That's nothing I'm skilled at, as you could probably tell. We have the horse; she could ride. And we'd deliver her back here in a fortnight and a half. Or certainly not more than a month."

He had to stop for a breath, and then, before anyone else spoke, he added the clincher. "By then everyone might have forgotten Namingfest Day."

"Oh, I really don't think . . ." Luna's voice faded.

To escape from Foolery for as much as a month! The idea was too tempting for Ariel to resist. Images spun through her head. She'd never been out of Canberra Docks. The tales Storian told about other places, however, were always exciting.

Buildings with towers. Hills of salt. Houses in trees. Once, a Fisher blown lost by a storm had sailed home months later with patterns drawn on his back and a musical instrument made from hundreds of tiny gold bells.

Elbert might have been hearing her thoughts. "Libros is quite different from here," he was saying, "a grand adventure for someone her age. There's a market where people trade sweets and a whole building filled with relics to look at. One little telling dart would be lost there."

Ariel could not imagine seeing anything from the old days more mystical than her telling dart—and then she could. Libros might have a bike.

Elbert let his words sink in, and then he looked squarely at Ariel. "I'd understand if she was too scared to go. Nobody travels much anymore, least of all someone young. A few Finders and the odd Tree-Singer, that's about it—them that aren't fearful of losing the way. Not many others are bold enough."

Sparks flew inside Ariel at the suggestion that she might be too scared. The whole proposal was terrifying, of course. It would have been scary with someone like Jeshua, whom she trusted completely. With Elbert and Scarl—! She felt faint. But the thought of treading distant hillsides awoke a yearning inside her, a fire in her gut under the fright. She wanted to go.

"And it wouldn't be easy," he continued. "Even with the horse, there's rain and rough country and bugs." He grinned, shifting his gaze again to Ariel's mother. "But I can assure you she wouldn't get lost."

"Goodness." Uncertainty wavered in Luna's normally firm features.

Holding her breath, Ariel watched her mother's face. Consent would mean entrusting herself to strangers who had given her nightmares. Yet denial would be worse, if only because it meant that nothing would change. She'd remain a girl with no talent and no future, a failure. Stung by that truth, Ariel's heart clamored to prove that she had a worth, even if it was only a willingness to step into the unknown. If she could not be a success, she could still be a rebel, breaking the unspoken rule that chained others to places they already knew.

"Let me," she whispered. And then she told the biggest lie of her life, and the only one she'd told more than once. "I'm not scared."

Surprised, Luna smoothed her apron. "There's really no need to consider," she told Elbert. "Whatever I thought, there's no way she could be ready to leave with you today."

"Hmm." Elbert scratched at his beard again. Ariel wondered if lice lived there, and whether she'd still want to go if they did. "We could wait until morning, easy enough," he said. "It is late to be starting today."

He added, "I confess, it would be more a favor to us than a reward. Maybe a little of both." His mouth remained poised to keep rolling. He stopped it with visible effort.

Ariel wanted to beg, "Mama, please?" like a toddler. She pressed the words back. Her eyes strayed to the dart in Elbert's hand, and a memory flashed in her mind. Zeke had told her the dart would fall into her keeping again. This must be how.

Thoughts of Zeke begot an idea. She tugged gently at her mother's arm and murmured, "Could we ask Jeshua?"

"Could you give us a little time to discuss it?" Luna asked Elbert.

"Of course, of course. I should have said that myself." He started to put the telling dart back in his pocket. He paused.

"Tell you what." He dangled the dart before Ariel. "So you

know that I mean it, you keep this until you decide. If the answer is yes, you'll already have it to carry."

She drew the brass gingerly from his fingers before he moved to the door.

"I'll be about, trading for provisions," he said. "Or Scarl's just there across the lane. When you've reached a decision, let one of us know."

Once he was gone, Luna turned to her daughter. A dozen arguments flicked over her face. She voiced only two. "They're practically strangers, Ariel. I'm not sure I can trust them. And I don't know if I can bear to be without you that long."

Ariel dragged her palms along her thighs. She had no idea how it felt to be away from her mother. She didn't want to imagine. It would confuse her too much.

"If I was going to apprentice with somebody else," she said slowly, "I'd be away, too."

"Not nearly so far. Not out of Canberra Docks."

"It's just a few weeks, though," Ariel said.

"Well, I have a mind about it," Luna said, "but I can tell that you do as well. Let me wash up our lunch dishes and we'll see if Zeke's father can guide us."

Word of the Finders' offer skipped from one neighbor to the next before Ariel and Luna even reached Jeshua's house. Two people they met along the way remarked on the reward, simply assuming that she would accept.

"Heavens, you can be a Healtouch next year," said one, "but you might never get another chance like this."

Another neighbor observed, "It's lucky for the rest of us, too, since it means the Finders will be back in a few weeks—more trading then!"

"We haven't decided yet," Luna told them, plucking uneasily

at one elbow. "It depends on what Jeshua and the sycamore say."
But Ariel could see the opinions of others nibbling at her
mother's misgivings.

As they neared Zeke's house, she kept her eyes on the
sycamore, silently begging its approval. Meanwhile, her skin
prickled with worry that the tree might actually give it.

CHAPTER
9

"I'm glad you came to ask me," Jeshua told Luna. He, too, already had heard that Ariel might go off with the Finders, but unlike most others, he didn't approve. After saying so, he added, "My opinion means nothing, of course," and went to sit for a long time alone near his tree. Ariel and her mother waited on the edge of the square, far from his voice.

When he rose and approached them at last, he looked somber. But he shared what the sycamore had said.

"It is best that she go. And she will."

Through the waiting, Ariel's own fears and her mother's had sneaked over her heart. The tree's answer sent relief surging through her and bolstered her nerve.

It seemed to have the opposite effect on her mother. "She will?" Luna demanded. "As if I have nothing to say about it? What does that mean?"

Jeshua shook his head. "I can't tell you. Regardless of my question, that is the answer I receive."

Luna drew Ariel to her. "I won't let her go. I can't do it."

Reaching a sympathetic hand to her arm, Jeshua replied,

"You know how I feel about ignoring their advice, especially when it's this clear. That always seems to cause trouble."

Luna smoothed Ariel's hair. Feeling too much like a pet, Ariel pulled away.

"I can't command you," Jeshua added, "but if she were my child, I would send her."

At that, Ariel's mother bowed her head, pressed her fists to her chest, and nodded. Ariel squirmed, a silent shriek of excitement vibrating through her bones.

She wanted to tell the Finders herself she was coming. Her mother insisted on knocking together at the door across the lane. When Scarl had been summoned, Luna didn't even say hello.

"Walk with me, please," she said, striding away. Over her shoulder she ordered, "Ariel, you stay here."

Scarl gazed thoughtfully after her. Then his eyes slid to Ariel.

Her breath caught. Could she really spend three weeks with those piercing eyes?

"The horse is around back," he said under his breath, "if you'd like to go make friends."

Ariel watched Scarl's long legs catch him up to her mother. He tipped his head toward Luna and clasped his hands at his back as he walked.

"There's that crow again," Ariel thought. If she didn't know that shape-shifters existed only in stories, she would have thought she had met her first one.

Seeing them hurry away, she abandoned the hope of overhearing their talk. Disappointed, she skipped from cobble to cobble, watching her mother's gestures from a distance before she took Scarl's advice.

Luna must have walked him ten times around the village square before returning. Meanwhile, Ariel found the horse tethered on a patch of scrubby grass. She stood lock-kneed at first, her heart thumping, until she could look at the horse without flashbacks of the forest on Namingfest Day. His enormous, warm eyes won her over. She stepped closer, first gingerly stroking the animal's nose, then slipping both hands into the cozy nook beneath his thick mane.

"Would you protect me, if I needed you to?" she whispered.

The velvety nose merely sniffed at her pockets.

Hearing footsteps, Ariel looked up. The two adults turned the corner of the cottage. Luna's eyes still crinkled with worry, no conviction clear on her face.

"His name is Orion," Scarl said, approaching.

"Is he smart?" Ariel asked.

Scarl shrugged. "Not really. He's sturdy. And kind. Have you ridden before?"

Ariel's eyes shot to her mother. Luna allowed a fraction of a smile to soften her lips.

Words could barely get out through the cramp of anticipation and fright in Ariel's chest. "No," she admitted. "But I've been on a boat and climbed a tree."

Scarl's lips twitched. "It's not much like either. You'll learn."

"Run to Madeleine's house now," Luna told Ariel, "and see if she'll trade with me for one or two of her birds. Scarl says that in a few days you could send me something tied to its neck. A bit of ribbon or string, so I'll know you are well. He thinks that since they've had practice, the bird would find its way home."

In fact, Madeleine gushed and nodded, round-eyed about

the idea. Ariel soon returned home with two birds in a grain
sack. Luna sat Ariel down with them sternly.

"This part is my idea, not his. Keep it secret." She waited
for Ariel's promise, then handed her several strings snipped
from an old fishing net. "The yellow means you're all right. The
black . . ." Luna kneaded her hands. "If anything is wrong—
anything at all—send me the black. Some Fishers will come
after you. You know they will if I ask."

Ariel nodded. Several of her father's old friends had looked
out for them since his death. The salty-skinned men would
become almost as ungainly as seals on land if they had to travel
far on their feet, but she knew that nothing would stop them.
Madeleine's birds might never reach home from farther away
than the Finders would take her by lunchtime tomorrow, but
Ariel didn't say that. Neither did her mother. The pigeons made
them both feel better.

Ariel spent the rest of the day getting ready, stuffing a knapsack with warm clothes and her new skirt to be worn in the
grand village of Libros, plus all the food that would fit. The sky
was dark by the time she flew around Canberra Docks, saying
good-bye to people she'd miss. She enjoyed the amazement on
their faces much more than the pained sympathy that had
shone there since Namingfest Day.

She couldn't find Storian, though. And she saved Zeke for
last. It was nearly bedtime before she undertook her toughest
good-bye. Tired, she passed through the square toward his family's cottage. The sycamore spread its shadow against the night.
She brushed her hand on its trunk as she passed, wondering what
else it knew about her or the future.

It must have been just about then that her mother changed
her mind.

CHAPTER
10

"It will feel like flying, I bet," Zeke decided, "riding up high on that horse." Jealousy pushed through the worried crimps in his face. "I wish I could go with you!"

"Me, too." Ariel and Zeke stood fidgeting just inside the door to his house. They both knew she needed to get home and to bed, but she couldn't push her feet outside. Her skin, wide-awake, itched for morning.

"Are you scared?" he whispered. His parents rested not far away.

She nodded. "But excited, too. Scarl said I'll see snowy peaks and rivers of flowers."

Zeke tugged a lock of his hair. "It'll be okay. My father would know if it wasn't." With a sidelong glance he checked Jeshua's expression. Perhaps not fully reassured, Zeke added, "Be careful of them, though. And don't fall off the horse. I'll ask the maple about you every day until you come back."

Shaking his right arm, he showed Ariel the tip of her bone dart hidden away in his splint. "I'll still keep this while you're gone, if that's okay."

She threw her own arms around him. "Bye, Zeke. I'll bring you a present if I—"

The door banged open, nearly hitting them both. Everyone in the room jumped.

Luna, a shawl flung over her shoulders, whisked inside. Her eyes swept the room. When she spotted her daughter, partly hidden behind the door, Luna reached both hands to pat her. She seemed to need proof that Ariel was solid and all in one piece.

"Oh, I'm sorry, Luna," said Zeke's mother, rising. "Zeke has kept her too late."

Gripping Ariel's shoulders in hands so tense they might have been wringing laundry instead, Luna rolled wild eyes toward Zeke's parents.

"Jeshua, I don't care what the tree says," she moaned. "I'm frightened." She lunged to grab the Tree-Singer's arm. "Something will go wrong, I can feel it! Will you tell the Finders I've decided against it? I'm sorry they've waited, but I can't do it!" Her head whipped in denial. Her hair, already let down for bed, swirled across her face.

Yelps of surprise and protest jammed in Ariel's throat. Jeshua took her mother by both arms and murmured her name, trying to calm her. Zeke's mother rubbed Luna's shoulder as well.

"No. No." Slipping into tears, Luna clung to both of Zeke's parents. "I ignored this same feeling the night before Remus was lost. I thought it was silly. I won't ignore it this time. I can't lose her, too." The words melted into sobs.

Zeke's mother and father exchanged a long glance while they mumbled soothing words. Jeshua's eyes found Ariel, standing stricken next to the still-open door. He rubbed his brow.

"All right, Luna."

She turned her reddening face to him. "You mean it?"

"I likely will rue it, but yes. We can't have you like this. I'll go see Elbert now."

"Wait!" Ariel cried.

Her protests sank into the flagstones. Zeke's mother walked her and Luna home while Jeshua took up his task.

Their own cottage squatted, familiar and dull, at the same place on the same lane in the same village forever. Ariel knew from past fits of temper that its door did not slam well enough to satisfy her. Instead she turned her back on her mother and flung chunks of peat onto the coals in the hearth. Angry sparks bounced and flew. The fire hissed, voicing Ariel's frustration and drowning out a whisper of relief she refused to acknowledge. Luna said little, but her wan smile begged forgiveness.

Not ready to give in but weary from days of emotional turmoil, Ariel hadn't the energy to speak. When the sparks had all disappeared up the flue and the fire would take no more fuel, she numbly got ready for bed.

The muffling bedclothes embraced her. Luna stood by the hearth, her eyes alternating between the flames and her daughter. Sleep was just filling Ariel's head when someone tapped at the door. She jerked back awake.

Once more, panic leaped to Luna's face. "Who is it?"

"Elbert, ma'am," came his voice. "I know it's late. It will take only a moment."

Luna covered her ears with her palms like a child. "Please leave. I'm sorry, but the answer is no. I won't argue."

"Oh no, I'm not here to argue. Not at all. I understand."

Luna's hands came down slowly. "Do you?" As if she couldn't believe it and had to see for herself, she was drawn to the door. Ariel rose on one elbow.

"Indeed. I only wanted to wish you well. No hard feelings. I'm afraid I do need the dart, though. I'd let her keep it, if it was up to me. But the man who sent us might not believe that we found it."

Luna spun to her daughter. Too exhausted to resist, Ariel reached for the knapsack still packed and ready at the foot of her bed. She handed over the dart, her face blank. Her mother cracked the door a few inches and poked the dart through.

"Thank you," Elbert said through the crack. "I'll bid you good night, good-bye, and good days, then."

"Thank you," Luna sighed. "And to you." Hanging on the door in relief and exhaustion, she pulled it open a few inches wider.

"You're a good mother, I can see. And the young one? In bed by now, I suppose?" He stuck his head through the doorway. His eyes fell on the table, the hearth, and Luna's workroom before alighting on Ariel.

"Ah. But not asleep yet. So goodwill, Ariel, and good night." His lips curled. "Sleep tight."

Elbert's slow smile in the flickering light would haunt Ariel's nightmares for the rest of her life.

Only wind remained in the doorway, however. Luna shut the door behind him and delivered her daughter a hug before retiring herself. With her mind numb already, Ariel fell asleep immediately. If she dreamed, it was only of darkness.

She didn't sleep long.

CHAPTER
11

Hands. A weight pressing, dragging. Darkness swirling.

Drowned in sleep, Ariel pushed to the surface. She broke free and awoke, struggling to breathe. The glow of embers in the hearth slashed across her vision in the dark. She flailed, not understanding how she seemed to be moving without use of her arms or her legs. Then her fingers recognized the cords of a fishing net tangled around her. An icy awareness stabbed into her brain: someone had hauled her from bed. Unknown arms crushed her against a hard chest. She wailed, but the cry couldn't get out. Her face was so firmly pressed into folds of net and a shoulder that she could barely breathe, let alone scream.

Chill air blew past her bare feet. Outside, that's where she was now—outside and being stolen away! Her lungs heaving to pull in a few gasps of air, she fought against her thief and the imprisoning net. Falling, abruptly free of the arms, she struck the ground on her back. Air whooshed from her lips. Her mouth yawned open to gasp for the breath she had lost. It found a cloth gag instead.

Sailcloth fell over her. Her captor whisked it beneath her

and scooped her up as if in a bag. Airborne again, she banged against something less firm than the ground. Two seconds later she jounced in time to the motion, she was sure, of a horse.

Ariel squirmed and kicked, trying to right herself. When she wailed against the gag, only moaning escaped. Tears of panic and outrage filled the back of her throat. They made it almost impossible for air to slip in. Her attempts to inhale resulted mostly in a wet, ugly rasping.

Wham! Something struck at the sailcloth, and through it, her ribs.

"Stop it," a voice hissed. "Unless you want to pass out. If you do, you'll have a nasty headache when you wake up."

Hatred took over Ariel's body and mind, numbing her fear and stilling her struggles. She bent all her attention on two things. The first was breathing. Relaxing her vocal cords helped. She sniffed and swallowed as best she could with a mouthful of rag. The more she focused on breathing, the easier it became. And that made it easier to think.

Her attention turned to the second item: escape. She shifted, every limb tangled in netting, her body more upside down than upright. As the horse moved into a gallop, Ariel used the sway and lurch of her bag to jostle herself into a less awkward position. Moving carefully, her fingers tried to make sense of their trap. In a net, struggling was the worst thing to do; she'd seen enough fish entangle themselves when they could have swum away if they'd only backed off. Her half-awake panic had snarled the net badly already. With small, slow movements, she drew one arm across her chest until she could reach that hand to her chin. Bending her neck as far as she could, she managed at last to hook the gag with one finger. She plucked it free.

A mouthful of air sent relief coursing through her. She didn't bother to scream. No matter which direction they'd gone, they'd already passed well beyond the last house in the village.

Ariel's ears strained for clues to her location. She couldn't hear the surging sea or anything other than hoofbeats. They'd been walking at first, probably so the thud of hooves didn't wake any neighbors. Now they galloped. Ariel had little experience with horses, but she often ran herself. These dull thumps sounded more like feet pounding through meadow or forest than skittering on sand or rattling over rocks. The rustle of sailcloth and clothing, however, blocked any other telltale sound.

Though she'd gained some movement with her hands, the net proved too tangled to allow her arms to explore any far-ther. The inside of the bag was so black in the night that she fingered her eyes to make sure they were open. She could tell by the bumping of muscle against her that the bag was slung behind the horse's left shoulder. The sailcloth must have been cinched there with rope. Through the lurch, Ariel couldn't even be sure if they were traveling in a straight line or not.

Her captor was Scarl, she was certain, and not only because she linked him with the horse. The few words hissed at her could have been from any man, but she remembered the feel of being trapped by arms against a chest. Bird claws, not bear hugs, came to mind.

A new terror wiped away Ariel's relative calm. If Scarl was with her, where was Elbert? Her teeth pinched her lip to repress a moan of despair. What had become of her mother?

She fretted and jounced for what seemed like an hour before the horse slowed and finally stopped. Ariel could not only smell the animal's sweat and hear the rush of its breathing, she could feel its damp warmth seeping in through the sailcloth. She waited, alert, as the rider swung off. Hands fumbled the bag, and it slid to the ground. Inside, Ariel yelped. She tried to brace for whatever came next. Perhaps he would unwrap the net enough for her to jump up and flee. She resolved to do nothing but glare until she could run.

Hands felt through the cloth for her head, then rolled an opening past her face. Fresh air bathed Ariel's skin, lifting the tears from her cheeks. She drew in a deep, sweet breath. The sight of Scarl's thin face tainted that small joy.

She tensed for action, but his hands closed about her neck so her limbs remained wrapped tight.

"Still alive?" he asked. "Good. And smart enough not to waste breath with screaming. That's good, too. So listen well, Ariel. This can go easy or it can go hard. If you make it too hard, Elbert—"

"Where is he?" That name had cracked Ariel's vow to stay silent. She whirled her head, peering into the night shadows. Elbert's absence made it too easy to envision him wrecking her house. "What did you do to my mother?"

"Stopped her from fussing, that's what. Never mind. You have enough to fear here. Elbert will be along soon and—"

"Is he—"

"Listen!" He shook her. Her teeth clacked painfully shut. "You said you weren't scared of me," Scarl said. Even in the dark, his eyes bored into hers. "You had best be scared of *him*. He talks honey, but he's made more of stone. He won't truck with wailing and fighting. He won't answer questions. He'll just cut your throat."

Doom draped itself over her. His hard face showed no pity.

"That's better," he said. "You learn fast. Now, do you want to ride astride or stay in the sack?"

Ariel's lips felt numb. She whispered, "Ride."

"Fine." Gripping her throat painfully with one long hand, he stood her up and stripped away the sail bag. With more trouble, the net came off, too. More than once, Ariel's heart whispered, "Run." Obeying that command would have strangled her. Unable to swallow, she heard the blood thump in her head under the pressure on her neck.

Black fuzz was erasing her shadowy view of the forest when he finally released her throat. He'd already trapped both her wrists in the other hand. Swiftly he bound them behind her back. With the long tail of the rope, he tethered her close to the horse. Then he mounted. Reaching down, he grabbed her under one armpit and hauled her up. Ariel cried out at the yank on that shoulder. Her legs flailed. Once she was seated before Scarl on Orion's bony withers, her shoulder throbbed.

Scarl tugged at her tether, which he'd lashed to a ring on the leather pad that protected Orion's back. He said, "If you jump, or even fall off by mistake, you'll be broken under Orion's hooves. Or dragged twenty feet before I can stop him. I don't recommend it."

"But I can't hold on!" She looked wistfully at the mane before her.

His arms reached around either side of her to take up the reins. "Use your legs. I won't lose you if you don't lose yourself."

Her legs clung against the horse's shoulders as best they could. She nodded.

"All right," Scarl told her. "Keep on like this and you might even survive to the end of our journey."

The thought of more horrors awaiting broke through her numbness. She dared a question.

"Where are you taking me?"

He nudged the horse into a walk, then a gentle lope. Even Ariel could feel how much more easily Orion moved, free of his lopsided burden.

The cold wind had pricked more tears to her eyes before Scarl finally answered her question. His voice might almost have been the night wind swirling into her ear.

"To your future."

CHAPTER
12

Ariel's efforts to remember their route proved futile. No moon or stars lit their way, and every shadowy tree they whisked past looked the same as the next. Now and then the horse veered or lurched up a hill, but otherwise they could have been crossing a kelp-shrouded seabed.

Though riding Orion was better than being cargo, the horse's withers rubbed blisters and bruises on Ariel's bare legs. More painful yet was the sore in her heart, put there by the knowledge that Canberra Docks was falling much farther behind her than anyone in the village had ever been.

As the sky finally paled for dawn, Scarl stopped the horse. Blearily, Ariel took in the world around her. The woods had given way to choppy hills covered mostly with scrub. The air smelled not of seawater but grass. Even if she escaped, she wouldn't know which way to run.

At Scarl's bidding and with his help, she scissored one leg over Orion's neck and slid down to her feet. At first, her legs nearly collapsed. They felt warped.

"You'll have time to stretch them," Scarl said, as he jumped down himself. "We'll be walking from here."

"Where are we?"

Instead of answering, he led her like a goat on a leash to a nearby patch of witch broom.

"Do your business, if you've a mind to," he said, turning his back.

"Here?" She cringed, loath to attend to such private matters with him standing so near.

"Unless you see a privy." The hiss of his own relief raked Ariel's ears. The sound also tugged at her bladder, which indeed ached from hours of terror and jouncing.

Flesh burning, she tucked herself as far behind the prickly shrub as her leash would permit. Some things were easier for boys. Squatting, she confronted a new dilemma.

"But I can't take down my drawers with no hands." Tears clotted her throat. This indignity rivaled any of the rough handling to which she'd been treated that night.

Expecting him to be as cold to this care as any other, she was surprised when he pulled her back to her feet.

"There are worse things," he said. But he untied her wrists and reknotted the rope with her hands together in front so she could manage the task. "Don't make me regret this."

"I won't," she promised. A flush of gratitude angered her.

Compared to the prospect of wetting her underpants, the lack of a wipe or washbasin seemed a minor concern. When she turned back to him, red-faced, she expected to see him peeking and snickering as the village boys might have done. Instead, he stared away from her to the approaching dawn, one hand clenching his nape as if he were disturbed by the rose-petal hues.

He led her to a rock outcrop with a spring bubbling at its base. After lashing Ariel's tether to another sturdy shrub, Scarl hobbled Orion's forelegs, wrapping them near the hoof with a short rope to prevent the horse from wandering far. Freed of his burden, Orion rolled gratefully and then plunged his nose into the spring, slurping and snorting. Bitterly Ariel licked her dry lips. The horse had more freedom than she did.

She shuddered inside her thin nightgown and curled tighter for warmth. Without the cruel shelter of Scarl's body or the heat rising from the horse, she was freezing.

"I'm cold," she said, when Scarl came to sit near her.

"Not much help for it before Elbert gets here. He didn't trust that I'd wait if I had any gear." He kicked off his boots and stretched his long legs before retying the far end of her tether to his own wrist. Ariel watched closely. She'd best learn the knot if she could hope somehow to untie it.

He lay back as if to sleep. With hope rising inside her, she scanned the hard ground for weapons—a rock to bang on his head, a stick to poke into his eye. Her chances of escape would shrink greatly once two men guarded her. But even after Scarl's lids closed, her slightest movement drew his attention. Hoping to lull him asleep, she held still for long stretches, but one of his eyelids kept flashing open. Finally she gave up and lay down herself, turning her back to her captor.

The ground drained out any warmth her body still had. Her teeth chattered.

A movement rustled behind her. "Here. Draw a bit closer."

She turned her head. He'd removed his oilcloth coat and spread it wide to cover them both. Ariel eyed it with longing. Then some harder emotion slipped over her heart. With a baleful glare, she turned back into her huddle. She didn't want to be any closer to someone so awful, not even for a measure of warmth.

After a moment, heavy oilcloth dropped on her. She whirled indignantly, squirming away. But he hadn't moved nearer. Without a glance in her direction, he lay back down where he'd been. Ariel had the coat to herself.

She drew it around tight, leaving herself just a slit to breathe through. Gritting her teeth to stop their chatter, she gripped her only touchstone to home, the green bead at her throat. With morning birds chirping as though nothing was wrong, Ariel waited to hear snoring.

Her head buzzed with exhaustion, but sore limbs and a sore spirit kept her awake. She yearned for her warm bed, her home, and especially her mother. Her chest felt as if vital fluids were flowing out from a hole in her heart. The longer it leaked, the more hollow the rest of her felt. Yet one burning irony remained: only a half day ago she had, impossibly, wanted to leave all those things that she loved.

Watching clouds mount on the horizon like an assembling rescue squad, Ariel told herself they hinted that someone was coming. A dread veil hid her mother's fate from her, but Luna wouldn't come searching in any case. She'd send others who were able to fight—Jeshua, maybe, along with some Fishers. Slowly warming under the oilcloth, Ariel fell into a half-waking dream where a band from Canberra Docks raced through the forest on a trail of hoofprints, shouting their rage. They might even have Elbert, bound and gagged, to lead them. They would never stop to rest but would hurry on, hurry on, until they found her and saved her. They could arrive anytime.

In the next days, Ariel clung to that dream like a dog with a bone. Slowly, gnawed by time and distance, it shrank.

CHAPTER
13

Thunder began rumbling midday as though answering Ariel's stomach. When rain splattered Scarl's clothes, he sat up and moved farther under the witch broom's meager protection. He shivered in the ensuing downpour. Afraid he'd take his coat back, Ariel pulled it more snugly around her and pretended to sleep.

She jerked when Scarl's hands moved to his coat. A whimper escaped despite her resolve not to give him the pleasure of knowing her misery.

"Rest easy. I just want something out of a pocket." He rummaged. Withdrawing a strip of dried fish, he tore it and passed half to her. The familiar salty taste redoubled her homesickness without really soothing her hunger.

"Can I get a drink?" she asked, trying to decide whether to scoop water with her bound hands or simply throw herself onto her belly and slurp like the horse.

Scarl retrieved a battered tin cup from another coat pocket. "Dip it shallow," he said, handing it to her, "and you'll drink less mud."

After quenching her thirst, she ventured another question. "When will Elbert get here?"

Scarl's dark eyes flicked to her. "When he does."

"Does he know where we are?"

One corner of his mouth twitched. "He'll find us."

He was not overly fond of words, plainly, but his responses were so prompt now, she tried again. She was afraid of the answer, but she couldn't bear the black uncertainty, either.

"Was he hurting my mother?"

Inhaling deeply, Scarl looked her straight in the eyes. "I told him to tie her and gag her, that's all. As long as it takes a while for her to be found, we'll have too much head start to be followed."

Ariel dismissed the head start. Her rescuers would overcome that. She wanted badly to believe the rest that he'd said. It would have been easier if his gaze hadn't slid to the wet ground the moment he finished speaking.

"I'm the one who has hurt her the most," he added, not looking up. "By taking you." His face never softened.

After both the rain and the brightest spot in the clouds had passed overhead, Ariel fell into an uncomfortable sleep. She awoke to voices in the twilight.

"—soaking wet, you dolt. You've gone soft." Ariel recognized Elbert's scornful rumble.

"I'll dry," Scarl said. "We've gone to a lot of trouble to let her die in her sleep."

"It's been fun, though. I left a few tokens for them to remember us by."

Alarm filled Scarl's voice. "Elbert! Like what? We don't need them on our heels."

Elbert snickered. "They couldn't locate us if they tried. I made sure of that."

Ariel jumped up—or tried to. Her body was so sore and stiff that it took several seconds for her to stand.

Both men watched from nearby. Ariel could see fatigue through the amused contempt on Elbert's face. He must have tramped hard to catch them.

"Where's my mother?" she cried. "What have you done?"

"I tried to convince her to come with us." Elbert smacked his forehead with the tips of his fingers. "I should have thought of that sooner. You could have both ridden the horse. But in the end, she decided she'd rather stay home and await your return." Ariel could have almost believed him, if not for the gleam in his eyes.

"I hate you."

He clutched his chest. "But I am so fond of you!" He winked. "My April Fool princess." From that moment, Elbert rarely referred to her as anything else. Ariel soon preferred Scarl's frank harshness to Elbert's charades.

With night falling, Scarl lit a fire using flamesticks from Elbert's overstuffed pack. His burden had included Ariel's boots and her knapsack, which she'd never had time to unpack. Elbert had already plundered her food, but she yanked out warmer clothes, pulling her sweater right over her nightgown. The sight of the yellow skirt her mother had sewn hitched Ariel's breath in her throat.

The messenger pigeons roasted over the fire. Glowering, Ariel refused her share. Scarl silently passed her crackers and cheese from their larder instead. She wanted to refuse that, too, but her hands wouldn't obey her. Wolfing the food, she soon felt ill.

"Are you sure you don't want some meat, princess?" Elbert

teased as the men ate. "It's delicious. The new Kincaller, I expect, would be pleased."

"Would you have done that if my mother had let me come with you?" Ariel demanded. "Would you still have tied me up as soon as no one could see?"

Elbert sucked a bone, debating. "Your friend Scarl there may not have let me. For a child snatcher, he's rather kindly, it seems." His eyes measured Scarl, who returned the gaze without expression.

"I suppose as long as you came along nicely," Elbert continued, "we could have kept up the game for some time. At least until I wanted pigeon for dinner, eh?"

"Keep eating," Ariel spat. "I'll pray that it chokes you."

Elbert's lips twisted into a grin that only emphasized the chill in his eyes. "Careful, my lady. You're the one who should be dead. My companion convinced me you might be worth more alive. Don't prove him wrong."

Ariel blinked, trying to understand. "Because I found the telling dart?" The notion seemed ludicrous. Why would that make them want to harm her—particularly once they'd taken it from her?

When Elbert ignored her, Ariel's gaze slid to Scarl. He avoided her look but gave her a curt shake of his head, not answering her question but telling her to drop it.

Too tired to make sense of it all, Ariel took refuge in spite. She yanked at her rope just as Scarl raised his hands to his mouth for a bite. Elbert laughed heartily. The first time, Scarl just shot her a warning glare. The second time, he jerked back hard enough to topple her over, then looped the rope under one of his boots to make slack between there and his wrist.

"Very good, princess!" Elbert said. "Merriment with our meal. You may earn the Fool name. Can you tell jokes? Sing a song?"

Ariel tried to think of a smart retort. She was too appalled that she had ever wanted to travel with them.

After eating, they settled to sleep. Ariel curled into an unfamiliar wool blanket. Closing her eyes, she sank like a stone into a pool of forgetting.

A tug at her leash awoke her the next morning. The men had already packed their gear on the horse. After a meager breakfast, they set off. Ariel didn't dare resist much, but she dragged her heels until the rope's pull at her wrists made them sore.

Their campsite dwindled behind her. She craned her neck to look back at what felt like her last bridge to home. Once that outpost had vanished, she truly felt lost.

Three days passed in a pattern of footsore days and uncomfortable nights. Ariel struggled to keep up with the men's longer strides. Orion bore her along with their goods every afternoon once her tired legs began failing.

The fourth morning, her captors led her up a ravine lined with spooky beech trees cloaked with black fungus. Small patches of their pale bark gleamed through like eyes, staring and hostile. As the sun heated the day, hornets crawled over the fungus, which must have been sweet. When the trio stopped for what Ariel called back-turning, she slipped cautiously behind a tree. The hornets ignored her.

Scarl held her tether and awaited her on the other side of the tree. Farther away, Elbert minded Orion and amused himself with shameful songs. If a classmate had sung such words, Ariel might have laughed, but in Elbert's bass tones they were only revolting. She tried to fill her ears with other songs from inside.

Orion decided his back itched. Shuffling beneath a low tree branch, he rocked, trying to reach just the right spot.

"Don't let him scrape off that pack," Scarl warned Elbert.

Just then one of Orion's hooves broke through the soil near the tree's trunk. A river of hornets flowed out. With their den breached, they rushed into battle, filling the air with black, droning bodies.

The horse reared and bucked, thrashing its tail. Elbert launched into similar motions. Swearing, he jumped for Orion's bridle before the horse bolted.

"Help me keep him!" he shouted.

Scarl threw Ariel's leash over a branch and he, too, lunged after the horse.

Ariel took only a second to think. She was no horse to be fooled by a rope that was looped but not tied. Batting her hands at hornets, she tugged the leash free, backed a few steps, and turned to run for her life.

The steep, narrow ravine provided few routes for escape. She darted back the way they had come, branches slapping her face.

Even beset by hornets and a mad horse, her captors weren't sluggish. Their shouts followed her quickly.

"I've got the horse, for the love of all sinners—get her!" Elbert's voice trembled with rage.

Feet thumped behind her. Ariel raced down the ravine, scrambling over tree roots and rocks. She was nimbler than Scarl, if not faster, and she heard him curse and grunt as he worked to catch her.

But the rope, still tied to her wrists, worked for its master.

She should have drawn in its end before running. Catching between boulders, her leash yanked her up short and right off her feet. She slammed into the ground.

Scarl was on her in a thrice. Grabbing at her sweater and one arm, he jerked her bodily into the air and upright. Ariel, who had sealed her lips against so much anguish already, burst into wails.

Scarl set her onto her feet long enough only to slap her so sharply across the face that she fell down again. Sobbing too hard to draw breath, she lay there, a stone cutting into her chin.

"Foolish girl!" he hissed. "Break a leg, crack your head, or if Elbert had caught you—! And where would you go." It wasn't a question. He stood over her, his breath raspy.

Days of pent-up fear, humiliation, and anger poured out in her tears. Pains in her body howled their presence. The greater pains in her soul immobilized her.

After a few minutes, Scarl raised her. When her legs wouldn't hold her, he slung her over his shoulder and picked a way back up their path. She hung limp, crushed at her belly and sobbing. Blood from the gouge on her chin dribbled down the Finder's coat.

Elbert met them, the glower on his face made more ugly by swelling.

"Did you beat her enough?"

"You want a go?" Scarl asked. Ariel choked. Scarl's blow had been bad enough. Fists as powerful as Elbert's could kill her.

A chill voice in her mind wondered if that might be best.

Scarl did not lower her from his shoulder, however. Slapping a persistent hornet, Elbert turned and stalked onward.

"I'll save it for later," he growled.

They traveled at least half a mile while the skittish horse calmed enough so that Scarl might safely shift Ariel to horseback. All the while, some animal part of her brain worked on a puzzle. By the time Scarl slung her sideways over Orion's back, she felt ready to stop weeping. Being lashed there like a corpse didn't feel good, but she didn't mind hiding her face against the warm, musky ribs.

She'd seen something in the rocks while she'd lain there, bleeding. In the agony of her recapture, she had not immediately registered anything out of place. Now, though, desperation pumped the knowledge from the underside of her mind to the top.

An apple core had been dropped in the rocks. It rested in a crevice, hidden except to a face very close, as hers had been. The flesh on the core had not yet turned brown.

Whoever had dropped it could not be far away. It could have been a stranger coming this way by chance, but not likely. Ariel knew her rescuers had finally come. She had to be ready.

PART TWO

SPECTER

CHAPTER
14

Ariel endured two more anxious days, primed for an ambush of rescuing heroes, while her captors hauled her through flower-specked meadows and an alpine pass. As the trio trudged over its crest, she gazed farther up toward snowy peaks and a sweep of what looked like white taffy pulled and stretched between mountains.

"Frozen river," Scarl said, noting her interest. "Ice that moves. If we were closer, you could hear it groan and break off at the end—slabs so big they would crush any house."

"Honestly, Scarl?" Elbert asked. "You've seen this before? I had no idea how well traveled you are." Ariel thought him sincere until Scarl threw an obscene gesture in reply.

Elbert chortled. "No, no, tell us more, wise one. Give the princess a thrill!"

Deafening her ears, Ariel bitterly remembered telling Zeke of foreign things she might see on her trip. Even now she could wonder at a frozen river, but that excitement felt frozen, too, locked in the ice crushing her heart. Silently she pleaded for her rescuers to hurry and melt it.

To her relief, since her attempt to escape she had not received another blow. Elbert's temper had faded, and no one had spoken again of her flight. Yet Scarl allowed her little rest and no privacy now, dragging her along every time he tended the horse or collected wood for a fire.

The extra movement tormented Ariel's feet. Stinging blisters rose on both heels, and even wearing two pairs of socks barely helped. Then a breakfast of fried brook fish gave her an idea.

Just before they started off that morning, Scarl bent to adjust the rope knotted at her wrists. He sniffed. His nose wrinkled.

"Did you put fish in your pockets?" he asked.

"No." Afraid he'd search her, she added, "I remembered the Fishers put fish oil on blisters. And I have a lot. So I rubbed the greasy bits of my breakfast on my feet."

His lips squashed a smile. "Clever. You may make a Farwalker yet."

She scowled. They'd already walked plenty far. "What does that mean?"

Tensing, Scarl straightened and spun her shoulder. "Unless you want that rope tighter, hush up and let's go."

As they descended from the pass that day, Ariel picked apart his odd comment. She realized she'd heard the term Farwalker before. One of the Storian's tales about the Blind War had included a song. It recounted how the people left after the war had put the world back together again. Forced to get along without sight, they honed senses they hadn't needed or heeded until they went blind. Tree-Singers began talking to trees then, and Kincallers made friends with the creatures of forest and field. Others discovered they could still find things, even blind, if they sought with some previously untapped part of their minds. Together, using skills they might once have called magic, the remaining few people survived. New trades grew around their uncanny gifts.

Storian's song celebrated heroes of that difficult time. Ariel couldn't recall most of the words, but she did remember one verse:

When large had crumbled down to small,
the Farwalker rose to span them all.
If knowledge is to rise again,
hope others can be found by then.

Unfortunately, Ariel had little idea what it meant, beyond the obvious clues in the Farwalker name. She sifted memories but ended no wiser, only sorry she hadn't paid more attention to Storian's lessons. The verse seemed to hint of another whole trade, a kind of teacher, perhaps. But teaching was the Storians' job. Besides, how much teaching could somebody do if they were walking around all the time?

The offhand remark may have been unimportant, but Scarl's reaction implied otherwise. And if the Finders had confused her with somebody else, or thought she held some Farwalker secret that she certainly didn't, more trouble might be coming when they got her to Libros and the mistake came to light. The rescue party from Canberra Docks had better free her before then.

Yet as one hour trod into the next, she couldn't think about her rescue too much. If she had, she could not have ignored her mounting fear that she'd imagined the apple core in the rocks.

Late that afternoon, Ariel spied chimney smoke. It drifted

past the treetops, rising on a breeze that also bore the jingle of distant cattle or goat bells. The hints of other people sped Ariel's heart.

"Is there a village below? Is that where we're going?"

"Not you, princess," Elbert said. "It's no more than an old roadhouse, left from the days when some few still traveled by road. Unlike us." He turned to Scarl, scratching one ear. "I'm thinking to drop by for a jar of beer. Maybe two."

"We look far too odd as traveling mates." Scarl tilted his head toward Ariel. "Let's just keep on."

"No, the beer is more persuasive than you are, my friend. You stay here with the horse and the two-legged luggage. I'll return soon enough. I'll bring you a swallow if I can talk them out of a jarful." Shouldering his pack, Elbert started downhill toward the smoke, picking through the boulders that littered the slope.

Scarl watched him go. Then he turned, checked the sun's low position, and considered Ariel at length, rasping one finger along the stubble on his jaw. "Hmm," he said. "Maybe I'll just put you to work."

He removed his coat and his shirt. Ariel's heart shot into her throat. With ribs lining his bare chest, he looked to be more sinew than muscle, but he'd picked her up bodily more than once. She knew exactly how little resistance she could offer if he'd decided that her clothes would be coming off next.

She had just opened her mouth to protest or plead when he tossed his shirt at her. It smelled of wood smoke and sweat.

"You can sew, can't you?"

She nodded, her arms limp with relief. Before long, she'd been tasked with stitching up several rips in his shirt. The Finder provided a needle from a small bundle of goods in his coat. He didn't have thread, so Ariel settled for a strand of horsetail. Orion didn't even flick his ears at her yank. Loosing one of her wrists, Scarl tied her snugly astride the horse, facing backward so she could lean over and pluck hairs as needed. Then he hob- bled the horse.

Freed from her and the leash, Scarl found a small pool of rainwater trapped among the hillside's many rocks. He bathed there discreetly, using one sock as a washrag. Ariel fought envy as she sewed. Her own skin felt gritty and sticky from too many days with no bath.

She was so filthy, in fact, she was attracting flies. That's what she thought when a horsefly flew into her shoulder, then another bounced off her leg. A third missile fell into the shirt fabric spread on her lap. Staring, Ariel saw that it was not a fly but a pebble. Orion stretched his neck to one side, fluttering his nos- trils at some unfamiliar scent.

Of course! Her confusion cleared. She'd almost missed the start of her long-awaited rescue. She glanced toward Scarl, who was busy dressing again. As casually as she could, she looked toward the apparent source of the rain of pebbles.

A flash of motion caught her eye. She sucked in a sharp breath. Zeke crouched beneath the curve of a boulder that hid him from the Finder.

Immediately Ariel stared at her sewing, resisting the urge to check Scarl's attention. If he were watching, that alone might give Zeke away.

Her mind raced. Why had her rescuers brought Zeke? Maybe he and the trees had helped them find her. Being smaller, too, he could sneak better than grown men. That had to be it.

She risked a peek at Scarl. He was donning his boots and

didn't seem to suspect. Amazed that he could not hear her heart pounding, Ariel pretended to rethread her needle, keeping her friend visible from the corner of her eye.

Zeke pointed to Scarl and made a series of gestures that included tipping his cheek onto his hands like a pillow. She understood perfectly: when the men slept tonight, she must stay awake. She nodded subtly to her lap. At her next stolen glance, Zeke was gone. And not a moment too soon. Scarl approached.

Ariel sewed, her stomach churning and her mind far from the needle. Scarl checked her progress, apparently not noticing how her fingers shook.

When she returned his shirt, she asked if she might bathe, too, afraid she would never sit still without a distraction. Agreeing, Scarl accompanied her to the puddle and turned a shoulder to her. Stirred up now, the water looked murky. Ariel heaved a rueful sigh and began splashing.

She'd long ago ripped her nightgown into a blouse, tying the remnant around her neck for more warmth. Now she used the makeshift scarf as a washrag, drawing it, sopping, under her shirt. The cold water stung less than the notion that she was wiping Scarl's grime onto her skin.

By the time she was done, though, she'd grown used to what might happen tonight. No longer terrified that she'd give something away, she thanked Scarl for letting her wash.

He nodded. "I wouldn't mention your bath to Elbert," he said. "He's likely to roll you in Orion's manure for a laugh. And I don't want to have to sleep next to that."

The last few nights had been so cold that her blanket had not been enough. This time, when Scarl had silently lifted the edge of his coat to share it, she'd swallowed her revulsion and wiggled beneath. Glad for the protective cocoon of her blanket, she'd discovered that his spare body heat, more than the coat, kept her quite warm. He'd told her the next morning that he would start kicking her back if she couldn't tame her flying knees and feet, and indeed, she'd been nudged awake more than once by an elbow. The warmth had been worth a few bruises.

Now Ariel pondered how to get farther away at bedtime without raising suspicion.

She found an idea.

CHAPTER
15

Elbert returned just after dark, in good humor and smelling of ale. He and Scarl shared more beer as the three of them dined on sausages Elbert also had brought. Scarl offered the beer jar to Ariel, too, but Elbert objected. She didn't mind. She would have drunk the bitter brew simply to help fill her belly, but tonight she wanted the men to sleep as heavily as they might.

As they prepared for bed, Ariel voiced her idea.

"Please, Scarl, may I lie atop Orion to sleep? He's warm, too, and you hurt me with your elbows. You can tie me to him as tight as you like."

"She prefers a horse, does she?" Elbert chortled, clearly feeling the effects of his beer. "What's that say about you, then, my friend?"

Scarl dismissed her hopes with a curt shake of his head. "His back needs the rest."

"Wait, I'm amused by this idea," Elbert said. "If she's atop and he lies down, he'll crush her." He slapped his thigh and got to his feet. "I say we tie her by the neck so short that if she falls off in her sleep, she'll hang herself. Two chances for fun. Care to wager on it, Scarl? What'll you give me if she's still kicking at dawn?"

"Don't be a dullard," Scarl replied.

"Why so fond of her, then?" Elbert demanded. "I'm starting to wonder if you've—"

"We won't get anything for her, dead."

"We won't anyway, if Mason is not as curious about her as you seem to think."

"Mason?" blurted Ariel, who had been listening with clenched stomach muscles, trying not to show how much she cared. "Is that who sent the darts? Are you really taking me to Libros?"

"Nobody knows who sent them, you little idiot, only who received them. Never mind." Elbert clomped over to untie Ariel's wrists from her leash. She feigned fear as he flung her up onto the horse. His frightening predictions might come true, of course, if she spent the whole night on Orion. She expected she wouldn't. Even if her captors woke midway through her rescue, her chances had to be better outside Scarl's reach.

"My blanket—"

"Sorry, that wasn't part of the wager." Elbert jerked her hands forward along either side of Orion's neck and secured her wrists together beneath it. The position tried Ariel's balance. Worse, Elbert tied a slipknot around her neck and looped the other end of the rope around the horse's belly just before his hind legs. Orion jigged side to side at the prickly binding. Ariel clamped her arms and legs tight.

After a moment, the horse snorted, uneasily accepting the rope. He dropped his head to crop grass, hopping with his hob-bled front legs and then catching up with the rear. The motion

jounced Ariel and tugged against the noose on her neck. She'd
never stay on all night. If she fell, though, the added tension
would choke her, cause the horse to buck his hind legs, or both.
Elbert had created a fearsome trap.

"A good trick," he declared, returning with a grin to his seat
by the fire.

"Fine," Scarl said through a frown. "I assume you're betting
she falls. And if she's still astride when we rise?"

Elbert fingered his whiskers. "If the princess stays on her
steed, you can have my hat."

Scarl coveted that leather hat, Ariel knew. It kept the rain
off Elbert's head when his own knit cap soaked through—as
did Ariel's forlorn yellow skirt, which she often draped over
herself like a shawl.

"No," Scarl said, surprising her. "I want the dart."

Elbert's eyebrows shot up.

"I know someone who will trade a lot for it," Scarl explained,
"knowing its story."

"Mason expects it. Are you Fool enough to defy him?"

Scarl shook his head. "Mason only wants to make sure its
message is not acted upon. She's from Canberra Docks. We can
tell him it fell into the sea when we grabbed her. We both saw
that it was damaged anyway. Even if it washed ashore and someone else found it, they can't know what it says. And remember
who this dart was sent to. We have her to present."

Elbert scuffed one foot on the ground. Ariel thought he could
barely keep up with Scarl's argument. Neither could she. The
dart had *not* been sent to her—why didn't they believe that?—
nor could she understand all the symbols it bore. She wasn't
anyone special, least of all some mysterious Farwalker mentioned in a crusty old song. Unless Mason longed to meet a

Naming test failure, he would be disappointed. And he or anyone else who wanted her cursed dart could have it.

"Are we on?" Scarl pressed Elbert. Ariel felt like a fish being quibbled over in a trade.

"You'll handle Mason?" Elbert asked. "Take the blame, if he's angry? And no whining if you lose and she's not worth hauling the rest of the way?"

Scarl tipped his head. "When have you known me to whine?"

"Then you're on."

Scarl gazed at Ariel as though gluing her to the horse with his eyes. There was no warmth in his face—only warning.

Clutching the horse's neck, she turned away. Her sausages roiled in her stomach. She hoped she hadn't just complicated her rescue.

Scarl rolled into his blanket soon after the wager, but his slit eyelids told Ariel he watched her. Elbert sat up late, pitching pebbles and clapping, trying to startle her mount. Although the horse flinched and hopped sideways a few times, she kept her precarious perch.

At last Elbert stretched out and dozed off. Eventually the gleam of Scarl's eyeballs vanished behind his lids. The night deepened, and despite her awkward position, Ariel found it harder to stay awake than she'd expected. Her own eyelids drooped.

She sprang back alert when Orion's neck tensed. Flicking his ears at some uncertain sound, the horse snorted gently. Ariel willed him to silence and blinked into the dark. Every flutter and scurry in the woods made her tingle.

One shadow proved more fluid than the rest. Once she spotted it, Ariel watched it creep forward, her ears tuned to her

captors' steady breathing behind her. Her brain tried to tell her
the slight form must be Zeke. She wouldn't believe it. Where
were the Fishers or his father? Soon, though, she couldn't deny
it. He appeared to be alone. The weight of the danger they
both faced, if there weren't men with weapons hiding just out
of sight, crushed out her breath.

Once he'd decided the shadow was no mountain lion, Orion
went back to his hop-along grazing. Ariel feared the horse would
outpace the boy, whose approach was painfully slow. When
Zeke's face finally drew near to hers, he held a finger to his lips
and began working on knots.

To Ariel's dismay, he did not start with the knot at her neck
but with the rope at Orion's belly. When it slipped free, the
horse tossed his head and relaxed.

Zeke bent to the hobble. Ariel had to mash her lips
together to stop herself from hissing at him. Instead she fluttered her fingers to catch his attention. They couldn't possibly
escape on anything as noisy as a horse. Zeke ignored her gestures for his own, suggesting that she watch the men. Helpless,
she obeyed.

With one hand hindered by his splint, Zeke took an excru-
ciating length of time to untie the hobble. To Ariel's astonish-
ment, when it came loose, he still didn't move to untie her.
Instead he slipped the hobble rope around Orion's throat, led
him two measly steps, and let the horse drop his nose again to
the grass. The boy hunkered against Orion's shoulder so his silhouette couldn't betray him if the Finders should awaken and
look up. Straining to interpret every sound, Ariel counted helplessly as Orion's teeth ripped five times at the grass. Only then
did Zeke lead him another few steps.

Her mind screamed: they'd never get away taking two steps for every five bites!

Yet Zeke's strategy had merits. Repeatedly one of Ariel's captors thrashed in his sleep. Twice she saw a head lift. All that could be seen were the dark shapes of a girl on a horse cropping grass, not far from where that horse first had been hobbled. Both times, the head dropped back into sleep.

A horseback rider never moved so slowly, nor a night so fast. Zeke began stealing anxious glances at the sky. Ariel had almost grown resigned to being captured a hundred feet from where they had started when her friend picked up the pace. No more grass for Orion. Soon they'd doubled their distance from Elbert and Scarl.

A few moments later, Zeke paused to untie Ariel's hands. She freed her own neck, and then Zeke tied that longer rope around Orion's nose in a makeshift halter. Fearing they'd never control the horse without something better than that, Ariel nonetheless took the loose end when he offered it. Her hands trembled. Surely this was the part when the night would begin erupting with shouts.

Zeke led the horse to a downed log, which he stepped onto. He breathed, "Help me up."

His familiar voice sent a trill of joy through her. She pulled on his arm as he clambered aboard behind her. She wanted to turn and hug him tight to her heart. Questions flocked to her lips. There was no time for either.

"Hang on tight," he whispered in her ear. He reached around her to grab a handful of mane and the halter rope so they both had a grip.

In terror, Ariel nudged the horse with her legs. Zeke added

a thump with his heels, and their mount picked up a lazy trot. In the darkness, even this gentle speed stuck Ariel's tongue to the roof of her mouth. Trees and rocks loomed, whisking past on all sides. Frequently Orion lurched left or right, stumbling on the uneven ground. If he lost his footing badly enough to go down, their fall could be deadly. Her heart pounding louder than the horse's hooves in the grass, Ariel clutched tight and bent low, afraid a branch would sweep one or both of them off while Orion kept going. Zeke tried to steer, tugging the rope, but clearly the horse was in charge.

As tense minutes passed without any sound of pursuit, Ariel felt safe to whisper, "Where are the others?"

"What others?"

Part of her had known it already, yet she cringed at the truth. "The Fishers! Your father! Is my mother all right? Why did you come by yourself?"

"Talk later," Zeke said. "Let's go faster." He bounced his legs harder against Orion's ribs. As the horse sped slightly, both riders struggled simply to remain mounted.

Ariel noticed that the horse mainly chose to descend. When they jigged out of the trees into a meadow, her heart flipped. She felt exposed to any Finders looking down from above.

"We can't just let Orion go where he wants," she told Zeke. "He might circle back to Scarl. Besides, we're headed the wrong way."

"I have an idea that might help."

Letting Orion slow and then stop, Zeke slithered down. He undid the makeshift halter and tied two knots a hand's width apart in the middle of the rope. Lifting the horse's rubbery lip, he shoved the rope into the gap in Orion's teeth where a bridle bit would have rested. The horse flopped his tongue around the strange thing in his mouth, but he didn't object. The knots on either side kept the rope from slipping through, so the riders had a rough set of reins. Ariel let herself feel a sparkle of hope.

"How'd you think of that?" she wondered.

"I've been watching and thinking a long while," he said.

As he rejoined her, Ariel studied the hills emerging from the darkness.

"We've got to cross back over the mountains," she said. "Do you see where we came down?"

"It was all I could do to keep up," Zeke replied, "so I doubt I can find the route back. But we've got to get away from them first. We can figure out which direction home is in later." He nudged Orion back into motion.

Ariel's mind raced. "Maybe someone at the roadhouse would help us!"

When she explained what she'd heard about that place, Zeke shook his head.

"That's what they'll expect," he argued. "They'll go there straight off."

"But, Zeke . . ." Her voice faded. The weight of their challenge fell on her heart. Whatever supplies hid in Zeke's small knapsack couldn't help much. How were two young people alone supposed to evade two angry Finders?

"Let's just keep going as fast as we can," Zeke added, tilting his face to the paling sky. "They'll wake up soon, if they haven't already."

Dread sliced through Ariel. It would take only seconds for Scarl and Elbert to see that Orion had done more than hobble away after grass. Cursing would fill the air. Then they'd search—and they'd find.

A hopeless calm settled over her dread. They'd be caught, with horrid results. Until then, they merely played a bitter game to see how long losing would take. The game held a twist of satisfaction, however: Elbert's cruelty had helped her escape. She wondered how the Finders would settle their bet. She'd won that round, her mind jeered. Pretending to play another made it easier for Ariel to think.

"Can't you ask a tree which way to go?" she asked.

When Zeke didn't answer, she swiveled. He shook his head curtly without meeting her eyes.

Afraid to break into his stony demeanor, Ariel looked for another idea. She knew the mountain pass had to lie nearly due west, but so did Elbert and Scarl. Some instinct told her that for this game—hide-and-seek—south would serve better. Her dangling feet twitched that direction like the needle of an inverted compass.

"All right." Taking charge of their rope reins, she goaded the horse and tugged on one side to turn him. "If you won't pick a direction, I will."

CHAPTER
16

Smoke stung Ariel's nostrils. Skirting a blackberry patch, she and Zeke nearly collided with an outhouse just past the brambles. They sidled into its shadow while their eyes picked out the rundown roadhouse nearby. Little more than a hut, it looked abandoned, but chimney smoke lay in the air along with an aroma of breakfast.

A blast of longing hit Ariel. A building with a roof spoke a different language from the one that had moaned to her daily of earthen beds and cold rain.

"If we told them we were stolen, wouldn't they help us?" she pleaded.

"Why should they?" Zeke crushed her quick hopes. "If Elbert says he's our father, how could we prove he was lying?"

Ariel stared at the empty promise of safety. A whimper leaked from her throat.

"Look." Zeke pointed. "A trail." A narrow path curled uphill into the trees on the far side of the roadhouse. Ariel's heart resounded as if she had known it would be there.

"If we take it, though," Zeke worried, "we might be easier to follow."

"It won't matter if we don't get farther away—and that's how!" She could no longer stand the feeling that Scarl and Elbert would soon grasp at their backs. She smacked her heels on the horse.

Startled, Orion leaped into the yard of the roadhouse, nearly leaving his riders behind. Ariel folded low and kept pumping her feet. Zeke clutched her, barely hanging on. Orion tore past the roadhouse toward the trail, his hooves thudding.

A pair of startled eyes may have appeared in the hut's lone window as they passed. By the time that uncertain impression filtered into Ariel's mind, the observer could have seen little but receding haunches.

Galloping felt glorious and terrifying. The only other time Ariel had gone so fast on Orion, she'd been stuffed in a bag. Branches reached to scratch them from alongside the over-grown path. The horse's hooves clattered on rocks. Too late, Ariel realized the noise might echo all the way to the Finders' ears. She decided she didn't care. As long as Orion could run, the space between them grew wider. Even Elbert couldn't travel as fast as a galloping horse.

They ran until sunlight crept down the hills. The horse heaved, nostrils flared. Finally his riders let him slow. The trail twisted through foothills, trees lining it most of the time, for which Ariel was grateful. It would make them harder to spot from a distance.

"Now tell me, Zeke," she said at last. "Why didn't anyone come with you?"

She felt him lay his cheek against her shoulder.

"I don't want to tell you," he sighed. "If I don't, when we get home, maybe none of it will be true."

Her throat clenched. Finally she swallowed the lump. "My mother—?" she whispered.

Zeke circled his arms around her. His head didn't lift off her shoulder.

"She's dead, Ariel. One of them killed her."

A buzz slid between Ariel's ears and her brain. It blocked the sound of hoofbeats and Zeke's nearby breathing. It drowned the cheerful chirping of birds. It could not, however, silence words she'd already heard.

Her mind found a crack she might slip through to escape. "No. You didn't see it. You couldn't. It was dark. She—" Her voice broke.

Zeke just hugged harder.

If only he had protested! If he had repeated himself or told her to stop it, she could have believed he was lying or teasing or wrong. His silence wiped away hope. For days she had felt as though vital juices were leaking out through a hole in her chest. Now the hollow space that remained collapsed hard, crushing what was left of her heart.

The buzzing took over Ariel's thoughts for a while. When it finally faded, she realized that Zeke had been speaking.

". . . under the dock. He didn't know that I saw, but I did."

"What?" she said crossly. "I didn't hear you."

Zeke shifted behind her. "Which part?"

"Any of it. Whatever you said. What was under the dock?"

He took a deep breath. "Never mind. We don't have to talk about it."

Clop, clop, clop rose from Orion's hooves below them.

"But why didn't anyone come after me?" Like a fishhook,

that puzzle tugged on Ariel's mind. It wouldn't let her sink back into the buzzing. "Even . . . even if . . . what you said before."

"Nobody knew you were stolen at first."

"But my mother . . ."

"They thought she'd gone with you. That's what Elbert told some of the Reapers that night—that he offered to take her along, too, and that swayed her. She wouldn't worry if she was traveling with you."

"Where was she?" The dull words formed by themselves.

"She—her body washed up under one of the docks."

The notion was so fantastic, Ariel could pretend it was one of Storian's tales. A silly story, that's what it was, about someone who didn't swim as well as her mother. Ariel did not need to cry. Tears were for girls whose mothers were dead.

Zeke added, "Windmaster found her on the late-morning tide."

A flare of anger seared up through her guts. "But if Windmaster knew, why didn't anyone figure out Elbert's lie? And chase us?"

"By then it was too late."

"You caught up! You found us!"

"That's not what I meant. It was too late for anyone to be brave enough."

"What are you talking about?" she demanded. "The Fishers are brave. And your dad—"

"Don't." What felt like Zeke's forehead dropped against the back of her head. "My dad is . . . it's like he's sick or sleepwalking. It's like the whole of Canberra Docks got stuck in a bad dream and they're too scared to even wake up."

Unable to add up this terrible math, Ariel just waited,

numb. By then she knew that awful answers came by themselves, whether she sought them or not.

A few heaving breaths later, Zeke spoke again.

"The Finders burned the sycamore when they left that night. My maple, too. She tried to speak to me a little before she—" His voice cracked. He swallowed. "They must have used flame-fix. The Flame-Mage wouldn't admit that she'd traded any to Elbert or Scarl. But one of them must have put something like that on the trees. By the time I saw the sycamore in the morning, it was all black and twisted, and grown-ups were wailing or stumbling around in a daze." A few more words shoved out of his throat, but Ariel could not understand them. They were too swaddled with tears.

They rocked with Orion's motion, each alone in their shock. A bitter slime rose from Ariel's heart to her mouth. She was glad to consider the horrible fate of the trees. It kept her mind from the black, buzzing corner where she'd stuffed any thought of her mother. The idea of burning a tree whipped Ariel's world upside down. For all of their cruelty, Scarl and Elbert still had been men. But only lightning or wildfire or other insane things could burn a tree still growing out of the ground. A person who did it must be as alien as the creatures that lived in the dark depths of the sea.

Ariel shifted one hand to cover Zeke's fingers. There was still another person nearby who was not such a monster. It was the only comfort she could give or receive.

But sharp thoughts began piercing her mind. Each sliced straight through to her heart: no more tender glances, no good night kisses, no arms to draw Ariel close. No skirts rustling at dawn to call her from bed. No and no. None. The no's hit her one after another, each knocking her down a terrible, bone-breaking stair. Each jolt left her breathless. No mother. No home.

"Don't cry anymore," Zeke whispered after a while.

Lost in *no*, Ariel had not been aware of her tears. She hadn't even known she was still riding a horse. The road had been lost behind glimpses of a mother who no longer awaited in a home that no more could be found.

"It'll be okay," Zeke added. He gulped, draining his words of conviction. "Someday."

"No!" Filled so full of that word, Ariel had to voice it. "No, it won't! Never!" Some of her pain squeezed out as anger. If he had not been behind her, she would have hit him. Zeke would go home to two parents. She'd lost the only one she still had.

She clenched her hands to her chest and curled over her stomach, not caring if she fell off the horse. A tuft of mane muffled her wail. "You can find a different tree!" she cried. "I can't find a different mother!"

A distant part of her cringed. Zeke didn't deserve her anger. Her heart turned away from that whisper of conscience, not able to heed it right now.

"No, I can't," he replied quietly. "But I know what you mean. I'm so sorry."

She let his words, which confused her, dissolve in her grief. Too stricken to make room for anyone else's pain, she didn't want to understand what he'd just said.

Miles passed beneath her, unknown and unnoticed. Eventually, drained to dregs, Ariel looked up and unfolded her limbs. She hated her own arms and legs for daring to ache. They seemed to be mocking her heart.

She twisted to look at Zeke. Anxiety sculpted his face.

"Why did you come?" she wondered.

"Because." His eyes slid away from hers. "Because I promised. And because nobody else would."

Hollow, she waited to be filled with more of Zeke's horrible knowledge.

"The burning made everyone crazy," he added. "It took hours before anyone noticed you and your mother were gone. And more till the Windmaster found . . . what he did. Then they knew you'd been stolen but they pretended you weren't. Even my—everyone. They were scared what else might happen, I guess, and they blamed your mother for ignoring the sycamore's advice. Besides, without the help of the trees, nobody knew which way to look."

"You found me," she murmured, grateful. What she'd heard made his presence behind her even more of a marvel.

"They sacrificed you," he growled. "Just like Fishers throw flowers into the sea during Fallfest. 'Please don't drown us this winter; here's some flowers instead.' And then they wanted to forget. That's what the maple tree said."

"Your maple? I thought they bur—"

"They did!" He shouted, hurting Ariel's ear. "But I ran there right away when I saw the smoke. She—" His voice gurgled. "The sycamore burned first, I guess. When I got to my maple, she hadn't left the world yet. She cried that I should help you. I didn't know how, but I promised I would. She told me to listen, that voices would help. Then she . . . she faded. Only scorched wood was left. And I'll hate the Flame-Mage forever. Forever!"

"I'm sorry, Zeke," Ariel whispered, frightened by the savage tone in his voice. "Sorry for everything. Except I'm not sorry you came. I am so, so glad. Even if they catch us and kill us, I am so glad to see you again first."

"I won't let them," Zeke snarled, with more outrage and fury than a boy not quite thirteen years old should be able to hold. Ariel believed him.

They never startled Orion into another gallop that day, but they trotted and walked many miles. They stopped only for water and to munch fiddleheads from a thicket of ferns. As their path climbed and day faded to night, they seemed to near heaven. Peaks cloaked the horizon. Stars pricked the black sky. Zeke pulled a blanket from his pack and wrapped it as best he could around both of them to ward off the chill alpine air.

Orion's hooves began dragging. Repeatedly one rider or the other jerked awake from a doze. Finally Ariel snapped alert to find the horse at a standstill, chomping grass. Waking behind her with a start, Zeke fell off into a hummock of springy salal.

"We've got to get off and sleep," Ariel mumbled. She slipped down beside Zeke and they tied the horse to a tree. Orion hung his head from the rope, trembling.

"Wait," Ariel said. Their mount's clear exhaustion and the night sounds of the forest roused her fear of pursuit. "We should get farther off the trail."

Zeke turned bleary eyes down the path, a paler swath in the night.

"They can't catch up that fast just walking."

Ariel tried to remember if she'd seen animal troughs at the roadhouse. The Finders couldn't ride cows, but she didn't think they would hesitate to steal a horse if they found one.

"You caught up when they had the horse," she said, fretting.

Zeke lay down, flapping a corner of his blanket to show he would share it.

"I had a boat," he mumbled, closing his eyes. "And help figuring out where to go." Before Ariel's next question, he slid into sleep. Yawning, she gave up and snuggled against him, unable to resist the same dragging tide.

CHAPTER
17

Though nightmares haunted both Ariel and Zeke, only hunger finally broke through their exhaustion to wake them.

When she opened her eyes, Ariel's brain took a moment to find her. Her first thought was a wish to relieve her tight bladder—despite a man at the end of her leash. With a flash of joy, she recalled that the rope and the man had both been cast off. Memories kindled, and her joy slid quickly to fear.

She bolted upright, searching for hunters like a small animal might.

"It's okay," came Zeke's voice.

The loss of her mother crashed down on her next. To endure it, she focused tightly on the world here, now, outside her. Her attention fell on the afternoon tint of the light.

Ariel moaned. "We shouldn't have slept so long."

"Too late now." Zeke was digging in his knapsack, which looked nearly empty. He sighed. "All I've got left are some walnuts."

Ariel took her share eagerly and cracked the shells with a rock. Only then did she realize that Orion was gone.

At her cry of despair, Zeke nodded glumly.

"I searched for a while before you woke up," he said. "We must not have tied him well enough, and he got hungry, too, I suppose."

"But what'll we do?"

He slipped one arm through the strap on his knapsack. "Same as I have been: walk every minute. Come on." Picking at his smashed walnuts, he headed up the path.

Ariel followed, nibbling her poor breakfast. Though the nut meat only mocked her hollow stomach, the long sleep and a beloved companion helped her body feel stronger than it had in days.

"We can't go as fast, but we won't be so easy to follow, either," she told Zeke. "Orion's tracks running away might confuse them. And if this trail gets very steep, he might not have been able to climb it. But we can."

Zeke only gazed at the stone faces looming above them. His expression spoke clearly enough: he didn't believe they would make it over the top, either.

Hoping to cheer him with a memory of success, Ariel asked Zeke how he'd caught up with her captors.

"I tried to get someone to come with me," he began. "Nobody would listen. The maple had told me which way to start, though. I followed hoofprints after that. It was hard. I would have lost you if I hadn't caught up with Storian right away."

"Storian! I thought nobody else came for me."

"They didn't. He didn't even know you were gone. He left before the Finders did. He thought he knew where they'd take the telling dart, and he meant to go, too."

Ariel remembered saying good-bye to friends her last evening at home. She hadn't found Storian. She had thought his burned roof explained that. She would never have guessed he was farther away than someone else's warm hearth.

"Did he tell you the truth about the dart, Zeke?" she asked.

"Only that it called certain people to a challenge, and that the Finders must have convinced themselves that you were one of them."

"It has something to do with Farwalkers."

Zeke stopped in his tracks to stare over his shoulder at her.

Alarmed, Ariel found her mouth filling the silence. "Scarl said something odd, like he thought I might be one. But it must be a giant mistake, don't you think?"

"Stop," he said. "What did Scarl say, exactly?"

When she told him, he mused, "There aren't supposed to be any Farwalkers left. Storian told us in class that the whole trade died out."

"But what did they do? I couldn't remember that part."

"They were guides," Zeke replied. "Messengers, connectors. They carried news and ideas, helped people trade goods, and brought 'em together into new villages when no one could see. And you—oh!" He dug in the end of his cast. "I meant to give you this."

He pulled out Ariel's whale bone needle.

She gave a cry of surprise. "You carried it all this time?"

"Can't really feel it in there. Kept forgetting. But look at the mark for who it was sent to."

Not really listening, Ariel stroked the bone. Tears for her mother pressed on her eyes.

"I don't know what the Farwalker sign looked like," Zeke added, craning to see between her fingers, "but that lightning bolt seems to go far, don't you think? Zigzagging all over."

Ariel blinked her wet eyes and peered at it with him.

Storian had not wanted to talk about that mark. The subject of Farwalkers seemed to make people nervous, perhaps because, like monsters and ghosts, they weren't supposed to exist.

"I'm thinking you might not be a Healtouch," Zeke told her. "You might be a Farwalker instead. Maybe Scarl is right."

"But it was only luck that I ever found the dart in the first place! It didn't fly to me."

"Sure it did," Zeke replied. "It just crashed into my maple tree first. She made sure you got it. She probably knew that if she stopped speaking to me, sooner or later you'd butt in and find it."

"Butt in?"

Zeke ducked his head, grinned, and began walking again. "Anyway," he continued, "when I told Storian what had happened, he wanted me to go with him. He didn't think we could take you back from them by force. 'Not one old man and a boy,' that's how he put it. We could help you better, he said, if we got to Libros before they did. Maybe he's there now." He shrugged. "But before he decided, we talked about a shortcut for following you."

"What shortcut?"

Zeke paused to scrape a wavy line in the dirt with his toe. Ariel recognized the headlands near Canberra Docks.

"Sailing up the coast and into this inlet cut off almost three days. Even after I ran back home for the boat." He brushed the marks away.

"Who gave you a boat?"

"No one. I stole a skiff from the docks."

Amazement huffed from Ariel's throat. This revelation, as much as anything else Zeke had said, showed her how chaotic their village had become—not to mention how determined he'd been. Never in her life had a boat, or much of anything else, been stolen in Canberra Docks.

"You sailed it by yourself?"

He nodded. "I told Windmaster where I was going, and I think he asked the wind to help." He didn't have to remind her why Leed Windmaster, of all people, might have found that much courage. "Once I landed, I kept hearing these whispers. Whenever I got confused, somebody—something—told me where to go." He gave her a sharp glance. "Before you say anything, I don't think it was trees. But I don't want to talk about that."

Ariel studied his back as he marched before her. Although troubled by glimpses of the pain Zeke was keeping mostly submerged, she felt lucky to have such a friend. Then she remembered that he'd also been keeping a promise.

"When we get home," she murmured, "I hope you find another tree right away. One that's almost as good as the maple."

Stiff shoulders gave his only reply.

In the silence, Ariel thought about Farwalkers. The thirteenth trade was extinct, and she hated the idea of being the only one of a kind. On the other hand, she had walked plenty of late, and she and Zeke kept plodding now, even after the trail became only a silvery thread in the moonlight. Ariel hoped it would reach a pass and start going down again soon. Otherwise, despite sharing a blanket, the pair could hardly stop without freezing.

Eventually the moon slipped behind a peak, but Ariel's feet still could feel the trail. Taking the lead, she gazed at the stars, like sparkles in black sand, and wondered how they could glitter at her and Zeke with so little sympathy.

Then she saw a star that didn't slowly slip away with its neighbors. This star got bigger instead. It wasn't a star, Ariel realized abruptly. A light shone through the dark.

At first the glow seemed to hover in a tumble of rock at the base of a bluff. As Ariel and Zeke approached, moving cautiously despite the cover of darkness, a mountain house took shape from the stone. One corner had been hewn right out of the cliff. Spires and sharp angles loomed from the shadows to form a building like none Ariel had seen. She couldn't fathom the purpose of such a great house, especially without a village around it. Light glowed from a window high above a big wooden door. The yellow candlelight flickered. Nothing else stirred.

Whispering, Ariel and Zeke decided that if they found nothing to fear, they would knock. Their hands and feet were already numb with the cold. Before taking the risk, though, Ariel wanted to make sure their pursuers had not, by some straighter route, arrived there before them.

The windows were too high to peek through. Circling the house proved impossible. But they discovered a very short wooden door embedded in its foundation. From a hole near the top, the smell of goats wafted out, along with an inquisitive snout.

"Let's go in, if there's room," Ariel said, lifting the latch. "I'm freezing. Nobody will look for us here."

Careful not to let goats escape, she cracked the door open. Zeke followed her into the warm, smelly hole. They were greeted by a chorus of confused bleats and rustling. In the utter darkness, it was impossible to tell how many goats were bedded down in the straw, but their body heat would keep the travelers warm. Ariel pulled the door tight and stuck her arm through its little window to latch it again.

Zeke's fingers found her hand. The lips of curious goats began nibbling at her.

"Crouch down so you don't bump your head," Zeke advised. "Come this way."

They followed the wall to a corner, where they'd be out of sight of anyone who opened the door in the morning. Sprawling, Ariel put her hand in something squishy. She jerked away, able to guess what it was, but told herself the warm hiding place would be worth it. After scraping her fingers clean in the straw, she made sure she could feel Zeke close beside her. Sleep stole between them, unnoticed.

Ariel dreamed she lay in a tomb. It should have been frightening, but this tomb was snug.

She awoke to a companion somewhat older than Zeke. His head propped on his hand, the teenage boy gazed at her face. Oddly, he wore a gray shift not unlike a girl's nightgown. One sleeve was stained red at the cuff.

Seeing her eyes flutter open, he smiled. When she bolted upright in alarm, he vanished. Only dirty straw rested beside her.

A rooster cackled somewhere nearby. Uncertain just when she'd stopped dreaming, Ariel whirled to find Zeke curled at her other side. Reassured, she looked about in the dim morning light sneaking in from outside. A dozen goats stood or lay in the pen. The tight space squeezed down in back where the uneven ground met the floor overhead.

A playful kid jumped on Zeke, drawing a muffled yelp from the boy. As soon as he shoved it aside, it circled to climb him from another direction. While she watched the goat game and tried to ignore the hungry twist in her belly, a moving figure too big for a goat caught the corner of Ariel's eye. She spun. In the gloom she saw nothing, not even a goat, but the straw beneath quivered. A cold draft swirled against the back of her neck.

"Zeke!" she whispered. "There's someone here with us! Besides goats, I mean!"

Zeke curled tighter, trying to discourage his new friend. "Oh, that. It's just ghosts. I could hear them whispering about us all night."

Gooseflesh rippled Ariel's arms. "Ghosts?" She hoped she'd misheard him. Storian had told tales of dead Fishers enslaved by the sea, and most of those ghosts were not friendly.

"They won't hurt us. They're just curious. Let me sleep a bit more."

Ariel's eyes darted. No wonder she could feel someone staring without seeing who. She couldn't hear any whispers, but the air prickled her skin.

A sound outside alerted the goats. As one they pressed toward the door. Zeke merely turned over, grateful for peace. Ariel clung against the wall to remain out of sight.

The door opened. Goats flowed out, butting and bleating. As their commotion faded, replaced by trilling birdsong, Ariel released her pent breath. No face had appeared at the doorway.

"Please come out, little goats," came a voice. Ariel's heart skipped when the voice added, "I've been expecting you."

CHAPTER
18

Ariel clutched Zeke. He lay frozen, his puffed eyes drawn wide.

A hand beckoned. "Come now. You can't eat the straw. Don't be afraid."

The pair exchanged doubtful looks.

"Still want to snooze? All right, sleepy goats. Come out when your stomachs want breakfast. Just don't wait until those who pursue you come striding up the path."

The mention of pursuit split Ariel's heart. One half feared that anyone who knew they were chased must have talked to, and might aid, the pursuers. The other half heard only a caution and the promise of breakfast. After two days with little food, Ariel could feel the wobble in her legs without even trying to stand.

Zeke crawled toward the door. "Anyone bad would have locked us in," he explained.

Ariel held back. "It might be a trap."

Zeke nodded. "It might be. But I've got to eat before I can fight or go on or even think. Don't you?"

He slipped out the doorway. No shouts or sounds of a

struggle ensued. Grimly, Ariel slid feetfirst toward the entry, poised to smash her boots into grasping hands.

None awaited. Ariel blinked in the light. The goats were already distant on the hillside. By day, the mountain house looked even more foreboding. Great stones formed the high walls, and clay chimneys poked through the slate tiled roof. Parapets and gables met in sharp angles, giving the place a hard, wild aspect that matched the stony peaks not so far in the distance.

The goatherd stood near the building's great wooden door, his hands in the pockets of a pale green garment that looked to Ariel like a dress. For an instant she thought this might be the young man she'd seen alongside her in the straw. But this man wasn't young. Well worn, his face crinkled. His smile displayed missing teeth.

Overcome with the weakness of relief, Ariel remained on the ground as the old man stumped back toward her and Zeke. He offered her his gnarled hand.

"You're more likely to carry me than me you, young 'un," he said. "Grab ahold, though, and come on inside."

He raised her up. Though his fingers felt like a snarl of frayed rope, she kept gripping them as they passed through the doorway. The stone entry echoed. Dark passages led away on all sides. Ariel took her hand back only once they were seated at a low stone table, awaiting a meal.

His name was Ash, he told them, after the tree. They'd found sanctuary in Tree-Singer Abbey. Hope surged into Ariel when she heard the name. Zeke's jaw slipped agape.

"I didn't think it was real," he murmured.

Ash left them briefly, returning with a sudsy washbowl as well as a food-laden tray. Goat cheese, preserved pears, hot tea, boiled eggs—Ariel and Zeke grabbed for the food. Halfway through her first slab of bread, Ariel looked up in shame. She'd ignored the washbowl as well as her manners. Ash just grinned his gaping smile and handed her a teacup.

"It's all right, little goat. The trees can eat sunlight. You and I must have something more solid."

Humbly, she thanked him and soaped her hands before going back to her bread.

"I knew you were coming, you see." Ash cackled. "The cherry tree in our courtyard began blooming night before last. An old tree, she is. Never blooms anymore except for visitors she wants us to welcome. She said there'd be two, but I wouldn't have guessed two so small. Are ye newly named Tree-Singers, then?"

Zeke deflated. His eyes dropped to his lap. "No."

Her hands wrapped on her warm cup, Ariel pondered his face. "One of us is," she said. "Zeke."

Tears glistened on the boy's lashes. "Not anymore."

Ash's eyes, which swam in a gray liquid of age, fastened on Zeke.

"Ah, so you're that one, then. I heard of the burning. A bad business. But the trees don't blame you, boy."

"Then why won't any hear me?" Zeke moaned. "I've tried and tried. Not many would answer before, but most of them listened. Now they won't even do that."

"You told me you heard voices, though," Ariel ventured.

Zeke's tears slipped loose. "I did! I would have lost you completely without them. But when I tried to figure out which tree was speaking, none would say anything more. When I sing, they all turn away!"

Ash rested his hand on Zeke's shoulder. The boy pulled his tears back under control. Ariel's heart throbbed, the pain of his loss awakening hers. No wonder he hadn't wanted to ask a tree for directions.

"We'll speak of that later," Ash told Zeke. "For now, eat."

Once they'd slowed in stuffing themselves, Ash Tree-Singer began asking questions. He didn't seem troubled that they'd come in the night or slept with the goats. What he wanted to learn was who followed and how far behind them the hunters might be.

"Finders," he mused when he'd heard. "I wonder. Two, did you say?"

Ariel repeated the names. "Do you know them?"

"Don't believe I know any Finders at all," Ash replied. "But what I know hardly matters. It's what our trees know that concerns me." His twisted fingers absently petted the tabletop as if he were placing pieces of an invisible puzzle.

"What if they come while we're here?" Zeke asked.

"I don't think they will," Ash answered. "They won't catch you until—" He broke off, shaking his head. "They won't catch you."

Ariel heard it again in her head, that one word: "until." If a Tree-Singer said it, you were hearing the truth. But Ash had said two things, or none. At once her breakfast weighed too much in her middle.

"Can't we stay here and hide? Please? They're awful! They tied me and—" Now Ariel's eyes filled with tears.

"My dear, you've misunderstood my creaky old tongue. Your path stretches long before you, indeed. I won't tell you a fib about that. But you will not spend another day with two Finders. That I can promise."

Ariel's chest began heaving with trapped sobs anyway. The swings of fear and relief were too much to bear.

Ash fluttered to comfort her. "Madrona?" he called.

Another green-clad Tree-Singer appeared, a woman a bit younger than Ariel's mother.

"What mother? You have none," whispered a stone lodged in her heart.

Ariel cried hard to drown out that whisper. Madrona fussed and then lifted her up, carrying her like a baby toward the doorway. The separation from Zeke prompted a quick flash of fear, but it gave way under Ariel's grief. She leaned into the soft bosom and wept.

Madrona settled on a stone bench in a courtyard and stroked Ariel's hair. Pink blossoms drifted past. Gradually, the soothing embrace lulled Ariel once more into slumber.

She dreamed again of the young man from the goat pen. He circled the cherry tree, head bowed, his gray tunic not unlike what the Tree-Singers wore. As he passed, his eyes flashed up to catch Ariel spying on him. Looking troubled, he extended a hand toward her, palm up.

"I can," he said.

"Can what?"

Her own voice awoke her. She lay stretched by herself on the bench, where apparently Madrona had left her.

Shivering, Ariel sat up. Cherry blossoms fluttered about the garden like lazy snowflakes. Petals landed on the bench beside her. While she watched, they shivered and twitched until they had aligned themselves into the shape of a hand.

She jumped to her feet, a scream caught in her throat.

"There you be. Awake again, then?"

Ariel whirled. Ash and Zeke stood in the courtyard archway.

"I've asked my friend Elm to heat water for baths," Ash went on. "Does a warm tub sound pleasant?"

Barely listening, Ariel glanced back at the bench. Her motion had disturbed the delicate petals, but they resettled, the shape too perfect to be accidental.

"Look!" She waved Ash and Zeke nearer and pointed to the hand outlined on the bench. "Is that a Tree-Singer trick? It's scary."

Ash took one look and chuckled. "Ah. You seem to have caught the interest of Misha," he said. "One of our ghosts."

"Told ya," Zeke muttered, when she shot him a wild glance.

"A lost soul, I suppose," Ash continued, "from times long ago. We used to catch sight of him often, drifting through the halls or this courtyard. He's been quiet for years, though. I rather thought he'd moved on."

"I could hear him whisper last night," Zeke said. "But I couldn't make out many words."

Ash tilted his head. "I knew you were unusual, Zeke. I suppose since you needn't sleep there again, I can tell you—the goat pen was once used as a tomb."

Ariel clutched her own arms to stop her skin from crawling.

"He can't harm you," Ash hastened to add. "He's just curious about you, I'll guess—someone new, and young like him. If you sit quietly, you may even see him."

Not sure she wanted attention from a ghost, Ariel gnawed her lip.

Ash patted her shoulder. "If you're scared, ignore him and he'll go away. He can't hurt you, I promise. No specter can."

Ariel hoped he was right. As Ash led her and Zeke back

through the dim, ancient hallways, she scanned gloomy corners and the rafters overhead to make sure they were empty.

"There was a time when Misha would get into mischief," Ash told them. "Handprints would appear on clean robes or squashed into meat pies—much to the torment of our cook, Juniper."

"Is everyone here named for a tree?" Ariel wondered. "Everyone alive, that is?"

"Indeed," Ash replied. "When Tree-Singers come here to stay, they take new names. There has been an Ash at this abbey for time forgotten. Many Cedars and Willows and Elders as well."

"Anybody named Horse Chestnut?" Ariel giggled. Zeke elbowed her, scowling. "I'm sorry," she added, trying to pull the grin off her face.

Ash winked. "You're forgiven. I think Horse Chestnut might be a bit awkward as a name. Though it's a beautiful tree."

Promising to call them when their bathwater was hot, he left them in a small room with two beds and a window overlooking the mountains. Zeke immediately flopped on one bed.

"Did you know about this place?" Ariel asked him.

"I thought it was somewhere Tree-Singers went when they died," he admitted. He shared some of what he'd learned from their host while she'd napped. The abbey had stood there, according to Ash, since before the Blind War, and maybe the war before that. The halls once had been full, but only a dozen Tree-Singers lived there now, and new arrivals came rarely. Madrona, the youngest, had taken a vow of silence.

"He told me she saves her voice only for singing to trees," Zeke explained sadly.

Watching his face, Ariel asked gingerly, "Did he make you feel better about . . . you know?"

Zeke stared out the window. "He told me I would never be a Tree-Singer again. He said I had something more important to do."

Ariel's breath caught. "You might be the Farwalker, Zeke! Not me—you!"

Zeke shook his head. "I asked about that. I will know my new trade when I find it—that's all he would say." He eyed her. "But I still think it's you. A wildcat couldn't have followed that trail last night once the moon set. And you're the one who led us to the path in the first place, too. I don't think that was luck."

Although he hadn't convinced her, she pondered Zeke's words until Madrona fetched them for their baths. Ariel had to admit she had found the way to the abbey almost as if something had guided her feet. But that didn't seem like a skill that could be traded for something to eat. Villagers exchanged news and goods with their neighbors, and most were too busy feeding their families to go farther afield, with a guide or without one. Besides, what news could she bear, if not the news that her mother was dead? No one cared. A Farwalker today would be unneeded, footsore, and hungry.

Dogged by these disquieting thoughts, Ariel sank gratefully into her tub. Madrona washed her hair and her back. The woman's soft touch summoned memories of home that stabbed into Ariel's heart. Tears leaked again onto her cheeks. Whisking them away, she pressed her hands tight to her chest, for that's where the leak seemed to have sprung. Madrona smiled kindly and pretended not to notice.

When the Tree-Singer left her to soak, Ariel noticed the looking glass hung on the back of the door. As if awaiting her gaze, handprints appeared in the steam coating its surface. Now that she could put a name to the ghost, it no longer spooked her so badly. It must be lonely, she thought, drifting without friends to speak to, good things to eat, or the comfort of a warm fire or tub. It sounded as forlorn as a Farwalker's life.

"I'm sorry you scared me before, Misha," she said. "I wish I could see you. Besides in a dream."

The hands in the mirror fogged over. She wondered if she'd said the wrong thing.

Disappointed, Ariel looked toward her toes at the far end of the tub. Steam still rose from the water around her. It did not, however, simply float toward the rafters. Even wet, the hairs on her arms rose. A misty bolt of lightning hung white in the air.

She drew her knees up to her naked chest and grabbed the glass bead on her necklace, needing something to clutch, if not hide behind.

"You know about the telling dart?" she breathed. "Or were you a Farwalker once?"

A breath puffed from behind her, whiffing the symbol away. She whipped her head that direction. She glimpsed nothing but space all around her—until her eyes fell on the misty mirror again. Drawn as if with a finger, the same symbol shone there. Handprints stamped around it. Ariel marveled.

She emerged from her bath into an oversize green robe. She snickered to see Zeke dressed the same. Ash sat with the pair near a fire, serving up warm milk and sweets. Ariel's stomach, still full from breakfast, gurgled with pleasure at more.

"Eat up, saplings," Ash told them. "I certainly don't begrudge you a roof and a bit of hot water and cheese." His smile became strained. "But I really think you should be on your way as soon as you can. Tomorrow, perhaps."

Ariel nearly spewed her mouthful of milk. She whimpered.

"So soon?" Scarl and Elbert were likely still hunting for them, and probably not far away. If the men had found Orion, they might be galloping now toward the abbey. Even tracking on foot, they could have closed to within pouncing distance, if they'd pushed hard. Ariel had no doubt they had—if only to catch her and kill her for vengeance. She could imagine Elbert's face when he'd realized she was gone. It must have looked like a storm driven over the sea.

"On our way," Zeke repeated, pinning Ash with a stare. "On our way where? We're not going home, are we? You don't think we are."

While Ariel gaped at her friend, an uncomfortable look slid into the old man's wrinkles. "Don't believe that, boy," he said. "You will find rest. I just think you have a long journey ahead first."

"What do the trees say?" Zeke demanded, his rude tone making Ariel cringe. "If something bad is going to happen, we might as well know."

"You're wrong there," Ash replied sternly. "Foreknowledge is far more dangerous than ignorance. But that's not the point. The trees tell us some things. They can't tell us the whole, they wouldn't if they could, and I can't imagine your father ever told you they did."

Chastened, Zeke dropped his stare. Ash crinkled his face kindly at Ariel.

"Trees feel the ebb and flow of the Essence, not each separate spark," he explained. "The world leaves it to us to stir sparkles ourselves, and it's precisely that striving that keeps the tide bright. Since no part of the world is detached from the rest, without brave efforts by all, the brilliant fire would go dim."

Ash would say no more about it. He told them Madrona would wash their clothes and fill Zeke's pack with food and warm blankets. They should eat their fill and rest while they could.

Desperate to wipe the dread from Zeke's face, Ariel told him, "Never mind. We'll be okay. I'm not scared." But she was.

CHAPTER
19

Even the first bed in almost a fortnight did not comfort Ariel. Too soon, morning had come, forcing good-byes. As she and Zeke crossed the high meadow toward the spires above, he walked backward, gazing down at the abbey.

"I wish we could have stayed there forever," he said.

Ariel glanced over her shoulder. The stone roof and chimneys seemed to melt into the sheltering bluff. If she hadn't just stood inside it, she would have thought the whole place a mirage.

"I'd rather go home," she said, although she no longer knew what that word meant.

Heaving a sigh, Zeke faced forward again.

Avoiding his anxious expression, Ariel studied the route ahead. She spied a creek tumbling down toward them, and her heart lifted to meet it. According to Ash, they should be able to follow its course to a saddle in the hills—their best hope of crossing to the other side. From there they could find the shore and head down the coast, keeping the sea on one shoulder until they got home.

If the steady uphill climb had left her with enough breath, Ariel would have sung. Even with the threat of pursuit, traveling toward home with a friend felt far different from marching as a prisoner. She watched the wildflowers nod as they passed. No breeze touched her face, yet the grass around her swooned and shivered in waves.

Zeke said, "Misha is with us again. Can you hear him?"

"No, but I wondered what was moving the grass. Why can you hear him and I can't? You could never hear ghosts at—oh! Maybe that's your new trade, the one Ash hinted at."

Zeke's expression grew guarded. "How could hearing ghosts be useful enough for a trade?"

"It helped you find me."

"That wasn't ghosts," he objected. "It's different. The voices that helped me follow you were more like hearing a tree—a vibration inside. Misha I hear with my ears. Right now, and last night again, too, before I fell asleep." Zeke appraised her. Ariel couldn't tell if the emotion tinting his eyes was jealousy or concern. "He kept calling your name."

A thrill ran beneath Ariel's skin, and she wondered what the ghost wanted. She didn't know how to answer his call, or even if an answer was wise. But the prospect of seeing him again, awake or in dreams, filled her with uneasy excitement.

She and Zeke climbed a long way. When the sky blackened, they stopped where a huge slab of stone had slid down the mountain aslant, creating a nook underneath. Ariel eyed that gap, afraid to go inside lest the slab fall and crush them.

"It couldn't fall, the way it's resting," Zeke said, knocking the rock with his arm splint. "Besides, it wouldn't smash us. It's friendly. I think it slid that way on purpose so visitors might come inside—foxes and such." He disappeared underneath.

The gray granite looked jagged to Ariel, not friendly. "Any animals in there now?" she called.

Teasing, he growled.

Zeke's judgment turned out to be sound. Their makeshift cave blunted the wind and gave them a view of the moon. Feeling snug, the two friends ate some of the food Madrona had packed them. When Ariel reached for more, Zeke stopped her.

"We don't know how long it might have to last."

Although she knew he was right, she didn't like what he meant.

"When we get to the sea, we'll find mussels and sea cucumbers," she argued.

"When we get to the sea."

A bolt of homesickness hit her. The sea, and all it meant, seemed only a Storian's tale. Needing tangible proof, she retrieved her whalebone needle from Zeke's pack, where she'd stashed it for safekeeping.

"The whale's spirit will help us get home," she told him, clutching the bone and hoping her words would be true.

Looking thoughtfully at the stone all around them, Zeke said nothing more. As Ariel grew drowsy, she tucked her needle back into his bag so she wouldn't lose it in slumber. Nonetheless, its comfort stayed with her. The feel of the whalebone lingered on her fingers. She hoped it would call her mother into her dreams.

It wasn't her mother who answered.

Ariel dreamed she had never left Tree-Singer Abbey. She wandered alone through its halls until a figure moved out of the shadows.

"What do you want?" she called nervously. She couldn't forget that Misha was dead.

He reached both hands to her—either pleading or welcoming, she couldn't tell which. Slowly her hand rose to take one of his. The grip chilled her whole arm, like sinking the limb into snow.

The abbey shadows throbbed with the beat of her heart. Smiling now, Misha turned and led her toward an archway. That's when she noticed that the hand holding hers was stained red. It had to be blood. Ariel tried to pull away, but his grip was too strong, and her legs wouldn't obey her. She trailed him through one dark passage and into another until an imposing wooden door blocked the path. Misha raised one hand as if to push through.

Ariel did not want to go through that door. It was the door to his world, she was certain—a door to the land of the dead. Even if passing through meant she might see her mother, she was too terrified she could never come back.

At last she tore her hand from Misha's. He turned with a wounded expression. Then his gaze passed beyond her. Raising his hand to his eyes as if against a bright sun, he pointed.

"Ariel, someone is coming."

She looked but could see only darkness behind them. His palm touched her shoulder, setting off a ripple of fear. But he didn't drag her through his doorway. Instead, he shoved her mildly back the way they had come.

The dark hall blurred into the dark nook under the rock slab. Ariel found herself sitting upright, still feeling that gentle push on her back. Zeke slumbered beside her.

"Someone is coming." She heard Misha's voice again in her head, though from far away now. "See there."

Ariel peered out of their shelter. The moon danced behind scudding clouds, now bright, now veiled. To Ariel's sleep-swollen eyes, many of the shadows below seemed to waver. Two shadows, however, moved steadily toward her. Scarl and Elbert were finding their prey.

The squeeze of dread in her dream seemed a caress compared to what now crushed her chest. She couldn't breathe.

"Zeke!" She shook him. He started awake. "It's them! They're going to catch us!"

As he blinked himself alert, Ariel gauged the threatening shadows, already closer. They would arrive in less than ten minutes.

Spotting them also, Zeke groaned.

Ariel's gaze probed the darkness behind them. "Can we hide deeper inside?"

"I think they'll know we are here."

"We've got to run, then! Back to the abbey!" As she said it, she could see that their pursuers would cut off their path. To circle around the men in the moonlight without being noticed would be nearly impossible. Their own moving shadows would stand out as much as the two she watched with such horror now.

"We'd have to be able to fly." Zeke's voice had gone dull. That scared Ariel even more than the relentless shadows. If Zeke gave up, her will to resist would fade, too.

Racing the Finders over the mountains was not really a choice. Even if they didn't plunge over a cliff in the dark, they couldn't outrun the men. Still, Ariel would rather fall to her death than be ensnared by the Finders again.

"Ash said they wouldn't catch us," she moaned.

"No, he didn't." Wise to the partial truths that Tree-Singers sometimes had to tell, Zeke added, "He said they wouldn't catch us *until*. He just wouldn't say until what. It's not his fault. If this is the path before us, we have to take it." Though his voice still sounded flat, it held a resignation that echoed almost like strength.

"We can fight." Desperate, Ariel scanned the debris littering the ground. "It's two against two. We can let them get close and then hit them with rocks." She scurried to gather an armful of stones.

Zeke didn't move. He sat with his hands pressed to his eyes.

"Zeke!"

"Shut up!"

Even in her terror, Ariel felt his rebuff like a slap.

He added, more gently, "Be quiet a minute." He got up, keeping his eyes closed, and wandered deeper into their shelter. One hand trailed along the rock that slanted overhead.

Unable to fathom his actions, she checked on the two shadows' progress and reached for more weapons. Even if Zeke wouldn't fight, she would. Maybe the men would decide she wasn't worth it, or be hurt enough that she and Zeke could escape.

Zeke's voice drifted from the darkness behind her. Ariel turned. He wasn't speaking to her. It was garbled and faint, but she thought he was singing.

Poor Zeke. Ariel's fear shifted to make room for sorrow. He'd lost first his maple, then his trade, and now this. His mind seemed to be straining apart like a rotten fishnet, spilling songs in a place without trees. She'd protect him, though, for as long as her arms could fling rocks.

Shortly the singing fell silent. Zeke hurried to drop to his knees at her side.

"Listen. I know what you must do," he said. He took a deep breath. "Let them catch you."

"Are you crazy?" Ariel hissed. "We—"

"Aagh!" he cried, so loud the Finders may have heard. Echoes bounced off the rock. "There isn't much time! Do you trust me?" He rolled his head, anguished. His eyes flashed. "Do you?"

"No," Ariel wanted to say. "You're acting too strangely." She had come so far from anything she knew that everything around her seemed warped. Her throat tightened. This was Zeke before her, she reminded herself, Zeke from home, and he'd never done anything on purpose to hurt her.

"Yes," she said instead, forcing the word out. "I trust you."

"Then let them catch you," he repeated, snatching his blanket and pack. "If they think you escaped by yourself, and they don't know about me, we'll still have a chance. Don't throw the rocks. Don't fight at all. If you make them mad, they might hurt you."

They would already be mad and they would probably hurt her regardless, Ariel thought, but she kept that fear to herself.

Zeke squeezed her hand. "I'll be near, and Misha will be with you." Darting around the lip of the rock slab and hugging the rock, he vanished.

Ariel drew her blanket close, curled into a ball, and let loose the tears crowding into her throat. The two men would soon reach the shelter. Misha might be there to see them, but he couldn't stop them from punishing her. And bad men could do unspeakable things.

Trembling in the moonlight, she waited for the Finders to come.

By the time their feet crunched in the gravel before the stone slab, Ariel's weeping had worn itself out. She lay near the entry, balefully watching their approach. They came directly but not too close together, as if they knew where she was but were ready to stop any flight. Just before they arrived, she buried her head in her arms and pretended to sleep. They may well have heard her crushed sobs, but if not, the less the Finders knew they'd been anticipated, the better.

The footsteps grew so loud she thought the men must soon tread on her. One pair of boots stomped past toward the back of the nook. All noise stopped. The silence was worse. To keep her eyes shut, Ariel had to clamp her lids so tight she saw shooting stars. She held her breath, awaiting a blow.

"She got a long way." Scarl stood over her, from the sound of it.

"If I had a horsewhip I'd give her a stripe for every mile." Elbert's voice echoed from the hollow behind her. "Plus a few more for the horse."

"He was my horse, not yours. But I still have his bridle if you'd like to try that."

"Don't tempt me. I might lash you for convincing me to take her in the first place."

"I know," Scarl said. "Listen. Why don't you go on to Libros straightaway in the morning? I'll follow with her. Save you the frustration."

"We'll see," Elbert growled.

The boot, when it came at last, only nudged Ariel's ribs. Overprepared for a kick, she jerked. She scrambled to her feet before her eyes fully opened. It wasn't hard to pretend to be panicked. She leaped for the entrance.

Scarl caught her arm, pulling her back and trapping her flailing body against his chest. Even once she stopped fighting, his arms remained doubled around her as though she were a sack of unruly potatoes.

"Princess! Forgive us for disturbing your rest!" Elbert returned from the back of the cave. Seeing his pale head emerge from the shadows terrified Ariel more than anything she'd ever seen of the ghost. His lips pulled back in a sarcastic smile that would have befitted a skull.

"We missed you. Didn't you enjoy our company?"

Resentment boiled into Ariel, almost replacing her fear. "Not half so much as I'd enjoy seeing your grave." Without thinking, she spat at Elbert.

Scarl laughed. Elbert's face buckled in fury. Ariel barely saw his fist coming. A flinch of Scarl's shoulder tipped her face away, but not far enough. Pain burst over one of her cheekbones. She slipped lower in his grip, the crook of his arm covering her face and nearly smothering her as she flung up her forearm. Knuckles glanced off the bridge of her nose, swept her arm out of the way, and ricocheted back across her eyebrows.

"Quit," Scarl growled. "You're hitting me more than her, and I'm not liking it much."

"Drop her, then, and give me a clean shot."

Ariel stiffened. Instead of releasing her, Scarl turned and carried her deeper into the niche where the moonlight and the breeze didn't reach.

"She's bleeding all over me as it is."

Ariel could feel blood from her nose drip over her lips. Although at least two of Elbert's blows had glanced off Scarl first, they still left her head buzzing. She sniffed back the blood in her throat.

"Best not to cry," Scarl murmured at her ear. Already sobbed dry, she had no intention of starting again. With the hand that was loose, Ariel wiped away blood.

"Oh, I plan to see a bit more of her blood once the sun rises," Elbert muttered. "In fact, we may see a grave, too, missy. Not mine, though. No indeed. I have a surprise for the morning."

Ariel opened her mouth, trying to think of a cutting reply. Feeling her inhale to speak, Scarl shifted his grip. His quick fingers found her bloody lips in the darkness. His thumb hooked her chin and snapped her mouth closed. He was telling her to be quiet.

"Yes," Elbert added. "We can all have a good time in the morning." He repeated that promise half under his breath, his voice falling flat to the earth.

Scarl put her down. Wrapping her in the blanket from his own pack so he didn't have to leave her unguarded for even an instant, he trussed her like a caterpillar in a cocoon. Once she was bound, he slid her farther back into the tight space and curled himself between her and the fresh air. Even if she had been able to move, she would have had to crawl over him to escape. Her lungs struggled. She wasn't sure there'd be enough air in the close dark for them both.

Her thoughts cried out to Zeke. How could he possibly free her again? Maybe he'd hurry back to the abbey for help.

The sixth or seventh time Elbert promised Ariel a good morning, she felt Scarl stir.

"Shut up," he called. "Get some sleep. Or your fine morning won't come."

She heard a rustle of his pack, then the slosh of a water jar. His hand felt for Ariel in the dark, patting as if to reassure himself that she was still there. Then a cold, wet bit of cloth slipped into the hand that could still reach her face. Wishing she would suffocate before sunrise, she pressed it to the parts of her face that hurt most.

Ariel lay awake even after the men's breathing took on the slow rhythm of sleep. The dawn still came before she was ready.

CHAPTER
20

"Come on out here," Elbert called cheerfully. "Out in the light. I want to make sure everyone can see." From the shelter's entry, he beckoned.

His eyes narrowing, Scarl sighed. He lifted Ariel, still ensconced, to her feet.

"Oh, untie her," Elbert said. "It'll be more fun if she can squirm."

Scarl took his time stripping off the bridle leather and blanket confining her. She pulled her arms gratefully loose. They'd fallen asleep in the tight constraints. Now they tingled. The feeling matched the apprehension in her belly. Elbert's voice had recovered its amusement, but Ariel didn't trust the dull light in his eyes.

He waited as Scarl escorted Ariel out. When she faltered, Scarl nudged her forward. She considered springing past Elbert down the hill. Falling and hitting her head on a rock might be better than whatever he had in mind.

She took too long to decide. She'd just shifted her weight to

the balls of her feet for a dash when Elbert stepped toward her
and grabbed her by the back of her neck.

"Oh, come along, princess."

He hauled her into the early light and then around the edge
of the rock slab. Ariel writhed and tried to jerk free from the
clamp on her neck. She struggled without much effect until the
spreading grin on Elbert's face told her she was only feeding his
pleasure. She made her limbs limp and heavy instead. They
matched her heart.

His grin fading, Elbert paused, looking over the slopes.

"So where is your little friend, then? The boy. Do you
know?"

Ariel gasped, unable to hide her horror.

"Sure! That secret is out," Elbert continued. "Are you surprised that we're not as dull as you think?" He shook her, his
big hand pinching her neck. The motion throbbed in the
swollen bridge of her nose.

"You were seen with him on the horse, at the roadhouse,"
Scarl said from behind them. "Ezekiel—am I right?"

Ariel slumped. Without Elbert's grasp she would have
dropped to her knees. If they knew about Zeke, she was lost.
Her remaining hope and defiance drained out. She should have
run and broken her neck while she'd had the chance.

"We'll flush him out," said Elbert. "For your sake, he'd better be close." Thrusting Ariel before him, he found a low edge
of the slab that wasn't too steep. He half pushed, half lifted her
onto the stone, then stepped up himself.

"A good view," Elbert said. "That's what he'll need."

Scarl hopped up behind.

Elbert tugged Ariel to the top of the slab. Beyond the edge
lay a ravine carved by the avalanche in which the slab had

originally fallen. Certain that Elbert planned to fling her down onto the sharp rubble below, she didn't resist. It would be over soon. She only hoped it wouldn't hurt too much. Her hands clasped the glass bead at her throat. Perhaps she would see her mother.

"That'll do," Elbert said, yanking her to a stop not far from the edge. He held her by the neck at right angles to the barrel of his chest. Cringing, she turned her head as far away as she could. She didn't want to see on Elbert's face the satisfaction she could hear in his voice. Surveying the meadows and cliffs, she couldn't help but look for Zeke, perhaps hiding behind a rock or a bush. Yet she would rather he be far away at the abbey by now, safe.

"Boy!" Elbert's bellow startled her. "You see this?" Like a dog with a rabbit, he shook Ariel by the neck. "We know you're out there. Can feel you, in fact. That's what Finders do. So no point in hiding. Come out."

Ariel scanned the mountainside. Other than a falcon in the distance, nothing moved. She wondered if even Misha had been scared away. Then she noticed that both Finders focused on the same clump of thimbleberry bush not far upslope, just beyond the rockfall debris. Unable to spy Zeke in the leaves, she looked away and hoped he'd gotten much farther than that.

"No?" Elbert called again. "Perhaps this will change your mind."

Expecting a push over the edge, Ariel held what she thought was her last breath.

Instead of shoving, Elbert brushed aside the flap of his coat. His hand returned with the long knife he kept sheathed at his belt. He raised it aloft. It glinted.

Fear slammed into Ariel like something important she had forgotten.

"You see this, as well?" Elbert hollered. His hand slashed downward, wrist flicking. A red line appeared against the dingy white of Ariel's left sleeve. Bemused, she gazed at it. A sting joined the mark along her forearm. Only then did she realize that he'd cut her. Once she knew what he'd done, burning pain slacked her knees. With a yank, Elbert held her upright.

She felt Scarl approach closer behind them, drawn to her blood like a shark.

"There's a bit more blood for us, hey, princess?" Elbert asked. "A bit neater than a fist, I'll admit."

Ariel clapped her right hand atop the crimson line. It welled up through her fingers. Though he didn't move, Elbert's next roar sounded fuzzy and distant.

"Boy! Show yourself now, while you can! Or watch something you might not want to see!" Elbert's grip shifted from Ariel's nape. His hand clenched her hair. Her chin cranked up to the sky. First she felt a startled twinge in the back of her neck—then the sharp line of pressure at her throat. Elbert's cold blade creased her skin just under her jaw.

Her eyes rolled at the blue sky. "No, Zeke!" she cried, as loud as the angle of her neck would permit. She feared the hoarse cry wouldn't carry. "Don't listen!"

Flick. The tip of the blade jumped to nip at her cheek before tucking back under her chin. Pain seared instantly this time. A tickle of blood coursed the curve of her jaw.

"Please," Elbert breathed. "Give me another."

"Elbert." Scarl's voice, close behind them, sounded hard. His usual hush had vanished.

"I'm busy," Elbert snapped. "Wait your turn."

"I don't think I will."

A hand cupped Ariel's jaw from behind. It yanked her upward and back, then down away from the knife, even as Elbert lurched half a step forward. She fell amid a tangle of legs.

Eyes darting, bewildered, she flattened herself on the stone. Had Zeke silently sneaked up to attack?

Scarl stepped over her, his left hand planted on Elbert's shoulder. His right hand wrapped the handle of his own knife. It had somehow become sheathed in Elbert's back.

Scarl withdrew it. The blade grated against bone. A splatter of blood hit the rock near Ariel's feet. Grimacing, Scarl plunged the knife back in and out again. Then his left hand gave Elbert a push. The big man crumpled to his knees on the stone, twitched, and tumbled out of sight over the edge.

CHAPTER
21

"I did not want to do that." Scarl's voice had returned to its usual murmur. "But I guess I've known for a while I would have to."

Ariel dragged her stunned eyes from the place where Elbert had disappeared. Scarl turned toward her. She skittered back out of reach.

"I'm sorry," he told her. "But he meant to kill you in any case. I could hear it in his voice. And he most certainly would have killed your friend."

Uncomprehending, her head spun. Feeling glued to the rock, she watched as he wiped the gory knife on the shin of his pants. The swish made her skin crawl. He tucked the blade back into its proper place at his hip.

"Zeke!" Scarl called. His voice rang across the hillside. "Come out, if you like. You needn't fear me."

His words unstuck her. "Don't listen!" Ariel cried again.

Scarl turned and raised one eyebrow at her. He took a step toward her. She scrambled farther away. She wanted to jump to her feet, but her legs couldn't seem to remember how.

"Shall I tend to those cuts," he asked, "or would you rather keep bleeding?"

"I'd rather be dead, too."

One corner of his mouth drew up. He dipped his head. "Suit yourself."

To her surprise, he stepped away down the slanted face of the slab, back the way they had come. She watched him jump from the low ledge and disappear around its base toward the nook where they'd slept, which was hidden from view.

Ariel stole a few breaths. Pain wormed its way through her shock. Wet rivulets ran from her forearm to stain her clothes and the stone. She cupped a hand to her bleeding cheek. The only sounds were chittering birds and a slight hiss of wind. The falcon she'd seen a moment before, still in the sky, circled closer. It seemed to belong to some other world.

Ariel edged partway down the rock, wondering exactly where Scarl was. A motion caught her eye. Zeke sidled into view not far away, descending from his hiding spot and circling around the slab toward her. When their eyes met, he gestured, asking if she was okay. She turned her palms up, uncertain, and then pointed in the direction where Scarl had disappeared. Zeke nodded. From his position, perhaps he could see the Finder even now.

Sudden nausea whirled in Ariel's stomach. A black buzz in her head warned she might faint. She scooted on her backside the rest of the way to the ground.

Zeke hurried to meet her. She threw her arms to cling to him, wobbly.

Stretching his fingers to her bloody cheek, he blurted, "I was so afraid I was wrong!"

"Where is he?" Ariel's head swiveled. She tried to decide whether to run, and if so, which direction.

"He climbed around to where Elbert fell and made sure he was dead. And took a few things from his pockets. Now he's just sitting by our cave, waiting."

"No. I got tired of waiting." Scarl had slipped, quiet as a breeze, around the front corner of the slab. He folded his arms to regard them. "You look about to pass out," he told Ariel. "Come and let me make up for some of the abuse that you've taken."

"You just want to trade me for something and not share what you get." Ariel's mind had begun working again, and she squared her shoulders alongside Zeke. "But it's two against one now."

A thin smile touched Scarl's lips. "I'll go you one better than that." He pulled out his knife again. Knowing how quick he could use it, Ariel quailed. But the Finder merely thrust it into the soil near his feet. He directed his next words to Zeke.

"I'll be sitting there, waiting, as you said." He held the boy's eyes for a long moment before he retreated again.

Ariel stumbled, weak kneed, to the knife. She found she did not want to touch it. Zeke didn't mind. He pulled it out of the earth and tilted it, appraising.

"I think he's not what he seems," he told Ariel.

"You don't know him. I do."

"I was watching. It looked to me like he just saved your life."

She shook her head, frustrated. Yet his words stuck, and memories flitted through her mind. Not all were welcome, particularly those in which Scarl had helped her stay warm or protected her, even subtly, from Elbert. Such reminders made it harder to hate him—but hatred had sustained her, and she feared giving it up.

By the time she and Zeke pushed around the corner of the slab, she was angry as well as in pain.

Scarl looked up. He sat on a stone just outside of where they'd slept. A few items from his pack lay scattered at his feet.

"Good. I shouldn't have expected either of you to trust me," he told Zeke. "I won't give you cause to use it, but keep that blade ready if you like. Come here, Ariel."

"Go ahead," Zeke murmured to her.

"Don't worry, I won't grab you." Scarl shook his head. "I can't trade anything for you. I never expected to."

"Why did you steal me, then?" Ariel demanded.

"The man who sent us would prefer you were dead. I've been trying to keep you alive. But I didn't get to you before Elbert caught up with me, and neither of us expected someone so young. That changed things."

"You're not really a Finder, are you?" Zeke asked. Ariel suspected he was remembering something Ash had said.

Scarl shrugged. "I can find. It's not all I know how to do."

"Like killing people?" she blazed. "And stealing children?"

Scarl rested his elbows on his knees and studied the dirt at his feet. "Both were easier than they should have been," he said softly. "But I think both had to be done."

"Why?" Zeke wondered. He and Ariel swapped a glance.

"I'll tell you as much as I know. But it will take time. Please, Ariel—who once would be Healtouch—if you won't let me, you'll have to do something yourself. You only have so much blood." He gestured to her arm.

She looked down at her crimson-soaked sleeve. Maybe she moved her eyes too rapidly. Certainly she'd had too much strain that morning and nothing to eat. Her head swam. Her knees buckled next.

Scarl and Zeke both reached to catch her. Scarl's arms were longer and he wasn't occupied with a knife. He settled her against the rock he'd been perched on. She didn't like it, but she no longer had the will to resist.

"Zeke, dig a jar from my pack and fill it with fresh water," Scarl said. "The stream's just over there. You can take your eyes off me for that long, I promise."

"I know," Zeke said, already moving.

Scarl ripped the slit in Ariel's sleeve wider and eased the gooey fabric from the wound. He winced.

"I can see the bone in there, girl. It must hurt."

"Not as much as my cheek."

His gaze moved to her face. "That's not so deep, at least. That one can wait."

At first, the icy water Zeke brought stung her more than the knife had. Whimpers pushed through her clamped teeth. Finally the cold numbed some of the hurt.

Scarl pulled Orion's horsehair from his mended shirt to make stitches in Ariel instead. To make it stronger, he doubled it over. Looking at the length of the gash in her arm, Ariel thought it a good thing she'd mended more than one place in his shirt.

As he threaded his needle, he warned her, "This is going to hurt, but it's got to be done. Zeke and I will try to give you something else to think about."

"The telling dart," she insisted. "I want to know why it matters so much."

He reached into a pocket. Ariel drew back, and her eyes

darted to Zeke. The knife hung limp in his grip. But when Scarl's hand reappeared, his fingers bore only the brass dart.

"It's yours," he said. "Take it."

She did. He bent to her wounded arm. She braced herself.

"Ready?" Scarl asked.

At her nod, his fingers squeezed the wound's edges together. She mashed her lips tight. A prick of the needle was followed by the sinuous drag of the horsehair. Those hurts were all but lost in the greater throbs that consumed everything below her elbow.

"What does the dart say?" she asked through gritted teeth.

Scarl shook his head as he stitched. "It's a summons, but I can't understand most of it. That's one of the reasons I needed Elbert. He seemed to know."

"Was he telling the truth when he said nobody knows who sent it?"

"Yes. You can see for yourself that the dart's tail end is blank. That's where the sender's mark should appear."

Storian had said the same thing. Blinking away the water blurring her eyes, Ariel checked again anyway.

"But I do recognize the sign for the receiver," Scarl added.

Zeke said, "The lightning bolt, right?"

"Farwalker," Ariel declared, mostly to see how Scarl would react.

"You've figured that out, then." He didn't look up from her wound.

Ariel exchanged a triumphant smirk with her friend. "But everyone thinks there aren't any left—" She flinched at an especially clear jab of the needle.

Scarl raised his eyes. "I meant it when I said it was yours.

There's one left—or I should say there's one yet to be. I'm convinced this dart came for you."

The respect in his gaze may have given weight to the words. Or perhaps she'd simply been drawn far enough from her old life to be open to one that was new. Ariel stroked the lightning bolt mark. It seemed to buzz under her fingertip.

"I don't know how to be a Farwalker, though," she protested meekly.

"Not yet, maybe," Zeke said at her side.

"You asked what I did besides finding," said Scarl as he stitched. "I often feel like a Fool. But they say a Fool sees the truth when wise folk don't dare, and I can see the Farwalker in you. You're on the path, Ariel. You just don't recognize it."

Ariel shivered. She looked closer at her mark on the dart, seeing it for the first time as equal to the trade marks below it, which showed who else had received the same message. She frowned. Another symbol had vanished.

"There were marks for every trade when we found it," she said.

"I saw them, too." Zeke peeked over her shoulder. "But now two are missing."

"The Judge symbol disappeared right away," Ariel added. "I noticed when—" She stopped. She didn't want Scarl to know about her copy. "The next day."

He may have assumed she merely was wincing. "If the person a dart is intended for dies, his symbol soon fades, along with the message. Elbert carried one completely blank dart. It had been sent to a Judge. What you've said tells me there's another blank one somewhere."

"Someone is killing them." Zeke's voice had dropped to a whisper.

Ariel gulped at Scarl. "Elbert. And you?" She wanted to pull her arm away from him. With the needle in it, she didn't dare.

"No, not me. Please believe that." He looked into her eyes. She stared back, unblinking, but she didn't feel like a good Fib-Spotter today. The lies seemed too tangled with truth.

"But why?" Zeke asked. "Kill them, I mean?"

"I can only guess, Zeke, without knowing precisely what the darts say. What I do know is this: besides your Farwalker's dart, another dozen went out. Thirteen in all. But not to just any-one. Elbert lied about that. They went to the strongest, the most skilled, the top of the trade, whoever that might be. The Tree-Singer dart went to Mason—"

"Who's Mason?" asked Zeke.

"He sent out the Finders," Ariel told him.

Zeke grunted, indignant.

"I'm surprised you don't know the name," Scarl said. "Appar-ently the trees speak well of him to other singers. Another dart went to an old Storian named Liam. They both live in Libros. Liam must have told Mason what the dart said."

"Or his tree told him," Zeke guessed.

Distaste twisted Scarl's features, but he didn't argue.

"Who got the Finder's dart?" Ariel asked. "You?"

Scarl snorted. "Hardly. Elbert." At her incredulous expres-sion, one corner of his mouth twitched. "It wasn't a dart for a good man," he added. "It was a dart for a very good Finder."

"I can't believe Elbert could understand all those symbols," she said.

"Oh, he couldn't. He had no patience for that sort of thing. But Liam Storian is known for his relics collection—Elbert mentioned it to you, I think—and our friend Elbert figured that was the one place where the dart might be worth something in trade. So he took his dart to Libros, too. That's how Elbert met Mason. Through Liam."

Ariel scowled at her dart, putting names to a few of the trade marks. "Well, that Storian's mark is one of the two that have vanished."

Scarl stopped stitching to peer at the dart for himself. His brow furrowed as he returned to his work.

"How'd you get in the story, if you didn't get a dart?" Zeke asked.

"Mason sent Elbert to round up a handful of Finders, including me," Scarl replied. "We were to collect all the darts, if we could, and make sure those who received them did nothing. Those were the instructions I got, anyhow. For speed, we scattered, each working alone."

"So you went around stealing everyone's darts?" Ariel wondered how many homes besides Bellam Storian's had caught fire.

Scarl winced. "Didn't have to," he said. "Most people can't understand them. Everyone I dealt with was happy to trade a confusing bit of brass for some finding. But I noticed the Farwalker sign among the others on the first dart I tracked down. That's when I started wondering what was really going on. We'd been told that the message was meaningless, but if a Farwalker lived, and the darts thought one did, that alone was news no one should ignore. Besides, I've spent much of my life searching for old knowledge and old ways, and I'd give a lot to ask questions of anyone who's traveled more than I have. So I went straight for the Farwalker dart."

Scarl knotted a stitch before he went on. "Elbert caught up with me first. He wanted to team up on the few darts remaining, and he insisted we go for the nearest. It had gone to a Judge. Do you know how Judges work?"

"Not really," Zeke said. "We don't have one in Canberra Docks."

"A good Judge can tell a lie from the truth in a voice or through the brush of a hand. That's one way they settle disputes. Anyhow, when we got to our Judge, Elbert held back and made me take the lead. Now I know why—he thought I'd fool her more easily, since all I knew was what I'd been told."

"Even I knew he was lying," Ariel said.

Scarl wagged his head. "Mm. That's why he needed me. But Mason is much more convincing, and I didn't yet realize how much I'd been misled, nor why. Still, the Judge knew something was wrong, and she wouldn't give up the dart. Thinking she might have some glimpse of the truth, I was waiting for a chance to talk with her alone. Before I got it, Elbert silenced her. Permanently."

"You didn't stop him?" Zeke sounded hurt.

Scarl sighed and rubbed one eyebrow with the back of his wrist. "I had no idea it would happen. And it's not easy to be on one side of a fight while pretending to be on the other. But I knew then that the Farwalker needed protection. If it wasn't already too late."

Ariel eyed the places on her dart that had gone recently blank. They gave her a chill.

"And that's when you came to Canberra Docks?" she asked.

Threading the needle anew, Scarl nodded. "At first I thought we'd come on a goose chase. The dart was broken. You just stumbled on it by accident. That's what Elbert thought, too. When you failed your Naming test, though . . . I had to give him some other options. I couldn't make the same mistake twice."

"So you snatched me." She couldn't keep the bitterness from her voice.

His gaze rose again to meet hers. "I was trading for time. I almost lit out with you when he went to the roadhouse, too, and I probably should have, but I worried he might get his hands on another horse to catch us. And we're still a long way from anyone I'd call a friend."

Ariel blinked as what he'd said meshed with things she already knew. This time, she did yank her arm from his grasp. She no longer cared about the added pain her jerk caused. Greater anguish had awakened within.

"You let Elbert kill my mother!" She hurled herself forward. Her fists pounded against him. "You knew he probably would, and you let him!"

He accepted her blows a long while, his eyes clenched in his wan face. Finally he wrapped his arms around her to contain her.

"I couldn't stop him," he murmured. "It was all I could do to stop him from killing you, and that's far more important. Though I don't imagine you'll understand that anytime soon."

"Never!" Overflowing with grief and anger and mottled confusion, Ariel sobbed and struggled against him. He let her go. She snatched up her dart from where it had dropped and hammered it down at him like a spike. He held her off, trapping her fist. She kicked him instead.

The blows dwindled as her rage sank back to sorrow.

Still holding her at bay, Scarl gave Zeke a helpless look. "Maybe you'd better finish her stitches."

Zeke blanched. With a sympathetic sigh, he put his free hand to his friend's shoulder. "Ariel, just let him get done with your arm."

"No," she moaned. But her struggling stopped. She drooped, limp.

Gingerly, Scarl released her, resting his hands on her shoulders. "I *am* sorry. I didn't want what happened in Canberra Docks. What Elbert told me made me sick. And I hated treating you harshly. I had to, if I was to keep Elbert's trust enough to keep you alive. If he had doubted me any more than he did, he would have finished you long before now. And it took me a while to . . . to face the idea of killing someone myself."

Letting go of her shoulders, he blew a long breath through pursed lips. "I could only hope the rough treatment was making you stronger," he added. "But I would make amends for as much as I can."

Unforgiving, she refused to meet Scarl's gaze. He reached again for her left arm.

Giving herself over to impulse, Ariel dodged. Without thought, she grabbed the knife from Zeke's slack grip and raised it. Two quick steps put the tip of the blade at Scarl's throat.

CHAPTER
22

"Ariel! Stop!" Zeke's plea didn't reveal who he most feared would get hurt.

Now that she held the knife at Scarl's throat, she wasn't sure what would come next. He might snatch the knife back. She was certain he could. His hands had frozen in midair between them, and she almost wanted him to grab for the weapon. For a moment, the shock of wild actions covered the hole in her heart.

Watching her face, he made his hands sink slowly again.

Those hands dropping made Ariel feel powerful. Stretching her arm, she pressed the knife's tip into the soft skin below his Adam's apple. A dimple circled the point. Scarl drew his neck back from the pressure, but otherwise he didn't move.

At last he whispered, "What now?"

It took a few seconds for words to flow into Ariel's mouth. "Prove it," she snarled. "Prove that you're sorry. Prove anything you've said. I don't believe you."

Scarl returned her fierce gaze. Ariel could hear her pulse

pound in her skull. She waited for him to argue or snicker or plead.

"I don't know how," he said finally. She felt the motion of his throat through the knife.

"I can take you to people who will vouch for me," he added. "Or I could take you to Mason, but I won't. I don't think either of us would leave Libros alive. Here, though, Ariel? I have nothing but things you've already seen. What proof would you have me give?"

Ariel glared, unable to answer.

"He's telling the truth," Zeke muttered behind her.

"How do you know?" she demanded.

"I . . . I don't want to tell you." Zeke shifted uncomfortably. "I'm not sure you'll believe me, either."

Ariel resisted the strong urge to twist her neck for a good stare at her friend. He'd rarely said anything so strange. How could Zeke possibly earn the distrust she gave Scarl?

"Try," she told Zeke. Her attention remained fixed on the Finder.

"The stone slab told me," her friend said. "I can hear it muttering to me even now."

Before her snort of disbelief faded, Zeke hurried to add, "I finally worked it out. The voices I've heard lately weren't trees— they were stones. I just never knew stones spoke. So it took me a long time to figure out what it was and how to talk back."

Scarl raised one skeptical eyebrow. Ariel did not want to share his reaction, but if she took Zeke on faith, she had to accept his assurance about the Finder.

Unwilling to retreat, she racked her mind for a way to test Scarl's word. She knew nothing of Judges. And other than a marriage ring, she could think of only one thing she'd ever seen given as proof of a vow.

"All right," she told Scarl, "if you're so sorry, bleed on it."

Zeke winced, but Scarl's regard never wavered.

"I will," he replied. "If that's what you want." His eyes dropped to the knife between them. "Do you want to do it? Or shall I?"

The knife abruptly felt very large and dangerous in Ariel's hand. Her classmates made blood vows with their fingertips and a fishhook—not blades half as long as her arm. If it had not rested against his throat, the knife would have trembled.

"You." Hastily she relinquished the knife. Only after it was out of her grasp did she wonder if she'd made any mistake in giving it back.

"He's bleeding already," Zeke pointed out.

Ariel saw what he meant. A red dot rose over Scarl's windpipe. She'd put it there.

Scarl swiped at the drop with a fingertip. "I doubt that will do. Will it?"

Ariel became aware they were playing a game. She didn't know how to win, but she wouldn't back down. Troubled, she frowned.

Scarl said, "I didn't think so. What will?"

Ariel shifted her feet and stared at the knife.

Watching, he cocked his head. "Ariel . . . are you testing me—or yourself?"

She wouldn't have given him an answer if she'd had one.

He nodded. "That's all right." His eyes swept to her left arm. "I'll tell you what—I'll match you. Fair enough?" Without waiting for any response, he yanked up his sleeve. The edge of the blade pressed his forearm. He snapped the opposite wrist.

Ariel looked away, but not fast enough. Her stomach flopped. When she looked back, red welled into the fresh slit in his skin. It spilled over.

"I have never lied to you and I never will," Scarl said softly. "There was a reason I let Elbert do most of the talking."

Ariel's gaze followed the crimson drops spattering the earth at his boots. Not even the blood from her own arm that morning had seemed to belong so much to her.

"All right," she sighed, suddenly tired and empty. She took a step back. Her legs wanted to fold.

"Ariel, look at me."

Reluctant, she raised her eyes again to Scarl's face. She expected a victorious smirk. Instead, a sad shadow hung in his eyes.

"Did you find out what you wanted to know?"

Ariel considered. He'd done what she'd asked, if not a bit more. She had some idea now how it felt to hurt him in return, and she'd enjoyed the bitter satisfaction of holding a knife on somebody else. But she did not feel like she'd won. She just wanted to be Ariel again—even if being herself meant having a heart and a conscience that could ache.

She nodded.

"There are men you would shame with your courage," he said quietly. "But I'm sorry that a girl from Canberra Docks had to pick up a weapon in vengeance."

Too drained to reply, she sank next to Zeke.

Scarl ripped the tail from his shirt and bound it tight around his arm. Then he offered the knife back to Zeke.

"I don't want it." Zeke shuddered.

"Will you take it just to rinse it for me? In the stream? I'll finish Ariel's stitches." He glanced at her for permission.

She examined her forearm. Many black lines and snarls of knot dotted her skin. Blood oozed, but she didn't see any mends that had broken. All but one gaping inch had been done. She held it out for him to proceed.

Seeing that, Zeke accepted the knife.

"Maybe when you come back you can tell us more about your talking stones," Scarl suggested.

Zeke reddened. "Maybe not," he muttered, hurrying away toward the creek.

Scarl found the needle where it had dropped. Rethreading it, he kneeled before Ariel and went back to work.

Feeling woozy, she tipped her head back and closed her eyes. She pretended the breeze drying the blood on her face could lift her away. Shortly, it did.

Ariel's eyelids didn't spring apart again until Scarl touched her cheek. Her arm had been wrapped snugly in cloth that seemed familiar, but her fuzzy brain couldn't identify it.

"You all right?" Scarl asked.

"Not very," she mumbled.

"Close your eyes again, then. I'm going to clean this cut on your face, but that's all. I think stitches will make a worse scar. I'm afraid when you look into a glass you might always be reminded of Elbert."

She shuddered. She knew he was right.

When Scarl finally left her wounds alone to throb, Zeke crept closer.

"Hurts a lot, huh?" he asked.

She nodded.

"I hope you're not mad."

"At what?" She stiffened. "Oh! You didn't say all that weird stuff about stones just so I'd drop the knife, did you, Zeke?"

She'd indeed be adrift, her last anchor lost, if her friend had begun lying to her, even for what might be a good reason.

"No, no. I couldn't have made that up." He gestured to her bound arm. "He needed a bandage. I looked in your stuff." Following his glance, she spotted her bag, which the Finders had hauled with them.

"That was all I could find that looked clean," added Zeke.

Recognition jolted Ariel. The cloth on her arm had been ripped from the skirt her mother had made her for Namingfest Day. Her fingers smoothed the yellow fabric as if she could touch her mother's hands through it. Tears fell on the cloth.

"It's all right," she murmured. "It's no good wearing a skirt out here anyway."

Scarl returned from the creek. He rubbed his face with his damp hands. "Feel okay?"

She sniffled. "I guess."

"If you know a plant that will dull the pain, tell me. All I need is a name. I don't have to recognize something to be able to find it."

Ariel scanned the meadow. The names of plants that might help were clouded by throbbing, and a Naming test memory, and shame.

"Maybe later," she sighed.

"Whenever you think of one."

Sinking to rest in the dirt across from Ariel and Zeke, Scarl let out a breath in a rush. "Well, that's done," he said. He pulled off his cap and ran a hand through his curls. "Now. We're all tired and you're heartsick and Zeke's talking crazy and I'm not sure what to do. But let's get one more thing out of the way. You've got a choice." His eyes flicked sideways, making sure Zeke listened, too.

"I don't think it's the right thing, exactly," Scarl went on, "but I will take you and Zeke home, if you want."

Ariel's heart leaped at the mention of home. It fell partway back when it struck against the knowledge of what wasn't there. Still, for the first time that morning, she noticed the sunshine. It glinted off the basalt rock and meadow grass around them.

"What's the other choice?" Zeke wanted to know.

Scarl regarded them both. "Let me take you to someone who might understand the summons on your dart," he said. "If we can figure it out, and it's not too late, I'll go with you to answer the summons."

"But we can't get the message inside," Ariel said. "Since it's broken."

"I know. We might fail."

"Who cares, anyway?" she grumbled, surprised by an odd sense that she had been cheated of some unknown prize. "Even if it isn't too late, nobody else will probably answer, according to you. The message is wasted."

Scarl pressed his palms together in front of his lips, choosing his words. Except that his eyes remained pinned on her, he looked almost as though he were praying.

"I'm not sure the message is what's most important," he said. "What's important is sitting before me. There's a Farwalker here, a young one, after everyone thought they were gone. And I can't believe it is only coincidence that those darts weren't sent until now. I think there's something you need to do."

He raised a hand to halt the questions that flocked to her lips. "I don't know for sure what it is. But I can tell you this from my travels: knowledge is shrinking. One village is becoming a myth to the next, because almost nobody passes between

them. Every Storian knows less than the person who taught
him. Every Healtouch dispenses more hope and fewer medi-
cines that work. I've been places with neither—hard, frightening places—because once there's no master there can be no
apprentices, and new masters never arrive. A Farwalker might
be able to fix that, eventually. And the dart is the first step to
finding out how."

Ariel tingled with both interest and dread. Although she'd
warmed to the Farwalker name, what he suggested sounded
arduous, uncertain, and scary. She rolled the troublesome dart
between her fingers. Its two signs for danger had shifted again,
leaving just one. Still, one was bad enough. Her curiosity
fought with a much-defied yearning for a measure of safety and
comfort.

"The dart says it's still dangerous, though." She pointed out
the ‡ sign her mother had shown her. "Even with Elbert gone."

Her statement caused a commotion before Ariel convinced
Scarl that she understood nothing more on the dart. Disappointed, he said, "Well, I don't need the dart to know danger
still lurks. The people in Libros believe Mason knows all, and
most of them will do whatever he asks. I wouldn't be here if
that wasn't true. It took a lot of effort—and wealth—to locate
so many Finders and tempt us so far from our homes."

Before Ariel could ask what had been promised, Zeke raised
a more practical question. "If we go home now," he wondered,
"will more Finders come?"

Scarl's teeth dragged at his lip. "Probably. Especially once
Elbert never shows up. I'll do what I can, but . . ." He shrugged.
"I'm alone. They won't be."

Even the thought of another stranger like Elbert sent a

tremor through Ariel's bones. Adventure and intrigue whispered from a distance; the pain in her arm shouted right here. It swayed her. She was afraid to go home, and it might cause the village more trouble, but Ariel longed to forget her unpleasant ordeals and return to familiar places and people.

She had just opened her mouth to say so when a breeze lifted her hair. Cold fingers slid over the slice on her face. But it wasn't merely a breeze.

Zeke pulled a sharp breath. "Look." He pointed.

On the boulder behind her, a bloody handprint appeared.

Scarl scrambled to his feet.

"Misha," Ariel explained. "He's a ghost."

As they watched, the wet print melted and ran, reshaping into a red bolt of lightning.

Shivering, Scarl rubbed the back of his neck. His gaze roved their surroundings, then returned to flash between the symbol and Ariel's face.

"You're not scared," he observed.

She shrugged. "He's done it before."

"If even the spirits are with you, then woe to those who oppose you," he said. "I certainly wouldn't. What do you want to do?"

Looking down, Ariel fingered her dart. A knot formed in her stomach. She knew why the handprint had appeared on the rock just as Scarl posed their choice. She didn't want to know, but she did. That glistening trade mark represented a purpose. She would never be able to forget that she'd seen it. A life catching fish might not be so bad, but she would always wonder what she had missed—or what she was meant to do. And she couldn't be a Farwalker if she went home to Canberra Docks.

The Finder saw her reluctance.

"I know it's a lot to ask," he told her. "I'm sure you must wish you'd never laid eyes on it. But that dart found you for a reason. Take up the path laid before you. I will help you as much as I can. But I might guess the world, and maybe the spirits, won't leave you alone if you don't."

Less concerned about spirits than her own nagging conscience, Ariel glanced at Zeke. He didn't look happy, but he nodded. She realized her decision must have shown on her face.

"I guess if I'm the only one, I'd better get to work," she joked, trying to drive back her fear. Zeke squeezed her hand.

Scarl didn't smile, but his eyes gleamed. Crouching before them, he reached his own fingers to cover Zeke's hand clasping hers. "You *are* the only one, but you're not alone," he said. "I'll do my best to keep the last Farwalker safe, and we'll try to find out together what the dart and your new calling means. It's the least I can do to help revive a lost trade—and atone for the ways that you've suffered. I'll try to make the rest of our journey less frightening and more pleasant than it has been. For both of you."

"No ropes," Ariel said.

Scarl winced. "Of course not. I'm sorry."

"And more food."

"I'll try." He chuckled. "I can usually find something, if you won't be too picky."

"And you'll take us home when we say. Whether we figure out the summons or not."

His amusement faded. He dipped his head. "Yes. I won't try to persuade you again." His gaze slid once more to the red mark beside her, and he ran a hand over his mouth. "I can't speak for him."

"I know. That's okay."

"We're agreed, then." Scarl's mouth twitched. "Do you want blood on those vows?"

Ariel groaned.

"I was joking," he added quickly. "I think we've seen enough blood for a while."

"For forever," Zeke muttered.

Scarl's eyes found him. "I hope you're right." He started to add something else. Changing his mind, he tightened his jaw.

"Can we rest here awhile first?" Ariel thought of the abbey, but she suspected that Ash would gently turn them away.

"Until you feel strong enough to walk." Scarl cast her a wry grin. "I somehow lost my horse."

She couldn't bring herself to smile back.

"I want something to eat anyway," Zeke announced. "Before we go anywhere."

Scarl rose to his feet. "I'll work on that."

Thus, long after Namingfest Day, Ariel took up the Far-walker name. It was assigned by a ghost, not won through a test, but she'd already faced far more pain and fear than any Naming test was intended to hold. She had little idea what her trade would require, nor could she look to any master to follow. By the next morning, though, she wanted to lose the ache of her arm in the rhythm of walking. Her instincts were emerging, even if she wasn't aware of them yet.

When she announced that she was ready to go, Scarl appraised their packs and transferred their heaviest items into his own.

"Where are you taking us, anyway?" Zeke asked him.

Scarl straightened and shouldered his pack. "To the best Storian I know, one I trust with our lives. He works in a place called Hartwater, about a week's journey from here. If anyone can figure out the dart's summons, it's him. So come on, Farwalker." He offered his hand to help her rise from her seat in the dirt. "Your future awaits."

Even his courage would have failed if he'd known where the Farwalker's path would take them. By then, though, Ariel had taken the lead.

PART THREE

STONE-SINGER

CHAPTER
23

Zeke lay on a boulder, his cheek against the sun-heated rock. Ariel and Scarl rested in the shade at its base, licking ground-melon juice from their fingertips. The tart liquid would have pricked tears from Ariel's eyes, but her body didn't have the moisture to spare. Over the past several days they had traipsed out of the mountains and into an arid waste of blowing sand and stone outcrops that Scarl called the Drymere. The wild melons helped relieve not only their hunger but the dogged thirst they could not escape.

"Want the last melon, Zeke?" Ariel called from where she sat cross-legged in the sand.

Zeke pushed himself from the stone and slid down to the ground. Ariel rose to brush rock grit from his cheek and hand him the palm-size orange fruit.

He took it automatically. "Men are coming this way," he told Scarl. "More than one."

The Finder, who had dropped to his haunches to eat, shot to his feet. He squinted to scan the horizon.

"Where did you see them?" he asked.

Zeke studied the groundmelon. "I didn't," he mumbled. "The stone told me."

"Don't sound so embarrassed," Scarl replied. "Did it say where?"

Zeke raised his splinted forearm to point north. Ariel saw nothing in the distance but puddles of heat. As best she could guess, the direction he indicated was almost opposite Canberra Docks, many miles and mountains away. The approaching men weren't chasing behind them, but might cross their path as Scarl led her and Zeke toward Hartwater.

"How far away?" Scarl asked.

Zeke wrinkled his face. "Distance is hard. Stones don't think about motion like we do. Half a day? Maybe less."

Scarl's gaze fell on Ariel, his eyes betraying his concern that the men were coming for her. "Best move on," he said. He gestured toward a rock ridgeline that had teased them for hours, seeming to retreat as they made their way toward it. "We need to reach the water hole before they do. Just in case." He crouched and motioned to Ariel.

She scowled. Scarl had taken to carrying her on his shoulders not long after they'd entered the Drymere. He'd crossed it before, he knew where water could be found, and the crossing would save them valuable time they might need to answer the telling dart's summons, if they could figure it out. He'd neglected to account, however, for traveling companions whose legs were not as long nor as hardened as his. They trudged without complaining, but together the three of them couldn't move quickly enough between water holes to prevent the spring sun from dangerously parching their bodies. It annoyed Ariel, though, that Scarl bore her, but never Zeke, when he wanted to move fast.

"I can walk quicker now that I've rested," she said. When he started to argue, she added, "And if I'm on your shoulders, and they're closer than Zeke thinks, they'll be able to see us from farther away."

"Good point. At least let me take your pack, then, stubborn." He stuffed her meager bag into his own, and they set off. Ariel panted to keep up. She pretended not to see the Finder glancing sideways and slowing his pace.

"The stone said something else, something odd," Zeke volunteered, also huffing. "Maybe I didn't understand right, but I think it said the men forgot with their hands and their feet."

"They for—? Oh." Scarl's strides faltered, then resumed.

"You know what it means?"

Scarl didn't answer. Having grown used to his taciturn ways, Ariel and Zeke simply turned their attention to the novelties around them. Never having been in a desert before, they were constantly amazed at the snake tracks and beetles, the spiked plants and odd patterns they found in the sand. Sharing their discoveries helped them forget the sticky thirst in their mouths.

Eventually, Scarl broke the silence. "Zeke doubted once that I was a Finder," he said. "Do you remember?"

They nodded.

"I apprenticed for a while as a Storian."

"You did not!" The disbelief burst from Ariel before she could stop it. She couldn't match her shadowy and usually silent protector to the only Storian she knew. Old Bellam was chatty and fond of tea at a hearth. Ariel doubted he could have killed a fish flopping on the sand. She'd seen Scarl kill a man.

He laughed at her reaction. "I'm sure your doubt is no compliment. But it's true."

"How old are you, Scarl?" Zeke wondered.

Scarl hesitated, either adding or considering whether to answer. "Twenty-nine."

Zeke and Ariel exchanged a glance. More than twice their age sounded plenty old, but from Scarl's closed, careworn face, both would have guessed older.

"I'm sure your Storian taught you about the Blind War," he said. "Did he tell you much about what happened after, once sight returned?"

"Not really," Ariel said, trying to remember.

"Only how the trades grew," Zeke added, "but that was mostly while everyone was still blind."

Scarl looked sidelong at them both. "We'll pretend my name is Scarl Storian, then, as it once was. I will tell you a story. It concerns the men we might meet. And it concerns you, Ariel."

She met his eyes. He looked away first, to the horizon.

"Imagine this," he said, using the opening to so many stories. "The Blind War has ended, its causes forgotten. For the first time in many long years, babies are being born who can see! The generations before them never lost hope that sight would return, so they'd devised clever tests, and soon the young children who pass speak of stars in the sky, distant birds, rainbows—things their parents know only from stories but the youngsters sense through their eyes. Yet some of the things that they're seeing confuse them: machines with mysterious purposes, devices their parents have heard of but no longer know how to use."

"They must have figured out a few things," Zeke said.

"More or less," Scarl said. "But the telling darts are a rather sad example. They seemed to be nearly alive. If you held one just so, symbols appeared and would shift with your thoughts. All that was needed to send it was to think of the receiver and fling it into the air. The Essence seemed to take care of the rest. Yet the meanings of so many symbols were lost, the darts became more of a plaything than a tool."

"Or a way to summon a Healtouch," Ariel said, remembering her mother's story.

"That's a better use than most," Scarl said. "And even things like the darts that worked for a while soon stopped, their power exhausted, or the knowledge and materials for repairing them lost. The Allcrafts didn't have time to fuss with curiosities. They could barely keep up with the basic goods needed most to survive."

Zeke sighed wistfully. "All that great stuff lying around—flying houses and darts and fire in a jar. I would have tried harder to fix 'em."

"There was a reason they didn't," Scarl said. "They weren't sure those wonders weren't responsible, in some way, for the war. And once the babies who could see had grown up, they were terrified of repeating their forebears' mistake. Life was so very much harder without sight. Nobody wanted to fall back into darkness, so few would risk meddling with anything left from the old age. What still worked, people busted. They collected up every device they could find and destroyed it."

"I wish they would have saved some of the bikes," Ariel said wistfully. She'd always dreamed of coming across one overgrown in the woods. Bellam's tales had inspired a longing in her, a wish to speed over the earth, hither and yon. Now, struck by this reminder, Ariel wondered if her interest in bikes had been an early hint of her Farwalker trade.

"Some people wished more than that," Scarl went on. "A

few believed we could all learn a very hard lesson. They argued for keeping as much understanding and as many devices as we could recover. If we were careful, they thought, we could use what was left to make life better, without fighting over the marvels or turning them to foul purpose. Those people—mostly Storians—were outnumbered by the rest. We've been struggling to survive ever since."

Ariel said, "But that sounds like . . . like maybe you made a mistake while reciting in class, so you just gave up and stopped going to classes at all."

"This had much the same effect," Scarl said. "It's been called the Forgetting, and we don't even know what we've lost."

They walked on in silence beneath the searing sun, contemplating legends of marvels and magic. At last, Ariel interrupted the lonely swishing their feet made in the sand.

"Your story . . . you said it concerned me."

Scarl started. "I'd better finish it, I guess. Perhaps you see why I ended up as a Finder." He glanced toward the horizon. His feet stopped. "We have trouble first, though."

Ariel followed his gaze. Five black blotches swam through the distant heat waves, first close together and then farther apart. Their motion gave them away as more than a mirage.

Scarl dropped to his knees in the sand. "Sit down and hold still. I don't want them to see you, if it's not already too late. And don't speak for a moment. I need to concentrate." He dug in his pockets and pulled out a clear disk the width of a plum. Zeke murmured appreciatively. Ariel had seen it before only in glimpses, but she'd guessed what Scarl cradled now in his palm: a Finder's glass.

He tipped it to get the angle he wanted and then stared at it intently. A picture was supposed to appear inside it, Ariel thought. She watched the glass as closely as he did—and surely she imagined the red sparks that burst in its center.

"Stop looking into it, Ariel," Scarl said, without turning his head. "You're interfering."

"I am?" A thrill of excitement gave way to the sense she'd been scolded. She gazed instead at the menacing blobs on the horizon. When she glimpsed a motion from the corner of her eye, she glanced back at Scarl. He'd dropped the glass back into his pocket.

"There's a big dead tree not far over that rise." Scarl tilted his head toward it. "Since we're not going to make the water hole in time, we'll go there." He gave a few curt instructions. Nervous enough to obey, Ariel hopped up to cling piggyback along with his pack. Since Scarl couldn't carry them both, he draped one arm over Zeke's shoulder, keeping the boy so close they sometimes tripped on each other. Thus the three of them might look from a distance like only one body.

They jogged in the direction of the unseen dead tree. Jouncing, Ariel began to doubt Scarl's finding. But at last they topped a dune with sun-bleached wooden bones jutting from the slope below. The dry winds had uprooted the skeleton and piled sand against its trunk. Scarl dropped Ariel near the snarl of roots.

He scooped at the sand along the trunk with his hands. "Dig yourselves in here like this, and cover back up as much as you can. Don't choke on sand."

Zeke obeyed, using his splint like a hoe. Ariel waited while Scarl returned her pack and offered a water jar, half full, from his own.

"Here's what we've got left," he said. "Try not to drink it all."

Her hands lifted to take it. Scarl didn't let go.

"Listen, and hear me," he said. "I'm going to cover some tracks, and then I'm walking out to meet them. If it's easy, I'll be back soon and we'll be on our way toward Hartwater again." His tongue ran over his lips, which were chapped from the sun. "If it's not easy, I may take longer. I might even bring them here and pretend to discover you—or betray you. Do you understand me? I will just be pretending, but it must be convincing. And you must be convincing as well."

"Should we act surprised?" Zeke had paused in his digging to listen.

Scarl's sinister grin set Ariel's stomach aflutter. "I'll try to work it so you *are* surprised," he said. "I'll give you as many clues as I can what I've told them. But the less you say, the better. Cower and wail and don't fight too hard. If they're looking for you, that's what they'll expect. If they're not, we won't have to do it."

Apprehensive, Ariel nodded. Scarl released the jar, but his fingertips rose to brush her scabbed cheek. The knife wound had begun to mend, but Zeke had told her it still looked bad.

"Lying is another thing I can do pretty well," Scarl said softly. "You may start to believe I really have betrayed you."

She gulped, but her dry throat refused to swallow her fear.

"I won't," Zeke declared. Ariel looked over her shoulder at him, both grateful for his conviction and jealous of it.

Scarl spun and ran three steps, then turned back.

"One more thing. If I don't return at all . . ." He peered up at the sun and swore before he continued. "If I'm not here by dawn, retrace our steps through the sand and try to find your way back to Tree-Singer Abbey. That will be your best hope." He sprinted up the rise and vanished.

"Do you really think he might leave us?" Ariel asked Zeke.

He gave her an odd look. "I wish you could hear the stones rumbling to one another as we pass," he said, digging again. "If he doesn't come back, Ariel, it'll be because he is dead."

CHAPTER
24

When she saw where Zeke was digging, Ariel moved closer to the splayed roots of the snag. "Scoot this way," she said. "We'll be hidden better."

He studied her chosen location and then joined her. Together they scooped out a nest, settled their backs against the tree, and drew sand over their legs. It would have been fun to be buried alive if the possibilities Scarl had posed hadn't sounded so grim. As it was, the ground sucked at their limbs.

"Have you heard Misha around lately?" Ariel whispered.

Zeke shook his head. "I don't think he likes all this sun. He likes dark places."

"Like dreams, I guess," Ariel mused. "Maybe he went back to the abbey."

"Maybe." Zeke looked doubtful.

Silence swelled around them again. The sand and the sky spun out together, an emptiness that canceled everything else. Amid too many reminders of death, something stirred in a walled-off corner of Ariel's mind. Gingerly she allowed herself to think of her lost mother: silky hair, work-strong hands, a quick embrace for her daughter. When pain seeped in, Ariel plied Zeke with questions to distract herself.

"So are you going to be Ezekiel Stone-Singer now?" she asked.

"I don't know. I guess so. Does it sound crazy?"

"Yes. I never heard of a Stone-Singer. Tree-singing is weird enough."

"It's kinda the same and kinda different," he said. "The stones are slower. More grumbly. And more . . . I hear them more in my bones. At home, I just assumed it was trees. Then when we slept in the abbey's goat pen, I told you I heard ghosts, and I did hear Misha. But now I'm certain the rest were the stones of the abbey."

Ariel's eyebrows jumped. "Rocks in buildings, too?"

"Sure. They think it's funny that we stack them up."

Ariel studied the grains of sand over her chest. She had enough trouble imagining a talk with a tree. Trees were like people—alive.

"I know it sounds stupid," Zeke said. "But every time I feel desperate, they help. When Scarl and Elbert were coming to take you prisoner again, the big stone slab over our heads said, 'Let the men have her. Letting them win for an instant, a blink, is the fastest way to regain your balance.'"

"Balance?"

"Yeah. Balance is important for rocks. I figured it was good for us, too."

"It was, I guess," Ariel said. "But when you were singing back there in the dark—no offense, but I thought you'd gone nuts."

"So did I, but I didn't have a better idea. And it worked."

"All right, Stone-Singer," she said. "I guess you'll be the first."

Zeke's grin faded fast. "And Scarl seems to think you're the only. Farwalker, I mean."

"That sounds crazy, too," she replied. "The only message I have to carry or share is the one on the dart, and I don't know what it is."

Zeke wiggled one foot, causing a small earthquake in the sand. "The stones don't know what it says, either, or they aren't telling me, so I sure hope the Storian in Hartwater can. But the big boulders know who you are—who we all are. I can hear them mutter about us as we pass. They speak of a great weight teetering with no certainty which way it will fall."

So the earth itself gossiped about her. Ariel shivered. "Falling any direction sounds bad to me."

"You're not a rock."

Glad for that much, Ariel watched night seep over the desert. A swollen moon took the sun's place, and stars pricked around it as the air against her cheeks grew chill.

Zeke asked for the water. They sipped carefully. Ariel's eyes searched the shadowy line of the rise. Surely the Finder would appear again soon.

"The sand is really just a million teeny rocks," she observed. "Can you ask them where Scarl is or what's happening?"

"Too many voices," Zeke said. "It's like . . . I don't know, ants in a pile, or drops in the ocean. They all speak in a roar. If I listen too hard it makes my head hurt."

A disturbance in the sand nearby caught Ariel's eye. What looked like a very large but half-shriveled spider dug itself out and scuttled toward her.

"Zeke! What is that?" She pointed out the yellowish creature with her chin. Its pincers made her think of a crab with no shell, but it had a sharp tail that hooked over its back.

"I don't know, but it's ugly," he replied. "It might bite."

"Stay still. Maybe it won't notice us."

In fact, the scorpion skittered right onto their laps and paused there, weaving. Ariel held her breath, grateful for their blanket of sand. Luckily, the creature decided they weren't interesting and hurried away into the dark.

Still, it rattled Ariel's nerves. What if another sand creature tunneling beneath them found a leg in the way? She squirmed. Sand cascaded off her.

"What are you doing?" Zeke asked.

"Feeling crawly," she said.

"Maybe we should try to sleep." He closed his eyes.

Ariel scoffed.

If she hadn't been scanning for things that might bite, she might not have noticed the dimple in the sand near her knee. She expected another creepy bug to emerge. Instead, the dimple began twirling, grains of sand spinning loose. The dent flipped inside out and rose in a tiny cyclone.

Ariel turned to awaken Zeke and found his eyes open, staring.

"Is it a baby tornado?" she asked. She'd heard that a bad storm could rotate the wind until it lifted boats right off the sea.

Her question fueled the swirling. Sand whipped into the air. She clenched her eyes shut as grains scratched her face. Zeke exclaimed, spitting. Through a squint, Ariel saw the dust devil collapse. The whirling stopped. She'd pulled one hand free to wipe her face when Zeke touched the top of her head.

She turned. Both of Zeke's hands remained buried. Yet Ariel could feel fingers and a palm on her head.

"Hey!" She craned her neck to peer up and back. Nothing

blocked the light of the stars. "I feel this hand— Oh. Misha is here."

The sand around them dimpled as if poked with a stick. Ariel wondered why the ghost hadn't made his usual handprints until she tried it herself. The sand was too coarse to hold any mark but a blob.

"Maybe I will try to sleep," she told Zeke. "I can talk to him in my dr—"

A light glared into their faces.

CHAPTER
25

The hands on Ariel in the next instant weren't ghostly. They were rough, and they yanked her and Zeke from the sand. Startled, but mindful of Scarl's instructions, she gasped and protested. It wasn't hard to sound frightened. Her gaze bounced from shadow to shadow, searching for his face. Those nearest her, all unfamiliar, grinned like barracuda—all teeth and no warmth.

When she spotted him at last, her insides went watery and nearly flushed from her body in an embarrassing way. A blindfold hid Scarl's eyes. His hands were thrust behind his back as if they were tied, while a stranger gripped his collar. His plans must have gone wrong.

"Zeke," she wailed.

The hand clamped on her arm shook her. "Shut up."

"Some Finder," laughed the man holding Scarl. He was stubby, his features and hands almost comically large. He cuffed Scarl across the back of the head. Scarl stumbled forward under the blow. "They were right under your nose."

Ariel looked at her feet to hide any hope in her eyes. Scarl hadn't told these five strangers the truth. That meant they still had a chance.

She expected to be dragged across the desert, kicking. Instead, the group settled on the downhill side of the snag. The torches they bore soon set it ablaze, lighting a half circle in the sand. Ariel and Zeke were dropped at its center. Nobody bothered to tie them.

The man who'd struck Scarl kicked him in the back of the knees. Scarl dropped to the sand with a grimace. Anger flared in Ariel's chest.

"Take a rest," the man sneered. "We'll deal with you later." He jerked his head at one of his comrades, who approached to guard Scarl.

Ariel surveyed the remaining faces. One belonged to a woman. She wore men's garments and her narrow face was weathered, but a long gold braid fell from under her hat. This woman took the water jar from Zeke, drank, and then passed it around to her friends. Ariel's dry tongue, which felt too big for her mouth, clicked in dismay. She and Zeke might as well have finished the water themselves.

"So." The leader approached Ariel and Zeke. His broad nose and doughy face reminded her of an old classmate's grandpa. If she hadn't just seen him kick Scarl, Ariel would have thought his round eyes looked kind. "My name is Gustav."

"Tell them the whole thing," Scarl called. "It's Gustav Fool, if I remember correctly." He paid for the words with another quick blow from his guard.

"You can call me Gust," the leader continued. "I understand you knew our friend Elbert Finder?"

Zeke shrugged. Ariel made no response at all.

"Where did you leave him?"

Gust awaited their answer for only a moment. Ariel saw the blow coming and ducked. Gust's palm grazed the top of her head to slap Zeke's ear. Zeke yelped.

"Perhaps that will quicken your tongues," Gust said. "If not, I can do it again."

"We got away from him in the mountains," Ariel said.

"You must be clever," he replied. "And you've come far without him. Where are you going?"

"I don't know. We were just running away."

Gust turned a small circle in the sand, pursing his fat lips. "I don't blame you," he said. "Elbert and Scarl are pretty poor friends. But there are others who would like to help you, you know. I think we can help you, in fact."

"How?" Zeke demanded. "By drinking our water and beating us up?"

Ariel fought a crazy impulse to laugh.

Gust's fleshy lips found a smile. "I apologize," he said. "I spend too much time around unpleasant men. No," he continued, sinking to one knee. "I think we can lighten your burden. One of you has a telling dart, do you not?"

Uncertain of a safe answer, they merely returned his stare.

Quick as a snake striking, Gust clamped a hand on Ariel's ankle and jerked her forward. Sand plowed up the back of her shirt. She couldn't muffle a squeal.

"Answer me."

"It's not the girl, Fool." Disdain filled Scarl's voice. "It's the boy. The girl is a Finder."

Gust froze. His eyes slid between Ariel and Zeke. His hand still tight on Ariel's ankle, he rose, arm extended, until she dangled upside down. Her hair swept the sand. Petrified he would swing her into the flames, she wrapped her head with her arms and tried not to struggle.

"A Finder?" Gust repeated.

"How do you think she followed us to help him escape?" Scarl grumbled. "I'm not as incompetent as you'd like to believe. She wears her glass on a string around her neck."

Gust shook Ariel as though pepper might fall from her head. The blond woman moved in, fumbled at Ariel's collar, and drew out Bellam's bead. Its green glass caught light from the fire.

Gust released Ariel's ankle. She dropped painfully in a heap.

"The dart's in that pack," Zeke said quickly.

Ariel rubbed her neck and wondered how things could possibly get worse. The telling dart *was* in her pack. They were fooling Gust about small things, but the big things mattered more. She was terrified she might have to watch him hurt Zeke, which would be worse than bearing pain of her own. And Scarl could do nothing about it. In fact, Scarl was the one who had put Zeke in her place.

While one of the men rummaged through her pack for the dart, Gust pulled her to her feet. She cowered as he fingered her bead on its ribbon.

"Not much of a glass," he muttered.

"She's not yet thirteen, what do you expect?" Scarl said. "That little vixen works on raw talent, not training."

"She'll get a chance to test herself, then." Gust shoved Ariel into the dark, where she stumbled to her knees on the sand. "Go on," he ordered. "Find your way home. If you can."

"She'll die, Gust, before she reaches the edge of the Drymere," said the woman.

"You think so? Too bad. The world can be harsh." Gust returned to the fire.

Ariel jumped up and ran before he changed his mind. She headed straight away so they'd think she was gone, and then she circled around to sneak up from the same direction they'd come. Dropping to the sand just below the top of the rise, she slithered like a snake to its crest. With the snag between her and most of the flames, she could spy down on them from the darkness.

Yet she was powerless to do anything but watch. At the center of attention, Zeke looked forlorn. Scarl huddled at the edge of the light. All control seemed to belong to the captors. Gust paced, twirling the dart in his fingers.

"I don't understand why you didn't just get rid of him," he was saying.

Ariel strained to hear Scarl's reply.

"I told you. I thought Mason would want to talk to him. Test him. Maybe keep him a while, see if he could be turned to some use. A Farwalker must be good for something."

Gust veered in his pacing to stand over Scarl on the sand.

"Your assignment was to collect the darts and make sure nobody fretted about what they said," he reminded Scarl. "You realize that by bringing this particular receiver with you, you were risking the exact thing Mason wants to prevent?"

"He's a kid," Scarl sneered. "He can't even understand the dart that found him. What's he going to accomplish?"

Gust kicked him. "He accomplished escaping from you."

"He had help." Pain tightened Scarl's voice.

"So did you. Where is Elbert now, anyway?"

"When the boy disappeared, we separated to cover more ground," Scarl said. "Thought we'd snare him faster that way. I haven't seen Elbert since."

"If that's true, he must be somewhere nearby," said the woman. "But we can't—"

"Only if you think he was any good as a Finder." Scarl snorted. "I don't."

"I may have to agree with you there," Gust said. Tucking the telling dart into a pocket, he moved to loom over Zeke. Flames reflected in the Fool's dull face. He added, "Elbert would be just the man, though, for the job that needs doing now."

Ariel moaned. She had a pretty good idea what Gust meant, and she'd rather die herself than lose Zeke. She'd better think of an alternative fast.

"Misha, can't you help us?" she whispered. Instantly, a hand fell on her shoulder. She whipped around on one elbow. No friend of Gust's lurked beside her. Still, neither a spectral touch nor dimples in the sand could help Zeke.

The faces around the fire all focused on him. Gust unsheathed a knife much thinner but longer than Scarl's. Zeke drew himself into a crouch, ready to run. With adults poised around him, Ariel didn't think he stood any chance of slipping past them all.

One of the men cleared his throat and said, "I wouldn't be here if I'd known this would get so rough, Gust. Do you really want a boy's blood on your hands?"

"No, I don't. That's why Matthias is going to do it." Gust reversed his knife and thrust its handle toward the man standing nearest him. "He understands the value of Mason's favor. As well as the pinch of his anger. Don't you?" He leered.

The man Gust had appointed nodded, but he shifted, uneasy. "We could just tie him up and leave him to thirst and the sun," he suggested.

"And sit here for a week, if it takes that long? Some of you might leave the world before he does. No. Quick and certain."

"Let me do it." Scarl pushed himself to his feet. "You're right, I should have seen to it sooner, and now he's caused me a fair bit of pain. At this point I'll be happy to cut that brat's throat."

"You?" Gust turned to appraise Scarl. Ariel's heart battered itself against her ribs. If Scarl could be untied, perhaps all was not lost. Yet a tinny voice in the back of her mind shrilled that with her free, the Finder might be willing to sacrifice Zeke to satisfy Gust and escape.

"I might actually have to respect you for that," Gust told Scarl.

"Don't get carried away," Scarl said drily. "You could just return my gear and let me go about my business."

Gust debated. Ariel twitched, barely keeping herself from tearing down the slope shouting the truth.

With a flick of his hand, Gust signaled that the prisoner should be unbound. He held his knife ready in case Scarl moved without warning. First the blindfold came off, then the rope tying Scarl's hands. Holding her breath, Ariel willed him to jump for the knife, swing a punch, or grab Zeke and run. Scarl only rubbed his wrists, glanced at Zeke, then fixed his gaze firmly on Gust.

Gust's eyes narrowed. Tension outlined nearly every form at the fire. Two other men gripped the hilts of their own knives. His lips twitching in wry amusement, Scarl was the only one who looked relaxed.

He shifted his weight, waited a breath longer, and then turned up his palm.

"Are you going to give me that, or did you change your

mind?" he asked mildly. "There's no point in waiting till morning. I could use a good sleep for a change."

Slowly Gust reversed the blade and extended the handle.
Scarl stepped to it casually, as though offered a cup of tea. His
fingers brushed the knife's handle, then drew back.

"Actually, I don't suppose I could use my own knife?" he
said. "It's done a similar job for me before. And it'll make a better keepsake—since I'm sure you'll want yours back."

Relaxing slightly, Gust jerked his head toward the woman.
She bent to a pack and soon held out the sheath with Scarl's
knife.

"Thank you. I appreciate that." Scarl took it. When he
straightened, a blade Ariel recognized glinted in the firelight.
Her breath caught.

"All right, you little cur," Scarl said softly to Zeke. He raised
the knife. "You remember what I told you before?"

Zeke's crouched body looked tight as a spring. His voice
only achieved a hoarse whisper. "I remember, scum."

In three strides Scarl was on him. He grabbed Zeke's shoulder and yanked him to his feet.

Ariel lost all control of her body. It leaped up and flew down
the slope toward the fire. Her screams of denial split the darkness. Sand that she'd clenched, unaware, in her fists sprayed out
toward the light. Startled faces turned her way. Her stumbling
feet churned up more sand around her.

Perhaps Ariel needed to provide that idea. Perhaps ghosts
just have excellent timing. As she swooped down the slope, a
rush of wind hit Ariel's back. She nearly tumbled onto her face
at its force. It lifted sand from the dune so the swirling air filled
with grit.

Ariel saw Scarl fling Zeke over the burning snag toward her. Then a billowing curtain of sand blocked her view.

"Zeke!"

The wind stole her cry and whipped sparks from the fire into the frenzy. Ariel's eyelids clamped tight against flying grit. Still running, she banged her shins into some unknown bulk and tripped hard. Sprawled on the ground, she raised one hand as a shield. The other tried to pry open her eyelids. Her watering eyes could see nothing.

A hand clutched her calf. She jerked it away.

"Ariel!" She could only just hear Zeke's voice above the scream of the wind and the skitter of sand lashing wood. They fumbled into each other and clambered together to their feet.

"Run!" Uncertain by now where the snag lay, the sand in the air was so thick, they clasped hands and struck out randomly. Their feet floundered in the soft dunes. They coughed, inhaling sand with the air, and stumbled over unseen rises and dips. Their legs slipped, then caught and drove on, lungs and muscles burning with effort.

Abruptly they ran beyond the edge of the sandstorm. Beneath stars once more, they risked a look back. Misha's whirlwind formed a large sandy blot on the otherwise crystalline night. The only sign of the fire was a slight glow in the haze. Everything else had been swallowed by the suffocating cloud.

"Scarl?" Ariel whimpered.

"He'll escape. He'll find us." Zeke's voice shook, though. He spat grit.

"I thought for a minute he might really kill you, Zeke."

"I—" Zeke swallowed. "So did I. Because you were already

safe. Until he said that about remembering. Then I thought, 'Maybe not.' But five against one . . ."

He shuddered. Sand cascaded out of his hair. More clung to his eyelids, his ears, and the rims of his nostrils. Ariel wiped sand from her own eyebrows and lips.

"I wouldn't have been so brave," she said. "I would have run as soon as Gust pulled out that knife."

"What are you talking about? You actually ran toward the danger."

She couldn't deny it. They'd resumed walking before Ariel had found any answer.

"Maybe that's something Farwalkers do."

CHAPTER
26

Guided by moonlight, Ariel and Zeke headed for the distant stone outcrop and its hidden water hole that Scarl had been trying to reach earlier. They agreed that the Finder would expect that. Besides, they wouldn't be able to rest anywhere less sheltered, knowing that Gust or his friends might still be hunting them.

Although the pair glanced back often, not a single figure emerged from the sandstorm. When the knot of flying sand finally dissipated, the dark desert looked empty. Listening only to their own grinding footfalls, Ariel fretted about what to do if Scarl failed to appear. Home now seemed impossibly distant, not only in miles but in events and emotions. A cramp of hopelessness seized her heart. She reached for Zeke's fingers, seeking comfort. He did not seem to mind.

When they set foot on the bedrock rising out of the sand, Zeke dropped her hand and took over. He led Ariel between wrinkles of stone to a tiny puddle of rainwater at the base of a twisting stone bluff. Once they'd licked the pool dry, he sank to rest among the scattered boulders nearby.

Still on her feet, Ariel looked up doubtfully. "Isn't there anywhere better? Rocks might fall on us here."

Zeke shook his head. "If any were getting ready to jump, I could hear it, I'm sure. And this bluff will protect us."

"From what?" No clouds veiled the stars, but any rain that did fall would pour right down on them.

"Anything—anyone—that would hurt us."

Ariel had trouble imagining how a rock could put up much fight. Sighing, she turned to gaze over the dark swells of sand they had crossed.

"It's a good place to keep a lookout for Scarl, I guess." She dropped beside Zeke and pressed her body against the stone's lingering warmth.

Her watch was short-lived. A troubled, half-conscious doze overtook her, molding her limbs to the ground and gluing her lids shut with sand. She couldn't move. When she moaned at the discomfort, hands came to pat her all over. The wind, or a voice, whispered jumbled syllables of her name at her ear.

"Ariel."

At last she dragged her eyes open. A man crouched before her, shaking her soundly. Ariel gasped and cringed against her stone bed. Fear rattled through her before she recognized Scarl.

He put a finger to his lips. "Careful," he whispered. "Our voices will travel far here."

She blinked and sat up, her mind clearing. Zeke snored beside her. The sun just breaching the horizon showed Scarl alone, his skin and hair yellow with sand. He'd lost his knit cap.

Without thinking, she threw her arms around his neck.

"It's all right," he whispered.

She released him as quickly, stuffing her willful hands into her armpits. Her impulse to hug him both shamed her and made her uneasy. Trust was one thing, affection another. She wasn't yet ready to forgive him for his part in the loss of her mother—a loss that had echoed when Scarl had stood in the firelight with a knife raised to Zeke.

They woke Zeke. Without saying anything more, Scarl waved for them to follow him. That's when Ariel noticed the sand-clotted slash across the back of the Finder's coat.

He led them deeper into the flowing river of rock. The stone rippled into folds and tight canyons where wind-driven sand slumped in the corners. The trio skidded down a slope and then clambered into a shadowy chasm. At the bottom, water bubbled up from a crack and filled a small pool fringed by ferns and green vines.

Grateful, all three slaked their thirst. Zeke submerged his whole head.

Giggling at him, Ariel turned to Scarl. Her grin faded. He'd removed his coat to rinse sand from his face and neck.

"You're bleeding." Seeing his red-soaked shirt, she was loath to learn what hid beneath.

"I know."

Zeke resurfaced with a jerk that sprayed droplets from his hair. "What happened? Did you kill all of them?"

"I don't know that I killed any of them."

The Finder may have misunderstood Ariel's frown. He added, "Oh yes, I tried. I'm not going to protect you from that. If it bumped me, I put my blade to it. I just had to trust that both of you had stayed out of the middle. Or at least wouldn't be jumping on me. But I couldn't see the knife in my hand, let alone any work it got done." He ran his fingers through his hair. Sand flew.

"And the first clear air I spotted, I ran for it," he added. "For

all I know, there could be five corpses in the sand or five pursuers behind us. The truth is probably somewhere between."

Zeke got to his feet thoughtfully and moved off a short distance. Guessing Zeke wanted to be alone to speak to the
stones, Ariel approached Scarl more closely.

"You'd better take off your shirt." She had to force herself
to say it.

Scarl lifted one shoulder and winced. He shook his head.
"Not much I can do about it here. It's better left alone."

"Not much *you* can do. But I can probably help it a little."

A grin split Scarl's face. "I don't know. You flunked your
Healtouch test."

"Shut up," she said. "That was your fault."

"I didn't intend it. I was as surprised as you were, and worried about what it meant." He shook his head. "But it's true I
wasn't quite disappointed."

Ariel had spent a lot of time watching her mother at work.
She'd learned more about dealing with injured people than
she'd realized until now. "You're stalling," she said. "Take it
off."

"It won't kill me before we get to Hartwater." Scarl gazed
east as if he could see through the rock. "Shouldn't, at any
rate."

She planted her fists on her hips.

He chuckled. "I don't know why I'm still surprised. It's hard
for me to look at you without seeing a young girl, I guess.
But . . . it feels pretty bad, Ariel. Are you sure you're up to it?"

With her jaw clamped, she nodded. He tipped his head in
submission, sat on a stone with his back to her, and unbut-
toned his shirt. When he had trouble peeling it back, she
took it and pulled. She tried to be gentle, because she could

see the bloody fabric sticking to him, but he still sucked air through his teeth.

When the shirt was finally out of the way, she sucked air through her own teeth. Her knees wobbled, too. She shoved them ramrod straight and pretended to be watching her mother. That helped.

A knife had sliced a long, ragged curve into his upper back. It looked deepest around the bottom of his right shoulder blade, as if the knife had slipped under the bone there before popping back out. The wound no longer bled, mostly because it was caked full with sticky sand.

"Well?" he asked.

"I don't think you'll be giving me piggyback rides again anytime soon."

"Good. You're heavy." His weak jest fell flat.

Ariel fumbled for a cloth and realized just how little they'd escaped with. "We don't have any of our packs."

"No, we haven't been so lucky as that," he said. "I do have the needle in my coat, though. Think you'll want it?"

"I'll be sewing until winter," she replied, trying not to be daunted.

She picked up his shirt and soaked it in the pool, rinsing out as much blood and sand as she could. Then she lifted it, dripping. Recalling how cold water had felt in the cut on her arm made her stomach flutter.

"This is probably going to hurt."

"It already hurts. Go ahead."

She drenched him, squeezing the cloth over his back. Gingerly, as some of the sand flowed away and she could see the wound better, she started wiping at it. Grit clung stubbornly in the torn flesh. She could tell by the way Scarl inhaled when the pain of her swabbing was awful and when it wasn't so bad. After a while, he braced his left elbow on his knee and leaned his forehead into his hand, his eyes closed.

Once she got past the distress of hurting him, Ariel slipped into an efficient coolness. She bent many times to the water and even, at the end, carefully slipped two wet fingers inside his sliced muscle to draw out the last grit.

"I bet you wish you'd hurt me more when you stitched up my arm," she said when she was done cleaning. She had remembered, almost too late, that talking might help distract him.

He took a shaky breath before he answered. "Are you going to enjoy yourself for much longer?"

"No. I'm ready to stitch it. But what should I use for thread? We could probably take the stitches out of my arm. It's healing pretty good. But I'm afraid the bits will all be too short." There wouldn't be nearly enough, either, but she didn't say that.

"Hand me my coat."

He pulled a coil of fish line from one pocket and removed the hook.

"That's awfully thick," Ariel said.

"It'll do."

"Not if I can't get it through the needle."

"Do I have to do everything?" At her silence, he added, "I was joking. You're doing fine. I'll put it back on the fishhook. Use that instead of the needle."

Ariel groaned. The prospect of running him through like bait nearly emptied her stomach.

"The only other choice is to leave it," Scarl said.

"It'll never heal without stitches." The wound gaped with every movement he made.

"You decide. I can't see it. You can."

She gazed sourly at his back and remembered that this had been her idea.

When she didn't reply, he said, "That's all right. Washing it out should help quite a bit. Where's my shirt?"

"No." She held out her cupped palm. "Give me the stupid hook."

He handed it to her. "You can do it. If I can put up with it."

Taking a deep breath, she rethreaded the hook and bent to the deepest end of the cut. Her mother, she thought, would have been proud. Her Fisher father also, perhaps. She blinked tears from her eyes and began baiting her hook.

It was the ugliest stitching Ariel had ever done, but slowly the gaping wound closed. Zeke came back and stood at a distance, watching and then looking away. Not long after she'd started, Scarl stopped her so he could pick up his coat. His hands trembled.

"I'll work on some finer threads," he explained. "So you can switch to the needle before I pass out." He began teasing threads from a raveled edge of the fabric.

She gladly took the oilcloth thread and the needle when she could. At that point, the stitching got easy enough that she could talk and distract him a little.

"Who were those people? Gust and the rest?" she asked.

"All but Gust are the other Finders I told you about, sent out by Mason."

"They were looking for me?"

"They were looking for me. Or Elbert, or both. To learn if we'd gotten our work done."

"They already finished theirs," she muttered.

"I'm afraid so."

Zeke spoke up. "I don't think they're coming after us here.

'Two have dwindled to dust,' that's what the stones say. The rest are still out there, but they're not getting closer."

"They'll probably regroup and try to catch us off guard," Scarl said. "We need to reach Hartwater as soon as we can. You'll be safer with more people around you. I thought I'd be enough to protect you, but nothing went as I expected." He sighed. "The worst of it is losing your dart. Now there's no way to find out any more about the summons, let alone answer it." He kneaded his forehead with the heel of one hand. "Too many mistakes."

Zeke caught Ariel's eye. Casually, he shook his right fore-arm. Ariel's whalebone needle still hid tucked in his splint. She'd slipped it back to him for safekeeping before they left the mountains because she hadn't wanted Scarl to notice it in her pack. Now she gave Zeke a tiny shake of her head. She wanted to keep that secret yet.

"Still," Scarl said, "you're alive. I've managed that much."

"It was a good thing Misha helped us," Ariel muttered.

"Well . . . your ghost makes me nervous," he replied. "If he stirred up the sandstorm, I have to give credit. But Zeke's cool head helped enormously, too. If he'd bolted too soon, they would have caught him for sure. And the way you swooped back, shrieking—it distracted them at just the right moment. Together those things probably saved all our lives."

Ariel said nothing. Recalling the last moments before the sandstorm brought a bitter taste to her mouth.

Some of her unease must have passed through her hands.

"Do you want to rest?" Scarl asked softly, after a moment.

"No. I'm almost finished."

By the time she tied the last knot, she felt drained and her stomach was churning. Scarl, his face drawn and pale, started to rise. He thought better of it. Instead he slipped down to one knee and carefully stretched out on his belly, resting his cheek on his left forearm.

"Wait. One more thing." Ariel eyed the plants that grew in the chasm and settled on a canterberry vine. "Are we going to stay here awhile?"

"If Zeke still feels we'll have it to ourselves," Scarl replied.

When Zeke nodded, the Finder said, "Good. We need the rest and the water. It's going to be a hard push to escape the Drymere without any supplies."

"Great," Ariel grumbled. She ripped the largest leaves off the vine, feeling as though invisible fingers were clawing at her, too. She shredded the leaves, made a paste with a few drops of water, and spread the mash over her stitching.

"There," she said finally. "That should help keep out infection. It's the best I can do."

Scarl waited until she crossed his field of vision to say, "Thank you, Ariel."

Tired and cranky, she didn't reply. To escape the sun, now high enough to pound into the chasm, she moved into a shadow that still curled around one side.

She'd just sunk into a comfortable nook when Scarl spoke again.

"If you'll look in the pockets on the left side of my coat, I think there may still be a few strips of dried meat there."

Zeke jumped up to check.

"What else have you got in that coat?" Ariel wondered when Zeke found the food.

"It pays to have lots of pockets."

Zeke took the meat first to Scarl, but the Finder shook his head. "Can't do it," he said. "You go ahead." Too hungry to argue, Zeke and Ariel split the meal. It took plenty of chewing, but Ariel's stomach welcomed each bite.

The meat made her thirsty again, though. A long drink didn't flush away the single thought that had been grinding away in her head while she'd chewed. As she returned to her nook, she noticed that Scarl's drooping eyelids had parted again at her motion.

"I want to ask you a question," she told him. She wasn't sure, in fact, that she did, but the suspicion gnawing at her wouldn't rest.

He didn't bother lifting his head. "I'll answer if I can."

Ariel took a deep breath. The question rushed out bitterly. "If you had to kill Zeke to save me, would you do it?"

Distaste cramped Scarl's features. "He's sitting right next to you, isn't he?"

"This time," whispered the shadow in Ariel's heart. She didn't relent. "That doesn't answer my question."

Scarl turned his face to the ground and sighed into the dirt. "I told you I'd never lie to you."

"You'd do it?" she demanded.

Finally he met her eyes. "If I had to, Ariel. Yes. But only if I had no other choice."

"I understand," Zeke said quickly.

"I don't." Ariel crossed her arms.

Scarl and Zeke shared a glance that left her out. A wave of fury rolled through Ariel's weariness. How could Zeke still look at the Finder with any respect? She stomped her heel against the stone in frustration.

"It's easier to be nobody," Scarl said. "But you're not."

She'd heard enough. Turning her back, she leaned into her

stone pillow, buried her cheeks in her palms, and closed her eyes.

But Zeke asked a question she had avoided. "Would you kill yourself to save her?"

Ariel shot him a glare.

"That's easier," Scarl told Zeke. "If I thought she'd be safe, with people who would help her, I'd do that before I'd ever hurt you."

Ariel moaned. She didn't want such information to get in the way of her anger. "But why?"

"Because everything and everyone I care about most might depend on you. But I'm not up to explaining right now. If it can wait a few hours."

"I don't care if it waits forever," she retorted.

The chasm filled with pained silence. Gradually all three of them slipped into sleep.

Or perhaps sleep hosted four, because at last Ariel met Misha again in a dream.

CHAPTER
27

Ariel dreamed she explored the halls of the abbey. Turning a corner, she heard her name and glanced up. Misha lay draped like a cat across one of the great wooden beams supporting the roof.

"You saved us," she said. "Thank you."

He smiled. She thought he might float down from above, but he didn't. A hand touched her shoulder. She whirled. Now he stood before her. Only cobwebs decked the beam where he'd lain.

"Don't. Please. That scares me."

Without reply, he took her hand and pulled her down the hall. Ariel guessed where they were going. As she thought it, the wooden door appeared. She wanted to pass through it no more than she had the first time she'd dreamed of it, but she knew she must. She owed him.

"That scares me, too," she whispered. "What's behind it?"

Misha only gestured an invitation to enter, then shifted like smoke, moving through her to stand at her shoulder. Apparently she must open it and find out for herself.

Her lips numb with fear, she murmured, "All right." Before

dread could leach out her will, she put her palm on the heavy
door and pushed.

Blinding light spilled over her. Ariel shaded her eyes and
stepped into a long, brilliant room. Its stone walls held aston-
ishing windows that stretched nearly from the floor to the high,
curving roof. Sunlight blazed through. Narrow wooden tables
stretched beneath them, casting shadows into the room. Ariel's
fear, primed for a tomb, dwindled.

"Where are we?" she asked.

Misha moved past her to trail his fingers through the dust on
one polished tabletop. The sunshine faded him to little more
than a gossamer outline. With a look of despair, he lifted his shim-
mering fingertips to her. The dust there was more solid than he
was, but she noticed again that his hand was stained red.

The suggestion of blood triggered a cascade of images in
Ariel's dreaming mind: wounds, stitching, Scarl. The attached
emotions pulled her out of the dream. She jerked awake.

The chasm swirled with shadows. The sky was pale, the
afternoon sun probably near the horizon. Ariel sat up with a
groan, rubbing a numb spot on her hip.

Zeke was gone. Panic welled through her before she spied
his silhouette near the top of the chasm. He was probably just
talking to rocks again.

Sleep still slacked Scarl's face. Ariel's eyes stole to his coat.
Her hunger had awakened with her, worse than before. She
argued with herself for a moment. Her honesty lost. Slipping
over the rough ground to the coat, she looked through its pockets for anything more there to eat.

She found a coil of thin rope, a pack of waxed flamesticks,
and his blackened tin cup, but nothing she could eat. She also
discovered, in a small pocket by itself, his Finder's glass. It

wasn't quite round, and one edge was chipped ragged. Holding it up to the sky, she could see a few bubbles in the glass, but nothing more.

"It's just glass."

She jumped. Her cheeks growing hot, she stuffed the glass back into its pocket and shoved the coat from her lap.

"I'm sorry." Resentment muddied her regret. "I was looking for food Zeke might have missed. I shouldn't have."

Slowly and painfully, Scarl curled himself up to a seated position. Crushed canterberry leaves fluttered down his back. Ariel watched the strain on her stitching. If it broke loose, she decided, she wouldn't tell him.

"Like to try it?" he asked. He reached for his damp shirt.

At first she didn't know what he meant. "Your Finder's glass? I don't know how."

"I'll give you a lesson. Bring it here."

She did so with reluctance, more ashamed to be caught snooping than if he'd been angry. He placed the glass back into her cupped hands.

"It's nothing more than a place to focus your attention," he said. "Although the more you use one, the more it reflects who you are." He slid his left arm into his shirtsleeve. "Look into it and concentrate on the thing you want to find. In the front of your mind, if you can understand that." He reached for his second sleeve and stopped, cursing under his breath.

Ariel's empathy swelled. "Here, I'll help you with that."

"Not yet." He brushed aside her hand. "Go ahead."

"Well, what should I try to find?"

"Anything that might be here that you can't see. Choose something easy."

"Something to eat." Her eyes dropped to the glass.

"That might not be so easy. Good luck."

Ariel gazed at the glass, exploring its thickness, its slight color, the pattern of bubbles inside it. Then she remembered to think about food, not glass. Mashed potatoes would be nice. She imagined a huge mound, sodden with butter and cream. Warm and dripping.

"Never mind." Unusually sharp, Scarl's voice cut through the roar of her hunger. "Help me with this." He struggled to slip his right arm into its sleeve.

Startled, she lifted the armhole so he could reach it. The instant his hand slipped through the cuff, he grabbed Ariel's wrist, making her jump.

"Where is it? Your food."

Her gaze bounced to a big rock on the far side of the pool, with no information in her mind to explain why.

Following her sight line, Scarl nodded. "Good. Look at the glass."

Red sparkles passed through it like fire drifting through water.

"It darkens for me," he said. "The trick is to think about it for so long, then stop thinking completely. Stay here." He rose and moved stiffly but silently to the spot Ariel's glance had picked out. He hovered there, his crow eyes scanning. With a quick flex of his knees, he dropped. His left hand darted into the shadow at the base of the rock.

When he raised his hand again, a wriggling lizard hung there by one hind leg.

"Very good, I'd say."

"Ugh. That's not food."

He slapped the lizard on the rock. It went limp. "You can't find a meat pie where one doesn't exist. How hungry are you?"

"Pretty hungry," she thought, but she grimaced.

"Tell you what," he said, carrying it back to her. "We'll take it with us in case we don't come across anything better soon."

She held out his glass. "You do it."

"I'm much more concerned about getting us out of the Drymere, and the glass will reflect that." He slipped it with the dead lizard into his coat. "But being hungry served you well for a first try, my little apprentice."

"I'm not a Finder," she protested, appalled. She didn't want to be like him.

"I think you'll need to learn a bit of everything, if you can."

"To be a Farwalker, you mean?"

"Just to survive. If you can do that, the farwalking skills will rise by themselves."

Although the thought of such skills reassured her, the word that echoed longest in Ariel's mind was that "if."

When Zeke returned from the top of the chasm, he brought a groundmelon with him. His bright orange lips made it clear that Ariel was not the only one hungry enough to be selfish.

"Where'd you get that?" Scarl asked as Zeke offered his fruit. Ariel took it.

"When I woke up, I climbed down to the sand over there." Zeke gestured vaguely.

Scarl's face clouded. "Don't go so far. You said yourself that Gust's band is still out there. And despite what either of you may think, I'm not eager to see you dead."

Ignoring his pointed glance, Ariel cracked open the melon. It wasn't ripe, but she suspected it still tasted better than lizard.

"We'll walk tonight under the moon," Scarl told them. "We'll get farther without water that way, and perhaps farther from our enemies, too. Drink up while you can."

All three filled their stomachs to sloshing. Scarl turned his coat inside out, knotted the end of a sleeve, and filled it with water. He watched the sleeve seep.

"This may not last long," he said, "but it's worth a try."

He entrusted his filled tin cup to Zeke, who held a melon rind overtop against spills.

They climbed to the top of the chasm. There Scarl paused, used his glass briefly, and then peered into the dunes behind them. When he was satisfied with the blankness of a certain swath of horizon, he turned.

"Ariel, you did so well at finding, I want you to try something else. I'm just guessing at this, but . . ." He shrugged and gestured forward. "Take us out of the Drymere."

"Me?"

Even Zeke gave Scarl a doubtful glance.

"You. I won't let you lead us too far astray."

She looked at Scarl's dripping bundle of oilcloth and the small cup in Zeke's hands. "But we don't have much water," she argued. "Or food."

"You'd best hurry, then," Scarl replied softly. He shifted his gaze to the eastern horizon.

Dubious, she waited. At last she said, "I'll need your glass, won't I?"

"You shouldn't. This isn't finding. You're a Farwalker. Walk. Follow where your feet take you. I think your path will appear."

"Ah. Go where the stones want you to go," Zeke said. "I get it."

Ariel listened with growing dismay. Scarl's request seemed unfair. Guiding them was his job, and the least he could do, if you asked her.

"Try it." Zeke said, nudging her.

"I'll give you two bits of advice," Scarl added. "They're true for finding, so I suspect they'll be true for you, too. Don't think too much and don't question yourself. Go."

She crossed her arms stubbornly, planting her feet. Scarl tried to hide a smile by casting it down to his boots. Zeke simply gazed at Ariel until she wanted to slap him.

"Fine." She spun and angled across the stone slope. If Scarl wanted her to get them lost so they all died of thirst, she would do it. Fuming, she marched toward the horizon.

Zeke caught up to walk alongside her. Scarl trailed behind like a shadow. After a while, soothed by the rhythm of her legs, Ariel forgot her annoyance and even some of her hunger. She and Zeke took turns sipping water as twilight sank into night. The staring moon watched their progress until it, too, fell behind them.

First the cup and then Scarl's oozing sleeve were long empty before Ariel's legs started to weary. They were growing stronger. But as dawn failed to come and the night only stretched onward, shivers began racking her shoulders. The desert chill seemed to mock the hot, sticky thirst in her mouth.

"I can hear your teeth chattering, Zeke," Scarl said. "Want my coat?"

"I'm okay," Zeke lied.

"Well, it's too big for Ariel alone; it'll hang down and trip her. Why don't you each take a sleeve? You'll warm one another that way." Scarl pulled the oilcloth from his shoulder, where he'd slung it once they'd licked off the last of the water. He passed it to Zeke.

"What about you?" Zeke worried.

"I'm feeling fever. Might as well use it."

Neither Scarl nor his coat was so big that the two friends

didn't bang shoulders and kick ankles at first. They soon fell into locked step, though, considerably warmer. And their nearness made it easy to whisper together.

"He hasn't changed your direction or stopped you," Zeke noted.

"He wants us to shrivel up somewhere like dried-out worms, that's all."

"No, he doesn't. He's just pushing you."

"Why are you sticking up for him?" Ariel's voice jumped above a whisper. "Have you forgotten your maple? If he'd told your father or Storian the truth about Elbert, the trees might not have burned. And we wouldn't be here."

Zeke stared at his feet. "I won't ever forget. But I don't think it's that simple. Besides, I like him, even if he would save you first. And the stones like him, too. They—"

"Enough about the dumb rocks, all right?"

That silenced him. Ariel regretted her words immediately. Zeke would not meet her eyes, and with him pacing so close alongside her, his hurt feelings spilled back onto her.

She tugged her arm free from the coat. "I'm sorry," she murmured, dropping her sleeve and pulling away. "I didn't mean that."

"Get too warm?" Scarl asked doubtfully from behind.

Ariel shrugged, in no mood to say more than she must to the Finder.

"Would you like a drink?" he added.

She spun, her frustration blazing. "You've had more water this whole time?"

"No." Scarl pointed. "You've been walking past a creek's tail for five minutes."

With effort, her eyes found the dark trickle in a swath of

wet sand. She ran to get there. It was maddening trying to fill her cupped hands without scooping up sand. The water tasted like rocks, but it still brought juicy joy to her tongue.

Zeke dropped beside her. Scarl arrived more slowly, surveying their empty surroundings.

"No hurry," he said. "We can rest here without fear of ambush." He sank to his knees. "By the way, Ariel, the head of this creek lies in Hartwater, so we can just follow it now. I've been here before—and I couldn't have found the route better myself."

Surprise lit Ariel's face. She looked back over their tracks, uncertain whether to feel foolish or proud. Then she realized that both her companions were smirking.

"Hmph. I told you I could do it," she said.

CHAPTER
28

Thirteen, Ariel thought to herself, was a number of power. The moon circled the earth thirteen times during a circuit of the sun, and young people took Naming tests in their thirteenth year. They'd once had a thirteenth trade to choose, too, but that was extinct—other than her.

She peeked at the Finder striding alongside her. The sun would soon heave itself over distant hills to glare in their eyes. Regretting some of her recent hostility, Ariel mustered the nerve to break the hush that accompanied their footsteps.

"Scarl?"

"Yes?" He did not look over.

"Was the thirteenth trade unlucky? Is that why there aren't any other Farwalkers left?"

He snorted. "You could say so, I guess. But the fault doesn't lie in the number. Blame the Forgetting instead."

When he didn't go on, she said, "I was hoping you'd finish the story you were telling before we ran into Gust."

He gave her a long, sideways appraisal.

She swallowed her pride to add, "Please?"

"Did the Farwalkers fight the Forgetting and lose?" Zeke asked.

"Just the reverse," Scarl said. "They helped, only to be forgotten themselves."

While people were blind, he explained, Farwalkers spread hope, and eventually, the glad news that children had once more started to see. By the time most everyone's eyes worked again, though, Farwalkers weren't nearly so needed. Villages had grown and could get along on their own. For a while, those in favor of Forgetting relied on Farwalkers to help collect and destroy the relics they found on their travels.

"Dumb," Zeke declared. "Why'd they help with that?"

"Don't be too hard on them," Scarl said. "A few saved what they found, or gave relics in secret to Storians, which is why we have any at all. But they had to eat, too, and perhaps they didn't realize where such a path led. After most of the old mysteries had been destroyed, the people who did it began discouraging Farwalker visits. Storians could be kept busy teaching children to count, but Farwalkers had become dangerous relics themselves. They'd seen too much in their travels, and their trade stood for sharing and remembering, not Forgetting. Attitudes shifted, and welcomes became chilly. Some Farwalkers ended hungry and alone. Others took up fishing or reaping, changing their names. Young people stopped asking for a Farwalker test on Namingfest days."

"So I'm some kind of outcast?" Ariel's heart flopped.

"If you were only an outcast," Scarl replied, "nobody would be trying to kill you. That's what Zeke's stone meant when it said Gust's band 'forgot with their hands and their feet'— wiping away the past and anyone, anything, that might bring it back. It seems Mason is so afraid of repeating mistakes that he shuns the old ways completely. He can't see, or doesn't care, how important a Farwalker could be for our future."

"But if the stuff left after the war is all gone or wrecked, how could one Farwalker make any difference?" Zeke asked.

"It's not just the relics he fears, Zeke. It's knowledge itself. That's the problem. People still stumble on better ways to do things, but we've lost the ability to share good ideas, so they fade again when the person who uses them dies. Villages are too far apart. Strangers are regarded with the utmost suspicion, particularly if they can't win friends by finding." He eyed Ariel. "Believe me, I know. A Farwalker could change that, although it could take a long time, because many places may be hostile from habit."

"Why bother killing me?" Ariel grumbled. "I'll probably die of loneliness anyway."

"Well . . . there's one other factor," Scarl said. "There was a story that once gave people hope. It spoke of a place underground. At the start of the war, or shortly thereafter, valuable things were taken there for safekeeping."

"The Vault!" Ariel exclaimed. "We know that story. It's supposed to be at the end of a rainbow. Or in a hole at the bottom of the sea."

"Or down a pink rabbit's burrow or beneath a circle of mushrooms or under the roots of a two-hundred-foot tree," Scarl countered. "There are dozens of versions. Every generation, a few Storians have chased what they thought were new clues. They've all given up or died in the wilds, losing themselves instead of discovering what they sought."

"Have you looked?" Zeke wondered.

Rue tugged at Scarl's features. "Long and far," he admitted. "That's why I eventually became a Finder. But you can't find what doesn't exist, Finders say. Certainly I've not found any store of old treasures."

"But . . . ?" Ariel prompted, her skin tingling.

"The telling darts," Scarl said. "I told you I don't understand most of the summons, and that's true. But I recognized one of the symbols, because I've spent much of my life searching for it. Your dart bore the mark for the Vault." He reached toward Ariel, a plea on his face. "I didn't mention it sooner because I feared you would think I was only hunting treasure. I couldn't care less about gold or jewels. I care about the Forgetting. It's gone on too long. And only the Vault can help us remember."

Ariel trod carefully through the gravel that had replaced the sand underfoot, feeling as though she walked a jetty surrounded by sharks. Scarl had been correct: if she had known from the start he was after the Vault, she would have rejected his proposal outright. Since then her mistrust had ebbed—and her commitment to her calling had grown. But his revelation still made her uneasy. So much was at stake.

"The Farwalker who spreads the news and contents of the Vault will be anything but an outcast, believe me," Scarl added. "Most people will be thrilled to learn the legend is true. And that is why Mason wants to kill you."

"But if somebody found it," Zeke protested, "and sent the darts to invite people to see it, that person must be dead now, since the sender's mark has faded."

Scarl shrugged. "There could be other reasons for the missing sender's mark. Perhaps it wasn't a person, for instance. I think the Vault itself might have sent them, like witch broom flowers shoot seeds. Maybe a certain number of years had to pass first. Or Ariel had to be born and grow up a bit. I don't know."

Goose bumps tickled Ariel's arms. "You think the dart says where the Vault is?"

"I doubt it's that easy. If it were, Mason could have already stripped or destroyed it. Especially with help from Elbert and Gust, who were probably easy to bribe. It's harder to imagine Liam Storian going along, even for wealth, so I can only guess that he argued and has since paid the price. Luckily, few people know I was once a Storian myself. And Elbert liked to talk. That's how I've pieced together as much as I have."

Zeke swatted his bangs from his eyes. "But my maple, and things Ash said . . . the trees think all this is important. A great Tree-Singer wouldn't ignore that. He couldn't do such terrible things."

"He may not think they're so terrible, Zeke. Mason seems to believe that we're all better off without anything that may be in the Vault. Everyone who favored the Forgetting agreed. And perhaps he fears that if the Vault is found, the world won't depend so much on Tree-Singers and trees. The people of Libros defer to him greatly. I'm sure he would not like to lose his place as the Farwalkers did."

"The world will always need Tree-Singers," declared Zeke.

"I can't believe any of them would commit murder to make sure of it," Ariel added.

Scarl's eyes slid to hers. "You're still young, Ariel. People sometimes kill for a lot less than that."

"Not in Canberra Docks!"

"No, I'm sure you're right. And that's exactly the argument used to justify the Forgetting."

"Maybe we *should* just forget, then."

Sighing, Scarl kneaded his forehead. "Let me show you some reasons for remembering before you decide."

"Like what?"

"You'll see soon enough. We'll be in Hartwater by nightfall day after tomorrow."

Ariel whimpered at the promise of food and a long rest for her feet. Zeke's grunt was more thoughtful.

"The Storian you want us to meet," he said slowly. "Were you his apprentice?"

"Yes," Scarl replied. "He's my grandfather. As well as the best Storian I know, now that Liam's apparently dead."

"Oh!" Ariel's feet stopped. "You're taking us to *your* village?"

"I know I can trust people there," he told her. "To fight for you, if need be. And my grandpop is sure to have some idea what to do next."

The sand and stones of the Drymere slowly gave way to scrub brush and thorns. When a stunted tree appeared, they stopped in its shade. Ariel flopped to the ground. Her stomach complained noisily.

"Ready for that lizard yet?" Scarl teased.

Her forehead wrinkled. "Well . . . can we cook it?"

"Yes." Scarl dug in his pocket. Instead of the lizard, he pulled out his glass. "But I'll see if I can find us anything better to go with it."

Ariel tried not to stare as he worked. Her eyes strayed to his glass anyway. Black specks burst inside it like fleas, then swarmed and melted together until the whole glass looked dark as obsidian. He pocketed it, kicked over a rock, and scooped something from the hollow beneath.

Ariel's face fell. Nothing he found under a rock could be better than lizard. She was horrified when he returned with his tin cup full of beetles.

"Ugh," said Zeke. "You expect us to eat those?"

Scarl whistled. "We probably could, Zeke, but if you do, you're more man than I am. They're buzzers. I was planning to use them as bait."

"The fish line's in your back," Ariel reminded him.

"I haven't forgotten for an instant, believe me. But I'm not baiting fish. Try to be quiet and still for a while."

He overturned the cup near the tree. The trapped insects buzzed angrily. Holding his coat in his hands, Scarl stood against the tree trunk and waited. Zeke napped, but Ariel couldn't. The beetles' noise scratched too loudly at her brain.

Shortly, a fat gingerbird changed course overhead and flapped down near the tree, approaching the overturned cup one wary step at a time. Scarl tossed his coat like a net. A quick motion later, their breakfast was ready to pluck.

"Can I try?" Ariel asked.

Scarl handed her his coat. "Throw when you think it's a moment too soon, or the bird will get the bait and be gone. I'll start a fire."

Passing gingerbirds couldn't resist. Ariel's first quarry flapped away with a croak. The second fluttered free from her arms. She awaited bird three as the mouthwatering smell of Scarl's roasting bird wafted past. Ready to give up and eat his, she found herself with an armload of angry bird in a coat.

"Now what do I do?" She hurried to Scarl with the bundle.

"Find its neck and snap it."

Ariel shuddered. "Will you do it?"

He hesitated. "No. If you want to eat it, you'd better learn how to kill it. But I'll make it easier, for the bird's sake." Reaching into the jumping bundle, he pulled the bird out and trapped its flailing wings under his arm. "Come beside me, grab its neck—watch that beak—and snap it as hard as you can. Hurry, now. Mercy."

The sensations of being snatched from her bed and stuffed into a bag returned to Ariel in a rush. She wanted to let the poor creature go, but its panic and Scarl's urging left no room to back out. Squeezing her eyes nearly shut, she did as he'd told her. Bones crunched. The bird went limp.

"I don't want to do that ever again," she moaned, scrubbing her palm on her leg.

Scarl dropped a hand on her shoulder. "That's why groundmelons and berries and wild carrots are nice. But they're not always there to be found."

Ariel only felt awful until the first bite. Even roast lizard didn't taste too bad if she didn't look closely. The gingerbird was delicious. They sucked up every scrap of the first bird. Scarl made them save most of the second.

"How long have you been wearing that splint, Zeke?" he asked.

Zeke ticked off fingers, calculating. "A little over three weeks."

"What?" Ariel felt as though months had passed since Zeke had fallen out of the maple.

"I think," he added. "I hope I haven't missed my birthday already."

In the end, they decided Zeke's count must be right. Since Scarl felt the splint should stay on a bit longer, he removed the bandage on his own arm instead. He rinsed it in the creek before rolling the meat in ashes from the fire.

"Yuck," Ariel said, watching.

"The ashes will wash off," Scarl said, wrapping the ash-coated meat in the cloth. "And they're fairly clean, compared to flies and dried blood and lint from my pocket and anything else that would otherwise get on the meat."

She sighed. He had an answer for everything. "The cut on your arm is healing, anyway," she said. The scar was pink and still swollen, but it had knit together reasonably well.

"It wasn't nearly as deep as yours." He glanced up. "While we're inspecting everyone's damage, we should probably remove some of your stitches."

"Hooray. They itch bad."

Zeke began snoring long before that task was done. Scarl cut the knots with his knife and carefully pulled out each bit of horsehair, tickling Ariel's sensitive skin. He was so intent on his work that she had a chance to study his face. He'd had no opportunity to shave it for days, and the stubble there made him look rougher than usual.

Ariel wondered if everyone in his village would resemble gangly crows. An odd thought struck her. "Scarl, do you have any kids?"

He paused to look squarely at her. "No. What made you ask that?"

"I don't know. Just wondered." It wasn't so hard to picture him tossing balls or giving piggyback rides. She'd had some of the latter, after all. She couldn't imagine a wife for him, though. He wasn't too ugly—just too hard and, at the moment, too ragged.

He bent back to her arm. Watching, she decided that the big knife so often in his hand didn't fit very well with sweethearts and babies, either. Still, a Finder might be able to find himself a wife if he tried.

"Would you want any?"

His dark eyes flicked up to hers and back to her stitches.

Ariel's throat crimped tight where it passed into her chest. Perhaps she'd asked the wrong question. But his refusal to answer put a cool silence between them just when she'd begun warming.

She was still feeling pinched the next day, despite a change in the landscape as healing as the first burst of spring. An army of pine trees had marched up to displace the desert's water-starved weeds. Mint and cinnamon smells rose from the sunbaked wood, and bearberries dangled from vines. The red kernels, although hard and not really ripe, caused tart explosions in Ariel's mouth. She tried not to let them sour her thoughts, but the strange forest seemed too eerily still. She missed the secretive rustling of ferns and the sunlight winking through a confetti of leaves.

As she gazed around the unfamiliar wood, she caught a dreamy half smile on Scarl's face.

"It's good to be near home," he explained.

She looked away quickly, stung by those words.

"Forgive me. I should have thought before I said that."

It was easier to be angry with him. They walked on, the silence broken only by their footsteps and the trilling of unseen birds.

"Do you have a song, Zeke, that you can sing for those of us who aren't stones?" Scarl asked.

Zeke looked startled. "Not really. What I sing to the stones isn't words, just . . . whatever sounds come into my head that I think they might like." He bit his lip. "I don't want to sing any tree songs. If that's okay."

"I understand."

Brown pine needles crunched under their feet until Ariel's defiance pushed her to speak. "I have a song," she announced. "Part of one, anyway."

"Do you?" Surprise spiked in Scarl's voice.

Inwardly Ariel smiled.

"Shall we hear it, then?" he added.

Ariel sang, sudden embarrassment squeezing her voice. Zeke and Scarl had to veer closer to hear. She'd started the song a fortnight ago, making up her own words for a tune of Elbert's to block out his rude lyrics. The verses had changed with her fortunes. The first time she'd sung it under her breath, she'd sung this:

> They drag me ever on and on,
> I'm all unwilling,
> Tied to a ragged crow
> Too far from home.
>
> Too far from anything,
> My feet are burning
> Walking so endlessly
> Lost from my home.

She'd added on to it since, so now she also sang:

> Walking ever on and on,
> Blood always spilling.
> Finders are awful men.
> Walk to the sun.
>
> Walk to the sun and back,
> My feet are burning.
> Zeke's here to help me now,
> Walk with the wind.

Ariel's voice halted. She'd played with more lines, but those weren't done yet. Acutely aware that her song mentioned both of the people alongside her, she kept her eyes on the ground. She couldn't remember why she had offered to sing it.

"That's pretty good," Zeke said. Ariel stole a peek at his face. Respect rode there.

When Scarl touched her opposite shoulder blade, she flinched.

"Yes." Scarl nodded. "A Farwalker's song."

She flushed and looked hastily forward again. It was infuriating, really. Every time she decided to dislike him, every time he pushed her and she meant to push back, she instead managed to make them both proud. Her own skills seemed to conspire against her. Maybe that reassured him, but it left Ariel uneasy about what surprise might come next.

CHAPTER
29

They marched long into the evening, dodging trees in the gloom, and began early again the next morning. As they climbed into foothills, Ariel began to dread another freezing mountain pass, this time with no blankets. Her worry so consumed her that small signs of human passage went unnoticed until the pines abruptly gave way to a cluster of little brown houses. She stopped in shock.

"They're all made of wood!" Zeke exclaimed, disapproving.

"We haven't so many stones here," Scarl said. "But old trees sometimes wish to leave the world and return as new saplings again. Our Tree-Singer usually can find one when we need."

"This is Hartwater?" asked Ariel.

"At long last. Come on."

He led them to the second house in the cluster. He didn't knock. He just opened the door.

A pale woman with loose, dark hair glanced up, startled. She shrieked Scarl's name. With two long strides, he scooped her out of her seat and into his arms. His face was soon covered with kisses.

Stunned, Ariel stared at the woman's vacated seat. She could only assume it was a bike. The seat of a wooden chair was affixed between two wheels larger than those on barrows back home. Ariel couldn't see any handles, but clearly the contraption could be wheeled about. When the woman's gaze finally shifted to Scarl's companions, he set her gently back into the seat.

"You look dreadful and I can tell that something is hurting you," she told him. "But I'll scold you later for that. Who are your friends?"

"Ariel, Zeke," Scarl said. "Meet Mirayna Allcraft."

Ariel dragged her attention from the bike to its owner. At home, she'd known only men who repaired roofs, mended boats, or built tables and chairs. But this Allcraft was neither male nor well. Mirayna might have been pretty, but hollows dragged at her cheeks and dark circles hung beneath her pale eyes. Even her hands looked as if the skin clung too close to the bone.

"Your wife?" Ariel asked, fumbling for a foothold.

"You might say so," Scarl said.

"No, you might not," countered Mirayna. The adults swapped an impatient look.

"Never mind that," Mirayna added. The wide smile she turned on Ariel and Zeke almost dispelled the haunted look in her face. "Please sit and rest."

While they perched on a bench near the fire, she asked, "Why has he brought you here? Where are you from?"

"The less you know," Scarl said, "the safer you'll be."

"I'm not interested in safe," she replied. "Tell me."

Scarl's jaw tensed. "They're hungry and tired, Mir. So am I. Can you argue with me after we take care of that?"

Her face softening, she reached to squeeze his hand. "I'm just glad you're back. You were gone for so long this time, I started to worry that . . . Well, let me put on the kettle." Placing her hands on the wheels alongside her, she pushed. Her chair turned and rolled to a pantry box.

Ariel could contain her amazement no longer. "You have a bike!"

Mirayna and Scarl both shot her startled glances. Then Scarl chuckled. Removing his coat, he sank into a chair by the window.

"Not a bike," he said. "A wheeling chair."

"My legs don't work anymore," the woman explained. "But your friend and I make a good team. He knew stories and could find things to use, so I was able to craft it."

"And that is one of my reasons." Scarl drilled Ariel with his eyes. "Wheeling chairs. Along with food keepers and better ways to stay warm, so winters don't mean somebody else we know freezes or starves. Plus devices to call for help in the night and cures that work better than crossed fingers and hope. *That* is the kind of thing we're Forgetting."

Ariel looked back at the wheeling chair. She'd thought of marvels from the past only as enticing, not important. But she could imagine what a difference this chair made for Mirayna. She longed to try it herself, even if it wasn't a bike. She knew she could never ask.

Fidgeting with his splint, Zeke asked Mirayna, "Did your legs break and not heal right?"

Ariel nudged him too late. Mirayna's smile barely slipped. But Scarl shoved his weight back out of his chair and crossed to the pantry box himself. He squatted and yanked it open much harder than needed. Mirayna touched his shoulder to soothe him.

"Not exactly," she told Zeke. "I have a sickness that stopped them working some time ago. But I get along all right." Her fingers tapped Scarl as her gaze returned to his back. "I see, however, where you're hurt. If it looks as bad under that filthy shirt as it does from out here, we'd better get the Healtouch for you."

"It'll keep," Scarl growled. He pulled out a half loaf of bread and a small dish of brown paste, banging both down atop the box. He paused as if he couldn't remember why he had taken them out. Twisting, he took Mirayna's hand from his shoulder and pressed it to his lips, his eyes closed. She laid her other hand on his cheek. Ariel could see that Scarl loved this woman terribly, ill or not, and Mirayna returned it. The knowledge wove a new thread through her understanding of him.

Squirming, Zeke kicked her ankle. To the relief of both, Scarl pulled himself from Mirayna to bring over the food, along with a spoon.

"Nut butter," he explained, setting the bowl on the bench next to Zeke.

"Come let me see what you've done to yourself," Mirayna told Scarl. She rolled herself toward the back room. With a glance at his charges, he followed.

Zeke swiped his finger through the unappealing brown paste and poked it into his mouth. When Ariel saw his blissful expression, she used the spoon. Within moments, they'd devoured the bread and licked up the last of the sweet treat.

"We should have left some for them," Ariel whispered.

"Anyone who can make a moving chair must be able to trade for more food than they need," Zeke replied. "She's lucky."

Ariel shushed him, hoping those murmuring in the next room had not overheard. She didn't know what illness troubled Mirayna, but there was nothing lucky about being so sick. She could guess now why Scarl hadn't answered her question about children.

When the adults returned and saw the empty nut butter dish, Mirayna laughed and set about preparing more food. Stirring the fire, she sized up Ariel and Zeke.

"I think I can find a few things that won't fit them too badly," she told Scarl, who'd reappeared in a clean, unripped shirt. Fresh clothes sounded more pleasant than Ariel would once have believed. But when Mirayna suggested that Scarl "show them the basin," she wondered how all three of them would share just one washbowl.

To her surprise, Scarl waved them outside and down a well-used path. Ariel braced herself for a cold bath in the creek and thought longingly of Tree-Singer Abbey.

They ducked under the sweeping boughs of a cedar to a mossy cleft in the hill where water spilled down a rock wall. Zeke stripped off his shirt, ready to stand in its shower.

"You can do that, Zeke," Scarl said, "but you might like this better." He led them up a stair in the hillside. At the top, water pooled before it found its way over the falls. An unpleasant smell of eggs rose from the pond.

"It stinks." Ariel wrinkled her nose.

"It's worth it." Scarl pulled off his boots and socks to plunk his feet in the water. "Ahh."

Gingerly, Zeke followed suit. He grinned and waded in to his knees, then turned to splash Ariel.

"It's warm!"

Soon the two of them sat chest deep in the basin, fully dressed, ducking their heads. One corner of the pool was too hot, but as the water flowed toward the falls, it cooled to a comfortable warmth.

While Scarl bathed more properly, Zeke ran back and forth between the basin and the chilly waterfall. Too lazy for that, Ariel lay back to float. Once she got used to the smell, soaking felt better than a cozy fire and a soft bed combined. Closing her eyes, she let the water leach away sorrows and pain—not to mention bug bites and grit.

A lone Hartwater resident appeared, perhaps drawn by Zeke's hoots each time he plunged into the falls. Scarl rose to speak with the man in low tones.

"What did you tell him?" Ariel asked, after the man had retreated down the path.

"I begged a few favors," Scarl said. "First, to give us some peace, and second, to keep a sharp watch for strangers, in case those we left in the Drymere have followed and are foolish enough to approach. I'd rather the whole village didn't know you are here, but I need them alert. Everyone will be safer that way."

When the dripping trio arrived back at the house, plates had been set on the table. Mirayna handed Zeke garments and asked Ariel to join her in the back room. The air there smelled of wood shavings and oils. Mirayna's crafting table and unfinished goods crowded her bed.

"I think we can tie this skirt under your arms for a dress," she told Ariel, pulling a soft brown wool from a beautiful chest. "With a sweater overtop to keep your arms warm."

She took the wet clothes as Ariel peeled them off. Ariel realized that the fingers of Mirayna's right hand never uncurled. She used it like a boat hook, not a hand, but so gracefully that Ariel hadn't noticed before.

"You're the Farwalker, aren't you?" Mirayna asked quietly.

At Ariel's guilty expression, she nodded and smiled. "I can tell by the way he looks at you. I'm a bit jealous."

She seemed so kind, and Ariel so yearned for a female friend, that she didn't try to stop her tongue. "Do you love him?"

Mirayna smoothed Ariel's wet clothes and set them aside before she answered. "Yes."

Pondering, Ariel wrapped the thick skirt around under her armpits. The woman reached to tie the drawstrings. Ariel felt connected to her in some uncertain way.

She murmured, "You know he's killed people?" Such a brash remark would have earned more than a scolding from her mother. But in the dim room, under the gentle touch, Ariel could ignore the rules that divided her from an adult and a stranger. Besides, she was starting to feel like an adult and a stranger herself.

Mirayna tugged and adjusted Ariel's makeshift dress. "He told me. It's dreadful. But I think I understand why he felt that he must."

"Why don't you want to be his wife, then?"

Mirayna's pale eyes lit on Ariel's face. "You see too much for your age." She stroked Ariel's shoulders. "The way here must have been hard."

Ariel gave a lopsided shrug. Her self-pity had been left far behind.

"Perhaps you can understand this, then," Mirayna said. "I don't want to make him a widower." Her wan skin and haunted eyes weighted the words so their meaning sank heavily into Ariel's heart.

"My legs were only the first things to stop working," Mirayna added softly. "Before long, perhaps, my illness will reach my lungs or my heart." She draped a sweater over Ariel's shoulders and summoned a weak smile. "If we have not been married, it will be easier for him to find some other wife."

Ariel listened to Scarl's voice through the wall as he murmured something to Zeke. She shook her head. "I don't think so." She didn't say more. She had realized, too late, that she had no business touching this wound.

They returned to the front room for a lunch of fried eggs and fish. Ariel giggled at the baggy pants tied onto Zeke and he mocked her dress. The clean-shaven Finder teased them both. Staring at her traveling companions, with soft clothes hugging her own freshly washed body, Ariel felt as if all of them had stepped into different skins.

Wondering who these new people were, she watched Scarl's eyes follow Mirayna. Plainly, this woman was the reason Scarl did anything, including killing Elbert and bringing Ariel here. She noticed, too, that Mirayna only pretended to eat. That, along with their whispered talk, tipped a decision Ariel didn't realize she'd been trying to make.

"Zeke, give me my needle."

Her friend paused, fish bones stretched between his fingers. His glance bounced off Scarl before landing on her.

"Now?"

She nodded. Curious, the adults watched Zeke dig greasy fingers into the end of his splint. He drew out the needle and gave it to her.

"A knitting needle?" asked Mirayna.

"Not exactly." Some of the charcoal had rubbed away, but Ariel could still make out the symbols. She passed it to Scarl. "I can't make amazing things like Mirayna, but I made this."

"What's it f—?" Scarl turned the needle. Catching sight of the symbols, he froze.

"It's a copy of the telling dart before Elbert took it," she explained.

The Finder pulled a long breath, let it out, and set down the needle very carefully.

Ariel's face puckered. She had expected him to be glad. Maybe she shouldn't have revealed her secret.

Rising from his chair, he circled the table. Ariel drew back as he reached for her head. Taking it in both hands, he planted a kiss on her forehead.

"That's for being so clever," he said. "I wish I had something better to give you."

"More nut butter," Zeke suggested.

Scarl laughed and held Ariel at arm's length. She blushed, unable to withstand his warm gaze.

"And for not telling me sooner, I'd like to shake you," the Finder added. A light scowl appeared with his grin. "We'll call it even for now."

Relieved by that glimpse of a Scarl she knew, Ariel smiled.

"What do the symbols mean?" asked Mirayna, picking up the bone needle.

Scarl returned to his seat. "I'm hoping my grandfather can tell us."

Mirayna's brow wrinkled. "He's not here."

At Scarl's exclamation, she explained that a man had arrived days ago—a Storian, if the rumors were true. Scarl's grandfather had decided to take a journey with him, as unlikely as that seemed for two such old men. Mirayna thought they had headed toward Libros.

Scarl slumped in his chair and tapped his fingers on the

table. Then he reached for the needle. "Ariel, would you entrust me with this? I can follow and catch them, but I want to keep you"—he caught himself, continuing—"the two of you far from Mason."

"No point in tangling your tongue," said Mirayna. "It's obvious who your Farwalker is. I could easily copy her symbols to a bit of wood for you. Except I don't really want to help any of you leave."

Relief washed Scarl's face. "Ah, good, yes. A copy will work." To Ariel, he added, "I can leave you here, with people I can rely on. You'll be safer out of his reach."

Dismay flooded Ariel. "No, if you go, I want to go with you." Grasping for words that might alter the Finder's stubborn expression, she added, "Ask your Tree-Singer what she thinks of us going together."

"Mason is a Tree-Singer," he muttered. "I'm not sure I can fully trust her on this."

"I could ask the stones," Zeke offered. "If any here will talk to me."

"Stones?" asked Mirayna.

"Please, Zeke, if you'll try," Scarl agreed. "Otherwise, I'll leave tomorrow."

Mirayna's face fell. "So soon?"

Scarl reached for her hand, but his eyes gave his only reply.

Ariel played with the bones on her plate and tried not to feel cheated. Once she'd given herself over to becoming a Farwalker, the dart, with its mystery, had taken on new importance to her. It seemed the one compensation she'd somehow traded, unwittingly, for her mother and all of her old life. It was a poor substitute, but she wanted all the more fiercely to claim it. The message borne by the symbols was for her, her alone, and Scarl couldn't take away this last consolation, no matter how good his reason.

She secretly vowed not to let him leave without her.

CHAPTER
30

After lunch, the Finder spent a long while with his glass. It seemed to tell him that the remains of Gust's band also had left the Drymere, but he decided they did not lurk near enough to be an immediate threat. That resolved, Mirayna insisted that all her guests visit the Healtouch. She arched her eyebrows at Scarl and said, "I'm not feeding any of you again until you've had attention from her." So he led his young friends across the small village.

"Oh, lass," murmured Pres Healtouch, when she examined the ridges where Ariel's arm and cheek had been split. Scarl had asked the wiry old woman to look after Ariel first, and the healer scowled at him now. "You deserve a whipping if this girl was in your care when this happened."

"I know, Pres. I feel guilty enough as it is."

"I'm afraid you'll wear scars," Pres told her. "There's nothing more I can do now."

Ariel fingered the wound on her face. "Can I see?" she asked, pointing to a small looking glass on the worktable.

Pres hesitated, but reached for the glass. When her eyes fell on it, Ariel exclaimed. It wasn't the pink scar that shocked her. She barely recognized herself. Too many days without quite enough food had thinned her cheeks, which also bore marks left by fear, grief, and strain. Ariel looked at least two years older.

"Don't feel bad." Pres patted her. "You're still young. It may fade."

Ariel glanced at Zeke. She'd seen his face every day, unlike her own, so she hadn't noticed that he had aged, too. Now that she looked, though, she could see it.

The old woman turned to Zeke next.

"Now, don't blame me for that one," Scarl said.

"He's well splinted, it would appear, so I guessed you had no part in that," grumbled the Healtouch. After examining Zeke and finding a sore spot that caused him to yelp, she replaced the splint and told him to let another fortnight pass before he removed it.

When Pres got a look at Scarl's latest wound, she chased Ariel and Zeke from her workroom. The pair sat on the front stoop, the sun on their faces and the open door at their backs. Curious villagers peeked at them through doorways and waved welcomes, but kept their distance, as Scarl had asked.

After a few moments, Pres stepped to her door and nudged Ariel with her toes.

"So it was you who stitched up the hole this foolish fellow put in himself?"

Ariel gulped. "I'm sorry it wasn't much good. I tried my hardest."

"You're a Healtouch apprentice, then, are you?"

Ariel's gaze dropped, her face burning. Zeke started to answer for her, but she overrode him. "No. I didn't pass my test."

"Well, you should have," Pres declared. "It's rough indeed,

make no mistake, and I'll need a good bit of time with him now. You might want to run off and return. But don't look so glum. I've seen worse stitching by grown persons, and none forced to use fish line to do it." She turned on her heel and disappeared before Ariel could shut her gaping mouth.

Zeke grinned. He squinted at the sun and rose to his feet.

"I'm going back to the waterfall," he said, "to see if the rocks there will listen to me."

"I don't want to stay if Scarl goes," Ariel told him. "I don't care what the stones say."

"Well, I do care. And I'm going to tell him the truth, if they'll answer my questions. It'll be for your own good."

Ariel scowled at his back as he sprinted away.

Sitting alone on the front stoop, she couldn't help but hear some of what went on inside. Whatever Pres was doing to Scarl must have hurt. Ariel gritted her teeth at the muffled sounds of his pain.

Yet she did not want to leave her cozy puddle of sunlight. To busy her mind, she pulled her bone needle out of her sock where she'd stashed it, much as she'd once slid the dart into her boot. Zeke's splint had served well to keep the copy a secret, but now Ariel wanted it within easy reach and preferably next to her skin. A touchstone to her mother, it comforted her.

She ran her fingers over the symbols. As it had on the dart, the lightning bolt tingled her skin as if vibrating gently. She smiled, sure the sensation had to be imagined, if not simply a barb left when she'd scratched it. None of the other marks even seemed rough, and a few were so shallow they'd become hard to make out. She decided she'd better rub more charcoal into several when they returned to Mirayna's.

Scarl had shown her and Zeke the mark that represented

the Vault. She peered at it and tried to imagine where it might be and what lay inside.

Each time the rod turned in her grip, the Farwalker mark caught her eye with a wink as though something shiny in its depths were reflecting the sun. That glimmer gave Ariel an idea.

Rolling the bone between her hands, she tried to remember everything Scarl had said when he'd let her try his Finder's glass in the desert. It was just a place to focus attention, he'd told her. That didn't explain how red sparks had appeared, or the black flecks when he used it, but Ariel supposed both could be caused by the Essence in all things. Perhaps her needle had some of its own.

She cradled the bone in both palms and gazed at it. Rather than focusing on individual symbols, she tried to see the complex design they all made together. Viewed that way, they looked like an assembly of ants, legs spread and tangled.

"Where does the summons want me to go?" she breathed. "Show me the way, ants."

She stared without blinking until her eyes watered. The ants blurred. A yelp from Scarl, inside, broke her attention. Ariel looked quickly away from the needle.

"Stop thinking completely," he'd said about finding. That was harder to do by herself than with his help. "Where?" Ariel asked herself, and then wondered if that counted as thinking. Her eyes stared at the dirt, drawn nowhere else. No secret knowledge rose inside her as it had when she'd found the lizard.

Ariel sighed and leaned back on the stoop. Clearly she'd just gotten lucky before. She was no Finder.

Her feet tickled in her boots. Ariel rubbed one against the other, but the itch grew. Unlacing her boots, she kicked them off and peeled away her socks to scratch, half expecting to find the ants she'd imagined. Nothing soothed the tingling until she nestled her bare soles into the cool dirt. An overwhelming desire to walk seized her legs. Unable to resist, she stood and took three purposeful strides before it dawned on her what she had done.

"Oh!" Ariel slapped her hand over her mouth, trapping Scarl's name, which had been next on her lips. As her mind raced, the urge to walk faded. She took another few tentative steps, just to see if that itch would return. If it did, she was trying too hard to feel it.

Ariel returned to the stoop and admired her wiggling toes. Could it be true that they felt a destination unknown to her mind? They'd done it before in the desert, though, without the least effort or knowledge on her part.

Drawing her socks and boots on once more, she wondered how to convince Scarl that her feet knew where to go. He need not go to Libros, unless that happened to be where her path took them regardless. She wouldn't know what to do when they got there, but if her feet led to the Vault, what else could matter?

She'd confide in Zeke first. He'd know the best way to win over Scarl. She'd rather wait until they'd all rested and she'd tested her feet a few times, but the Finder had sounded intent on a speedy departure. She couldn't wait past that evening to tell him.

When she heard Scarl's footsteps behind her, she slid her needle back into one sock, ready to leave. But Pres stopped him not far from the door. After she gave him instructions for tending his newly mended wound, she added, "One more thing, boy."

Ariel smothered a giggle.

A hush entered the Healtouch's voice. "Don't go wandering away again soon."

"I likely will need to, Pres. I'll be all right."

"It's not you I'm concerned with."

Silence leaked though the doorway. His voice, when he found it, carried more of a groan than a question. "Mirayna?"

"Don't make that girl leave the world without your help. Be here to hold her."

The muscles in Ariel's face and neck strained tight. In her mind she saw the hollows beneath Mirayna's eyes.

"How long?" Anger roughened Scarl's words.

"You know I can't say. But a new moon is coming and that's often the mark."

In the next silence, Ariel imagined Scarl's jaw clamping tight. She'd seen it often enough for less cause.

"Thank you for warning me," he murmured finally.

"She'll be upset if she learns that I have. But it's best for you both."

Scarl emerged to trip over Ariel. Cursing, he demanded, "Where's Zeke?"

She scrambled out of his way, afraid to look at his face. "Trying to sing to your stones."

He closed his eyes and nodded. When he spoke again, he was gentler. "All right. Come along, then."

As they walked back to Mirayna's home, Scarl kept his eyes on the path. Halfway there, Ariel gave in to an impulse. She slid her fingers into one of his hands, which hung limp at his sides. He didn't react. She thought he was too sealed in sorrow to notice.

He withdrew his hand just before they arrived. First, though, he gave a brief squeeze.

Ariel spent the afternoon watching Scarl with Mirayna and mulling what had happened on the stoop of the Healtouch.

Now that her elation had faded, she was afraid to test her feet's sense of direction, worried she'd imagined the whole thing. Besides, Scarl made little sign of preparing to leave the next day.

She was about to fetch Zeke from the basin to discuss it when he returned, looking troubled.

"Any luck?" Scarl asked.

Glancing at Ariel, Zeke shook his head. "Not really."

Scarl only nodded thoughtfully and returned to Mirayna's workroom to help her finish a project. Ariel couldn't blame him for not recognizing what she did: Zeke wasn't telling the truth.

She didn't get him alone to find out why until bedtime. Pres Healtouch had offered the use of her sickbed, currently empty. So when Ariel and Zeke began yawning, Scarl walked them back to her house. Pres arranged the pair at opposite ends of the deliciously soft bed so that only their feet overlapped. Zeke's big feet tickled and shoved against Ariel's.

Pres blew out the candle and left, leaving the door ajar. Ariel sat up.

"Tell me what the stones said," she whispered to Zeke.

"Oh, nothing much."

"I know that's not true, Zeke. So stop it and tell me."

Zeke sat up, too, meeting her in the middle of the bed. He plucked at the blanket.

"They didn't say Scarl should leave here without us. Just the opposite. 'Restless young feet will press distant bedrock,' they said. 'His will pace this ground a few moments longer.' Somehow we're leaving without him."

"He can't leave Mirayna yet," she said, reluctant to explain further. She already felt as if she'd stumbled on something that should have been private. The message Zeke had received from the stones shot even more dread through her heart, though. It recalled things Zeke's father had said about her departure from home, words that burned in her memory. "It is best that she go," Jeshua had told Ariel's mother. "And she will. Ignoring the advice of the trees always seems to cause trouble." Often in the days since, Ariel had wondered: if her mother hadn't changed her mind and withdrawn her permission, would she still be alive?

"We'd better go on our own," she said, "before Gust or someone else comes and takes us, and people get hurt."

Zeke nodded sourly. "But to where? Home?"

"No." Too aware that the cushy mattress beneath her wouldn't be there for long, she hugged the blanket to her chest and told him what had happened that afternoon. "I think my feet can take us to answer the summons," she told Zeke. She swallowed to firm her voice, which wanted to waver. "If your stones will help us."

"I believe you," he said, "but Scarl will never let us leave by ourselves. I bet Mirayna won't, either."

Ariel knew he was right. That meant they'd have to sneak away and move fast. But how could they stop the Finder from chasing after?

"Perhaps I can help," came a voice from the doorway. Both young people jumped.

"I'm not going to beg your pardon for overhearing," said Pres, slipping inside. "You're in my sickbed—that makes your troubles my business. Zeke's voice carries better than yours, lass, but I didn't figure he was talking that much in his sleep." The edge of the bed sank as she rested upon it. "Your friend Scarl was planning to deliver you elsewhere, was he?"

Nudging Zeke under the covers to be quiet, Ariel nodded. "But I heard what you told him this afternoon. So we can go by ourselves." The new knowledge that she looked older than her years pressed confidence into her voice. "I'm just afraid he'll come after us, so he won't be here when . . ." She didn't want to make the pending sorrow more real by saying the words.

Pres nodded. "I can take care of that, at least for a while. I'm less sure of you. I can see you've been down some difficult paths with him, but are you sure you'll be—"

"We've done it before," Zeke assured her.

Trying to recall exactly what Pres may have overhead, Ariel took a chance. "We can find our way home." She told herself it was only a half lie because she hoped it was true—even if home was not where she expected to go first. "It'll just be easier if you'll help."

"Perhaps I can arrange for someone to go with you part-way," Pres mused.

"We'd rather go by ourselves than with a stranger," Ariel argued.

"You're as stubborn as your friend Scarl, aren't you?" Pres sighed. "As I might expect."

They worked out a plan. After Pres left them to sleep, Ariel and Zeke only lay back and gazed at the ceiling. His toes, warm against her calf, seemed to say all that was needed between them. This night in a real bed would be the last for a long time to come.

CHAPTER
31

Scarl believed it the next morning when Zeke and Ariel told him Pres had chores for them to do in trade for their bed. Their deception was sealed after Zeke mentioned that he'd tried again with the stones.

"'Don't roll before rain falls,' they said." He glanced up at the cloudless blue sky to hide his discomfort in meeting Scarl's eyes. Zeke had more trouble with untruths than Ariel did.

Relief lit Mirayna's smile. Scarl had told her about Zeke's unusual trade.

"Really? Wait for bad weather?" The Finder rubbed his jaw. His gaze wandered back to his love. In a distant voice, he added, "I had thought . . . but perhaps just as well."

His distraction eased their departure. Afraid Mirayna's loaned skirt would hinder her too much, Ariel located the clothes she and Zeke had arrived in and spirited them out of the house. She also made certain she had her bone needle, which the Allcraft hadn't yet copied. Shortly, the two runaways returned to meet Pres, who had blankets and a pack of food ready. At least a full day would pass before Scarl even knew they were gone, and Pres promised to insist that he stay near Mirayna thereafter.

"That boy may be a Finder, but he hasn't found the one thing he's looked for most," the woman said with a sigh. "Some lost magic that would keep that girl in the world, since this old Healtouch hasn't been able to save her."

Mindful of the Vault, Ariel wondered if it wasn't too late.

"I hope I'm doing the right thing in sending you off," Pres added as they departed. "You're sure you know the way? Don't follow the deer trails crisscrossing these woods. They don't really go anywhere, and the wolves run them at night."

Ariel held very still. She'd never seen a wolf, but she'd heard them howl from afar. They sounded hungry. Before her courage failed or the old woman could change her mind, she nodded and waved, then nudged Zeke toward the trees.

"Goodwill, youngsters," Pres called. "And good-bye."

Pierced by that word, Ariel's heart tripped. Seeing Mirayna and Scarl that morning, she had longed to embrace them both in a heartfelt farewell. She never would have believed just a week ago that she would feel so bad, and so vulnerable, leaving Scarl behind. His trust in their words, and the cause of his distraction, only glossed her discomfort with guilt. She managed to abide it until she and Zeke had slipped out of sight. Then she grabbed her friend's arm and raced away from good-bye.

They ran until rough ground forced them to slow. Ariel spent a few moments absorbed in the symbols on her bone needle, then let her feet tread where they wanted. The sensation of preference was so strong that she wondered if it was totally new or if she'd just never noticed at home, where it may have been muted by familiar paths. The more she thought about it, though, the less clear her direction became. She began nursing a terror that she would run them in circles or lose them for good.

Pushing the lump from her throat, Ariel asked Zeke, "Can the stones tell you if we're going the right way or not?" She held her breath for his reaction.

Zeke kicked a tuft of grass. "I doubt it," he said. "They can feel where we'll most likely end up, but that doesn't mean you meant to go there. Besides, it's more obvious to them that the world is a ball, so directions for them are more . . . curvy. But I can try, if you want." He raised his eyes to her. They held no accusation or worry. "Shall I, Farwalker?" he added softly.

"Maybe later." His confidence boosted hers. Remembering Scarl's advice about not thinking too much, she forged forward.

They did not stop for nightfall. As the woods became black, the trees thinned and gave way to stony alpine meadows that rolled before them like swells on a dark sea. Clouds obscured the stars. Ariel hoped the hidden moon was still fat. If she could, she would have fed it her share of the food to stop it from dwindling.

Her feet began wanting to veer west, but the forest crouched that way, a dark animal waiting to pounce. If they returned to the trees, they'd never see to keep walking. So instead she led Zeke on a route that twisted across boulder fields.

She should have heeded her feet. As she twined her way between upthrust stones, a sudden emptiness opened before her. One boot slipped in loose shale. Instinct flung her weight back, where she fell to an abrupt seat. Behind her, Zeke grabbed her collar. Only air lay under Ariel's heels.

"Careful!" Zeke said. "That was close!"

Hands clutching the ground, she strained to see. A sharp

ravine yawned just before her, its bottom lost in the dark. Ariel's stomach soured as adrenaline flowed through her. They retreated carefully from the crumbling edge of the cliff. Faced by the need to backtrack, though, she lost her drive. She suggested a rest. They settled into a niche between stones, where they'd be hidden from any observer not nearly atop them.

"I don't want to sleep long," Ariel said, fear of pursuit already replacing the shakiness of her near fall.

Zeke offered to stay awake while she napped. Then they'd trade before moving on. Before she lay down, Ariel retrieved her bone needle and clutched it to her heart.

She slipped quickly into her dreams. The bone needle went with her.

Perhaps Misha was most comfortable in surroundings not unlike the abbey; Ariel's clearest dreams of him always came when she slept amid stones. She found herself sitting on an abbey bench with the ghost. He pointed to her fingers, which clutched a bone knitting needle. Instead of her charcoal-filled scratches, the symbols on this one glowed gold.

"It's my telling dart," she explained. "But I can't understand it."

His palm turned up to receive it. He whispered, "I can."

His claim sent a thrill through her. Of course he could. Who knew how long ago he had lived? Misha may have sent and received telling darts himself. As if fired by her excitement, the gold symbols grew in brightness until Ariel squinted. That unnatural glow—something was wrong. She moaned. Discomfort and unease seeped into her dream and dragged her from sleep.

Zeke slumped opposite her, his mouth slack and his eyes shut. But what alarmed Ariel more was the glow—not from the needle still in her fingers, but bouncing off boulders not far away. She sucked in a tight breath. A campfire burned nearby.

Reaching to nudge Zeke, her hand froze. Male voices blew to her ears on the breeze. Although the sound was distorted by echo, one voice came through clearly.

"They're here somewhere, I tell you!"

Trembling, Ariel awoke Zeke and pointed. The whites of his eyes flashed as he made sense of the threat. He gestured for her to stay calm and eased toward the source of the glow on his belly. She slunk behind.

More argument wafted to them. ". . . it's them? I didn't . . . to leave the village so . . ."

". . . too stupid to wait like a cat at a rat hole."

"Maybe you are, and we're just chasing deer mice . . . not the best Finder I've met."

Their chins in the dirt, Ariel and Zeke peeked over the edge of the ravine. Two male silhouettes shifted around a roaring fire below. A third hunkered nearby—or was that just a shadow? One man piled wood on the flames. The second brandished a burning branch. Their argument dwindled to mutters between them.

"Sure, if we make it till dawn," snapped one.

Ariel flinched when Zeke touched her and pointed across the ravine.

"Wolf," he breathed in her ear.

She couldn't see anything until it moved. The dark form of a large dog crouched on the far rim, its snout trained on the bottom. Leaping, it skidded partway down the gulch to a new, lower lookout. Stones rattled beneath it.

Shouts erupted below. The man with the torch thrust it into the dark. It revealed more canine shapes just beyond the light's reach. The nearest retreated, but perhaps not for long. The pack knew daylight was coming. If they wanted anything near that fire, they'd have to close in and take it.

Ariel yanked Zeke's sleeve and wiggled back from the edge. Once shrouded by darkness and boulders again, they rose and first tiptoed, then scrambled, away. Groping through the rock rubble, they followed the ravine west toward the tree line.

"That was a dumb place to sleep," Zeke whispered when he felt safe. "Hard to escape, and easy for something to jump down on you."

"I'm glad they picked it!" Ariel replied. "If they hadn't, the wolves may have come after us! And if not for the wolves, the men might have found us instead. It was Gust or his Finders, don't you think?"

Zeke shrugged. "Too hard to see against the fire. But who else would be out here?"

Grimacing, Ariel scurried on. She was certain from their builds that none of those men was Scarl. As far as she cared, anyone else could be wolf food—particularly anyone hunting for them.

Birds began welcoming dawn sooner than Ariel expected. Shortly the sun, though still under the horizon, bounced enough light into the sky that she and Zeke could move faster without stumbling and banging their shins. Allowed to follow their own path again, Ariel's feet pushed hard. When the ravine dwindled and grew shallow enough, she and Zeke slid into the gulch to cross it. Ariel stared up its length, half expecting men or wolves to bound down it in attack. The silent draw gave no hint of events deeper inside.

Beyond the ravine, they headed northeast. Sunlight poured over the mountains to cheer Ariel's heart. She didn't care if it meant they'd be more visible. She was more afraid of dangers that came out of the dark.

"Scarl probably knows now," Zeke said later that morning. They'd paused to nibble oatcakes Pres had packed for them.

"How long do you think it would take him to catch up, if he won't stay with Mirayna?"

He considered. "Two-thirds of the time we've been gone, maybe less." By late evening, then, a pursuer could be breathing at their backs—if those from the ravine weren't already. Ariel would much rather see Scarl, but her conscience pricked her as sharply as fear. By leaving without saying a word, she and Zeke had undoubtedly made Scarl's difficult place even harder.

The moon that peeped over the mountains that night was too lopsided for Ariel's comfort. Weary, she and Zeke stopped at last, dropping into tall grass near a creek bend. She had hoped to find bedrock or a cluster of boulders, but the earth hadn't obliged. The peaks to their right were too far away. The wooded hills and meadows had given way to a grassy basin, beyond which a tongue of the Drymere licked at the mountains. Streams trickling through the grassland ensured plenty of water for now, but other than wet pebbles, she and Zeke didn't have stones. The stems waving over their heads would have to suffice to hide them from anyone, man or wolf, who was looking.

Ariel yearned for another dream of that gold-engraved needle. Wanting a dream and finding it, however, were two different things. Though her grass bed was softer than usual, she lay awake a long time. The smell of damp soil reminded her of the sea. Her chest thrummed with longing for people and things out of reach.

When at last her mind let go of waking, Ariel wandered a shadowy forest. Eyes glinted in the dark. She thought some belonged to people she trusted, but she couldn't tell those from the eyes of wolves. She had to keep moving to stay out of their teeth.

The trees thinned until one stood alone. Ariel recognized its shape from the abbey—but this cherry had died. A bloated moon gleamed on its branches, where shriveled leaves clung. They rustled a warning. A dark blot oozed down the trunk to the earth.

Its touch stirred dust or ashes below. From the cloud, the shadow rose into the shape of a young man, but with no face. Ariel shuddered, fearing it would leap and take hers.

"Misha? Is that you?"

The shade moaned with the wind. "You did not bring it. The bone."

"Yes, I did." Her hands, though, were empty. Searching with the twisted logic of dreams, she checked both her socks for the needle and then pushed up her left sleeve. Instead of a scar there, Ariel stared at an unhealed slash in her skin.

A black hand gripped her wrist and yanked down. Her arm bones sprang out through the wound.

Gasping to scream, Ariel froze. Symbols etched the larger bone of her forearm. The telling dart's message had been carved into *her*.

"I understand all." The shadow moved closer, exhaling rot. Its voice thinned to a hiss. "Shhhall I shhhow you?"

Fear sucked Ariel's heart into her belly. This dreadful thing was no kind teenage ghost. It stank not only of death but of absence and loss, forgetting and pain. A distant part of Ariel's mind knew she was dreaming, but nothing would change if she woke herself up. This raw Misha would embrace her the next night, or the next. Always there, endlessly waiting.

Certain she was asking to die, but unable to resist what that primal dark offered, Ariel stepped into the blackness. "Yes. Show me."

Not long before dawn, she awoke. One cheek rested on clammy, wet earth. Her left hand dangled, numb, in the creek. She jerked upright, her heart thudding, and spit mud from her lips. Ariel yanked at her sleeve. Her forearm bore merely a scar.

Grateful to be alive and inside her skin, she hugged her arms to her chest. Handprints, not all of them hers, tracked the mud all around her.

Without bothering to wipe the muck from her face, she crawled to Zeke where he snored in the grass. Before the sun rose, they were walking again.

Her dream lingered, both hounding her and leading her on. For the first time since flunking her Naming test, Ariel Farwalker knew where she was going and what lay ahead.

PART FOUR
FARWALKER

CHAPTER
32

"Uh-oh. Look."

Ariel glanced back. Zeke had stopped. Shading his eyes, he squinted at the horizon ahead.

"I saw something flash." He pointed. "There, again."

A small cry escaped her. Something moving in the distance had reflected the sun.

"It's coming toward us," Zeke added. "Do we have to keep going this way?"

Ariel gritted her teeth. "This is the right way."

From the moment she had awakened yesterday morning, she had been seeking a spire among the eastern mountains. She and Zeke had soon left the grassland and now minced along the gravel-strewn border between mountain and desert. Every mile forward revealed new peaks, but not yet the one that she wanted. Like a fang, it would be more pointed and sharper on one side than the rest, fringed, if not shrouded, with cloud. A voice in a nightmare had hissed its name: Cloudspear. Ariel's skin prickled when she thought of that voice.

The alarm now in Zeke's voice troubled her, too.

"This won't be the right way if it leads us to Mason or Gust!" he exclaimed. "I don't think Scarl could have passed us to be doubling back. Find some other route, Ariel, or a good place to hide, right away. Or I will. If we wait too long, whoever it is will be able to see us."

Ariel had no intention of turning into the desert, so she frowned instead at the rumpled land to her right. A wet glimmer traced the bottom of a ravine. A swath of lavender flowers tinted a ridge. If not the path her feet wanted, then which way instead? Frustration warped her face. She hated that their safety depended on her.

Then something like the pull of a tide drew her feet toward the creek-threaded gully. They'd inclined northeast for days, but now that she had a reason to detour, her instincts responded.

When he and Ariel reached it, Zeke splashed into the stream with his boots. The water drained from the gulch like blood from a scratch, the slopes above too loose with shale for easy walking.

"This is good," he said. "We won't make any tracks."

Behind him, Ariel wavered. Once they entered the gully, she'd lose the vistas that would reveal Cloudspear. Besides, she didn't want to get her boots wet.

"What are you waiting for?" Zeke stared back at her.

"I'm coming," she growled. It was crazy to worry about wet boots when whatever approached might want to kill them. She got nearly ten steps before the cold water seeped in.

With Zeke regularly twisting to gaze back toward whatever had flashed, they began a slow jog. The gorge's tight bends hid much of what lay ahead. Bear grass and briars straggled across the steep hillsides. The smell of wet stones made Ariel think of her nightmare.

When the vacant, hissing blackness had offered to show her

the telling dart's message, she had known it would give her a view through a window belonging to Death. All things, made and unmade, succumbed to that void, and Ariel feared to approach. But the symbols had become part of her somehow, a message both to her and of her, and she wanted, she needed, to be shown.

Blinding her eyes, engulfing her in an icy embrace, the dark shape had swallowed her whole. Its cold voice had wormed into her ears, and Ariel had tried then to scream. The hiss poured instead from her own open mouth. Her last rational thought had been, "Lost." The world, lost, and her friends, lost, and her soul, lost: all lost.

As she drowned in that word, drifting in blackness, an image appeared in her mind. A fang, she thought, one that would bite. This fang pointed up, though, standing alone.

Her dreaming mind clutched another idea. "Stone," she thought. "Mountain." The peak anchored her in the swirling dark. The hiss faded. The growl of a predator slipped overtop.

"Cloudspear," it said. "The mouth of the mountain. Come united. A message is caught in a throat."

Like water through a gap in a boat hull, reason flowed back into Ariel's mind. She asked the darkness, "That's what the telling dart said?"

"What was outside is known or has fallen behind you. The inside still speaks."

The darkness receded. The image of Cloudspear remained like a glimpse of the sun in eyes that have closed.

When it, too, faded, Ariel found herself sprawled near the dead cherry tree. Dressed once more in the form he had taken in life, Misha sat cross-legged near her. One of his hands gleamed a wet red. The other raised a—

Knife blade! Ariel jerked away. Her alarmed motion woke

her, casting her to the muddy bank of the creek where her dream and her night's sleep had ended. The dream sent one last image, almost too late. It wasn't a knife in Misha's hand after all. He'd gripped only a large pale feather.

Now, two days later, Ariel splashed upstream next to Zeke, wondering what kind of mouth could belong to a mountain. It might be a source of uncanny noises, like blowholes in sea cliffs. Or it could be a cave, a big crack, or lips formed of stone. Perhaps such a mouth could speak of lost treasure or open to reveal the Vault. She just hoped it wasn't able to bite.

Feeling as though one set of teeth nipped at her heels while another waited ahead, Ariel looked over her shoulder. She couldn't see very far.

"Ask some of these rocks if anyone's behind us," she suggested to Zeke. "And how close."

Without stopping, he pointed ahead. "I'll try when we get to that outcrop. We'll be more hidden there, and the big ones are easier to hear."

To drown her worries and help lift her waterlogged boots, Ariel began humming the song she'd sung for Scarl and Zeke. She tested some new phrases under her breath.

Walk where the nightmare leads,
Looking for Cloudspear.
Follow the water's path.
Don't walk, but run.

Rainwater running now,
Dripping from Cloudspear.
Look for the mountain's mouth
Far from the sun.

"How do you keep doing that?" Zeke asked. "Thinking up fresh words, I mean."

"I don't know. They just show up in my head. But they don't rhyme much."

"They don't need to."

Ariel wasn't sure she agreed. She preferred songs that rhymed. But this one fit well with the rhythm of her feet.

Zeke's outcrop was farther away than it looked. By the time they arrived, the afternoon had begun to wane. Nibbling dried fruit, Ariel tried to sit still and rest. Even a few moments without motion made her nervous. She was too certain Gust or his Finders dogged them.

Zeke patted the stone bluff tentatively, as if greeting a strange dog. He gave Ariel an embarrassed glance.

"Don't listen, okay? My songs don't sound as good to people as yours."

"I want to hear, though. I would never laugh, Zeke, honest." She couldn't talk him out of his self-consciousness. Finally she stuck her fingers in her ears and said, "All right, all right. I'll hum to myself."

When his lips stopped moving and he approached her, looking glum, she unplugged her ears.

"The stones here aren't very friendly." He sighed. "But there are definitely people behind us. 'People crawling everywhere,' it told me, 'like ants.' It was complaining, and that's all I could get it to say."

"Fine," Ariel grumbled. "We'll crawl away and leave it alone." With an anxious glance downstream, she led on.

Tucked as they were in a fold of the land, twilight arrived early. Clouds settled onto the peaks, where tendrils of mist glowed in the last light.

"Let's go up there for the night." Ariel pointed to a ridge above.

Zeke looked dubiously at the treacherous slope and then back the way they had come.

"I know we'll be visible from farther away," she added. "But we can't sleep in the creek, and I'm sick of being down in this crack where we can't see things sneaking up."

When she insisted, Zeke gave in. They hauled themselves up to a hollow protected from the worst of the wind. Darkness flowed uphill behind them, so their new vantage revealed nothing but night. They wound themselves in their blankets and huddled close to share warmth.

Ariel woke to raindrops slapping her face. Next to her, Zeke mumbled and pulled his blanket over his head. Lightning flashed. In that half second of vision, Ariel saw angry swirls of storm trapped against the higher peaks to the east. Thunder rolled as though the mountains were falling around them.

Clutching Zeke's arm, she pressed her face against him. "I hate thunder."

"I'd rather have thunder than—"

A threatening new sound tore the night. Ariel bolted upright. A roar like an overstoked fire rose from below, accompanied by the hollow clunking of rocks.

"I think that's the creek!" Ariel said. Another flash of lightning gave them a glimpse. Rushing gray water scoured the streambed, clawing high up the banks. Neither Ariel nor Zeke had witnessed a flash flood before, but both knew the fury of storm-driven waves.

Ariel tugged her damp blanket tighter. "If we'd slept down there," she said, awed, "we'd be drowned."

"Or at least swept away. I won't argue the next time you pick a campsite. That must be a Farwalker skill."

Zeke cocked his head. Ariel's ears caught it, too. Someone downstream was shouting.

"They're close, Zeke!" she exclaimed.

"Not for long, if they're caught in that water," he said. "Nothing we can do now, anyway, except hide. It's way too dark to start walking."

Early the next morning, the two picked up their blankets to hurry away. Obstacles had only begun to emerge from the gloom, so Ariel and Zeke couldn't move fast, but by the time the sun cleared the horizon, they'd put several more miles under their boots.

When they crossed a scree field beneath a bluff, Ariel touched Zeke's arm.

"Think one of these cliffs might tell you how much farther to Cloudspear?" She was starting to fear it would never appear.

He turned, halted, and groaned.

"I guess it doesn't matter," Ariel whispered, when she'd followed his gaze. Two figures tracked a slope they had crossed themselves not an hour before.

CHAPTER
33

By midmorning, capture seemed inevitable.

"I don't see how we can outrun them," Zeke said, panting. He and Ariel jogged as often and as rapidly as the landscape would allow, but each time they crested a hill and looked back, their pursuers loomed closer. They were men, it was clear now. They weren't moving as fast as Scarl would, Ariel thought, but the men must have run sometimes, too.

She convinced Zeke to keep fleeing. The bleak hills offered nowhere to hide, and she would rather drop from exhaustion than turn to face defeat. Her silent appeals to Misha proved fruitless. The ghost had not appeared to her since their last frightening encounter.

As Ariel and Zeke trotted past the base of a cliff, its face hid them briefly from those behind. Zeke peered up. The basalt's geometric columns formed a jagged staircase of stone.

"Quick, let's try to climb this," he said. "I'll give you a boost."

"Are you serious?"

"If we can reach the top before they spot us, maybe they'll pass underneath. Then we could double back and escape."

"If we don't, they'll just wait at the bottom until we both die of thirst!"

"Do you have a better idea?" Zeke grabbed her as if to toss her to the first shelf, willing or not. Deciding she'd rather die of thirst than become a prisoner again, she accepted his help.

They rapidly gained the lowest ledges. When the climbing became harder, Zeke slipped past Ariel, finding it easier to pull her from above than to push from below. He sang under his breath as they climbed, presumably pleading for permission or help. Snatches of his voice spilled down to her, but so softly that she wondered if the stone could hear him at all.

Before they had scaled more than a dozen feet up, they got stuck. The narrow steps in this staircase were farther apart than they looked from below. Slippery moss clung in cracks that suggested the stone couldn't be trusted—it might fall off in slabs. While Zeke searched for handholds over his head, Ariel clung to the wall, trying to keep panic from shaking her limbs. She wanted to check on their pursuers, but she hardly had space to swivel and look without tumbling off backward.

"The stone thinks we're brave to climb up here," Zeke gasped. "But it doesn't know how it can help." He turned his voice back to song.

Ariel slid one hand down her calf to the bone needle tucked in her sock. Though she no longer needed it, touching it still gave her strength.

"Zeke," she said, not really expecting to break through his focus. "I'm climbing back down. They only want me. They'll let you go, maybe. Stay here." On solid ground, she could fight. If she surprised them, perhaps she could stab her broken needle into somebody's eye.

She reached carefully with one leg to the foothold below.

"I don't know what trouble you're brewing up there, Ezekiel, but come down at once!"

Ariel recognized the voice before she could turn to its owner. "Storian!"

"Ariel? Is that you? I wasn't sure from afar."

"Wait!" cautioned Zeke. "Who's that with him?"

Heedless, she scrambled down, tumbling the last feet into Bellam Storian's arms.

"I'm so glad to see you're unharmed." He embraced her and then held her at arm's length. "Not unharmed after all," he added. "You look battered, poor thing."

Zeke's warning belatedly found a hold in her mind. Ariel's eyes jerked to the second man. Even older than Storian, he leaned on a staff and reached to rub one of his knees. Something about his shoulders looked familiar, but she was certain he was no one from home. More important, he was nobody she'd met in the desert with Gust.

Ariel turned back to Bellam. He looked worn, thinner, and bent, but the sight of him still flooded her with homesickness.

"What are you doing here?" she asked.

"I will return the same question to you," he replied. "The two of you led us on a bit of a chase. These tired old legs are about to give out."

"We didn't know it was you. Zeke!" She tipped her head up. "Aren't you coming down?"

"He's just being careful," Storian said. "I can't say I blame him, with all the ill that's afoot. The last time I saw him, he was searching for you. He succeeded, that's clear."

"I must interrupt," said the other man. "It was hard for me to hear that my grandson may have stolen a child. Is it true?"

"You're Scarl's grandfather?" Ariel cried.

"Answer my question before I will claim him."

Ariel tugged a lock of her hair. "Well, he did snatch me," she said. The old man put a hand over his eyes.

"He was trying to help, though." Zeke slid down from his ledge. "To protect her from murder."

The grandfather drew his palm from his eyes to his lips. "This tale grows more grim in the telling. First Liam goes missing, now this."

His name was Derr Storian, he told them, when they'd all settled to rest. It was something he owned that had flashed in the sun yesterday—an oblong tube like a hollow rolling pin. Glass gleamed inside. When Derr raised it, Ariel could see his eye through the glass, looking twice as big as it should.

"Old men have old-fashioned tricks," Bellam explained. "We saw you through this from afar, Zeke, but I couldn't tell who you had with you or where you thought you were headed. I feared you were looking the wrong way for home. But it took us a while to catch up."

"And to make sure you hadn't drowned last night, too," Derr added.

"We heard you shouting," Ariel said. "We thought you were Gust."

At their blank looks, Zeke offered, "He wants to kill us. That's who we were running away from."

Confusion and alarm creased both elders' faces. "We did no shouting," began Derr.

Bellam broke the air with a clap. "Stop. I believe you both learned your lessons better than that. This is no classroom, but I must ask you to recite the story properly, from the start. Don't leave anything out."

Ariel's fingers rose to her collar and the green story bead

there. The gift from Bellam had found its own story, she realized. She just didn't know yet how it would end.

The two Storians listened in disbelief while she and Zeke
described their adventures with Scarl. When she admitted that
they'd snuck from Hartwater, Derr gazed doubtfully southward.
In turn, the old men explained that they'd visited Libros, hoping the Storian there would have news of the darts—or that
two Finders would show up with Ariel.

"But we found Liam's home in disarray," added Derr, "and
few of his neighbors would talk."

Ariel told them that, according to Scarl, Liam Storian had
received a dart of his own, but that his mark on hers had since
vanished.

"He's dead, then." Derr sighed. "Despite the dart's warning."

Ariel exclaimed. "You know what it says?"

Bellam gave her an apologetic look. "Only the outside. I told
Derr what I knew, and I'd memorized the symbols I didn't. We
worked those out together. I'm sorry, Ariel. I never dreamed the
summons was intended for you. With the Finders after it, I
thought you'd be best off not knowing anything the dart said.
Little good my caution did."

She waved off his regret. "So tell me that part of the message!"

"It said, 'It is past time for the Vault to be found. Come take
up this challenge no later than Beltane. Timekeeper is counting. Expect riddles and risk.'"

"When's Beltane?" Zeke asked.

"Mayfest," Derr replied. "Five days from now. Of course, it
won't matter, since we haven't the rest of the message inside."

Afraid they wouldn't believe her, Ariel shared what she'd
learned in her nightmare. They greeted her revelation with

astonished excitement. Derr assured her that Cloudspear rose not far away.

"We could get there tomorrow," he said.

Despite legs that were already trembling, she insisted they go far enough to glimpse it that day. When she crested a hill a few hours later, the view beyond stopped her breath. Flags of mist fluttered from a black spike of stone lording over the valley. Moisture gleamed on the rock like the blood of gored clouds.

Tears of relief pricked Ariel's eyes. She didn't need Derr, climbing slowly behind her, to introduce Cloudspear.

Coming up alongside her, Zeke pointed, not to the spire but lower on its flank. A black slit gaped there.

"The mouth of the mountain," Ariel murmured. "At last."

The Storians pleaded old bones and tried to dissuade her from trekking farther that day. Nothing would do but for her to keep going until she'd reached that frowning mouth.

By then, all four were footsore, and their shadows had merged with the twilight. Although much wider than tall, the cave yawned over their heads as they entered. They dropped their gear just inside, amid a rubble of rock.

"Are there great rooms back in there?" Ariel asked, peering into the blackness.

"I've never come in," Derr replied. "According to stories, it slips around the flank of the mountain, breaking through now and then like the tunnel of a great mole." He nodded toward the northwest. "The true mouth of the mountain opens that way, facing Libros. Most people would say we've come to the tail end instead."

"If there's truly a message here for you, Ariel," said Bellam, "we may have to pass all the way through to find it."

"We can't without torches," Derr said. "We can walk to the

mouth on the outside instead and collect fuel on the way. We'll have to take care where the ground falls in, like that." He gestured. Over their heads, the ceiling was cracked and riddled with chimneys. When the moon rose, its gleam trickled through them, the only relief from the dark.

Before they all lay down to sleep, Zeke slipped past the puddles of moonlight to sing softly in the cave's complete darkness. Too tired to await the results, Ariel found a smooth spot away from the cave mouth and out of the chill mountain wind. Her eyes closed. In the cave's spooky echoes, she hoped not to dream of Misha or anything else.

Not enough hours later, Ariel woke with a start. A glow reflected around her, too near to be sunrise. The Storians hunched alongside a small fire.

A well-honed instinct for danger spiked in her mind. Her shoulders jerked up. "What are you doing?"

Her voice woke Zeke. He blinked, his face rubbery.

"Nothing to trouble your own rest," Bellam said softly. "Old bones just don't sleep when they're driven so hard."

Ariel imagined the fire shining for miles, a bright eye in its socket. "If the others are still after us, they might see it!"

"They'll only see that you're no longer alone," Bellam soothed her. "They won't dare attack you with us here."

Zeke's hand clamped her elbow. She followed his gaze to the gloaming outside.

A single person approached. From his shape, she could see it was Gust.

CHAPTER
34

A whimper escaped Ariel. She leaped to her feet.

The old men moved less quickly. Bellam rose to stand at the cave's mouth, his hands on his hips. Derr retreated to join Ariel and Zeke.

"It's all right," he murmured. He hefted his wooden spyglass like a club. "Looks like he's alone. Even with a weapon, he can't just walk up and take you."

"That's far enough," Bellam announced.

Just outside, Gust took several steps more. "How about a 'good morning'?" he called.

"No point in playing games," Bellam replied. "Go back where you came from and save us all trouble."

"Oh, I've had so much trouble already, a bit more won't matter." Gust resumed walking directly toward Ariel and Zeke.

Bellam brandished Derr's walking stick and started toward Gust.

Fingers darted from the darkness behind Ariel to grab at her collar. She wrenched herself free. Zeke sprang away to her

right. A grunt of surprise was cut short by a dull crack. Derr
groaned in pain.

Alarmed, Bellam glanced back from the entry. That lapse
was enough. Gust dashed forward. Though he tried to resist,
Bellam was neither young nor had spent his life working his
muscles. Gust yanked the staff free and cracked it against the
Storian's legs. Bellam dropped. Stretching the staff between
both hands like a rope, Gust slipped it over Bellam's head to
choke him. Bellam's fingers clawed at the staff, but his face
quickly glowed crimson.

Gust smiled toward Ariel and Zeke, frozen on opposite sides
of the cave mouth. He stood between them and freedom.

"That wasn't much trouble at all," Gust said.

"No," someone agreed.

Ariel whirled. Slightly farther back in the cave stood one of
Gust's Finders, who had failed to grab her. Derr slumped at his
feet. Somehow the man had slipped in behind them.

Flapping his arms weakly, Bellam choked, "Run."

"Only if you want to give these old men more pain," Gust
told Ariel. "If you're smart, you'll just sit. I don't want to kill
any old men, and I won't—if *you* don't."

Ariel teetered on the balls of her feet. She couldn't see a
clear path to slip past him.

Zeke cautiously lowered himself to one knee. His frame
remained taut. Ariel had seen him win enough footraces to
believe he could still burst free. But she wasn't nearly so speedy.
Even if they bolted together, not more than one of them would
escape.

To gain time, she mimicked Zeke's stance.

"Good. You see, I'm not the killer your friend Scarl is." A

gurgle of pain squeezed through Bellam's pinched throat. Ariel winced. "Not yet, at least," Gust added. "Matthias?"

The Finder hauled Scarl's grandfather to his feet. Derr's eyes rolled, and relief trickled through Ariel's terror. Groggy, the Storian couldn't stand on his own, but he clearly fought to gather his wits. His captor dragged him between Ariel and Zeke to the front of the cave, joining Gust. Together the men blocked the entrance completely.

Ariel considered a dash back into the dark. If they hid, would Gust search? Or simply wait until thirst did his work?

"Pray to any god you like, boy, it won't matter." Gust sneered. Ariel stole a glance at Zeke. His eyes were on the stone over their heads. His lips moved.

"Tie up these geezers," Gust ordered his companion. To Ariel and Zeke, he added, "I had a gift for the two of you. Perhaps we'll give it to your friends instead, shall we?"

His sarcasm drew a curtain in Ariel's head, veiling her terror and shock. Only hatred and instincts for survival were left in front of that drape. She watched coldly as Matthias bound first Derr and then Bellam. Gust drew a jar from one pocket of his coat.

"If you'll come closer, you'll have a better view," he suggested. "We picked up a few pets in the Drymere."

A rattling sound crossed to Ariel's ears. Goose bumps rose under her clothes. She could guess what squirmed in the jar—the ugly brown creature that had skittered toward them when she and Zeke had lain buried in sand.

She found her voice simply to slow down the chaos. "What is it?"

"Scorpions."

"No, thank you. I don't want a pet."

"I insist. I don't make a habit of repeating mistakes. But your pets don't enjoy their jar, I'm afraid. If we let them loose—say, into a collar—they're likely to sting."

Bellam struggled feebly. Matthias yanked loose the collar of Bellam's shirt and took the jar, prepared to upend it. If he did, its contents would drop against the Storian's skin.

"Don't!" Though loud enough to echo, Ariel's voice sounded distant in her ears.

"No? Very well," Gust said. "Here is your choice. The two of you lock hands, march straight to my friend here, and stand still to be tied. If you do that, these old men can go home, or wherever they were headed before your paths crossed.

"If you don't," Gust added, "the scorpions sting. Watch them die. It's painful, I'm told. And you're next."

Ariel clenched her fists. "What happens if you tie us up?" She had little intention of making a deal, but she grasped for every moment that kept the threat in the jar.

"I take you to Hartwater. Oh yes, I know where Scarl Finder lives. I will make sure he watches while Matthias ends both of your lives. I don't know which of you he most wants to protect, and I don't care. It won't hurt much, I promise. At this point, I'm more interested in hurting him. He killed a man I admire and a woman I—never mind. But I will burn every little wooden house in Hartwater to the ground, if I must, to draw him out."

Gust truly was a Fool, Ariel thought, if he expected them to submit to either awful choice he'd described.

"So what will it be?" Gust continued. "Here now? Or Hartwater later?"

"But what if Scarl's not there?" She imagined villagers rising to fight.

"If he's not there . . ." Gust shrugged. "Your deaths and

some burning will hurt him enough. If I leave you there, I can be sure he'll eventually find out. That isn't true here. With that small satisfaction, I can go home and collect what I'm owed and be done with it."

"You could just go home now," she pointed out.

"No," he said softly, "I can't. Make your choice."

Ariel drew a deep breath. If she screamed, would Misha hear and respond? But the ghost hadn't made his presence known for days. As the breath left her again with nary a whimper, so did her resolve not to bargain. She couldn't bear to watch her gentle Storian suffer.

Ariel forced the words out. "All right. We'll go with you." If Gust didn't kill them right away, they might still escape. She rose off her knee and edged toward Zeke.

"Gust."

Ariel jumped, startled as much by the end of Zeke's silence as by the command in his tone.

Gust narrowed his eyes. "What is it?"

"I have a question for you first." Even Ariel could see that Zeke was stalling. But a hard and confusing confidence lay over his face. In her distant, cool thoughts, Ariel realized she was glimpsing the man Ezekiel Stone-Singer might become, if he still got the chance.

"Ask it and be quick."

"All right," Zeke said slowly. "I will. Here's my question, then: before you grabbed our Storian, and before you got the staff away from him, and before we were even really awake—how did your Finder get in behind us?"

Before Gust even opened his mouth, the answer came from the darkness behind them.

"The same way I did."

CHAPTER
35

The familiar voice at her ear whisked aside the cloak over Ariel's emotions. With a choked cry, she started to turn.

Derr blinked and said the name for her. "Scarl?"

A hand yanked Ariel farther into the dark. She felt his body glide past as he drew her behind him. Losing her balance, she started to fall. A screech stuck in her throat. More hands, Zeke's this time, caught her. The instant Scarl had moved forward, Zeke had jumped toward her, keeping Scarl between them and the rest of the men.

"You wanted to see me?" Scarl's voice lilted, soft and deadly. He slipped his pack off his shoulder. His knife was already out.

Sudden fury flashed in Gust's face. A cold mask snapped overtop it.

"How convenient," he said. "You've saved me a trip."

Scarl's gaze shifted between Gust and Matthias, the tip of his knife rocking lightly. He advanced.

Matthias asked, "What do you want me to—"

"Just get out of the way," Gust growled.

With a quick motion, Matthias opened the jar and emptied it into Storian's shirt.

"No!" Ariel's scream and its echoes drowned any sound Bellam made. He jerked, either hearing or feeling the scorpions' release. Gust shoved him aside and leaped with the staff raised for Scarl.

Still screaming, Ariel didn't realize she'd jumped toward them until Zeke slammed her into the cave wall and pinned her. His voice joined the bedlam. Although he, too, was shouting, more than pure emotion poured out. The Stone-Singer was singing as never before.

The stone around them answered.

Zeke shouted just a few recognizable words. "Scarl, get back!"

With a thunder more akin to the sea than the sky, the cave mouth collapsed.

The blast knocked Ariel and Zeke to the ground. For a moment no air seemed left there to breathe. Ariel's lungs fought to work, her eyelids clenched with the effort. Sheer will pried her eyes open again.

Dust swirled. The wash of dawn's glow through the entry had vanished. In its place, weak light trickled down from above. Ariel pressed her chest off the ground with one hand. Grit clung to her face. Her elbows, knees, and hip bones throbbed where they'd jolted against the stone floor. No rocks crushed her, though. Her arms and legs informed her they were all still attached.

"Zeke?" Her voice trembled.

He remained splayed on the rock, but he coughed.

Ariel's own coughing answered. As the dust settled and fresh air flowed in from above, their dry rattling faded. Only then did Ariel notice the utter stillness around them. Her eyes scanned the gloom where the cave entry had been. Jumbled rock filled the space from bottom to top. The adults had all vanished.

"The mountain answered," Zeke mumbled. He sat up. Any trace of the man Ariel had seen in him a moment ago had departed. Stunned by what he'd unleashed, the boy stared at the pile of rubble. "I didn't think . . ."

"Are they outside?" Ariel asked, not wanting to believe the report from her eyes.

Zeke's lips writhed as he tried not to cry. He shook his head.

Ariel spied the tail of a coat sticking out from beneath a boulder. A man had stood in that coat. She didn't know who.

Her propping arm folded beneath her. She fell back down to her belly with a *whoompf*.

"Storian!" Ariel wailed. Ever practical, her mind suggested that stones might have been better than whatever a scorpion did. She wanted to scratch that thought from her brain. "No!"

"Not Scarl, too?" Zeke moaned. "Please, I thought he was back far enough! Scarl?"

Something shifted near the edge of the rockfall. A stone clunked. An arm emerged. A cascade of rock crumbs slid off it, raising more dust.

"Scarl!" Zeke jumped toward the arm. Ariel remained frozen, too frightened of what she might see. Crushed bodies and gore lay invisible under those rocks. The vile knowledge washed through her. One of those squashed was the Storian she had known all her life. She didn't hear the hitching, dry sobs that escaped her.

Zeke brushed mounds of rock shards from Scarl's head and chest until the Finder's one free hand grabbed the boy's wrist so tightly that Zeke squeaked.

"Stop it."

"You're okay!" Zeke reassured him. Tears thickened his voice. "One of you, at least, is okay."

"No." Scarl wheezed, a tight sound filled with both dust and pain. "Dead would be better." His head turned through the swirling murk toward them. The whites of his eyes popped from the grime coating his face.

When his gaze struck Ariel's, he closed his eyes and turned his face back toward the ceiling. That silent rebuff stung. Nonetheless, she stepped closer, staring in shock.

Scarl lay on one hip. Zeke's hands traced the lanky arms and legs amid the strewn rocks. At first he found only bruises, and Scarl drew both arms to his chest. But the Finder's lower right leg disappeared completely beneath the edge of a slab.

Though Ariel's stomach was already empty, her gorge rose to make certain. She could only imagine the crushing force on that unseen ankle and foot. A cold sweat popped onto her skin.

"Can you move this leg?" Zeke asked Scarl, his hand trembling over but not touching Scarl's shin.

"I can see, so there must be some cracks overhead," Scarl said. "Look around. Can you climb out from here?"

"Don't know," Zeke muttered. He sized up the rock on Scarl's leg.

"If not, you'll have to walk through the dark to the hole I dropped in through. It's not far. Keep one hand on the side of the cave and go slow until you see sunlight over your heads. If you help each other, you should be able to climb out."

"We might be able to lift this," Zeke told Ariel. He positioned himself on Scarl's far side. Hands skimming the anvil-shaped slab, Zeke raised his eyes to meet hers. "Are you going to help me or not?"

Zeke's wounded regard jolted Ariel loose from her stunned disbelief. She jumped to join him.

"Don't even try," Scarl warned.

"What are you talking about?" Zeke demanded. "We might be able to get you out."

"You'll just hurt yourselves," said the Finder. "Even if you can move it, Zeke, all you're going to do is put me in a lot more pain. If I don't bleed to death, the shock will probably kill me."

"He might be right," Ariel whispered, hating the words. She'd once seen a fisherman with a shark spear through his biceps. He'd hardly bled—until the spear was removed. By the time Luna had stanched what flowed then, he had barely survived.

"Does it hurt a lot, Scarl?" she asked.

He swallowed. Watching his Adam's apple move, she could see him decide how much to lie. He chose not to answer at all.

"We've got to try," Zeke argued. "You'll die here for sure if we don't."

"There are worse things." The bitterness in Scarl's voice gave Ariel a chill. Not wanting to consider what caused such a tone, she moved to find a handhold on the slab. Acting was easier than thinking or feeling.

If she had said anything first to alert him, Scarl might have stopped her. Shifting without warning, she didn't see him grab for her ankle until she'd already stepped past his reach.

"It's not flat on the bottom." Zeke showed her. "It's big, but if we can tip it, we might be able to pull his leg out." He slid his hands under the edge. Immediately he straightened to tear the bandage off his right arm. Dropping the splint, he flexed his hand and found a grip he liked better. Scarl lay silent, his eyes closed the whole time.

Ariel slid her hands under the slab, too, terrified that she and Zeke would fail.

"I'll ask the stone to help if it can," Zeke told her, without much hope in his voice.

"You could ask for a few more to drop from the ceiling instead," Scarl suggested. "Pretty impressive the first time. Although it showed how little faith you had in me."

Ignoring him, Zeke drew a deep breath and released it, his palms flat on the slab. Half words and nonsense flowed out on his breath.

"All right," he added. "I'll count." Ariel braced.

With a sigh that ended in a curse, Scarl lifted his uninjured leg to press his boot sole against the lower edge of the slab. Praying that his shove might boost their power, Ariel let herself hope.

"One, two, *three*."

She felt they were lifting the world.

CHAPTER
36

Grating, the slab tipped. One edge jumped a few inches before the contours of the underside stopped it. Startled by success, Ariel and Zeke shared a confused glance, not sure what to do next. They couldn't ease off their effort, yet Scarl's leg remained trapped. Aware that Zeke couldn't possibly reach it, Ariel swept one of her own legs sideways and back. Her heel caught the Finder's pinned calf and dragged his foot from under the rock.

A terrible cry rose from Scarl. It echoed. Ariel lost both her grip and her balance and stumbled backward over his leg. But as the slab thumped back into its original place, nobody's limbs smashed beneath.

"We did it!" Zeke crowed. Puffing, he whirled to Scarl's slack face. "Did we kill him?"

"No," Ariel said, confirming the slight rise and fall of Scarl's chest. "He passed out." Glad she couldn't hear that scream again soon, she scrambled to right herself. Her hands found the crushed leg before squeamishness could stop her. Mercifully little blood oozed into his sock. The skin at its cuff looked as translucent and fragile as flower petals, but as near as she could tell, no leg bones were broken. The odd angle of his foot on his ankle, however, meant that one or both had been crushed. Bracing for another howl of pain, she drew his foot into a more normal position. Scarl remained unconscious and silent, but Ariel whimpered at the pulpy feel of the joint. Her fingers jittered over his bootlaces. She decided to leave the boot on.

"Find me something to wrap this up with," she ordered Zeke. "Is our pack—?" Zeke thrust her the two halves of the splint he'd only just removed from his arm. Grateful for that good fortune, Ariel loosened Scarl's bootlaces enough to slide the narrowest ends of the splints right into the boot on each side of his ankle. Zeke's bandage she wound and tied overtop to hold them in place, trying to finish before Scarl woke up.

"Do we have any water?" she asked.

When he looked, Zeke found both their pack and Derr's uncrushed, where they'd slept. Scarl's rested nearby where he'd dropped it. Ariel grabbed a blanket, taking the steps she knew to protect Scarl from shock. She hoped they'd be enough. His shallow breathing turned to groans and his eyes began to roll under his lids.

Ariel glanced toward Zeke, who stood motionless nearby.

"I saw blood oozing from under a rock," he said. His voice wavered. "It could have been Stor—"

"Never mind that." Her heart broke at the guilt on his face. But she couldn't join him in grief, insisted something inside her. Not yet. "We're alive, Zeke, thanks to you. Scarl, too. Now, go find a way out. Or ask the mountain to make one."

Zeke winced. "But . . . we can't carry him."

"We can be crutches, and we've got to get out of here as soon as he can move. Please, Zeke. Don't give up now."

Looking dazed, he drifted away. A soft sound in the dark,

not singing but sobbing, wafted to Ariel's ears. She willed herself not to hear it. If she thought of the dead, she'd be overcome, too. There were still more pressing tasks if the three of them were to survive.

If Ariel had never heard the cursing of Fishers, her ears would have been burning the moment Scarl awoke. Instead she was relieved by the strength in his voice, even if it did come in gasps.

His motions, on the other hand, struck at her heart. He shoved off her hands and rolled away from her onto his side.

"You've done enough," he muttered. "Let me be."

He wouldn't take the water she offered. Instead, he breathed deeply, flexed his three good limbs, and gathered his strength. In slow portions he worked his way to a seated position, leaning against a rock with his eyes closed for a long time once he'd gotten that far. His face looked more ghostly than Ariel had ever seen Misha's.

Her stomach fluttery with concern, she tried to lead him back from the edge of the faint that threatened to reclaim him. The only lifeline she knew how to throw him, since he rejected her touch, was her voice. She described what had happened since she and Zeke had last seen him. His face gradually gained color and tension, but he made no response to her chatter. Ariel didn't mind. She feared the answer to the only question she might have asked.

Awkwardly trying to keep filling the silence, she paid too little attention to where her words led. She said, "It didn't take you too long to find us."

"I didn't come to find you," he snarled. His tone surprised her even more than his words. "I came to find Mason's thugs. Slitting their throats in their sleep seemed the best way to fulfill a promise I'd made."

"A promise?" Ariel couldn't recall him ever using that word.

"To somebody other than you. A last promise."

Warmth seemed to leak from her body and into the rock. Two small sounds leaked out with it. "To . . . who?"

Ariel wished she could call those syllables back. With effort, Scarl raised his head to regard her. Even in the low light, she could see the pain swim in his eyes, overlaid with a dark sheen of fury.

"Don't play the child with me. You know who I'm talking about."

His hostility took her aback. Terribly afraid she deserved it, she twisted the fingers of one hand in the other.

"Mirayna?" she whispered.

Closing his eyes, he let his face drop back against the stone.

Even the scorching anger he'd directed at her didn't stop Ariel from feeling his grief. The last drop in a cup already full to the brim, it spilled over. Everywhere she went, she left a trail of death. Her mother, her Storian, and now the Allcraft who had been so kind to both her and Zeke. Ariel pressed her knuckles hard against her lips to keep her anguish from escaping. Silently it dribbled out down her cheeks instead.

To her surprise, Scarl spoke again. This time his voice matched the flat, cold angles of stone all around them.

"I found Gust and his jackals quickly enough, all right. But the shadows of wolves made them cautious. They never all slept at once. So I could never get close enough—until they finally got this close to you." He snorted. "Dullards. I thought I was going to have to point you out to them. But the fire did it at last."

Ariel sat in a helpless silence that froze both her limbs and her heart. After wishing he'd speak, now she cringed at his voice. She was bound to hear anything he chose to say, but she dreaded the creeping awareness that Scarl might never forgive her deception. Not because the truth would have kept Mirayna in the world, but because his last hours with her must have been tainted by distress and distraction. And if Scarl wouldn't forgive her, Ariel could never forgive herself—or her calling.

He began rubbing his leg, but without reaching below the knee to the damage.

"There was only one fault with you stealing away," he told her. "She wouldn't let me ignore or forget it. I had to go after you. She couldn't bear the danger you'd put yourself in, even if I could."

Ariel ventured, "I thought Pres would help, so you could stay with her."

"Pres." Groaning the name, he glanced up again. Though still rimmed with pain, now his eyes mostly looked weary. He ran a hand across them.

"Get over here and help me stand up."

The order caught Ariel by surprise. She rolled to her feet and obeyed, crouching alongside him. Scarl gripped her shoulder too hard. She held still despite a spike of alarm.

"When I refused to leave her," he said, bracing his other hand on a boulder, "she proved who was stronger." He drew his good leg beneath him, sucked in a breath, and gave Ariel a nod. She straightened and he pushed himself up. Fighting dizziness, Scarl leaned heavily on both her and the stone.

"What do you mean, stronger?" she asked. Unable to bear his long pauses, she wanted him to deliver his painful words and be done.

"I wouldn't leave Hartwater. So she . . . she left instead."

"She left?" How far could a sick woman in a wheeled chair go?

"Pres had given her foxglove." Now the words rushed out. "In case a day came when Mirayna's body would no longer obey her at all. Do you know foxglove flower, Ariel? What it's good for?"

She didn't want to say it. "It's poison."

"Yes. If I wouldn't come after you while she was still breathing, she said, she could fix that. She didn't tell me, of course, until the foxglove was inside her—"

Though Ariel had guessed what was coming, her own moan surprised her. Scarl shot her a sharp glance.

"Too late to argue," he added. "Too late to do anything but hold her and watch her leave the world. And make—" His voice broke. "And make wretched promises to her about you."

He released Ariel's shoulder. Any more abruptly, and she would have called it a push. He took a hobbling step. A yelp of pain stuck behind his lips, but he stayed upright. Fearful, she moved up alongside to steady him if needed.

"Her time would have been short enough." Looking askance at her, Scarl rubbed his face. "And mine seems too long."

"I'm sorry," she whispered. She didn't say it from guilt, though a few pangs throbbed low in her belly. She said it from understanding.

He gripped her shoulder again. He kept his eyes straight ahead. "Not half as sorry as I am."

They didn't speak again for a time. Leaning on her, Scarl minced his way beyond the rockfall. Most of his movement amounted to hopping.

"Where's Zeke?" His eyes roved the chimneys and gaps overhead. Increasingly bright, they hinted at sunshine outside.

"Looking for a way out."

"Call him. I don't have the breath."

Ariel hesitated. Her tongue felt too large in her mouth.

"Do you wish you'd let Elbert kill me?" There, the words had been loosed. Now that this barbed question was out from inside her, she thought she could hear whatever answer he gave.

He gave her a long unblinking look. She could feel, like a vibration, the consideration behind his eyes. He was not concerned about her reaction, she saw. His debate was strictly over what to admit—not to her but to himself.

By the time it came, the answer may have surprised them both.

"No." His hard hand on her shoulder neither clenched nor relaxed. "No. I don't."

CHAPTER
37

The dismal look on Zeke's face when he emerged from the darkness told Ariel he'd overheard a great deal of her conversation with Scarl. He could barely meet the man's gaze. Sighing, Zeke only pointed into the black tunnel and said, "We'll have to go that way."

He hefted Scarl's pack. Ariel shrugged on their own. Despite a search, Scarl's knife sheath remained empty, but Zeke did manage to pry Derr's staff from the rockfall. Scarl took it to lean on and sent the boy to retrieve Derr's pack, too.

"We don't really need it," Zeke protested. "You're hurt and—"

"He was my grandfather, Zeke." More threat than sentiment edged Scarl's voice. "Bring it here." Zeke obeyed, reluctantly lifting it onto Scarl's back.

With the staff supporting Scarl on one side and Zeke propping him on the other, they turned their backs on the shafts of sunlight and shuffled into the dark. Ariel led them, Zeke holding her collar to keep them together. In the absolute darkness inside the earth, they could not see their own limbs, let alone the stony debris they stumbled against.

"Keep to the left," Scarl said. "I don't remember tripping so much there. Hit my head twice, but I'm taller."

A hop and lurch at a time, they progressed. The utter blackness seemed to ooze against Ariel, not only rendering her eyes useless but gnawing her face. She began wishing for light. Even the pale specter of a ghost, she thought pointedly, would be welcome. Misha, if he heard such thoughts, didn't answer.

Scarl did, though, it seemed. "Stupid!" Halting, he swung Derr's pack down from his shoulder. "My grandfather often carries a candle for starting fires in the rain. I should have remembered sooner." Carefully, he bent to dig after it.

Feeling terribly alone in the dark, Ariel listened to the rustle of Scarl's blind search. Her hand, clutching nervously at her throat, found the glass bead there. She gripped it and prayed with all her heart that he would find what he sought.

They all cheered when he announced that his fingers had closed on a few flamesticks.

"Light one," Ariel urged.

"No. I don't want to waste it. It won't help me see into the pack much anyway." His rustling continued, growing rough and frustrated.

"Ariel?" Zeke's voice floated to her. She glanced toward him but couldn't see his face well enough to know what he wanted. With a gasp she realized she was seeing at all.

Scarl's hands stopped. Ariel saw that, too—a pause in a gray flutter of motion.

"There's light here," Scarl said. "Or is it just me who sees it?"

It had sneaked up on them all. A sickly dim glow separated them from the dark.

"It's on Ariel," Zeke said.

Dumbfounded, she looked down at herself. The fingers clenching her bead relaxed open. The gold flakes at its heart twinkled through the green glass, casting a dim golden glow almost shocking after the blackness. Scarl grunted in surprise.

"How are you doing that?" Zeke asked.

"Finding, perhaps?" Scarl mused. "Without knowing it? What are you seeking?"

"Light. That's all I wanted." She held her breath, afraid the glow would blink out if she so much as twitched.

"You can't find what doesn't exist," Scarl insisted. "Or my hands would be on a candle by now."

"Who cares," Zeke said. "Make it brighter. We won't need the candle."

"I don't know how!" Ariel wailed.

After a snort of amazement, Scarl lifted Derr's bag once more. "I don't know how you're doing it at all, but let's use it while we can. Keep wanting light. Maybe the Essence will keep winking at you."

Wanting came easy. The dim light revealed little more than shadows, but the contours of the rocks in their path rose before them. They made faster progress with far fewer bruises. Perhaps ten more minutes had passed when Ariel's eyes picked out a brighter speck of sky far ahead.

The glow from her bead abruptly went out.

The daylight fortified their hearts, though, if not their strained eyes, so they soon reached the sinkhole.

"I need to stop here a spell before we climb out." Scarl lowered himself to the ground and eased his crushed foot, boot and all, into a pool of brackish rainwater. The muscles in his jaw jumped.

A beam of sunlight streamed down from above. Testing, Zeke clambered partway up the lumpy stone wall toward its source. He jumped down again.

"It might be hard for you to climb up there with only one leg," he told Scarl.

"Don't have much choice, do I? You're the one who decided I needed to live." Closing his eyes, the Finder lay back on the rock while the icy water numbed his foot.

Now that their escape seemed assured, the anxiety that had kept Ariel moving deserted her. In the silence, her ears seemed to fill with the roar of stone slabs collapsing. A lump rose into her throat as she breathed a silent good-bye through the darkness to Bellam and Derr, left forever behind. The shadows throbbed with the malice of other, evil men crushed by rocks. To banish the memories and horror, Ariel found her own pool of water, which looked a bit cleaner than Scarl's. She filled her jar, sipped some, and filled it again. Dabbling her hands, she pressed her wet palms on the cave wall. Drips echoed musically off the walls.

Zeke looked up from poking around the bones of a deer that had fallen into the sinkhole long ago. "Calling Misha?" he wondered.

She shrugged. She would have liked for Misha's handprints to appear alongside hers, but she doubted the ghost still kept company with them.

"Better get moving, I guess." Scarl pushed himself to his feet. He wavered, clutching the staff. "This is going to be hard."

Ariel thought he spoke mostly to cover his dizziness, but he went on. "Once we get out, take all you want from the packs—all the food. If I can make it back to Hartwater, I will. Return there when you're ready, and I'll try to find someone to take you back home, if you like. If I'm not there, I'll be gone from the world, but tell Pres the truth and she'll help in my place."

"Aren't you coming with us?" Ariel asked, her heart picking up speed. "We can go slow, or wait a few days while you heal. But we still have to get to the mouth of the mountain."

He looked up at her wearily. "Why?"

Ariel's lips sputtered, empty. No response could have surprised her more.

"I told you. The telling dart—there's a message. The Vault . . ." At his expression, her voice trailed off.

"I don't care anymore," he said. "I promised to try to protect you from Gust. He can't hurt you now—so I'm done. You go where you want. Clearly you can."

"But we need your help!"

"No, you don't."

Left out of the argument, Zeke looked on with dismay. "One of Gust's gang is still out there," he said. "I'm pretty sure there were three when we saw them with the wolves."

Scarl waved off the objection. "Washed away, if not drowned, in the flood. Didn't you hear the shouting that night?" He picked up a pack and hopped with the staff toward their exit.

Aghast, Ariel watched his back. Reality itself seemed to have slipped from beneath her: Scarl had given up.

"You can't!" She grabbed his elbow, nearly knocking him off his one-legged balance. "You started it," she insisted. "You want to find it worse than I do. It can't help Mirayna, not now, but you still—"

Spinning to seize her arm, he snapped her up onto her toes. Ariel's teeth cracked together painfully. She held back a whimper, sure she was in for a shaking. Zeke jerked protectively toward her.

That motion broke the wave of Scarl's anger. With a grimace, he splayed his fingers and released her.

"I'm sorry," Ariel whispered, not sure what for.

"No. You don't deserve that. If anyone is wrong, it is me. But hear me, Ariel. . . ." He tore a ragged breath, closed his eyes, and shook his head. When his eyes opened again, they stared over her head. "I know my own actions have caused what I feel. I didn't try hard enough to stop a death delivered to you—your mother. I put what I wanted first. And now you have hastened a death delivered to me. Two, with my old grandpop."

Zeke groaned. "I did that! I didn't mean to, but . . ."

Scarl ignored Zeke and refused to meet Ariel's eyes. "It's only justice, and I'll take the punishment I deserve." He turned away. "But that's enough pain for us both. Let's stop there."

The closed look on his face sank into her heart. The tearing sensation it left in Ariel's chest felt in some ways worse than any before. When Zeke had told her that her mother was dead, there remained a faraway cottage where that death might not be real. This time, she couldn't tell herself that the words might be wrong. Worse still, no matter how dead her mother might be, Luna had not chosen to die. Nothing between them had pushed her to leave Ariel intentionally.

"You really won't go with us?" Her voice trembled. "We could—"

"No."

Her eyes filling with tears, Ariel's gaze swung to Zeke. He looked stricken as well but had no help to offer.

Ariel flung the last argument, the last hope, she had. "Coward."

He flinched but did not turn.

"Call me what you will, Farwalker," he said softly to the wall before him. "I'm not you."

In silence, Scarl boosted both Zeke and Ariel out of the cave. Gulping hot, racking sobs, Ariel climbed desperately, scraping her elbows and knees to avoid needing more of his help. She didn't want him to touch her. Then Scarl tossed up the packs and his staff, along with a rope knotted under his armpits so Zeke could tug from above. With that help, he managed to ascend. He could not, however, stifle a few cries as he bumped or put weight on his foot.

Ariel waited in the sunshine, looking elsewhere through water-blurred eyes. The whole morning's grief spilled out in tears she didn't bother to hide. Hearing pain echo out of the earth, she felt it reverberate through her heart.

CHAPTER
38

"Come on, Zeke," Ariel said, once all three of them were out of the hole. The tunnel's course, a grassed hump, stretched clearly before them.

Zeke turned troubled eyes on Scarl. "Are you sure you'll be okay?" he asked, low.

"Good luck and good days." No cheer lifted Scarl's voice. "You may catch up to me after the farwalking is done."

Zeke sighed. "Does it ever get done?"

"Go with him if you want," Ariel called over her shoulder. She didn't mean it, and everyone knew it. Zeke gave Scarl a farewell and hurried after her.

For an hour, Ariel fought the impulse to turn and look back. When they'd left Hartwater, she had taken comfort from the possibility of Scarl coming behind them. Now his silhouette could only be moving away. Before her, shrubs and brush dotted hollows as she and Zeke traversed to a wetter side of the mountain. To Ariel, though, this land felt emptier than even the Drymere.

The pair walked in silence most of the day. Tears slipped

now and then down her cheeks, but she made sure they fell without sound.

As the sun slid to the earth, Zeke wondered, "How much farther do you think it is?"

The feeling that her feet were being tugged had returned, but it had never hinted how far she'd be drawn. Ariel shrugged.

A few steps later, she said, "It's for me, Zeke. A message for me. I have to go get it, if I can. If we just go home now . . ." She couldn't push past the dread images that arose in her mind: an empty stone cottage. No Healtouch in Canberra Docks anymore. The only surname for Ariel there would be Fool. She could imagine the village without her mother, but she no longer wanted to see it. Not until she had nowhere else left to go.

"I know," he said. "It's all right."

The sigh in his voice jolted Ariel's sympathy loose. "Thank you so much, Zeke, for sticking with me. Do you miss your family awfully?"

Zeke clenched his teeth, trying hard not to either cry or shout at her, Ariel wasn't sure which. "Yes," he said finally. "But you didn't see my dad after the burning. I—I don't know if he'll be there when we get back, not really. Not *him*." Zeke turned to her swiftly. "And you know what? Whenever we get back, *I* won't be there, either. That's almost the worst."

Ariel thought she knew what he meant. She pushed back an urge to tell him she admired Ezekiel Stone-Singer far more than the Zeke she'd known in Canberra Docks. The words would have eased her guilt, but she wasn't sure they would make him feel better. So instead she rubbed his shoulder and suggested they stop for a rest.

They snuggled beneath a large candle-wax shrub in the lee of the mound made by the tunnel beneath them. The late-afternoon sun soaked into them pleasantly. Zeke took bites of their food, but Ariel didn't feel hungry, only tired. Instead of just resting, they both fell asleep.

When Zeke blinked and yawned a few hours later, he could not shake Ariel awake.

Her dreams only gradually twisted. At first, she sat near the hearth back home, aware that her mother stood just around the corner in her workroom. Ariel smiled, eager to see her, but she felt thirsty, very thirsty indeed. Her throat grated when she tried to swallow. So instead of visiting her mother, Ariel headed outside to the well.

The village square, where the well should have been, held a graveyard. A dead tree guarded each mound. Misha wandered among the graves as if looking for one that he wanted.

Her thirst made more sticky by dread, Ariel cowered, barely breathing. If Misha noticed her there, he would invite her into a grave, and she knew, in that case, she must go.

A bird winged past her, the size of a raven but with feathers as gray as a dove's. It lit on Misha's shoulder. Another bird circled the far side of the graveyard. Perhaps because Ariel had thought it, the second bird *was* a dove. It fluttered in midair, not sure it wanted to perch. Misha raised his hand. Flapping uneasily, the dove dropped to his fingers.

A sea fog rolled in, cloaking Misha and the birds. A new figure emerged a few paces ahead, regarding the graves just as Ariel did. She could not see his features, but she knew it was Scarl.

"Ariel?" he called across the graveyard. She was too stiff with fear to respond. Besides, she didn't want attention from anyone—or anything—there.

The mist parted, and Misha stepped from behind the nearest dead tree, his lips curled in distaste. Scarl backed away. The ghost muttered words that did not reach Ariel, and then he glanced over his shoulder to the tree. Both gray birds perched on its bones.

At Misha's look, the gray raven hurtled toward Scarl. He flung one arm over his eyes. The bird hit him in the chest, talons slashing.

Recoiling, Ariel clapped her hands to her face. She peeked out between fingers.

Scarl and Misha both jerked their heads toward her, two sets of eyes staring into her own.

Before she could speak, a monstrous wave rose from the sea, snatched her up, and carried her off.

CHAPTER
39

Ariel could not figure out why she couldn't wake up from her bewildering dreams. Zeke had awoken from his nap; she knew because his face kept looming over hers, asking questions she couldn't hear. After a while, Scarl's face appeared, too. She felt hands on her, hands all the time, so she supposed Misha also was there, though she did not see him again.

"Go away," she told them all. "Let me wake up."

She wanted to get to the mouth of the mountain, but her stomach hurt. So did her back and her head. Perhaps she shouldn't have fallen asleep in the sun. It had given her a headache and strange, thirsty dreams, as if she and Zeke had stumbled back into the Drymere.

After a while she dreamed solely of water: the creek where the pollywogs lived, the Hartwater basin, the sea. She once felt water in her mouth, cool when she felt so hot. The water rushed back out, warm. Her stomach didn't want it. Only her dreams wanted water, it seemed. In watery dreams she was drowning.

Ariel lay blinking at the stars a long time before she realized they were not sparkles deep in a well.

She turned her head to the right. It hurt to move, and her skull felt full of mud, so she didn't move it back. She just let her eyes wander.

She recognized nothing about the hollow where she lay. The candle-wax shrub was gone. She could have reached one foot to the ashes of a fire, though. Perhaps the shrub had burned. Beyond the gray mound, a slender form curled in sleep—Zeke. If he slept now, maybe she was finally awake.

She became aware of the hand resting flat on her chest, rising and falling with her breath. Hands again! She moaned.

Something next to her lifted. Automatically she swiveled her head toward it, wincing at the bolt of pain that quick motion caused.

"Ariel?" Scarl propped himself on one elbow. The sag in his face hinted that he'd been asleep alongside her. "You're awake?"

As much as she hoped that was true, it didn't seem possible. She and Zeke had left Scarl when they'd climbed out of the cave, so this must still be a dream. Mustn't it?

He shifted his hand to her forehead, checking her fever. She wanted to brush it off, but her limbs felt all watery, too. If she lifted her arm, her hand might slide right off her wrist.

Scarl turned away briefly, then back. His cupped palm hovered over her mouth. Drops of water tickled her chin. Suddenly nothing was more important than catching those drops with her tongue. They'd done this before, more than once, Ariel realized, as water dribbled into her mouth. This time, it stayed down.

"More?"

She nodded slowly so the mud wouldn't slosh so hard inside her skull.

His tin cup came to her lips. His other hand cupped the

back of her neck so she could sip. The water swished joyfully down her throat, even if her head throbbed from the lifting.

He took the cup away too soon. "Careful," he said. "Only a bit at a time."

Dull anger blinked in her chest and went dark. It took too much effort. But the inside of her mouth felt mobile again.

"What—"

He laid damp fingertips on her lips. "Just rest. Another drink soon, if you want it."

Ariel wanted each sip he gave her until the stars were absorbed into the dawn. The water slowly leached the mud from her head. By the time Zeke groaned and rolled over, Scarl had helped her sit up, propped against one of the packs.

Zeke's eyes went round when he saw her. "Are you finally better?"

Scarl answered for her. "She's decided to stay in the world, anyway."

Zeke scooted around the fire, which Scarl had relit, to pat both hands on her arm.

"Geez, you scared me," he said. "First you wouldn't wake up, then you— It's been more than three days!"

A part of Ariel's brain that hadn't worked for a while told her she'd been not just dreaming but sick—so sick she had no idea what had happened since she'd fallen asleep next to Zeke.

His explanation of the things she had missed filled the morning. Zeke's attempts to rouse her had failed. She'd only garbled a few words and shoved off his touch. When she still tossed and mumbled the next morning, he'd realized she was more than just tired.

"You drank the water in the cave, didn't you?" Scarl asked

her as Zeke told his story. "I should have paid more attention. It was foul, obviously."

Memories swam back into Ariel's fogged mind. With them came a sense of betrayal.

"What are you doing here?" she asked. Her body, recovering, let her voice snap. She turned to Zeke. "Did you go and get him?"

Zeke shook his head. "I would have tried, but I was too scared to leave you alone."

"I came on my own," Scarl said. "It just took me a while to catch up."

Ariel looked at Scarl's foot. He hadn't moved far enough from her side for her to gauge how badly he limped. But the wood splints were gone, the crushed foot bandaged inside its boot.

"It's still bad," he said in response to her glance. "You and Zeke didn't move at all for a couple of days, though. When I saw how ill you were, he and I tried to get you to Libros. We had to risk it. It isn't that far, but I just couldn't do it lame."

"So I went by myself," Zeke said. "Yesterday morning."

Ariel turned a stunned look on her friend.

"I had hoped he could bring back a Healtouch," Scarl explained, "without Mason catching wind of it—or of me."

"But the Healtouch I found wouldn't come," Zeke said. "Or give medicine to 'a strange ragamuffin with nothing to trade.' That's what he told me."

Scarl muttered something about trading for some of Zeke's courage. Zeke blushed.

"He told me that if I wanted a handout, I ought to ask Mason," the boy continued. "Or if Mason advised it, he'd come.

I didn't listen, of course, but I did spy on Mason's house. People were lined up to see him. The Healtouch made it sound like they would wait standing on their heads if he said so." Zeke shrugged. "Anyhow, the best I could do was to bring back fresh water for you. We were out."

"But that water helped break your fever," Scarl told Ariel. "Zeke probably saved you."

Solemnly, Ariel thanked her bold friend. She said nothing more for a while, nibbling a morsel of dry bread and trying to imagine all that commotion. She realized that a big piece of the puzzle still hadn't appeared. Strengthened by the bread, she summoned her nerve to unearth it.

"Why did you follow us?" she asked Scarl. "After everything you said?"

The Finder's gaze dropped. His fingertips traced circles on the water jar in his hands.

"I had a visit from your ghost friend that first night."

Ariel sucked in a breath. Snatches of nightmare swept back into her mind. Shivering, she guessed, "In a graveyard in Canberra Docks."

Scarl's head jerked back up, unease rippling his face. He whispered, "You were there . . . weren't you?"

"What happened?" urged Zeke.

Scarl yanked at the tail of his shirt and drew it up over his ribs. Expecting slashes from talons, Ariel cringed. Then she blinked at his bare chest. The skin was unbroken, but it wasn't unmarked. An angry red welt glowed over his heart. It could have been formed by a burn or, more likely, a sharp slap—because the welt took the shape Misha favored: a handprint.

"He told me my work and my obligation to you was not done," Scarl said. "To my shame, I needed reminding. And he gave me a token so I wouldn't forget or think it was only a dream."

"Misha," Ariel murmured. So the dead boy could do harm, if he chose. Or his raven friend could. She wondered if Scarl had spied the dove as well as the raven.

"Does it hurt?" Zeke asked.

"Not on the outside." Scarl tucked his shirt smooth again. "It woke me up, though, I can tell you. That's when I turned around and came to find you."

Ariel studied her knuckles. She wanted to say that she and Zeke didn't need him. Obviously that wasn't so, but she resented the truth.

Her thoughts must have shown on her face. He reached to touch one of her elbows.

"I know I frustrate you greatly," he said. "But I've never known a Farwalker before, least of all one who's still mostly a child. That confuses me more than you know. First I underestimate you, then I expect too much. I keep making mistakes."

He caught her eyes so she would meet his regard. In their brown depths, Ariel found herself recalling mistakes of her own.

"Me, too," she whispered.

"I don't know if you'll find anything where you want to go," he said. "I don't know if I even still care. I—" He looked away. Ariel reached a hand to his arm, and the touch seemed to brace him.

"But I'll walk beside you and help you as best I can," he finished, "for as long as you want me to be there. Or I will leave again if you'd rather. That's all I know how to offer."

Ariel's fingers tightened on his arm. What she most wanted was to leave turmoil behind and find something steady to cling to.

"You can't find what doesn't exist," she said. The saying

tumbled from her lips more in response to her own thoughts than to anything Scarl had said. But it seemed like a hard truth between them, a heartache they shared.

He wrapped her hand with his own. "You seem to be able to," he replied.

CHAPTER
40

If stones could see—and Zeke assured Ariel they felt movement so well it amounted to the same—Cloudspear watched them, uncaring, as they limped haltingly toward its mouth. Even after a full day of rest and food, Ariel could only travel in short bursts as her strength returned. Though he said little about it, Scarl struggled as much.

"Your foot's not getting much better, is it?" she asked him. Her mother had told her that limbs that were too badly damaged had to be cut off if the person was to survive. But Ariel couldn't imagine doing such cutting.

"The evening after we climbed out of the cave was the worst." He shuddered. "If I hadn't lost my knife you'd see one foot, not two. But the pain eased a little from there. As long as Zeke's willing to keep serving as my legs for finding our water and food, we're all right. If Mason suspected we were here, he'd be on us already."

"Still, you should let me look at it." She didn't want to see the mangled flesh under Scarl's boot, but she felt it was her job to offer.

"And do what?" A sour grin softened the truth they both knew. "No. If it turns black, toss a flower on me when it finally takes me out of the world. If not, I'll live with it."

They pushed on, finding new reserves of endurance once they'd glimpsed the end of their quest. From this side, the hole in the mountain looked indeed like a mouth. Round and gaping, it gave the hillside an expression of amazement that matched Ariel's own: they'd actually made it this far.

As they drew near, the roar of falling stones echoed in her memory.

"It's not going to collapse again, is it?" she asked Zeke.

"No." Miserably he kicked a dirt clod out of his path. "I asked it to do that before. I didn't think it would listen. Not like that. I was just hoping one or two rocks—little rocks—I didn't mean to kill everyone! I didn't really mean to kill anyone!"

"You have no cause for guilt, Zeke," Scarl said. "You were only defending Ariel and yourself the best way you knew how."

"But Storian and Derr . . ." Zeke drew a ragged breath.

Scarl squeezed the boy's shoulder. "I know. You just didn't understand your own power. And stones aren't fine instruments, either. But killing seems to be part of living. It's a hard lesson you should hope not to use often. Sometimes, though, the world gives us little choice."

"Made and unmade," Ariel whispered, thinking she'd heard it in some dream.

Scarl nodded. "Sunlight and leaf pass to firelight and ashes," he said. "And back once more to leaf. So the Tree-Singers say."

"They do." Zeke sighed, but he nodded.

As if the cave heard and had an opinion to share, its foul breath hit them. Ariel's throat clenched shut.

"Ugh. What is that smell?" Zeke asked, clutching his nose.

Scarl buried his own nose in the crook of his elbow. "If I'm not mistaken, it's death."

They found the source of the stink just inside the cave mouth. A body, once human, slumped beside a large pack. Ariel, who had seen beached, bloated seals, was grateful this corpse had been dead long enough to look shriveled rather than squishy.

It was not hard to tell how the person had died: a wide slash split the neck from one ear to the other. The blunt end of a telling dart stuck out of the wound.

Ariel groaned. "When I dreamed about the mouth of the mountain, Misha told me the inside of my dart said, 'A message is caught in a throat.' That's not it, is it?"

"Don't know," Scarl replied. "I was thinking we may have found Liam." He picked up a splinter of stone. "Don't watch."

Neither of his companions obeyed. Scarl snagged a brass fin with the splinter and drew the dart out. Maggots clung to it, squirming. Ariel's gorge rose. She whirled away. When she looked back, her stomach still quivering, the dart had fallen to the ground. Scarl scuffed it clean in the dust before he bent to inspect it.

"Blank. It must have been his." Scarl checked the abandoned pack. "Looks like a Storian's belongings to me. It has to be Liam. Perhaps he came here with Mason or Gust. Maybe both." He turned to Ariel. "If there was any other message to be found here, Mason may already have it. Clearly this dart was left as a threat."

With a scowl, she stared into the shadowy cave. Her feet wanted to wander farther inside, so she let them. A gurgle of water rose to her ears. Following it into the dark, she stopped when the splashing seemed to surround her. Her hand fell to her green bead. She wondered if she could make it twinkle again.

"Don't go any farther," Scarl called.

"I'm not." She closed her eyes and wished for light. When a glow lit her eyelids, it wasn't her bead. Zeke and Scarl approached, torches in hand.

"Liam came prepared," Scarl explained.

The flames lit water pouring from a crack in the ceiling and carving a channel downhill into darkness. They followed the stream until it pooled in a basin the size of a rowboat. The water gurgled and spun there before it disappeared down the funnel of the whirlpool.

"It goes underground?" Zeke said.

Scarl lowered his torch near the whirlpool's surface. Wet, polished stone glinted beneath. Though the water was clear, his light did not reach to the bottom.

"The mountain's dark throat," he murmured. "Slide down that and you're swallowed forever."

"Oh!" Ariel cried. "The message is in there. It's caught in *this* throat!" Her feet wanted to slide into the water, and not only to cool her burning soles. She sat and untied her boots.

Scarl knelt to explore the pool with one arm.

"There must be a ledge or hole down there," Ariel said. "With something inside."

Wet to the shoulder, the Finder straightened. He shook his head. "If so, it stays where it's at."

She gaped at him. "We have to try to get it." She glanced to Zeke for support. He looked dubious, too. "I'm a good swimmer," she added. "It doesn't look all that deep, and the drain hole might not be big enough to fall through."

"It doesn't matter," Scarl said. "You'd be trapped against it by the force of the water. You'd drown just the same."

"Tie the rope on me. You can pull me back out."

"No, I don't know that I can." He propped his torch against the wall. "I want you to feel something." Dropping his staff and his pack, he dug for a rope. A sweater also emerged. Stringing the rope through its collar, Scarl tied it on snug, like bait on a line. Then he handed Ariel the end of the rope.

"Hold tight." He flipped the sweater into the whirlpool. It spun twice before the stream slurped it under.

The rope jerked Ariel's arm. She lurched forward. Scarl grabbed her.

"Now pull it back up," he instructed.

Zeke had to help. The reeling in of their bait took more effort than she cared to admit. When they finally landed it, sloppy, Scarl bent to untie the rope.

"You felt the tug on the sweater," he said. "The force against your whole body would be considerably stronger."

She opened her mouth to protest.

"No," he repeated. "I trust your instincts that something is there. But I'll not drown you for it. I don't care if it's the very door to the Vault."

It wasn't. Something small beckoned from under the water, Ariel thought, small and enticing, like the tingle still left in her feet. She muttered, "You would have drowned someone for it before."

He looked away for a few seconds before returning her gaze. "I won't now."

Ariel crossed her arms and stared at the whirlpool. After the tug on the sweater, she knew he was right. She didn't want to be trapped by that deluge. But to come so close and be forced to walk away empty-handed!

As she and Scarl had argued, Zeke had wrung out the sweater and walked a few steps upstream. Gripping tight to one sleeve, he plopped the sweater across the course of the water. The stream backed up behind the wet wool.

"Look," he said. "Could we stop up the water? Make it run deeper into the cave or outside instead?"

They watched as, for an instant, the whirlpool dropped. Then water flowed around the sweater and found its channel again.

Ariel leaped on the idea. "A rock dam would block it!" Unfortunately, unlike the tail of the tunnel, this end was barren.

"That's probably why your dart said, 'Come united.'" Scarl studied the narrow stream channel. "With a dozen others, an Allcraft, ropes and wood and strong backs—maybe. With three of us . . ."

Ariel could see him consider it. That was victory enough to encourage her.

"We've got rope and your staff and our three packs," she said.

"Four," said Zeke, "counting the dead guy's."

Scarl regarded the corpse and rubbed his jaw with his knuckles. When he took off his coat, Ariel grinned and ran to empty their packs.

Zeke volunteered to play beaver. Only Scarl had enough weight or strength to act as the anchor. That meant Ariel would drop into the whirlpool. She would have fought for that role anyway.

The Finder took out his glass. When he put it away, he turned to her.

"Where are you drawn to?" he asked.

Facing the whirlpool, Ariel closed her eyes to better grasp the sensation. One foot itched to slide forward and down toward her right. She pointed. "Around there, on that side."

"I think so, too. If it's a hole, as you said, and you have to reach far inside, you'll need to be very careful not to get stuck. How deep, do you think?"

She had no idea. "Um . . . as deep as you are tall, maybe?"

He pinned her with his eyes. "Twice that, by my reckoning. So if we can't lower the water a lot, I don't think you can get down there, put your hands on whatever it is, and still come back up."

"I can hold my breath a long time—watch." She demonstrated. Scarl counted.

"Okay," he said, when she finally released her pent breath. "I have an idea how soon to yank you back up, anyway. It'll go faster when you're struggling and cold."

She bent to stick her hand in the water. She yanked it out again hastily.

"You can still change your mind."

At her impatient gesture, Scarl added, "Well, I'll change it for you if Zeke's dam doesn't work."

Zeke had located a spot along the creek where the surrounding floor dipped and the water might be encouraged to veer out of its channel. The three of them stuffed into their packs what spare clothing they had and all the brush they could scavenge from outside. Zeke braved the stink to snatch Liam's pack, too. Scarl lashed three packs together, leaving the fourth and his coat for stopping up chinks.

The boy eyed the corpse wistfully. "We could use him, too, flop him right in the creek. Except I don't want to touch him."

Scarl nixed that idea, worried about contaminating water that Ariel might gulp. But he did find a tightly rolled grain sack among the things Zeke had dumped from Liam's pack.

"He must have hoped to carry home treasures," he said. Shaking it open, he discovered that the burlap had been lined with thin animal skin. By carefully splitting it along a seam, they created a tarp. Scarl and Zeke plotted how best to use it.

When Zeke stood ready, Scarl tied the rope under Ariel's armpits. Her feet were bare and she'd removed her trousers, too, to reduce the drag of the water.

"That's so tight I can hardly breathe," she complained.

"It won't slip off, then." He tugged the rope. "Jerk it twice, like this, if you're ready to come up before I make you."

He planted himself where he could brace his good leg against the wall. Wrapping himself with the rope, he took up the slack, leaving her little more than a dozen feet to dive with.

"I'm going to holler at Zeke," Scarl said. "Don't go until the water drops and I tell you. Then, unless the dam works even better than we hope, I'll count to forty. No more."

Determined, she steeled herself against the icy water. "I'll get it."

The instant Ariel hit the water, she was squeezed by the heart-stopping cold and dragged by the immense undertow. Her legs and elbows banged against the sides of the pool. Her eyes flew open. Zeke's dam had worked well enough that she could see a wavering torchlight through the water swirling over her head. She couldn't see a thing in any other direction. Panic spiked through her. Bracing her palms against the nearest stone surface, she recovered her grip on her thoughts. She didn't need to see, she reminded herself. She needed to feel. She closed her eyes again to shut out the blindness.

Letting the water pull her down, she scoured the rock with her hands, forearms, and feet, searching for a crack or a hollow. She felt only water and slippery stone. Her chest grew heavier each second. Her toes wanted to stray farther right and still deeper, so she squirmed to orient herself head down to reach with her arms. Although she moved with the current, not against it, the effort used up most of the air in her lungs.

She clamped down tight against the burning urge to breathe. Back and forth, up and down coursed her hands. It was here somewhere. If only she could breathe. The current felt weaker than when she'd jumped in, but water still rushed past and against her.

One of her fingers jammed painfully. Sweeping back again, her hand crossed something not stone: an eyelet of metal. She scrabbled her fingers around it. It wasn't a hole or niche as she'd expected, but a length of thin chain. Her hand slid down it and struck something larger.

Ariel clutched it. Her air-starved brain couldn't identify it. Only concepts flashed in her mind: round, hard, smooth, breathe oh breathe. She'd found what she'd sought, but the chain didn't want to let go. She had to get out. Scarl had to pull now, because she must change the air in her lungs. But she couldn't bring herself to relinquish the prize. Trying to find an angle where the chain could slip free, she twisted herself all around it, tugging feebly.

A sharp wrench on the rope nearly knocked out her held breath, but it didn't pull her away from the eyelet. The rope's pressure grew. Pain swelled through her chest and flowed through her arms.

A fuzzy darkness crept over the pain. Just before Ariel gave in to the command to breathe, water or no, she felt another fierce jerk. She flew through the water, scraping on rock. Her legs kicked, bashing her toes. The water broke over her head. She gasped. Air and water both rushed down her throat. She choked, not wanting to inhale again but unable to stop herself. More water caught in her windpipe. Coughs racked her.

Scarl dragged her clear of the water. Spluttering, Ariel landed in a painful heap on the edge of the pool. A smack between the shoulder blades startled her into an instant of stillness. The next round of coughing cleared her throat better. Air found its way in.

"Are you hurt? What was stuck? Is anything—" Scarl's hands roved her limbs, searching for damage. They stopped at the thing locked in her arms.

"Well, bloody no wonder! I thought I wasn't going to get you back up! You just about did us both in, wrapping yourself around that!"

Ariel focused on her prize: a milky jar with a clamped lid. Corroded metal sealed the lid and formed a few links of kinked chain—including the rusted link that had finally broken. It was entwined with her lifeline where it tied at her chest. Her arms alone never would have kept the jar against Scarl's strength, but the entangled rope had held on to it for her.

Zeke raced up, soaked and squelching and demanding to know if she was all right.

"She's better than I am." Scarl exhaled hard. His hands shook as he removed the rope from them both. "That scared the life out of me." He ignored the information from Zeke that his half-healed back was bleeding again.

Ariel cleared her sore throat and wiped rivulets from her face. Water lay everywhere—puddled all over the ground, dripping from Zeke, and rushing alongside them. Though Zeke had done well for a moment, the whirlpool swirled high again.

"I got it, though." Her fingers tapped the heavy white glass in her lap. She couldn't suppress a victorious smirk. "Just like I said."

A grin split the lingering strain on Scarl's face. "You sure did, spitfire. Let's see what it is."

CHAPTER
41

Ariel shook the white jar. Something rattled inside. Excitement sizzled through her. But the metal clamp on the lid had corroded solid. It could not be undone by any of them.

"Break the jar," Zeke suggested. "I'll do it."

They took it out into the light. Zeke rapped the lid against a stone, gingerly first, then with more strength. The jar's contents clattered with each strike.

"Don't smash whatever's inside," Ariel said.

At last the glass shattered. Amid the white shards rested another brass telling dart.

Zeke groaned. "If this is just like the first one, I'm going to bash my head on a rock."

"It's not." Ariel drew it from the pile of glass. The brass was smooth and nearly blank, its sharp tip unbroken. Suddenly terrified that she would somehow ruin it, she thrust it at Scarl.

He turned it so all eyes could see. Only two symbols marked the outside. Ariel recognized both.

"Farwalker," she said, pointing. Her heart swelled into her throat. "And Tree-Singer. The message must be inside?"

"Should be." He passed the telling dart back to her. "Only you or a Tree-Singer can open it, though."

"I don't know how."

"Press on those blades with one hand and twist with the other." He demonstrated. "Gently. It should pop apart in your fingers."

Zeke cupped his palms beneath hers. "In case it holds jewels," he explained.

Sure she would accidentally break it, Ariel pressed and twisted. Some hidden catch clicked. The dart seemed to come alive in her hands, the shaft splitting lengthwise and springing into a curved strip of brass. Gray dust showered into Zeke's palms. He gasped.

Ariel slid a fingertip along the concave strip, leaving a smooth trail through the dust. The inner surface was unmarked.

"It's blank!" She checked again. Her eyes shot to Scarl for explanation or help. "Oh—what day is it? Mayfest?" She counted on her fingers. "The day after? The first dart said 'no later than Beltane.' We might be too late!"

Scarl, too, inspected the strip. "From what the Storians told you, I got the impression you had to get started by Beltane, not finished," he said. "But I could be wrong." He reached to pinch the gray powder in Zeke's hands.

"It's not shiny enough to be silver," Zeke said.

"It's nothing but dust," Ariel wailed. "Isn't it?"

"I think," Scarl said, sniffing his fingertips, "it's actually ashes."

"Ashes? All that for ashes?" Zeke started to tip the ashes into the wind.

Scarl grabbed his wrist. "Maybe it has some significance we're not seeing," he said. "Get one of our water jars, Ariel. Dry it out. We can save this and—"

"And what? Toss it into the air and make wishes? Cast it onto the sea so a mermaid will rise? Forget it." Ariel slumped. "Whatever it was, it burned itself up yesterday. We can't make it unburned. So we might as well let the wind have it."

Scarl gnawed his lip but found no argument. Silently, he released Zeke's wrist. Zeke parted his hands and let the ashes trickle away in the breeze.

"The Vault is in ashes," Zeke murmured. " 'Sunlight and leaf pass to firelight and ashes.' "

Ariel moaned. "It's a horrible joke."

"Way too much trouble for that," Scarl said. "And I'm not convinced it contained anything different yesterday or last week."

"What else, then? What could it mean?"

Scarl studied the mouth of the cave without answering.

Ariel nudged him. "You know."

"I might." At her exasperated look, he continued. "I don't know why the other darts weren't sent until now. This one has been in that pool a good while, and clearly human hands placed it. But maybe the contents of the Vault burned long ago. Maybe that is the message a Farwalker needs to spread. So people like me will stop wasting energy looking for it."

"You can't find what doesn't exist," Ariel muttered.

"Mmm." Scarl closed his eyes and pinched the bridge of his nose. His voice thickened. "You can spend your time more wisely, perhaps."

Ariel's face crumpled by degrees. She carefully set down the sprung dart and drew her knees up to her chest, wrapping her arms around tight. She hid her face in her lap, and she wept. All the grief on the twisted path from Canberra Docks to the mouth of the mountain caught up with her, and she gave herself over to sobs.

Zeke and Scarl exchanged a pained look. Zeke helplessly patted Ariel's shin. More practiced with grief, Scarl did a bit better. He reached an uncertain arm around her shuddering shoulders.

Ariel turned her face to his chest and threw both arms around him. His embrace tightening, he rocked her. His chest muffled her wails.

Some corner of Ariel's mind may have known even then what the latest message truly meant. Perhaps the Farwalker inside knew what Ariel did not—that neither her body nor her heart could do what was needed, not then. At that particular moment, Ariel's young body needed food and plenty of rest if she ever was to regain her strength. And her heart desperately longed for the chance to cry like a child in the arms of someone she loved.

That's what she did.

CHAPTER
42

Ariel stopped crying eventually. The trio found their way to the outskirts of Libros, where a family of Reapers took them in. They slept in a corn shed still empty from winter. Scarl told a halting story: the two young people had lost their mother to poison, by her own hand. One look at their ragged father, a lame and impoverished Storian, was enough to explain why. His wife's family had hounded him out of their village, but he would not surrender his kids. To feed them, he would trade any plain labor no one wanted to do for themselves, as long as it could be done with a limp. It was far too dangerous to practice his true trade within rumor's reach of Mason. Ariel thought it a pretty good story, and it earned her and Zeke more sympathy than questions. Anyone who knew their ages would not have believed it, but the miles had been hard on them all. Scarl looked the part.

They were nervous about being spotted until Zeke reassured them.

"The stones say to stay here awhile," he explained. He'd spent more than an hour poking in the pile of rocks the Reapers had removed from their field. "Well, what they really said was, 'You've tumbled enough. Let moss grow to hide you. Rest and grow ready before you tumble again.' I'm sure that means we'll be safe here for more than a couple of nights. Don't you?"

So one week bled into the next, and even Scarl began to relax. Pulling weeds and hauling water from sunrise to sunset, the Reapers had little time to gossip with neighbors. Their guests tried to make themselves useful without attracting attention. They pulled weeds and hauled water, too, but when they could, they gave more valuable help. Zeke became skilled at following the Finder's whispered directions, and the subtle advice of stones didn't hurt. He and Ariel pretended to merely chance upon honeybee hives, medicinal plants, and piles of deer droppings for fertilizer. Though the Reaper family had little enough bounty to spare, nobody suggested the newcomers leave.

Then one day the Reapers reported a stir in the village. A Finder had stumbled into Libros, raving of whirlwinds, phantoms, and floods. He'd been swept from the mountains into the Drymere, nearly drowning before the torrent that had caught him sank into the desert. There he'd wandered for weeks before locating the way back to town. Thinking him crazy, nobody paid much attention—except, perhaps, the man who had sent him.

When he heard this, Scarl wanted to leave immediately. He feared the Finder's return might give Mason questions that local trees could too easily answer.

"But you still limp really badly," Ariel pointed out. Scarl's foot hadn't turned black, but it was only starting to bear his weight. "If someone comes after us, they'll catch us anyway."

He had to admit she was right. He considered sending her and Zeke back to Hartwater alone. She convinced him that would raise too many suspicions, after the story he'd told. So they remained, sticking closer together than ever, and Scarl took to leaning on a scythe instead of his staff. He barely let Ariel out of his sight, and he prodded Zeke for warnings that the stones didn't give.

They still had to eat, though. Not long before sundown one evening, the three of them slipped through the cornstalks to the river that meandered along the Reapers' fields. Hidden beneath a veil of weeping willows, they hoped to catch fish.

Finding an eddy, Ariel took off her boots and waded, collecting periwinkles for Scarl's hook. She and Zeke giggled at the strange way he flung his bait into the water and yanked it back out. They stopped laughing when he landed a fish. He was just unhooking another when footsteps approached on the bank.

"A Fisher now, instead of a Storian? Your trade changes swiftly."

Scarl whirled. A hand parted nearby willow fronds, and a girl Ariel's age stepped through. She led a small, mincing man by the hand. Short, black hair clung to his scalp, and his narrow shoulders were draped with an extravagant blue cloak.

Scarl's eyes darted, scanning the riverbank for henchmen and gauging the distance to his scythe. It hid in the grass out of reach, not far from the intruders' feet.

Ariel gasped. "Mason?" She was less frightened than angry— no stones had warned Zeke!

The man cocked his sharp chin to her voice. Only then did Ariel spy the milky sheen in his eyes and the lazy droop of his lids.

"Mason Tree-Singer, yes. You must be the Farwalker. Alive." He nudged the girl at his side, who stood staring. She led Mason closer.

Scarl gestured quickly for Ariel and Zeke. They splashed to him.

"He's blind," Ariel whispered.

"No less dangerous," Scarl muttered. He herded his companions a few paces upstream and searched again for movement in the green curtains around them.

"No less aware," Mason added. "I might have expected a visit from Scarl Finder on his latest arrival in Libros. Not courteous, really, to make the blind man seek you. I believe you owe me an explanation. At the least."

Before he replied, Scarl tapped Ariel and pointed across the river, his eyebrows raised in a question. Zeke nodded for her. She realized what Scarl was suggesting. She bobbed her head, too, but turned a troubled scowl back to the current. She could swim to the far bank, but she wasn't sure about Zeke, who ran fast but floundered in water. And Mason couldn't follow regardless, but what of his guide?

She tugged Scarl's sleeve with objections. He raised his palm: wait.

"If you want an explanation," he told Mason, "I suggest you ask Elbert." He drew Ariel and Zeke several steps farther away. "Or your favorite Fool. Perhaps even Liam can—"

"Stop slithering from me!" Mason hissed. His command startled Ariel, but not so much as what followed. Without a breath of wind to cause it, the willow arched over them shook.

Zeke eyed the tree and backed away from the dangling fronds.

"I would have brought more than this girl to guide me," Mason added, "if I planned to finish the work you abandoned."

Scarl bristled. "The work I abandoned involved telling darts. Not murder."

"Take care." Mason wagged his head. "Take care whom you accuse, and of what. Some of your sloppier comrades got carried away, that's all. I can't control men like that."

"You sent them," Zeke grumbled.

"Ah. The third voice. You must be the youngest son of Jeshua Tree-Singer. Both of whom the trees now ignore."

"Shut up." Without thinking, Ariel rose to her friend's defense. Scarl's hand fell on her immediately. She ignored his warning to add, "You don't know anything."

"On the contrary." Mason fumbled for a riverside boulder and eased himself to a seat. He waved off his guide, who retreated. "But there is one thing, I admit, that you know and I don't," he continued. "I know you spoke with the mouth of the mountain. Tell me what it said."

"Send your thugs home first," Scarl retorted. He had finally spotted the other people he'd anticipated would be hidden nearby. Following his gaze, Ariel saw the shape of a man behind a tree trunk. Zeke pointed out another farther away through the fronds.

"They're here to protect me, not harm you," Mason said. "Several men we both know have left the world unexpectedly. I'm told they had your help. You're a fine one to cry murder, I must say."

Unable to stand Mason's disdain any longer, Ariel said, "That's your fault. He was only protecting me."

"Hush." Scarl squeezed her shoulder. She pulled from his grip. This was about her, after all. She wasn't going to be silenced like a student who had talked out of turn.

Mason's attention fell wholly on her. "What is your first name, Farwalker?"

So the trees did not tell him everything. She decided it

couldn't matter and told him herself. "And you might as well leave us alone," she added. "The message we got on Cloudspear was blank."

"Was it? I wonder."

Ariel opened her mouth to say that the dart's devastating silence had been broken only by the insult of ashes. Something held her tongue, and it wasn't Scarl's growing agitation. Ariel was gaining trust in her instincts, and she heeded them now. She took a few steps closer to the Tree-Singer, mostly to prevent Scarl from quieting her with his hands.

"Check the dart for yourself if you want," she snapped. "I'd give it to you now, but it's back in my bag. Or did you already snoop through our things before you followed us here?"

Surprise and irritation fought on Mason's face. Clearly he was unused to such hot retorts.

"I didn't follow you. I just asked my green friends where you were. I've known for days you'd taken shelter with Reapers."

"You'd better not hurt them," Zeke growled. "How can you call yourself a Tree-Singer, anyway? What trees are friendly with you? Trees would never say that killing anyone was okay."

"Just because I value their help does not mean I always take their advice," Mason replied. "The trees do not realize how foolhardy humans can be."

Zeke snorted. "Oh, I bet they know just from talking with you."

"Silence, boy! I won't take insults from the likes of you."

"Be careful," Ariel told Mason, giving in to a temptation too great to resist. "He's killed more people than Scarl has." She ignored Zeke's wounded glance, but at Mason's startled expression, she added, "There's a lot the trees don't seem to have told you."

She couldn't have picked a sharper or more dangerous weapon. Mason only lowered his head and curled his hands into fists, but the two men in the distance edged closer. Scarl reached to yank her shin deep into the river.

"I'll tell *you* something, you impudent kitten," Mason growled. "You scratch at me now from your grave. The trees have already told me your search ended on Cloudspear. No Vault has been revealed for a Farwalker to blather about. That is the *only* reason you are not dead."

The willow above them didn't shudder this time. It convulsed. Fronds snapped up and back down like whips. Gray-green leaves filled the air. Everyone on the riverbank gawked.

When the wind and water had borne the fluttering slivers away, every dangling frond between Mason and Ariel had been stripped bare.

"I heard that," Zeke said. Belatedly Ariel realized he meant more than the swish and flutter of leaves.

Mason's face glowed with fury. "Willows," he muttered. "Frothy and sentimental, particularly over idiots and children."

Zeke stepped back out of the river to stroke a leafless stem. "No, it's not just the willows. They all will forsake you if you try to hurt her now. I just don't know why they haven't already. You've been warned before."

His lips working, Mason flicked leaves from his shoulders and hair. "I'd get rid of you anyway," he told Ariel, "if I thought you were lying to me."

"But what are you so worried about?" she asked. "What if we had found the Vault?"

"He's blind," Zeke said. "He doesn't want anyone else to see wonders, either."

"No, I'm not nearly so vain. But I am blind, and as a result I see some things more clearly. I can tell the difference between what people need to be happy and what they only think that they need. We do not need anything that might be in the Vault. Worse, it would unleash greed and envy. The very idea of treasure sparks evil in people like Gustav Fool. Besides, treasures turn our attention from what's in our hearts to what's in our hands. The trees agree with me there. So if a few lives were lost to keep the attention of everyone else on their hearts, so be it. More lives were saved."

"People are too stupid to learn or make wise decisions or share?" Scarl asked. He shook his head.

"We have proven it over and over again."

"You're wrong," Ariel said. "And the trees think so, too." She didn't mention the stones. She still couldn't understand why the world had so often helped them in a quest that had ended only in disappointment. "But it doesn't matter, I guess."

"No, it doesn't," said Mason. "You sought the Vault and found nothing, only a hoax from the past. Spread the truth, Far-walker. Put the legend to rest." He sneered as he rose. "You can say Mason Tree-Singer sent you. That will mean more than the word of an orphan with no master."

Stung by his words, Ariel only glared. He rang a small bell sewn into the hem of his cloak. The girl who had led him reappeared. She barely dared to peek at Ariel as she took Mason's hand and guided him from his stone seat.

"Were you ever kind?" Zeke wondered. "Why do the trees hear you at all?"

Mason stopped and turned back. "I was kinder before I understood that people can be ruined by kindness. The tree that knows only sunshine uproots at the first storm. And when action is needed, fear drives it better than kindness. But I will show you that I am not the demon you think. I will help you, Farwalker, and rid Libros of you at the same time."

Mason called a name. One of his henchmen approached. Though his face bore no threat, Scarl shifted to stay between Ariel and the stranger.

"I can hear from his gait that your caretaker is lame," Mason told Ariel. "I will give you a horse and what food you may need to go home. Or wherever you will, outside of Libros. I have not enjoyed dealing with any of this, and I long to forget a few names—including yours. Tell my guard here what you might need. It will be delivered tomorrow. Make quick use of it."

Mason shuffled back up the bank with the girl. His second guard followed after.

"I won't say a 'goodwill' we all know would be false," Mason added over his shoulder. "But good-bye."

Once he was gone, Scarl eyed the assistant with mistrust.

"He can be harsh," the man murmured. "But he's usually right."

Scarl waved him away. "Go. We don't need his gifts. It's enough that he'll let us keep breathing."

The man winced at the sarcasm.

Ariel shifted. Standing in the river, her feet had grown numb, but the rest of her pulsed with strength. She hadn't realized how much the shadow of Mason had darkened her days. Now he'd walked away. She understood Scarl's resentment, but she decided that wasn't reason enough to refuse Mason's offer.

"Enough food for two weeks of travel," she told the man. "And a horse big enough to carry a rider, too. That's all we need."

Nodding, the man trotted away.

Scarl gave Ariel a cross look. "I don't know why I keep thinking I am in charge."

"Me either," she said. For what felt like the first time all summer, she laughed.

A horse was tied outside their shed the next morning. The Reapers praised the generosity of their Tree-Singer, and nobody bothered to contradict them. The three friends simply wished their hosts a good harvest and began riding south.

The old cart horse was neither fast nor as nimble as Orion had been, but he was large enough that all three could sit on his back with their packs slung over his withers. In a few days, chimney smoke greeted them over the pines. Riding in front, Ariel noticed no difference in Scarl. But Zeke, sandwiched in the middle, felt the Finder's body tense as they rode into Hartwater.

They went to Derr's empty house, where Scarl collected a few things. They stayed long enough only for a warm bath apiece. On their way back out of the village, Scarl reined in the horse before the door where Mirayna had lived. That home also stood empty—for his return or for someone who wanted it more.

Ariel and Zeke sat with their own memories while Scarl gazed a long time at the house. Both started when he spoke.

"Her wheeling chair is inside," Scarl murmured. "She told me, Ariel, or tried to, how I could take it to pieces and use them to make you something like a bike."

Both touched and appalled, Ariel turned to stare at him.

"I doubt I can do it," he continued. "But I might be able to pass her words to another skilled Allcraft who can."

"That's okay." She shook her head. As much as she'd always yearned for that thrill, no speed or wind could wash away the sadness of a bike made from Mirayna's sick chair. "I mean, thank you," she added hastily. "But someone else might need a wheeled chair."

He sighed. "Maybe so." He nudged the horse into a walk.

As they drew near Canberra Docks, Ariel understood better why Scarl hadn't wanted to linger in Hartwater. Her insides cramped and her skin crawled with apprehension. The familiar smells of cottonwoods and the sea, the distant cries of gulls, the salt-damp air on her cheeks all welcomed her home. But they also reminded her that while these wild things remained, the most significant face of her home had been lost.

The horse crested a rise, and its riders looked down on the docks. With the sun low, boats angled back from the sea. A few roofs winked in the distance. Ariel realized with a start which one had been hers. Slate shingles were missing, snatched by some storm. No one had replaced them. No peat smoke rose from the chimney, no herbs hung to dry from the eaves. The windows were shuttered, the rear garden bare. Behind this sharp reality flickered an image Ariel had seen in a dream: the village square as a graveyard. It wasn't unreal enough.

"Stop," she said, her voice shrill. "Scarl, stop!"

He reined in the horse.

"I don't want to go in," she whispered.

"I do," said Zeke. "For a little while. Maybe not long."

"They'll lynch me if they see me," Scarl said. "I'd planned to set you down about here and say good-bye."

"No." Ariel clutched his arm where it reached around her for the reins. "You can't."

"Where else could I take you?" Scarl asked quietly. "Surely you've seen enough of me."

Where else indeed? The question wormed through Ariel's mind.

"Ashes," she murmured.

Like a telling dart springing open, the Farwalker dozing

inside her snapped awake. Ariel twisted hard on the horse, nearly knocking Zeke off with her elbow. She beamed up at Scarl. They hadn't spoken of the dart since their meeting with Mason, but its riddle, understood, now shone in her eyes.

"You can take me to the Vault," Ariel said. "It does exist, and I know where it is."

CHAPTER
43

At Tree-Singer Abbey, only the seasons had changed. Goats grazed the hillside. Ash knelt plucking weeds from a garden. He straightened to see two young people and a Finder crossing the yard on a horse.

"Oh, great boughs and branches!" he cried. "My lost goats, are you safe?" He peered with suspicion at Scarl. "My old limbs can't fight, but the trees on these hills hear me well. Shall I beg them to thwart this man's path?"

Ariel threw her leg over the horse's neck, slid to the ground, and ran to give Ash a hug. "He's my friend," she told him. "We've come for a visit."

"If anyone here is a prisoner, good Tree-Singer," called Scarl, "it's me."

A smile lit the Tree-Singer's face. He returned Ariel's hug, then spread his arms wide. "Welcome, then! I didn't expect you this time. The trees have their secrets yet."

Impatient with courtesies, Ariel broke in before Scarl and Ash had even finished introducing themselves.

"We know about the Vault," she announced.

"Vault?" Ash repeated. "The Vault of long legend? The trees laugh at those who ask about it, you know." He genuinely didn't seem to know more.

He insisted on serving them tea. When he'd heard the barest bones of their reason for coming, Ash again shook his head.

"Storians have come here before," he said, "though it's been a long while since the last. They spend a lot of time in our goat pen. There's nothing there but goat droppings and ghosts. I've lived at the abbey for most of my life, and I've never found a hint of any other mystery, either. Not within these walls."

His bewilderment scratched Ariel's confidence. Until then, she'd known absolutely that the second telling dart pointed here. Zeke had said it: "The Vault is in ashes"—not the dust of a fire, but the place of someone named Ash. Ash's home, Ash's abbey. And Ash had told them himself that his name had been used at the abbey for long generations.

"Has Mason Tree-Singer ever come here?" Scarl asked.

Ash's wrinkles shifted subtly. "Mason? No. A few of our group are from Libros. They may have spoken with him in the past. But not here, nor recently. And not me."

Ariel studied Ash's kind, watery eyes. She didn't think he was lying, but he knew something about Mason that had not been said. Perhaps Mason had changed his mind about letting her go. She couldn't believe Ash would harm them, but coming here still may have been a mistake. A knot of anxiety formed in her belly. She was tired of fleeing, of living in dread. And she wasn't sure she could bear to have her hopes dashed again.

Her fingers sought the bead at her throat. Having seen her through many difficult trials, it renewed her faith in her instincts and skills. She reminded herself that this particular Ash needn't know it for the Vault to be there.

"Can we look around, anyhow?" she asked.

"Of course." Ash gestured to the doorway. "Wander as you like."

As they rose, Zeke asked if the Tree-Singers had seen or heard Misha lately.

"Not since you left," Ash replied. "We'd noticed that our rafters had emptied."

"He came with us," Ariel told him.

"I suspected as much. Either that, or you scared him away!" Ash's smile faded. He dropped a hand on Ariel's shoulder. "Spirits may be drawn to great good or great evil. I feared for what you would find with him on your shoulder."

"Both," Zeke muttered.

Ash studied his face. "If you will, Zeke, and you have time, come find me. Let us chat as we did before. I'm curious about things the trees have hinted to me."

Zeke glanced at Ariel, then shrugged. "We can talk now."

He and Ash returned to the hearth, leaving Ariel and Scarl alone in the hall.

"If you're waiting for me, don't," Scarl murmured. "If pure finding could do it, it would have been found long ago."

"I'm not sure where to look." That wasn't quite true. Ariel wanted to start with Misha's grand, sunlit room, if it truly existed. She doubted, however, that the Vault simply awaited on the far side of a door.

"Don't look for it at all, Ariel. You're the Farwalker. Walk to it."

Ariel asked her feet where they wanted to go. Not sure of

their answer, she drifted down the hall. Scarl followed a few paces behind.

They wandered to the cherry tree's courtyard. Entering it again under sunlight, rather than dreamlight, made Ariel smile. Then her eyes fell on the stone bench. An entire handful of long, pale feathers lay there.

Seeing the smile drop from her face, Scarl touched her arm. "What?"

Ariel shivered. Hoping Misha had left them as a sign, she picked them up. They whispered to her fingers of creatures long dead.

They also, it seemed, whispered to her feet. A familiar tugging drew at Ariel's boots after long weeks without it. She crossed the courtyard and ducked back inside, passing several wooden doors. None were the one that she wanted.

Turning a corner, Ariel stopped. Misha's door stood before her, no dream. Feeling his absence like a missing tooth in her mouth, she raised her palms to rest them flat on the wood. Its carved whorls seemed to speak.

She pushed, confident she had shoved it open before.

The room behind it didn't blaze with light as it had in her dreams. Many of the windows had busted, their cracks carefully pasted, bigger gaps plugged with bits of cork or carved wood. A few were shuttered instead. Nonetheless, sunshine gleamed on the many long tables. They were just as empty as Ariel had seen them before.

A motion behind the door caught her eye. Expecting Misha, Ariel stepped eagerly in. A startled squeak escaped her. Tucked in the corner beneath one of the windows, Madrona Tree-Singer regarded Ariel with surprise. The table before her was spread with tanned goatskins. Ariel would have guessed the woman was busy making boots but for one thing—her fingers cradled a feather.

Madrona smiled. With a swish of the feather, she invited Ariel and Scarl closer. Dishes on the table held what looked like strong tea, but in colors: red, white, black, two greens, rust, brown. Paint, Ariel guessed, though she'd only seen whitewash on boats. This paint created trees on the goatskins, sweeps of color evoking trunks, boughs, and leaves.

Madrona dipped the stem of her feather in a dish. It lifted a few drops of red. The woman shifted her arm and the drops became cherries on a tree.

"Ah." With compliments on the beautiful work, Ariel handed Madrona the feathers she'd found in the courtyard. Dipping her head in thanks, the woman set them on the windowsill, which already held an entire collection. Many were stained with paint on their feathery edges.

While Scarl lingered near the Tree-Singer to watch, Ariel wandered the length of the room. Confused but not yet despairing, she trailed her fingers on the tables just as Misha had done. She could imagine him in a room full of painters, all bent over goatskins. But how many paintings of trees could even an abbey of Tree-Singers need? Something didn't fit.

She paced, her legs restless. Her boots tapped overloud on the flagstones. *Tap-tap, tap, tap . . . tap.* With a self-conscious glance toward Madrona, Ariel tried to step more softly. Fortunately, the echoing sound of her footsteps seemed to be irritating no one but her.

At the far end of the room, she grasped why. She turned suddenly to Scarl.

"I want Zeke."

When Zeke learned what Ariel wanted, he simply picked a spot on the painting room floor, stretched out on his belly, and laid his ear against a flagstone. He closed his eyes. His lips moved. Ariel struggled to remain quiet and still. Her feet wanted to jitter.

Sooner than she expected, Zeke raised himself on one hand. "Bits of dead trees and dust."

"There's something else under these stones," Ariel insisted. "A tunnel. Or—" A Vault, she wanted to say. She bit the word back, not trusting herself.

Zeke shrugged. "That's not what the stones say."

Ash and Madrona stood near her worktable, watching somberly.

"Lift one, if it will please you," Ash offered. "Nothing but their weight holds them in place. It may not be easy, though. They have lain there for many a tree's life."

Ariel turned a pleading look toward Scarl. Doubt cramped his face, but he cracked his knuckles.

"We can try." He surveyed the floor. "Is there one you want most?"

Ariel's feet crossed the floor for at least the tenth time. The dark flagstones came in all sizes. The skill with which they'd been matched together had left little space for even dust to fall between them.

Ariel stopped. "This one." Not much larger than the sole of her boot, it filled a spot between two greater brothers.

Scarl glanced at Zeke. "It can't hurt to ask for a little cooperation," he said.

After Zeke whispered an appeal to Ariel's choice, Scarl knelt beside him. With a new knife he'd gotten in Hartwater, he scratched at the gap around the stone to try to make a purchase for fingers. Then he wedged the knife into the crack.

"You pry with this and I'll try to get a hold beneath," he told Zeke.

"No, let me pry it." Ariel flounced down to join them, wrapping her fingers around the knife handle.

"The blade may snap," Scarl warned. "Watch that it doesn't fly up and cut you." He twitched an eyebrow at her. "You may owe me another knife in a moment."

Zeke crowded nearer to Scarl, his hands also ready. After another warning about broken fingers, the Finder gave one more instruction.

"You did well enough in the cave, Zeke. You count it now."

As Zeke whispered, "Three," Ariel put her weight against the knife.

Either Zeke still didn't know his own skills, or the stone Ariel had chosen had long wished to shift from a tiresome place. The knife rocked the edge up immediately. Scarl's fingertips caught a grip. His wrists and forearms strained to keep it. A half-formed plea escaped Zeke and the flat rock abruptly flipped backward, banging against Scarl's knee.

"Ouch."

"Strong work!" Ash, who had stepped up to watch, clapped his hands. "But it doesn't look as though anything lies beneath, does it?"

Ariel pawed at the flattened dirt. She uncovered nothing but more soil. To make sure, she slid the knife blade straight into the earth. It slipped in to the hilt. Drooping, she resisted the desire to yank it back out and throw it across the room.

"Ariel."

She looked up at Scarl's soft call. He'd drawn back to rub

his bruised knee. Now his fingertips coursed the flat underside of the rock they had moved.

A handprint, once crimson but darkened with time, neatly marked the smooth stone. Overtop and along each of the fingers, spidery symbols had been added in white. They easily could have been drawn with the tip of a feather.

Although Ariel didn't know what it was, excitement skittered through her. "What's it mean?"

"Fives," Scarl mused. "I think it's a lesson. Look. Five fingers. Dots of five colors, with symbols next to each—the names of the colors. White lines on each finger, counting up one to five, and symbols next to those—the names of the numbers. Five shapes, five trade symbols, five little animals. It looks like something you might use to teach children. But instead of reciting the names for each thing, they'd learn symbols."

He handed it to her and turned to pry up another. The absence of the first made it easy. The second stone was covered with much more complex markings.

"Oh, how I wish my grandfather could see this." Scarl traced the signs with one finger. "We'll need a host of Storians to explain these. But what a find." He set it aside to flop over another.

"Is it just stories, though?" Zeke asked. "And symbols for kids? That's not treasure."

"It's more like secrets," said Ariel, still poring over the markings atop Misha's palm print. Her fingertips trembled at their age and mystic importance, and she silently vowed to learn every one. "But I like secrets. Don't you?"

She pulled her eyes away from the Lesson of Fives long enough to survey the length of the floor. "There might be a lot of them here."

"Bark beetles and beavers, who knew?" said Ash. He bent to peer at a flagstone that Scarl had overturned. "We've been treading on relics. No wonder the trees laugh at us."

"Zeke," Scarl called, from three flagstones away. "You say it's not treasure, but listen. Can anyone explain to you how a telling dart works? Even a wise tree or stone?" Flashing a grin, he turned the flagstone in his hands to show the diagram there. At the heart of a web of symbols sat a familiar outline: a brass tube with three vanes and one end that came to a point.

"I think this can."

CHAPTER
44

Excited, they overturned the next dozen flagstones in less than ten minutes. Quite a few displayed Misha's red hand under part of the writing, but others bore the print of a thumb, four dots in a square, or other distinctive designs by their makers. The tight rows of tiny symbols on some stones made Ariel's eyes cross, but others included drawings and maps. There were depictions of devices with so many parts that all she recognized were the wheels. There was a sketch of an unhappy boy with plants drawn all around him. Ariel recognized enough of those to suspect that each cured a different complaint. One stone bore a map of constellations she knew, but the stars were accompanied by other marks whose meanings she couldn't guess.

As rich with mystery as the floor turned out to be, it was not the only treasure revealed. Beneath a series of stones running the length of the room, they found a long trench in the dirt. There, wrapped in crumbling cloth, were the remains of dead trees that the flagstones had mentioned to Zeke. Sheets of wood thinner than splinters had been stacked and bound together with planks.

Images and scratches of paint filled both sides of each sheet. Scarl pulled dozens of these stacks from the trench.

"Like voices from a grave," he breathed. He caressed the pages, fragile as shells. "It may take a lifetime to figure them all out."

"The trees may offer some help," Ash told him. "These things wouldn't be here if they hadn't been made by Tree-Singers of some sort long ago. And little that Tree-Singers do escapes the notice of their favorite trees."

"Or friendly rocks," Zeke said. "I think each stone may know what it bears." He spread his hands on one, obscuring the diagrams there, and let his lids droop. "This one tells how to move things with steam, like from a kettle." Flying back open, his eyes sparkled, and he added, "The stone mostly wonders why people like to move things so much."

Forgetting the disappointment of no gold or gems, he shuttled from one flagstone to the next, announcing the story captured on each. His friends didn't know what he was talking about much of the time, and neither did he. But his grin only grew wider.

Ash watched Zeke and the hubbub in gentle amusement. But when twilight replaced the sun pouring in through the windows, he made the stone flippers stop for a meal.

"I hope you don't mind a few more visitors, Ash," Scarl said as the Tree-Singer passed around bowls of thick barley soup. They sat around a grand hearth, the fire the only light in the room. "The secrets, as Ariel calls them, need to be revealed and shared."

Spoons froze as both his younger companions were struck by similar thoughts.

"What about Mason?" Ariel asked.

"What about him?" Ash said. Again, a closed look had fallen over his face.

Scarl studied him, trying to decide how much to trust him.

Ariel took less time. "If he finds out what's here, he'll try to get rid of it—and us, too."

"I don't know what loyalties you have to him, Ash," Scarl said hastily. "But he's done more than threaten Ariel's life. She'll be in danger from him. Everyone here may be."

"You don't . . . no, of course not. How could you?" Ash pulled at one oversize ear. "I forget that not everyone hears the gossip of trees. What you've said makes me sad, but there's no need for concern. Mason Tree-Singer has passed out of this world."

Their cries of surprise and relief bounced off the rafters. The echoes mingled with a flurry of questions.

"I only know what the trees tell me," Ash said. "That depends on who I ask—unusual, to say the least. Only one thing seems certain: Mason fell in a river near Libros and drowned."

"We saw that river," said Ariel. "But how?"

"I should not tell you more, I am certain," Ash replied.

"I think she has a right to hear it," Scarl said, "after all that he's done. You don't know half of it."

Ash debated, tapping his spoon on his chin. "I may know more than you think." He sighed. "But perhaps not. Please, may my words stay in this room? Never to be repeated?"

When he was satisfied with their promises, he gazed into his soup. "The pines say a willow pushed him," he said. "The willows claim they only gave him no warning, that they stood by in silence while a young apprentice gave the push. The cherry says he tripped by himself on his own folly. The alders won't say at all, but they do not mourn. They once would have."

Ash pursed his lips, appraising Ariel and Zeke. He directed his next words only to Scarl. His voice dropped, but perhaps not so far as he might have liked.

"The apprentice was a girl. Perhaps Mason behaved wrongly toward her and gave her a reason to push him." He shook his head grimly. "At any rate," he added, "I tend to believe the willows in this case."

The others shared a glance. After what they had seen on the riverbank near Libros, they believed the version told by the pines. Vindicated, Ariel wanted to whoop. She contented herself by letting her feet dance, out of sight under the table.

"It does not matter, in the end," Ash declared. "He was a great Tree-Singer, I'm told, but greatness creates its own temptations. The trees think poorly of humans who rank their own wisdom too highly. It sounds to me as though Mason overstepped his bounds, snapping even the patience of trees. But he's had nothing to do with this abbey."

"He must not have guessed what was under your feet," Scarl said.

"The better for us, I suspect. But to finally answer your question, we welcome all visitors who respect our trees and our ways."

"Even if they pull up your floor?" Ariel asked.

Ash smiled. Without being asked, he took her empty bowl to refill it.

"I knew before the first time you came here that change would be hard on your heels," he told her, handing it back. "The trees warned me not to let you stay long, lest the changes bring more harm than good. I never imagined you'd be back, though, or that the abbey itself would be more than a brief haven for you."

"Oh, she brims with surprises," Scarl said. He gave her an appreciative look that she couldn't meet for long. Instead, Ariel beamed at her soup. It always pleased her to defy expectations. Certainly no one ever would have expected a girl who had failed her Naming test to discover what she had today.

"Why do you think nobody found this stuff before?" Zeke wondered. "I mean, it's not an actual Vault with something inside like everyone thought. Still . . ."

"We were too stuck on our notions of treasure, I guess," Scarl mused. "Seeking too hard for things we could carry away. Or the problem might have been seeking itself. What was needed was . . . walking. Wandering, even."

"Having a Stone-Singer helped," Ariel said. Gratitude purred through her bones, lighting the grin she gave Zeke. She knew she would have been lost without him.

"Without doubt," Scarl agreed. "But that's the Farwalker's trade—connecting people to accomplish what they could not alone. Carrying hope, crafting the future." Aware he was embarrassing her, he tweaked a lock of her hair. "You've done all of that, Ariel. Whether you meant to or not."

Ash murmured agreement. Blushing under their admiration, she could only slurp her soup. Its warmth couldn't compare to the pride burning inside her.

Later, she took a candle and wandered the abbey alone. She discovered that the empty halls gave resonance to her voice, so she worked on two new verses for her song:

The path leads me on and on;
My feet are willing.
Follow the falcon's flight;
Walk with the wind.

Walk with the wind and sun;
My heart is willing.
Follow the river's song;
Walk with a friend.

As if her last verse had summoned him, Scarl came to find her.

"Ash feared your candle would burn down and you'd get lost in the dark," he explained.

In fact, her taper was little more than a nub. She shrugged. "I know the way."

He nodded. "I told him Farwalkers didn't get lost. But they might need some rest."

She agreed readily enough. The beds Ash could offer were no more than straw mattresses, but their pillows were filled with fragrant balsam-fir needles. Ariel couldn't wait to snuggle her face into one. A night free from dew, dirt, and crawling things would pass pleasantly indeed. She thought she'd miss only the stars.

As they ambled back to the great room where Ash and Zeke awaited, Ariel sidled closer to Scarl. She tucked her hand into his.

"I'm sorry we didn't find it sooner," she said. It almost certainly wouldn't have mattered, but she wanted to say it regardless.

Scarl failed to hide a wince. It would be a long time before he could smile again when he thought of Mirayna. But he squeezed Ariel's fingers.

"If we hadn't found it at all, my life would not be so different," he said. "Yours has been uprooted completely. I don't expect you to forgive me for my part in that, but I hope that one day you will feel all the joy in your song. It has changed quite a lot."

Her ears burning, Ariel stared at the low flame of her candle. She hadn't realized he'd heard her. A few paces later, she decided she didn't mind.

"Where will you go now?" she wondered.

"Nowhere for a while, if Ash will allow it," he said. "But then I'll go find Storians to bring back, all who will come, and learn from them as much as they'll teach me. After I return Zeke to his family, of course."

His eyes turned to hers. "But you, Ariel? Where do you want to be? Do you know?"

The answer rose from her feet to be confirmed by her heart, but it stuck in her throat. She feared the words sounded childish. She pushed them out anyway.

"With you, walking."

He shook his head, bemused, but his legs stopped. The hand not occupied with a candle drew her into a hug. The closeness made her think of her mother. His embrace was neither as soft nor as snug, but the rise and fall of his chest against hers stanched the leak that had sprung near Ariel's heart on the night she'd been stolen from home. The old hole remained, but at least Ariel's life had stopped dribbling out.

"With me." Wonder threaded Scarl's voice. He rested his chin in her hair. "You'll change your mind as you get older, I think. But I told you before—I will stay at your side, if that's what you want, or take you where you long to go, if I can. When stones speak and ghosts walk and the Vault can be found, then I guess a child snatcher can become a protector."

"A father," she whispered.

"Careful." He gripped the scruff of her neck and shook

gently, like a dog with a pup. "I'm a Finder, that's all. But I can find work for a Farwalker. Many people will want news of your discovery today."

Afraid to lay too many words on her feelings, Ariel simply nodded. She fell alongside him again, hugging his arm. But before they had taken too many steps, the elation inside her spilled out:

Wandering near and far,
My feet will guide us.
Carry the news to all;
Walk till the end.

She sang it with confidence, even knowing their path would be littered with hardships, because it would also be blazing with purpose and pride.

With Scarl matching his stride to her rhythm, they turned to collect Zeke and stretch out on the beds Ash had offered. Ariel hummed her song as they went.

Read on for a sneak peek of Ariel's next adventure:

The
TIMEKEEPER'S
MOON

The moon refused to hush or come down, so Ariel Farwalker was forced to climb up.

She kicked aside her blankets and abandoned her straw mattress. Ariel slipped through the dim hallways of Tree-Singer Abbey to its great wooden door, the cool flagstones soothing the itch in the soles of her bare feet. Lifting the latch, she pulled the door open, soundlessly this time. She didn't want to disturb her friends' sleep. Not again.

Arise, walker. Hither. The full moon kissed Ariel's face, but its silvery voice needled her. *Arise. Hasten. Late, late.* Despite its name, Thunder Moon shone from a sky free of clouds, and rather than growling, it hissed. Its voice, stealthy and barbed as a porcupine quill, pierced her thoughts, caught there, and pulled. Dragged from her bed by that moon, Ariel thought she knew how the tide felt.

She hurried outside and along the stone wall to a corner. Her nightgown fluttered in the brisk mountain breeze, which was cool even though it was summer. Moonlight drenched Ariel and gleamed on the abbey. Although she did not have the talent for speaking with trees, the Tree-Singers' grand hall had become her home over the past year. Tonight, instead of shelter, the rough-hewn stone building could serve as her stairway to the moon.

She fitted her strong fingers and toes into the quoins' deep mortar joints and hoisted herself up. Her muscles complained, but she pushed them. Although she was only thirteen, Ariel was a Farwalker—the sole member of a trade once thought extinct—and she'd endured a great deal more strain in earning that name than she could face climbing a familiar stone building. The danger would never have stopped her, but if she hadn't been so desperate to quiet the moon, she would have recognized the folly in her risky ascent.

The moon whined and wheedled, urging Ariel to hurry. *Hear, walker. Heed.* Each word tugged at her feet, which throbbed restlessly even as she crept up the wall. Although usually friendly, the stones of the abbey nipped, too, their sharp edges biting into her soles.

Ignoring the sting, Ariel gained the cornice. The overhang stymied her for only a moment. She gripped the stone gutter and hung there from both hands, her feet dangling. With a kick, she swung them up onto the slate tiles. As they so often did, her feet found a way of their own, and her sturdy legs levered her onto the roof.

She huddled there briefly, catching her breath, and then rose unsteadily to her feet. The slant made her teeter. Emptiness yawned between Ariel and the earth, twenty-odd feet below and swirling with moon shadows. A pine scent wafted over the meadow to tickle her stubby nose and twine in her dark, blunt-cut hair. Her soles, slick now with blood, slid on the smooth slate with each step. But Ariel's attention fixed again on the moon.

That round, silver face looked almost as far away as before. It leered at her failure to reach it.

Half only, half only. Unripened. Undone. The syllables circled and blurred, their insistence more clear than their meaning. *Hurry.*

"I'm trying!" Ariel scanned for the best route to the peak of the roof. As a Farwalker, she was accustomed to letting her feet lead her wherever she needed to go, without thinking too much about it. Her skills did not seem to be helping now, though. Of course, her farwalking usually took place on earth.

As she searched for firm footing, a glimmer below caught her eye. She eased toward the end of the roof and looked down.

The moon also shone below her.

One full moon taunted her from above, in the southeastern sky, but another swam on the surface of the abbey's stone well. With an insight twisted by exhaustion and moonlight, Ariel realized she could reach her goal that way instead. A few running steps and a leap would plunge her into that wavering light. The moon's sly face would burst as it received her, silver droplets a balm for her aching head and stinging feet. The moon, which had tormented her all spring, would shut up—and Ariel might finally sleep.

"That's better," she murmured. "I'll meet you."

She gauged the distance to the well and backed along the gutter, working out the angle and how many steps she could take before launching herself off the edge. Four long strides and a good kick should do it.

Running feet pounded below. Zeke Stone-Singer burst into the abbey's dirt yard. Despite the darkness, Ariel could tell it was her friend not only by his lanky silhouette, but also by his speed.

"Ariel!" Zeke whirled and peered up. "What are you doing on the roof? You might fall!"

An exasperated grunt escaped her. "I was trying so hard to be quiet! I didn't mean to wake you, Zeke. Sorry."

"You didn't. The stones woke me. They're worried about you. Now come down!"

Ariel scowled. No one but Zeke could have heard such a warning from stones. It wasn't always convenient to have a best friend with his unique talent.

To her greater dismay, another dark figure joined Zeke. Her friend must have roused Scarl, the man who served as guardian to them both. Scarl's limp had prevented him from arriving so swiftly, but he'd not come empty-handed. He clutched a dark bundle.

Zeke pointed her out. "There," he said, as if Scarl Finder couldn't have found her quickly enough by himself. Few things eluded a Finder who sought them.

"It's okay," Ariel called down to them. "Go back to bed. I've just got to hush the moon, that's all. And then I can—"

"Ariel, hear me."

She flinched at the snap in the Finder's usually muted voice.

"Stop right where you are," Scarl ordered. "Sit down."

Distant trees murmured. Something wasn't right, Ariel knew. It wasn't just that she'd disturbed her friends' rest yet again. Scarl sounded upset. Ariel hadn't heard that tone from him in a year, not since they'd discovered the Vault and its treasures hidden there at the abbey. She'd almost forgotten how sharp Scarl's voice could be when he raised it.

Still, his command echoed dully compared to the whisper slicing down to her from the sky: *Half done, whole undone . . .*

done undone . . . and die. She didn't have to understand for the last word to scare her. It wasn't the first time the moon's whisper had threatened.

"Don't be mad at me, Scarl," she said faintly. "Please. But I can't."

"She's sleepwalking or something." Zeke's moon shadow jittered behind him, drawing Ariel's attention upward again.

"I don't think so. Ariel!" Scarl cursed when she didn't respond.

"What should we do?" asked Zeke. "Should I ask the stones to help somehow, or—?"

"Here, take this. Quick."

Their frantic voices drifted to Ariel from a distance. She was caught in the moon's skewed stare, one of its round eyes looking on from the sky while the other stared up from the well. Her feet didn't just itch now, they burned—and only reaching one moon or the other could cool them. Neither moon was quite right. One was too distant, the other too wet. But—

Heed now. The moon pulled harder than uncertainty, harder than pain. To silence it, Ariel shoved herself into a run.

Joni Sensel is the author of *The Timekeeper's Moon*, the sequel to *The Farwalker's Quest*, as well as *Reality Leak* and *The Humming of Numbers*. She also works as a communications consultant. When not writing for children, she climbs trees and chats with boulders at the foot of Mount Rainier, near her home in Enumclaw, Washington.

www.jonisensel.com